IN OUR STARS

IN OUR STARS

THE DOOMED EARTH: BOOK ONE

JACK CAMPBELL

ACE
NEW YORK

ACE
Published by Berkley
An imprint of Penguin Random House LLC
penguinrandomhouse.com

Library of Congress Cataloging-in-Publication Data

Names: Campbell, Jack (Naval officer), author.
Title: In our stars / Jack Campbell.
Description: New York: Ace, 2024. | Series: The Doomed Earth; book 1
Identifiers: LCCN 2023030379 (print) | LCCN 2023030380 (ebook) |
ISBN 9780593640630 (hardcover) | ISBN 9780593640654 (ebook)
Subjects: LCGFT: Science fiction. | Novels.
Classification: LCC PS3553.A4637 I5 2024 (print) |
LCC PS3553.A4637 (ebook) | DDC 813/.54—dc23/eng/20230707
LC record available at https://lccn.loc.gov/2023030379
LC ebook record available at https://lccn.loc.gov/2023030380

Printed in the United States of America
1st Printing

Book design by Daniel Brount

To Leigh Brackett, Andre Norton, and C. J. Cherryh,
who lit the beacons into space that the rest of us
still follow to the stars

/////

For S., as always

IN OUR
STARS

CHAPTER 1

12 June 2180

A S THE WEAPON DETONATED ON THE SURFACE OF THE EARTH, A COLLECTIVE, wordless moan of despair sounded from the crew of the Unified Fleet heavy cruiser *Pyrenees* in orbit near the Moon. Lieutenant Selene Genji stared, unable to accept what she was seeing, as the initial burst of weird, hideous light expanded with horrible speed, growing and racing across the surface of the planet. Oceans instantly evaporated, the surfaces of continents vanishing, billions dying in the blink of an eye as the weapon consumed all of human history and art and hope.

The Spear of Humanity had won. Earth had been "cleansed," destroyed in the name of saving it.

"We're getting odd readings on all of our instruments." The voice of the weapons officer sounded strange, choked by grief.

"Light is being bent," another officer gasped. "Like space-time is being distorted. Energy release is off every scale we've got."

Boring beneath the surface, the destruction reached Earth's core.

What remained of the planet exploded.

In the seconds remaining to her, Genji watched the enormous

oncoming shock wave, part of her wondering at how the image warped mysteriously in places. More free quarks than the universe had seen since its birth, invisible to the human eye, and the remnants of the outer atmosphere driven outward by inconceivable energy, the death throes of Earth formed a tsunami of brilliant blue shading into ultraviolet as the explosion expanded at incredible velocity. Earth's dying moment was beautiful in a very strange and extremely frightening way.

She only had time to form two words in her mind before the shock wave hit.

If only . . .

6 February 2140

Ninety-nine watches out of every hundred were boring and monotonous, and often the one hundredth one was as well. Lieutenant Kayl Owen realized that he had managed to snag the watch with something "interesting" happening.

Hazards to navigation were not supposed to pop up out of nowhere. That sort of thing could happen on Earth, but not in space, not where the instruments aboard the Earth Guard ship *Vigilant* could spot everything within literally millions of kilometers. Something could pop out from behind the Moon, but from where the *Vigilant* currently was in a Cislunar/High Earth Orbit, the Moon was nearly twenty-five thousand kilometers away.

But there it suddenly was, stubbornly refusing to abide by common sense and experience, which said it couldn't be.

"Turn off that alarm!" At the best of times, Captain Garos seemed to regard the universe as a perverse thing dedicated to making his life difficult. He always seemed to regard the crew of the *Vigilant*, and Lieutenant Owen in particular, in the same light.

"Why didn't anyone report that object to me before it got within a thousand kilometers of us?"

Everyone else on the bridge either tried to look busy or looked at Lieutenant Kayl Owen, who was the officer of the watch. Knowing the captain's wrath was already focused on him, Owen tried to keep his voice professional, calm, and assured. "Captain, the object did not appear on any of our instruments until now."

Captain Garos's glower grew deeper. "Meaning you didn't notice it until now!"

Sometimes, Owen let the captain's rants slide off him. But in this case, his whole watch team might also catch blame. He had to stand up for them. "Captain, the system backup records will confirm there was no indication of that object being there before the alert sounded."

"Then where did it come from and why didn't our instruments see it?" Garos demanded.

"I don't know, Captain."

"Of course you don't!" Garos switched his attention to Lieutenant Francesca Bond, who had just arrived on the bridge. "What is it? Maybe *you* can tell me something."

Bond squinted at the readouts. "It's definitely artificial, Captain. Uncontrolled tumbling. Visually, it looks like a wreck."

The executive officer, Commander Ilya Kovitch, had also arrived, and shouldered Lieutenant Bond aside to personally study the images. "A piece of a wreck, you mean. It looks like part of a larger ship."

"Where did it come from? What is it?" Captain Garos shouted.

Everyone looked at Owen again.

"I don't know, Captain," Owen repeated.

"Find out!" Garos pointed a rigid finger at Owen. "Take a boarding party, examine it, and give me a full report! Don't screw up!"

Kovitch gestured to Lieutenant Bond. "Take over the watch."

Owen rapidly filled Bond in on everything she needed to know about the ship's status. Normally, he and Francesca got on without too much friction, but right now she was on edge because of the captain's rant and because she knew he and the executive officer were watching, so she got through the turnover as quickly as possible with no wasted chat.

Before leaving the bridge, Owen called the deck division head. "I need the ship's boat ready to go and a boarding party assembled."

"That's going to take an hour," Ensign Vivaldi complained.

Owen took a quick glance toward the fuming Captain Garos. "The captain wants the boat to go without any delay. Would you like to tell him it'll take an hour?"

"No," Vivaldi said quickly. "Umm . . . we'll get it ready as fast as possible."

/ / / / /

THE *VIGILANT* WAS A *DEFENDER*-CLASS CRUISER, AND AT THIRTY-ONE YEARS OLD was about the average age of Earth Guard ships. Because the Universal Space Treaty hadn't been challenged for longer than the *Vigilant* had existed, her main armament of four Penetrator particle beam weapons and two Shrike missile launchers had never been used for any purpose except target practice and the removal of obstacles to safe space navigation. Three hundred meters long, the *Vigilant* resembled a cylinder with a rounded bow and a big bulge amidships, as if the ship were a snake that had swallowed a massive meal. Most of the Earth Guard personnel aboard *Vigilant* were younger than their ship, and equipment improvements over the last few decades had been incremental, so they could have been using the same devices their mothers and fathers had worked on.

Though technically a warship, in practice the *Vigilant* (like every other Earth Guard ship) was basically employed in search and rescue and keeping orbits cleared of dangerous debris. Boredom was the worst enemy her crew had ever battled.

None of them, Lieutenant Owen especially, had any idea how much that was about to change thanks to a piece of wreckage that had appeared out of nowhere.

/////

"GET IT MOVING, VIVALDI." LIEUTENANT COMMANDER SINGH HAD COME DOWN TO hurry along the launch of the ship's boat. "We'll have it ready for you pretty soon, Kayl," he said.

Owen nodded gratefully, trying not to fume over the tongue-lashings Captain Garos had given him during the half hour so far already spent getting the boat ready.

"Boat launchings are supposed to be scheduled," Vivaldi grumbled.

"Ensign Vivaldi," Singh said, "what's the purpose of our patrol?"

"Uh . . ." Harry Vivaldi struggled with the question. "Safety, security, uh . . ."

"Protect the Earth and its people against all events and actions that may threaten them," Lieutenant Commander Singh stated. "Carry out search and rescue, and support law enforcement actions whenever possible. There's nothing about a schedule in there. You need to be able to react quickly when *unscheduled* things happen."

Singh shook his head at Owen. "Too many officers think the purpose of a patrol is to simply carry out the patrol. Anything that causes us to deviate from the preplanned schedule is a problem, rather than being the reason why we're patrolling in the first place."

"Like this wreckage, sir?" Owen said. He liked Singh, who had more than once stuck his neck out for him out of a simple sense of duty.

"Like this wreckage," Singh said, shaking his head again. "It's the weirdest thing I've ever encountered, appearing out of nowhere like that. We ought to be jumping at the chance to find out as much as possible about it. But after you've carried out the inspection of the wreckage required by Guard regulations, I have no doubt it will be handed off to someone else as fast as possible so we can get back to our routine activities and continue on the patrol so everyone can celebrate another successful completion of a patrol on schedule. Find out as much as you can, Kayl."

"I will, sir." It was the closest Singh could come to openly complaining about Captain Garos's attitude to a more junior officer.

Fifteen minutes later, Owen sat in the pilot position of the ship's boat, his arms crossed over the front of his Suit, Space, Exterior, Mark XV Mod 2. He wasn't really driving the boat, which was running on automatic pilot, but he was supposed to be ready to take over control if the autopilot glitched.

Next to him, in the co-pilot position, sat Chief Petty Officer Gayle Kaminski from engineering, and behind them, two sailors. The boat couldn't hold much more, and room had to be left in case any survivors were found, though no one expected that to happen this time.

"Out of nowhere?" Kaminski asked Owen.

"Out of nowhere," Owen confirmed. "It wasn't on any instruments, even visual, and then it was."

"I'm pretty sure that can't happen, Lieutenant."

"I'm pretty sure you're right, Chief. Somebody forgot to tell the wreckage, though."

Kaminski was a decent sort, a professional who didn't let the example set by Captain Garos and Commander Kovitch impact how she acted around Owen. Some of the other chiefs did, trying to see how far they could push things.

Owen gazed at the stars outside the boat, trying not to let his bitterness fill him. Ten years ago, a new ship commanded by his father, Captain Cathal Owen, had exploded in a disaster that had cost a lot of lives and embarrassed Earth Guard. Even though he'd died along with much of his crew, Cathal Owen had been charged with responsibility for the disaster, but the case had fallen apart when an independent investigation placed the blame on design decisions in the new ship that had been pushed by Earth Guard brass to save money. Despite that, his name was still linked to the disaster, and to this day Earth Guard had never officially accepted the investigation results.

Owen had joined Earth Guard burning with ambition to restore his father's reputation with his own achievements. But a lot of senior officers still blamed his father, and it was no secret that they would look favorably on anyone giving an Owen a hard time. Owen's plans had foundered on unofficial barriers, including in his present job. Due to a shortage of officers, all it took to make lieutenant in Earth Guard was to be breathing and have a core body temperature somewhere above sixty degrees Fahrenheit / fifteen point five degrees Celsius. But he'd never gain another promotion, even if the constant efforts of officers like Captain Garos and Commander Kovitch didn't succeed in finally forcing him to make a crucial mistake.

He hated knowing people like that would win.

The autopilot beeped a warning as the boat neared the wreckage. Thrusters fired along the boat's hull, matching the motion of the slowly tumbling wreck.

This close, the mystery of the wreckage wasn't any easier to solve.

"Can you tell what kind of ship that piece came off?" Owen asked Chief Kaminski.

"No, sir. See that section of outer hull plating, though? If the curve of that is any indication, that was a big ship before it got broken. Where's the rest of it?"

"Nowhere we can see," Owen said. How did one large piece of what must have been a pretty big ship end up on its own in space? The more he thought about this, the less sense it made.

Owen and the others had done boarding drills many times in training. Seal suits, check suits, double-check suits, remove atmosphere inside boat, open hatches, send across tethers, check tethers, double-check tethers, confirm communications between suits, and finally head over to the wreckage. Owen led the way, going hand over hand along the tether.

Ship interiors had a certain similarity about them. Rooms or compartments, none of them typically all that large because of the risks of losing atmosphere or of fire. One hand gripping the edge of a hatch to hold himself motionless as he looked about the wreck, Owen felt sure this section had once been the bridge or some other control center. Any emergency lights must have been destroyed or run out of power, the only light inside coming from the suits of the four Earth Guard personnel. With no atmosphere to spread the light, anywhere the lights fell was brilliantly lit, with sharp edges leaving the shadows beyond totally black. Even for someone experienced in boarding wrecks, it was a spooky experience, their skin crawling with the sense that wraiths or ghosts of the vanished crew were lurking in those black pools.

He shook it off, focusing on what needed to be done. The general layout of what Owen could see seemed familiar enough, but there were differences he couldn't account for. On the remains of one bulkhead, a motto was still visible in large letters. WE ARE ONE. That didn't ring any bells for him, but maybe a later search would find which ships might have displayed that slogan. "Chief, see if you can identify anything about this wreck from the equipment."

"Yes, sir. Kang!" Kaminski called to one of the sailors. "Get over here and help me try to pry open some of these consoles."

Owen gestured to the other sailor. "Da Costa, check over that area for anything important." He watched Da Costa pulling himself hand over hand, moving carefully through the wreck, before Owen himself turned and pushed off in the other direction.

And almost immediately found a body.

There was a large rip in the abdomen of the protective suit, made by a hefty, wicked-looking metal fragment that had pinned the body to a bulkhead. Some blood had welled out before it froze. Owen stopped his motion to examine the body, forced to grab on to one rigid arm to keep himself from drifting away. The suit was an unfamiliar design, but there were enough private companies running spaceships that it wasn't unusual to encounter differences like that. Some of the components seemed remarkably small, though. Had someone made some major improvements in efficiency?

He carefully recorded all details of the body, trying not to think about the person it had once been. At least death had probably been extremely quick. "*Vigilant*, this is Lieutenant Owen. We found some remains, but they're going to be hard to get free."

Commander Kovitch answered. "We can see that on your feed. Get a DNA sample and leave the body for a cleanup crew. We've already reported this wreckage needing to be cleared from orbit by the salvage engineers. This is all their responsibility now, not ours."

"Yes, Commander. There are a lot of things on this wreckage that we can't identify. I recommend that we—"

"We have a patrol to complete, Owen. This wreckage is the responsibility of the salvage engineers. Understand?"

"Yes, Commander."

"Why are you taking so long to complete your survey of the wreckage, Owen?"

"I am following Earth Guard safety and exploration regulations and guidance, Commander." That was an old trick, trying to get him to rush things so they'd have cause to hammer him.

"Lieutenant?" Chief Kaminski called. "We got some access panels off, but everything inside is fused. Just lumps. I don't know whether that was caused by whatever destroyed this ship or some sort of power surge inside the ship when it was destroyed."

"Lumps?" Owen asked. "Can you tell anything about the designs, the circuitry?"

"I can take back some samples and analyze them for metals and other composition, but that's it. This stuff isn't just fried. It's melted into globs."

"Okay, Chief. Record everything you can and get some samples."

"One more thing, Lieutenant. I'm pretty sure some of these are weapons controls, though I can't place what exact kind of weapons they're for."

This had been a warship? Only Earth Guard operated warships inside the solar system. And nothing about this wreck identified it as being associated in any way with Earth Guard.

Owen pushed off again, gliding deeper into the wreckage on this side, sailing over a heavy panel partly wedged against a bulkhead.

There was something behind it, almost invisible in the pitch-black that reigned wherever his suit light wasn't shining directly.

Owen twisted to get a good view.

Another body, one that had apparently been protected by this heavy panel wedging itself in place.

He tried to pull himself down behind the panel, attempting to get close enough to examine this set of remains.

An alert suddenly pulsed on his suit.

What the hell? Life signs?

He pulled himself closer, checking the unfamiliar space suit. Nothing on it appeared to be working. But his suit stubbornly insisted that whoever was inside it was still alive.

"*Vigilant*," Owen called. "We have a survivor. We'll get them back to the ship as quickly as possible."

It should be cause for celebration, but Owen knew his discovery wouldn't be greeted with joy. Dead remains were easily dealt with or passed on to someone else to deal with. Living survivors could be a pain, possibly requiring *Vigilant* to deviate from her patrol route to get the survivor to necessary medical assistance. Even worse, they could die after being brought to the ship, necessitating a detailed investigation. As Lieutenant Commander Singh had said, actually conducting search and rescue got in the way of completing scheduled tasks on schedule.

So it was that, fifteen minutes later, as Owen helped bring the survivor, still sealed in their suit, aboard *Vigilant*, he wasn't surprised to be greeted with scowls instead of congratulations.

AN HOUR AFTER THAT, OWEN FOUND HIMSELF OUTSIDE COMMANDER KOVITCH'S TINY stateroom, which was about the size of a closet in a house on Earth.

"She's alive," Kovitch informed Owen. "Commander Darius has no idea how, but she's awake and able to talk. Get down to sick bay and get a statement from her. I want the ship that piece of wreckage came from identified so we can file a final report and close this out."

Owen didn't bother asking why that particular piece of wreckage and this particular survivor had become his special responsibility. It was out of the ordinary, it was a pain in the neck, so he got handed it.

Commander "Doc" Darius seemed distracted when Owen arrived at sick bay, peering at displays showing test results. "The survivor is in there," Darius said, waving Owen toward the tiny "recovery room" off of sick bay, which was barely big enough for a single bunk and a pullout seat that doubled as a toilet. "A young woman. Mid- to early twenties, I'd guess."

"How'd she survive?" Owen asked.

"Beats the hell out of me." Darius leaned back, rubbing his neck with one hand as he studied the test results. "My best guess is her body went into some kind of hibernation state. That's not unheard-of on Earth. Mammalian diving reflex. You've had some training in that, right? But this seems to be something well beyond that."

"Commander Kovitch told me to get a statement."

"Feel free. She was disoriented earlier. I'm not sure how lucid she is."

/////

LIEUTENANT SELENE GENJI, LYING ON A NARROW BUNK IN A TINY COMPARTMENT, stared at the overhead, her mind still filled with images of Earth's death and a flash of confused chaos as the shock wave hit her ship. Where was she? There were fragmentary impressions of a ship's sick bay and a man peering down at her in mingled surprise and concern. What ship was this? Whose ship was this? The few pieces of equipment that she could see appeared to be museum pieces. But it was definitely a ship. She was in zero g, a strap holding her in the bunk.

How had this ship managed to survive the shock wave that had destroyed her cruiser? Maybe it had been in the shadow of the Moon, though there was no telling how much was left of the Moon. Probably nothing. Memory of the shock wave's immeasurable power made her shudder for a moment.

Did where she was matter now? Did anything matter now?

Any Unified Fleet ships that had survived the destruction of Earth would be heading for Mars, where any remaining Spear of Humanity warships would also be gathering for a final battle over the fate of what little was left of the human species. If the colonies on Mars had survived. How powerful would that shock wave still have been when it reached Mars?

How had any surviving Spear of Humanity believers in space reacted when their destruction of the "polluted" Earth hadn't been followed by the miraculous reappearance of a "pure" Earth? Her only solace was imagining their pain when they realized how badly their faith had betrayed them.

Hopefully the Tramontine had gotten far enough away from the solar system for their ship to ride out the spreading shock wave.

She wasn't sure how far they had gone in the two years since boosting away from the asteroid belt, twelve years earlier than they'd planned. Their hope had been to defuse the anti-alien hysteria, but it had only amplified with their departure, the Spear of Humanity warning of aliens still here, hidden everywhere.

Someone knocked on the side of the doorway before pulling themselves inside.

She released the strap holding her to the bunk and pulled herself erect, determined to face down whoever it was. The first thing she noticed was that the young man wasn't wearing the dark-gray-with-red-trim uniform coveralls of the Spear of Humanity. But he also wasn't wearing the medium blue with gold trim of the Unified Fleet. Instead, his coveralls were light blue with silver trim, a uniform that felt oddly familiar but that she couldn't place at the moment.

The young man smiled reassuringly. "I've been asked to get a statement from you. Do you feel up to it?"

"A statement?" Genji took a deep breath, wondering at the man's relaxed attitude. How could anyone be so calm after witnessing the death of Earth? Even the most fanatical Spear of Humanity stalwart should be showing some reaction to the horrible event. "Who are you?"

"Lieutenant Kayl Owen, Earth Guard."

Her eyes locked on him, studying the uniform, finally realizing where she'd seen it before. "Earth Guard? You can't be serious."

Lieutenant Owen held himself still using one corner of the bunk. "Why wouldn't I be serious?"

"Because Earth Guard ceased to exist over ten years ago. Why did you think I wouldn't know that?"

Owen's open expression grew concerned. "But . . . this is an Earth Guard ship."

"An Earth Guard ship?" Genji asked, making her skepticism clear. "Which one?"

"*Vigilant.*"

"*Vigilant?*" She felt anger flare. "How dare you mock the memory of their sacrifice!"

Owen stared at her. "Sacrifice? What, uh, I mean, umm, maybe you should tell me who you are."

"Lieutenant Selene Genji, Unified Fleet. That's all you'll get from me."

"Unified Fleet?"

"Unified Fleet," Genji repeated, gesturing to her uniform.

"Uh . . . what was the name of your ship?"

"Lieutenant Selene Genji, Unified Fleet."

"What were you—"

"Lieutenant Selene Genji, Unified Fleet."

Lieutenant Owen acted startled and confused. "I'm not your enemy, Lieutenant Genji. I found you still alive on a portion of your ship. Earth Guard wants to find out what happened and notify anyone concerned about your fate."

"You're concerned about my fate?" Genji said before turning her voice into a lash. "What are you really? If you're Spear of Humanity, congratulations. You won, and may you all roast in hell for eternity. Don't play games with me. Just go ahead and space me. I won't tell you anything. Not that it matters anymore."

"Uh . . ." Lieutenant Owen stayed silent for a few moments, his face reflecting uncertainty. "You're not a prisoner. Do you think you're a prisoner? You're not. We rescued you from the wreckage of a portion of your ship," he repeated slowly. "Do you know what happened to your ship?"

Her gaze on him sharpened. She wanted to shout. Fighting back tears, she wanted to throw a punch that would toss Lieutenant Owen out that door, but somehow she kept herself still and her voice under control. "The *shock wave!* My ship was destroyed by the shock wave!"

"What . . . shock wave?"

"From the destruction of Earth! What is the point of pretending you don't know what I'm talking about? You know what I am! You can tell by looking at me! Stop playing whatever stupid game this is!"

He stayed silent for nearly a minute, his eyes on her, no hint of hostility in them, just worry and disbelief.

Lieutenant Owen was an excellent actor.

He finally released his grip on the bunk, nodded to her with every indication of uncertainty, and left.

Should she fight her way out of here? Find out how many of these Earth Guard pretenders she could take down before they ended her?

But what was their game? Why pretend this way? And if these people were Spear of Humanity, why were they allowing an alloy like her to even be inside their ship, "polluting" it? It implied there was still something important left for her to fight for.

Stay alive, Genji told herself. *Watch and wait.*

She lay down again, her eyes on the overhead.

OWEN RUBBED HIS EYES AS HE TRIED TO REREAD WHAT HE'D WRITTEN. HE WAS DUE back on watch in an hour, his mandated rest time devoured by the mission to the wreckage and then interviewing the survivor and writing up this report.

But instead of seeing the words of his report, Owen kept seeing the survivor, Lieutenant Genji, and hearing her words. *You know what I am! You can tell by looking at me!*

What had that meant? The size and shape of her eyes had definitely been unusual. Had he ever seen that before? And the surface of her skin had been oddly smooth and sort of glowing under the lights in the recovery room. It was probably some new cosmetic treatment, and certainly not different enough to explain Genji's statement.

The destruction of Earth! She had sounded so certain, those unusual eyes haunted by what they had seen.

But of course, that was ridiculous. Earth was out there. A goodly distance from the *Vigilant* at the moment, but definitely there.

What had that strange statement about the sacrifice of the *Vigilant* meant?

Why was she acting like a prisoner of war instead of a rescued survivor?

Despite her lucid appearance, Lieutenant Genji was clearly irrational, perhaps as a result of emotional and physical trauma from whatever had really destroyed her ship. The only logical thing to do was recommend she be transferred to an orbital station and then taken down to Earth to get the treatment she needed.

Except that left unexplained just what her ship had been. Owen checked the report from Chief Kaminski again. Given the curve of the surviving outer hull section, the whole ship must have been of a diameter that didn't match any known spacecraft. Kaminski had also run searches on the exteriors of the equipment on the wreck and hadn't gotten any matches. Lieutenant Genji herself had a uniform that didn't match anything Owen had been able to find searching through the ship's database. Nor had that *We Are One* slogan shown up in any context that would explain its appearance on a spacecraft.

She'd survived by some means Doc Darius couldn't explain.

And that piece of wreckage had appeared out of nowhere, none of the rest of the ship it came from visible anywhere. And no ships anywhere near that size had been reported missing.

Nothing about this made sense.

Hearing a sharp knock, he turned his head to look as Lieutenant Sabita Awerdin stuck her head inside Owen's living compartment.

"Hey, Kayl, what's the story with that survivor?"

"Why? What happened?"

Awerdin spread her hands in bafflement. "Francesca and I were told to make enough room for the survivor to bunk with us until we could transfer her off the ship. But just now the executive officer told me that wouldn't happen, and when I asked why, she just about bit my head off."

Owen sighed, rubbing his eyes again. "That's not that unusual when it comes to Kovitch. But maybe it's because the survivor is crazy."

"Crazy?" Sabita Awerdin's eyes widened. "Like dangerous crazy?"

"I don't think so. But she insists Earth was destroyed and that she's part of some fleet that doesn't exist."

"Earth was still out there last time I looked," Sabita said. "I guess—"

The general announcing system burst to life, the words echoing with unusual force. "Lieutenant Owen to sick bay, on the double!"

Both he and Sabita stared at the nearest speaker for a moment, startled.

She recovered first. "On the double? You never tell an officer to go somewhere on the double!"

"They did this time," Owen said, unstrapping himself from his chair. "I guess I'd better get to sick bay."

"Kayl . . ." She shook her head worriedly at him. "Be careful."

"Always am," he said. His usual reply, as usual pretty much meaningless.

In sick bay he found Doc Darius waiting for him in a sealed isolation suit and came to a halt in the doorway, staring.

Darius took a step toward him. "Did you touch it?"

"Did I . . . ?" Owen looked about him, confused. "Did I touch what?"

"That!" The doctor pointed toward the now locked door to the recovery room, a bright yellow sign warning QUARANTINE pasted across it.

"I did touch the door—"

"Not the door!" Doc Darius calmed himself with an obvious effort. "The creature."

It took a few seconds to realize what he meant. "You mean the survivor? Lieutenant Genji?"

"Yes. Did you make physical contact with . . . the survivor?"

"No," Owen said, shaking his head, thinking that the doctor's face showed more sweat on it than short confinement in the suit should have generated.

Darius relaxed, his body sagging. "Good. I didn't think you had touched the creature, but if you had you'd be ordered into isolation just like me to protect everyone else on the ship."

His surprise fading, Owen felt growing outrage replacing it. "Doc, did you call her a creature?"

Darius gave him a half-hostile, half-pitying look. He pointed to a large display on one bulkhead. "What is that?"

"A genetic readout," Owen said. Everybody learned about those in high school biology.

"And what does this signify?" the doctor demanded, pointing to an odd symbol poised above one gene.

In fact, Owen saw the symbol placed above a bunch of genes. "I have no idea."

Doc Darius pointed again, his stiff finger appearing ready to impale the offending gene. "It means that is not a human gene."

"Not—" Owen swallowed hastily. "That's impossible. My sister works in genetic research. Putting nonhuman genes into humans has been prohibited for—"

"Listen to me!" Darius gestured again, the motion as sharp as if he were swinging a knife. "It's nonhuman and cannot be linked to any genetic source on Earth or elsewhere in this solar system. Do you understand? Alien. That thing in there looks human," he said, giving a fearful look toward the recovery room, "but it's not. A substantial part of its genetic makeup is alien."

"What? What?" Owen struggled to grasp what he'd just been told.

You know what I am! You can tell by looking at me!

Was that what Lieutenant Genji had meant? But how could anyone link her appearance to inhuman genetics?

Then his mind fastened on something else.

Thing.

"Sir," Owen protested, adopting formal speech, "Lieutenant Genji is not a thing. I talked to her. She's a person."

Darius blew out a disgusted breath. "Think with your head instead of whatever part of you is attracted to the survivor's looks, Lieutenant. It's not human, but it looks human enough to fool all of us. Do you think that's a coincidence? How would you infiltrate a world inhabited by another intelligent species?"

"But . . . she . . . Humanity has never encountered any aliens!"

"Just because we've never found them doesn't mean they couldn't have found us. If you're smart," the doctor said, "you'll forget anything about what's in that recovery room except for this." He pointed to the genetic readout once more. "There's your warning and all you need to know about . . . the survivor. Have you talked to the captain yet?"

Still trying to get his head around what he'd learned, Owen had trouble grasping the sudden question. "About . . . ?"

"That." Darius gestured toward the recovery room. "I'll pass on the captain's orders since you haven't gotten them yet. Not a word. Not to anybody. You know nothing about this. There is nobody and nothing in there."

"Yes, sir." The words came out automatically, the doctor's attitude clearly conveying that Owen had been dismissed. Owen pushed his way out of sick bay, floating a couple of meters down the passageway before his mind caught up with his body.

An alien? A . . . spy?

Why would an alien spy wear an unfamiliar uniform and claim

that Earth had been destroyed? Weren't spies supposed to blend in and try to not attract attention?

That thing. It. The creature.

He hadn't been able forget the anguish in Lieutenant Genji's eyes, in her voice, as she spoke of Earth being destroyed.

The smart thing to do would be to follow orders. To forget he'd ever seen or talked to anyone named Selene Genji.

Yeah. That's what anyone primarily concerned about protecting himself would do.

Screw it. It wasn't like he had a career worth protecting. But someone else needed help.

GENJI HEARD A SOFT CHIME. SHE SAT UP, HEARING IT REPEAT.

There was an old-fashioned panel on one bulkhead near her, a light blinking on it.

She looked toward the door, which had a small translucent window in it. The guard she had seen posted there had disappeared a while back, the sick bay beyond going dark as if it, too, had been closed off to seal her in.

Earth Guard, hell. These people were acting just like Spear of Humanity fanatics, afraid of contamination. Why hadn't they just killed her already?

Maybe whoever was calling would provide an answer.

Finding the right control to respond to the call took some fumbling, but she finally located it.

To see an image of a troubled-looking Lieutenant Owen gazing out at her. "Umm, hello, Lieutenant Genji."

"Hi, Lieutenant Owen," Genji said, wondering if Owen was going to continue his clueless act. The clumsy opening certainly felt like it.

"They told me not to talk *about* you, but they didn't tell me I couldn't talk *to* you," Owen said. "This is a backdoor channel through the regular communications system, so we're not being monitored."

He was going to pretend these were unofficial communications? Why? "What's the point of this?" Genji asked.

"You're . . . alien?"

He sounded so sincerely disbelieving. She silently mimed applauding his acting. "That's right, Lieutenant Owen. I'm an alloy, as I'm sure you saw the moment you looked at me."

"An alloy?"

"A Human-Tramontine alloy," Genji said, tired of talking around things. "First generation, procreated by genetic engineering. As I'm sure you already know."

"Tramontine?"

She lost what little patience was left in her. "Are you an absolute idiot? How can I believe you don't know who the Tramontine are? Do you need me to remind you of basic facts like First Contact with the Tramontine in April 2140?"

He stared back at her wordlessly. This was a waste of time. She was moving to cut off the call when Owen spoke abruptly. "It's February 2140. February seventh, 2140."

Genji froze in mid-motion.

"All those things you told me," Owen said, the words spilling out in a rush. "They haven't happened. Earth Guard exists. This is an Earth Guard ship. And Earth itself is still out there. It hasn't been destroyed. Why do you think it has?"

"I watched it," Genji said slowly. "I watched Earth die. On the twelfth of June 2180."

"That's . . . that's impossible."

"You're telling me it is now February 2140?"

Lieutenant Owen nodded.

Genji shook her head. "What is the point of this? Why are you carrying out this charade? What possible thing could you want from me that would justify you claiming and trying to convince me that it's forty years ago?"

Owen glared back at her. "Why is this on me? Look, I know what a raw deal is, and you seem to be getting the worst one I've ever encountered. I want to help. But I can't if I don't understand any of this. You're an *alien*?"

"An *alloy*. Part alien."

"Fine," Lieutenant Owen said. "A Human-Tramonate—"

"Tramontine."

"—alloy. So explain any of this to me," Owen said, looking frustrated. "If your human appearance is supposed to let you move undetected among us, if you're a spy, why did you show up in a uniform that's totally wrong, claiming to be part of a fleet that doesn't exist, and claiming that you witnessed Earth being destroyed forty years from now? How does that help you hide among us? Am I missing some special spy tactic?"

Was Owen that good an actor? Genji looked at him, trying to find an answer in his appearance, his movements, his eyes. "I'm not a spy," she finally said. "I'm an officer in the Unified Fleet."

"There is no such fleet," Owen said with a certainty that seemed impossible to fake. "There never has been."

Further words stuck in her throat. A ship filled with equipment that seemed to have been pulled out of a museum. Officers claiming to be part of an Earth Guard whose remnants had dissolved a decade before, and claiming that this ship was the *Vigilant*, which had been destroyed in late 2175. Claiming that Earth still existed. Apparently shocked to learn she was an alloy, and acting totally ignorant of the Tramontine. Claiming that it was the year 2140.

Those reports as the shock wave approached. Light bending as space-time flexed. Her own sight of reality warping as the shock wave got closer.

Genji shivered as the implications hit her. If the destruction of

Earth had created conditions that had hurled her back in time, if this really was 2140, if Earth still existed, if the Tramontine hadn't made contact with humanity yet . . .

Her uncompleted last thought as the shock wave approached finally finished. *If only . . . someone had been able to prevent this.*

If it really was the year 2140 . . .

Genji felt herself trembling as an insane hope grew inside her. She fixed Lieutenant Owen with a rigid gaze. "If you're lying to me, I will kill you very slowly. That's a promise."

Owen twisted his mouth in a sardonic expression. "I'll keep that in mind. Is that all you're going to say?"

"No. Do you want to help me save the Earth?"

CHAPTER 2

HIS ROOMMATE, JOE, WAS ON WATCH WHEN SABITA AWERDIN STUCK HER HEAD into Owen's stateroom. "You got time to talk?"

Owen yawned as he nodded. "Sure. What's up?"

"That's what I want to know." Sabita lowered her voice. "The survivor. What do you know?"

"Not a thing," Owen said, scowling. He couldn't risk confiding even to Sabita his secret conversations with Genji. "What survivor?"

"You're the last person I'd expect to go along with that. Aside from Doc, you're also the only person who talked to the survivor, and Doc is acting a little psycho since then." Sabita gave him a pleading look. "Why are we being told there wasn't a survivor?"

"Sabita, you don't want to get into this."

She paused. "Rumor among the crew is the survivor isn't human. Some kind of monster. Is that true?"

Owen hesitated, unwilling to let that statement go without an answer. "That depends on what your definition of human is. I think she's human."

Sabita surprised him with a short laugh. "Are we back to that?"

"Back to what?"

She indicated herself. "There was a time when people with skin this dark, my ancestry, weren't considered human. Or at least not as human as other people."

"This isn't . . . exactly . . . like that." He looked at Sabita. "She's human."

"Okay." Sabita gave him an arch look. "Rumor also says she's beautiful."

"What?"

"Is she? Is that what makes her human? That she's hot?"

"No. I guess she's okay as far as that goes. But that's it."

Sabita studied him. "When you think of her, what do you see?"

That one was easy. "Her eyes."

"Her eyes?"

He'd surprised her. "They look like they've seen things . . ." He took a deep breath. "I don't see a monster looking out through them."

Sabita nodded, her eyes hooded with thought. "You're looking at the right place to judge a person, anyway. Kayl, everyone calls the survivor 'it' or 'that' or something. You're the only one who says 'her.'"

"She's a person," Owen said in a low voice. "Just like you said."

"I guess I did." Sabita hesitated again. "Do you need help?"

"No." Owen suddenly blurted out more. "She does."

"Oh. Oh, man." Sabita's voice grew sharp. "Tell me you're not going there. Tell me you're not thinking that."

He started to say something, but the words caught, so he stayed silent.

"Kayl, think really hard before you do anything. Will you promise me that?"

"Sure." He met her eyes. "Believe me, I'm thinking."

"Don't forget that you're the one who told me she was a couple of tons short of carrying a full load of reaction mass. *You* said she was nuts."

"I haven't forgotten that."

After Sabita Awerdin left, Owen leaned back, closing his eyes and trying to think.

Selene Genji seemed to have accepted that the year was 2140, but what proof did he have that she had come here from 2180? There was her DNA, and the strange events surrounding her rescue from the piece of wreckage, but there could be other explanations for those things that he wasn't aware of or hadn't thought of. Including the apparently official belief that Genji was an alien spy or saboteur or something else nefarious.

What could he do even if he decided to do something? Sick bay was sealed off except for an occasional trip closely supervised by Doc Darius to pass ration packs into the recovery room via the isolation tray. Two sailors were always on sentry, complaining and bored but nonetheless there even though officially they weren't guarding anything. Captain Garos and Commander Kovitch would slap him down hard if he went to them about his concerns for Lieutenant Genji. How could he help her even if he decided to do that? A quixotic charge trying to press the issue would just get him relieved of his duties and probably confined to his stateroom, if not locked up in the coffin-like brig.

Especially since Captain Garos and Commander Kovitch had apparently decided Owen might have bungled his interrogation, which officially hadn't happened, of the survivor, who officially didn't exist. Frustrated at being unable to openly blame him for failing at something that officially was not, both of them were being even more hypercritical of Owen than usual.

Owen had tried sounding out Lieutenant Commander Singh, only to be quickly shut down and told the subject was too hot for anyone to talk about. Even Sabita had just shown that she didn't want him to do anything.

For now, the best way to help Lieutenant Genji was to remain free and able to act if an opportunity presented itself. Though exactly what he should do, what he could do, remained very vague in his mind.

/////

"LIEUTENANT OWEN, SIR!"

Leaving the bridge after his latest watch, Owen turned to see Chief Gayle Kaminski approaching. "What's up, Chief?"

Kaminski nodded in greeting as she reached Owen. "Just something I didn't get a chance to pass on to you. I know we're not supposed to talk about . . . anyone on the wreckage, but there haven't been orders about the other stuff on it. I've analyzed the samples we took of the melted-down electronics, and it's kind of strange."

"Strange?" Owen said.

"It's the proportions and types of elements and materials in the samples," Kaminski explained. "If I melted down everything inside some of our gear, I wouldn't get results like that. I don't know where that equipment came from, but based on the composition of the samples, it's not anything made anywhere that I can find out about."

"That is strange," Owen said. And, perhaps, evidence to support Lieutenant Genji's claims to be from the future. "Thanks for telling me, Chief. Have you heard anything about what's happened to the piece of wreckage?"

Chief Kaminski shook her head. "All I know is there's a salvage tug on the way to intercept it. Now, if it was me, I'd haul that thing in and analyze it every which way. But if the salvage engineers only have orders to remove the body and scrap the wreckage, that's all they'll do. As you are aware, sir, nobody wants any questions raised about that wreckage. I could try to see what I can find out, though."

As you are aware, sir, was the special phrasing used by noncommissioned officers to remind officers of things they should already know and needed to be thinking about. Owen took the hint and shook his head. "I don't want you getting keelhauled over this because you asked questions, Chief. If you happen to hear any-thing, though, I'd be grateful if you passed it on to me."

"No problem, Lieutenant." Kaminski turned to go but paused. "Sir? There's something I've meant to tell you for a while."

"What's that?"

"I had a good friend aboard the *Sentinel*," Chief Kaminski said.

Owen couldn't stop himself from stiffening at the name. *Sentinel* had been his father's ship, the new vessel that had suffered cat-astrophic failures on its first patrol.

"A real good friend," Kaminski repeated, her face shadowed by memories. "He was among the dead. I wanted you to know, Lieu-tenant, that I dug into things after that disaster. You know me. I took a real good look at everything, and I never believed the official line that it was your dad's fault. I think he and the rest of the crew on that ship were handed a ticking time bomb. I just wanted you to know that I lost a really close friend on the *Sentinel*, and I never blamed your dad. I wanted to tell you that. I should have done it when you first reported aboard."

"Thank you, Chief," Owen said, his voice choked despite his attempts to control it. "That means a hell of a lot coming from someone like you. It really does."

"I just wanted you to know," Kaminski repeated, looking awk-ward. She nodded again before turning and heading back down the passageway.

Owen watched her go. He'd never before heard the compro-mised design of the *Sentinel* referred to as a "ticking time bomb," but that characterization of the flawed ship felt very apt.

Come to think of it, "ticking time bomb" might also be an apt way to describe Lieutenant Selene Genji.

HE SHOULDN'T SPEAK WITH HER. EVERY TIME HE DID, HE RAN THE RISK HE'D BE detected. Earth Guard was complacent about a lot of things, including hacking, which had allowed things like the unmonitored back-channel line Owen was using to speak with Genji. But that didn't mean the automated security systems might not spot him. He had no illusions about how he'd be treated if he was caught.

But he called whenever he could, and he talked to a Lieutenant Genji whose earlier despair and defiance had been replaced by an earnest eagerness. *We have to make some plans. We have to do something.* She said "we" a lot, assuming that Owen would be part of any effort to "change the fate of Earth." And who wouldn't want to save the Earth and every person and other living thing on it?

If she wasn't crazy. He pried more details of the "future" out of Genji, hoping for contradictions that would let him dismiss her story as a fantasy.

But it all kept hanging together.

"What are the Tramontine like?" Owen asked her during one of their clandestine chats, he in his stateroom, she still confined in the recovery room inside sick bay.

"You mean their personalities?" Genji asked, puzzled. "Individuals vary, just like humans."

"I mean their appearance."

"How could you not know? Oh." Genji furrowed her brow in thought. "Humanoid. A lot like us. Not close enough that a Tramontine could walk down the street and not be noticed instantly. But basically shaped like humans. That was one of the big reasons why they were eventually accepted after First Contact."

"And First Contact is in April? Of this year?"

"Of 2140," Genji said, watching him as if expecting that might cause him to make a mistake.

So they were still testing each other. "April 2140," Owen confirmed. "You have to agree that your story of being from the year 2180 is pretty hard to accept."

Genji met his gaze. "From my perspective, your claim that it is now the year 2140 is pretty hard to accept."

She had a point, Owen realized. "How'd that go after the Tramontine were accepted?"

"After a lot of early misunderstandings, it went pretty well for a little while, according to the histories."

"'According to the histories'?" Owen asked. "You don't have firsthand knowledge?"

That earned him a weary, exasperated look. "I wasn't born until eighteen years after First Contact. And my memories of my first five or six years are a bit hazy. Were you trying to trip me up again?"

"Yes," he admitted. "When did things go bad?"

"Not all at once," Lieutenant Genji said. "Slowly, and then suddenly. Starting in the late 2140s, through the 2150s and 2160s, major institutions, things like Earth Guard, started crumbling. I don't know all the details. It was decades ago, and I wasn't born until 2158. I know people lost faith in institutions and started turning to fanatics and frauds. That led to the wars. The aliens were convenient demons to blame for everything. The Spear of Humanity took advantage of that to gain support and followers."

"How many wars were there?" Owen asked.

"That depends on how you count," Genji said. "Some people counted individual conflicts, like the Lunar Incursions in 2174. Others just lumped them all under the name the Universal War. Because it seemed to be everywhere and one war just followed another."

"We end up fighting the aliens?"

Genji gave him a look of disbelief. "Did you really ask that? No. The Tramontine aren't involved in any of the wars that make up the Universal War. It's all humans fighting other humans, for a variety of reasons that increasingly include the belief that some humans, and the aliens, are the cause of all the problems and don't deserve to exist." She paused. "I owe it to you to explain that alloys, people like me with some alien DNA in addition to my human DNA, fed the fears. We had to be wiped out. That's how some people thought."

It felt like a nightmare, described by Lieutenant Genji in the resigned tones of someone reliving bad memories.

"How many died?" Owen asked.

She looked at him. "Do you mean before billions died along with the Earth? I remember the headlines when the global death count passed three hundred million. I stopped paying attention after that. It was bad enough counting the dead in the Unified Fleet."

"But . . ." Owen didn't want to believe this would happen. He tried to find arguments to prove that what Genji said would come must be wrong. "Why does Earth Guard crumble? And other institutions? We're doing pretty well, aren't we? Aside from limited border clashes, there's been peace for decades. I don't think we're perfect, but what could lead to collapses like that?"

"Wow." Lieutenant Genji said the word without any inflection or feeling. Just a single, flat word.

"What's that supposed to mean?" Owen demanded.

"It wasn't an attack on you."

"It sure felt like an attack."

Genji sighed. "You know history, right, Lieutenant Owen? Did you ever study some period of history before everything fell apart and ask yourself why, when the people responsible for things were shouting warnings, no one seemed to care as their world teetered on the edge of a cliff?"

"Yes," Owen said.

"And have you thought, man, those people must have been stupid?" Genji looked at him again. "Lieutenant Owen, I've talked to you enough to know you're smart. To know you're observant. And even you can't see it. You think Earth Guard is pretty near perfect, with no systemic problems. How could it slowly collapse? But it will. I don't know all the reasons why—some of that stuff was thirty and forty years ago for me—but it will."

Owen shook his head. "I know perfectly well that Earth Guard too often promotes the wrong people for the wrong reasons. And that it's been rewarding people for pursuing bureaucratic measures of success rather than doing what we're supposed to be doing. And that—" No. He wasn't going to discuss his father's case with her, the hushing up of major mistakes that had led to a disaster. That was too personal. "Lieutenant Genji, if you think I think Earth Guard is perfect, you need to rethink what you're thinking."

She raised one eyebrow at him. "Have you always talked like that?"

"No. In fact, it seems to be a side effect of talking to you."

For one of the few times since he'd met her, Lieutenant Genji smiled for a moment before getting serious again. "Lieutenant Owen, I know a few things I can try to change. Like problems that developed around First Contact. I can fix those. But other things I don't know or don't know how to approach. Together, we might be able to figure out ways to try to identify and tackle those problems, too. Anything that might prevent Earth from being destroyed on the twelfth of June 2180."

"You're saying 'we' again, Lieutenant Genji," Owen said. "What makes you think I'd be a good partner in this plan of yours?"

"Because, Lieutenant Owen, you are the only person on this ship with the guts to talk to me," Genji said. "And that means you're the only person on this ship who will listen to me. I'm used to dealing with people who don't want to share oxygen with me, an alloy. You're not like them. I think we can work together."

"What's so bad about being an alloy?" Owen demanded.

She looked at him as if he had suddenly grown a second head. "If you don't know the answer to that, I have no idea how to explain it to you. In the 2170s, there'll be a lot of people who could explain it to you. Lieutenant Owen, we need a way for me to get off this ship to where we can start trying to change things."

Once again, "we" needed to do something. "Lieutenant Genji, we're still on patrol. If I broke you out of sick bay somehow, and you managed to steal the ship's boat, you'd be spotted within minutes, and you'd be tracked and intercepted. We need something that will give you a reasonable chance to get free." Had he just said "we"? "I'm trying to come up with something. I'm watching for opportunities."

She watched him for a moment before nodding. "All right. As long as you're working on it," Lieutenant Genji said. "I have faith in your capabilities." She seemed perplexed by his reaction. "Why is that funny?"

"Let's just say I haven't heard that very often," Owen said.

"Why not?"

"That's a long story."

"At the moment," Genji said, "I've got nothing but time."

"I don't," Owen said. "I've got another watch coming up."

"Already? How much sleep are you getting, Lieutenant Owen?"

He stared at her, amazed to see that Lieutenant Genji appeared to be genuinely concerned. "Not enough. Why do you care?"

Genji looked away. "I guess I'm starting to think of you as a shipmate. Even though I'm a prisoner and I still can't fully believe it's really the year 2140."

"What will it take to convince you the Earth is still there?" Owen asked, his guilty memory prodding him about the way he'd told Genji at their first meeting that she wasn't a prisoner. At that time, she hadn't been, but her status had changed very quickly after that. "Will you have to stand on the surface before you believe it?"

"Probably."

He found himself enjoying their talks more and more and kept cautioning himself not to get personally involved with Genji. He also felt more and more guilty as each day went past, unable to figure out any way to help her while the *Vigilant* was on patrol.

The next day, the decision was taken out of his hands.

THE "WARDROOM" ABOARD THE *VIGILANT* WOULD BE CALLED A "BOOTH" IN A RES-taurant back on Earth. But that still made it one of the bigger places on the ship to hold meetings. Which was why Owen found himself wedged in among the other officers while Commander Kovitch glared at everyone for not being able to shrink small enough to fit in the wardroom even though, since they were in zero gravity, the officers could literally fill the entire space from top to bottom instead of crowding along the deck.

"Attention on deck!" Kovitch called out.

Captain Garos pushed himself up to the wardroom, stopping in the passageway. "I want everyone to listen up. You are all aware that we had a *routine* encounter with a *normal* piece of space junk and that we did not take *anything* off that piece of space junk. However, we've been ordered to divert from our patrol route long enough to rendezvous with a courier ship, to which we will transfer . . . an item. I don't want one word of gossip about the diversion, not one word about the courier ship, not one word about *anything*! Owen!"

The sudden shouting of his name startled Owen enough that he took a second to respond. "Yes, sir."

"Did I wake you up, Lieutenant Owen?"

"No, sir."

"The . . . item . . . requires an escort," Captain Garos said. "You will transfer to the courier ship to ensure it reaches its intended destination safely. *Understood?*"

Owen nodded even though his thoughts were churning. "Yes, sir. How many others will be in the escort, sir?"

"Just you, Lieutenant. Just you." Spinning about, the captain pushed off down the passageway.

"Dismissed!" Commander Kovitch shouted.

"Commander?" Owen called out before Kovitch could leave. "Where am I supposed to take the courier ship? What exactly am I supposed to do?"

Kovitch eyed him as if the questions were absurd rather than sensible. "The courier ship will be on full automatic. All you have to do is monitor things. That is all you will do. Monitor the autopilot until the courier ship reaches its destination, and then follow the orders you receive there. Is that clear enough for you?"

"Yes, Commander," Owen said, trying not to sound and look as angry at the dismissive words as he felt.

Roughly half of the officers aboard *Vigilant* took their cues from the captain and avoided speaking to or dealing with Owen unless they had to. Most of the rest had some sympathy for him but weren't willing to go out on a limb for a lost cause.

Which was why, as the other officers hurried off, only two remained with Owen: Sabita Awerdin and his roommate, Joseph Gish.

"It looks like they're giving you a few days of vacation," Joe commented. "Keep your guard up, man."

"I will," Owen said. "Do you have any idea where Lieutenant Commander Singh is? Why wasn't he at the all-officers meeting?"

"He's on the bridge. Why?"

"I just . . . wanted to ask him a few things."

"Don't be an idiot, Owen," Sabita warned him. "Not this time. Lieutenant Commander Singh will tell you the same thing. If this is a chance to get the thing that isn't in sick bay off the ship, let it go."

"She's not a thing."

"Fine. That alien that isn't in sick bay. Which is not worth risking your career over and maybe even your life."

"Sabita, why are we out here? What's Earth Guard's mission?"

"To protect and help people," she said.

"Yeah," Owen said. "To protect and help people."

"*People*, Kayl. Not aliens."

"I hear you," Owen said.

"Which isn't the same as agreeing with me! Try not to get yourself court-martialed."

/////

COURIER SHIPS WERE SUPPOSEDLY BUILT TO QUICKLY TRANSPORT NEEDED ITEMS. It was an open secret that they were almost always used instead for exclusive transits by Very Important People who wanted to travel in style without mingling with the average Earth Guard sailors. As such, the living areas on the ships were divided into a fairly small forward compartment for the pilot and navigator / flight engineer, and the much larger compartment behind, in which the VIPs would reside.

The courier ship having docked on full automatic, Owen headed toward the boarding access. There was no one to see him off except a single sailor monitoring the hatch to ensure it closed properly. He was about to climb down into the pilot compartment when his phone chimed.

He paused to check it, ignoring the pained look on the face of the sailor.

Joe had forwarded a message to him. Check this out! Owen stayed on the ladder, reading quickly. A large object entering the solar system had been detected slowing its velocity in ways no natural means could account for. Tracing its trajectory back through the vast dark between stars led to a place of origin that was one of the stars humanity had tagged as having habitable planets.

The object had been declared likely extraterrestrial, likely alien. On its current vector, it would reach the inner solar system in April.

First Contact with the Tramontine in April 2140. Lieutenant Genji had been right on the button.

Her story was sounding more believable. He had to tell someone. But how?

And how long had this information about the alien ship been known before it was publicly announced? Did the arrival and assessment of that ship have anything to do with this mysterious errand on the courier ship that seemed to be centered on Lieutenant Genji?

Owen continued down the ladder, the sailor slamming the hatch behind him with unnecessary force.

The pilot compartment, as advertised, wasn't luxurious. Two regulation chairs before the control panels with regulation padding, a pulldown bunk on the bulkhead behind them so the crew could alternate sleeping, and a pullout toilet without even a privacy curtain.

He ached to see whether Lieutenant Genji was inside the VIP compartment, whether she was on board at all, but the standard security device in the door separating the compartments was solidly locked.

Any attempt by him to crack that lock would be recorded by the ship's systems. He was probably being monitored full-time by the cameras in this section of the ship, which could well be relaying their observations back to *Vigilant* or ahead to his destination. He needed to know what he was going to do before he broke open that lock.

An alert warned him just in time to strap into the pilot's chair. The courier ship broke contact with *Vigilant*, thrusters fired, and then the primary propulsion kicked in to hurl the courier ship onto a vector for Galileo Station, a large orbital facility that included a major Earth Guard base.

When the burn ended, Kayl checked the projected track. Frowning, he checked it again.

Instead of steadying on a vector direct to Galileo Station, the courier ship had settled on a vector swinging below the station, much closer to Earth. A midcourse correction burn would be required. "Navigation, why aren't we on a direct vector for Galileo Station?"

The AIs on Earth Guard ships were widely mocked, but they

could usually handle simple questions. "Pilot, the chosen vector avoids other traffic approaching Galileo Station."

Owen viewed the situation display, not seeing any traffic heading for Galileo that would require the maneuver. But it was hardly worth overriding the AI's navigation. The chosen vectors looked safe enough, and the longer flight time wasn't a problem as far as he was concerned. It would give him more time to think, more time to decide what he had to do.

Painstakingly going over every square centimeter of the pilot compartment didn't help him decide what to do, but it did keep him busy. He ran diagnostics on every system and got perfect results. There weren't any signs of trouble.

What would happen if he broadcast the information that someone with alien DNA was in Earth Guard's possession, someone who had accurately predicted when the alien ship would reach the inner solar system? Most likely he'd be discounted as one of the UFO kooks and arrested as soon as he got to Galileo Station. That wouldn't help Lieutenant Genji.

Was she even really aboard this ship, or was this an unusually detailed attempt to get him to openly violate orders?

This courier ship wasn't designed for atmospheric entry, only for flights in space. Where could he try to take it in space that wouldn't result in him quickly being intercepted and thrown in a brig?

Think! What can I do? What should I do?

Half an hour until the vector correction burn was scheduled.

Owen pulled himself into the pilot chair, trying to sort his thoughts.

He blinked, wondering if he'd just micronapped.

He felt really sleepy. Which wasn't surprising given how little sleep he'd gotten in the past week.

Another wave of sleepiness washed over him like a gentle tide.

This didn't feel right. His eyes went to check the life-support readouts, seeing that everything, including air quality, was solidly in the green.

But he was really, really sleepy. Owen fumbled at his seat harness, thinking if he got up it might pass. Wait, his harness wasn't even fastened. He tried to push himself up, but a wave of darkness washed over him.

/////

"LIEUTENANT OWEN! LIEUTENANT OWEN! WAKE UP!"

Something hit the side of his suit helmet, rocking his head a bit inside.

His suit helmet?

Owen blinked himself back into consciousness. He had a splitting headache and his vision was a bit blurry, though it seemed to be clearing. He was sealed into a suit, all the markers blinking green except for the one monitoring the exterior atmosphere. That glowed a solid, deadly red.

Gazing anxiously at him through her own helmet was Lieutenant Selene Genji. How had she gotten into a suit? How had he gotten into a suit? How had she gotten out of the locked area in the back of the ship?

All of the questions jammed in Owen's still foggy brain, producing only a single word. "How?" His voice sounded frighteningly hoarse.

Genji waved her gloved hand around to indicate their surroundings. "The air in here has a lethal level of carbon monoxide."

"What?" Owen managed to turn enough to view the ship's controls. The life-support lights still all shone green. But his suit's external air sampler agreed with what Genji had just said.

"I . . ." She hesitated. "I felt something was wrong with the air, so I hacked the lock."

"You hacked the lock?"

"It's a really old design."

"It's state-of-the-art." Owen winced as the pain in his head flared. "And then you got into a suit?"

"And got you into a suit," Genji said.

What he'd experienced were classic symptoms of carbon monoxide poisoning. "If you hadn't done that, and done it fast, I'd be dead."

Genji looked away for a moment. "I need your help," she finally said.

"Lucky for me, I guess." Owen managed to straighten up in the pilot's seat and started another diagnostic on the life-support system. While that was running, he checked their position. "What the hell? The ship was supposed to do a vector change to put us on an intercept with the orbital station we were heading for. It didn't. It made a wrong vector change."

Somehow, he wasn't surprised to see that the autopilot was also reporting that it had no problems.

Genji was peering at the movement display. "It looks like we're heading for atmospheric entry on . . . on Earth." Her voice sounded incredulous for a moment.

"Yeah." Owen checked the data with growing worry. "We're going too fast for safe reentry."

"And we're coming in at a bad angle," Genji said, proving she knew her space maneuvers. "Can this ship handle that?"

"No," Owen said. "This is pretty much a 'never do that' situation with a ship like this."

The diagnostic on life support finished, reporting no problems.

So did a diagnostic on the autopilot.

"It's my understanding that a life-support system can be programmed to produce carbon monoxide, but it can't happen by accident," Owen said.

"That's how they work in 2180," Lieutenant Genji said.

Owen reached to punch the emergency beacon.

Nothing happened.

"Manual maneuvering?" Lieutenant Genji suggested. She'd strapped into the co-pilot seat next to him but was studying the controls as if she didn't know the layout at all.

Owen tapped the thruster controls. Nothing. He flipped up the cover and mashed the manual override. Nothing. Without pausing, Owen reached for the manual main propulsion control, hitting it hard.

Nothing.

The green lights on the control panels shone merrily at him, assuring Owen that everything was perfectly fine. But nothing worked.

He activated the comm system and set it to emergency broadcast. "Any ship, any ship, this is the courier ship VX-401. SOS, SOS. All systems unresponsive." He released the control, looking at Genji. "We should have heard that message over our suits' communications system. We didn't. Nothing went out."

"What are our options?" Lieutenant Genji asked, her voice calm.

How could this be happening? "I . . . I don't . . ."

"Lieutenant Owen, you know this equipment. I don't. What are our options?" She was right. And, given the competence with which Genji was dealing with this, her claims to be a combat veteran were becoming a lot easier to believe.

Evaluate the situation. Owen scanned the information before him. "Assuming this display of space traffic in our vicinity is accurate," Owen said, "nobody can get to us before we enter atmosphere. Automated tracking systems should have caught on immediately when this ship didn't carry out the planned vector change and instead headed for atmospheric entry. They should've sounded alerts. That's if," he added bitterly, "those systems haven't also been monkeyed with."

Now what? Evidence. Pulling out a spare data drive, Owen plugged it in. "Since they left the diagnostic systems working to fool us, I should be able to download all the system data so we'll have proof of what happened that we can hand over to the right people."

"How do we survive long enough to do that?" Genji said, still sounding unruffled.

"We've still got the lifeboat. There's a capsule tucked under the ship for emergency atmospheric entry. Its systems are totally independent of the ship's for safety reasons. If whoever messed up this ship forgot to plug the lifeboat into the ship, it won't have been infected by whatever malware has crippled the ship and should work."

Lieutenant Genji studied their vector. "Can we launch it on a vector that gives us a chance to survive entry? We're coming in hot and wrong."

"I think there'll be a window we can launch in that gives us a chance," Owen said. "We'll probably have to launch on gut instinct, though."

"I agree on both counts, Lieutenant Owen."

He looked at her. "We may have a lot less than an hour to live. My name is Kayl."

"I'm Selene. Hey, Kayl, how about we survive this, get drunk later, and laugh about it?"

"I like the way you think, Selene."

She surprised him with a laugh. "At least I lived long enough to hear someone tell me that!"

"We've got about ten minutes until this ship starts coming apart." Owen unbuckled his harness and led the way into the main compartment, where the escape access was located. On the way there, he paused in front of an emergency locker. "What the hell. Let's wear these, too. The way things are going, we might need backup to our backup."

"What are those?" Lieutenant Genji asked.

"Parachutes."

"Parachutes? *Parachutes?* With fabric and rope? Where are your impellers?"

Owen shook his head at her. "I have no idea what you think an impeller is. But right now I like having an emergency device that I can activate." He indicated the ring as he helped her strap on the parachute over her spacesuit. "If it doesn't open automatically, and you see mine open, pull this."

Her eyes followed his directions. "Got it."

"Help me here." Owen yanked up a section of carpet, revealing a hatch in the deck. Raising a T-lever built into the top, he strained to open the hatch, Lieutenant Genji adding a surprising amount of strength to the effort. As the hatch rose, Owen leaned down to check the connections. "We're in luck. The lifeboat isn't plugged in to the ship. They didn't think of that."

"They thought we'd already be dead from carbon monoxide poisoning," Lieutenant Genji pointed out. "This hot atmospheric entry is about getting rid of the evidence."

That sounded both grim and all too plausible.

Wearing the chutes made them bulkier, but fortunately VIPs tended toward plus sizes, so the accesses were large enough to let them through. As Lieutenant Genji worked to get her harness fastened, Owen activated the lifeboat's systems.

"Is this what I think it is?" Lieutenant Genji asked, looking about her with a worried gaze. "This seems to be a very primitive capsule."

"It is," Kayl said, flipping some switches and pressing buttons. "The basic design is nearly two hundred years old." The courier ship suddenly began trembling as it hit the highest edges of the atmosphere. "We've got maybe two minutes to launch this lifeboat before the ship is torn to pieces." The upper hatch cycled closed as Kayl raised a protective cover off a big red button. "When one of us hits that, explosive bolts will kick us free. We have to judge when the trajectory that will put us on is survivable."

Lieutenant Genji nodded. "If we're lucky, there'll be a survivable trajectory."

"If we seem close to one, call out. I'll do the same."

Owen poised his hand over the red button, feeling the courier ship pitch and buck as the atmosphere thickened rapidly. The ship suddenly yawed, a prolonged screeching transmitted through the hull marking a substantial part of the ship tearing free. Owen felt his stomach lurch as the courier ship suddenly whipped nose upward and around.

"Now!"

Owen realized he and Genji had shouted that at the exact same moment, his hand already slamming forward to mash the red button, the explosive bolts kicking the capsule free, a moment of relative calm, and then the atmosphere caught the capsule and started playing pinball with it.

He'd been in simulators. He'd experienced difficult reentries. But nothing like this. Suddenly grateful that he hadn't had a chance to eat anything so far today, Owen felt himself being whipped painfully back and forth and up and down and every other direction as the capsule tumbled uncontrollably.

But the capsule's automated systems were firing thrusters, trying to steady the descent. After one particularly vicious swing, the capsule settled down, swaying slightly as it fell deeper into atmosphere, the air outside glowing red as it leaked over the edges of the heat shield, the temperature inside the lifeboat growing uncomfortably warm. Kayl fought down his fear, trying to control his breathing.

He looked over at Lieutenant Genji to see how she was taking this and was surprised to see her lips drawn back in a tight smile. Noticing his gaze, she turned her head toward him. "What a ride, huh, Kayl?"

It suddenly struck him how very easy it would be to fall in love with a woman like Lieutenant Selene Genji. "I'll let you know how I feel about it after we reach the ground," Owen mumbled.

Owen felt a jolt as the drogue chutes deployed, the capsule

jerking violently as they opened. After a few minutes, the main chutes blossomed above, lowering the capsule's descent to a safe speed. "I can't believe we survived that," he said. "So far, so good."

"Don't jinx us," Lieutenant Genji warned.

As the interference from superheated atmosphere around the capsule subsided, the capsule's systems began scanning the area.

And almost immediately beeped an urgent warning.

Owen checked the alert. "Two airborne craft on collision course with us. There's nothing to worry about. They must be search and rescue birds."

Genji's hand reached past him, one finger stabbing at the data readout. "Look at the speed and size of those objects heading for us! They're not SAR birds, they're missiles on intercepts aimed at this capsule!"

He stared in disbelief at the data. "But . . . but . . ."

"Lieutenant Owen, we've got twenty seconds!"

CHAPTER 3

ENJI'S PRODDING JOLTED HIM INTO ACTION. OWEN'S HAND MOVED WITHOUT conscious thought, hitting another button, bolts blowing away the emergency hatch next to him. He reached over and yanked himself out of the capsule, holding there for a moment as Lieutenant Genji reached the hatch and without pausing launched herself away from the capsule.

That seemed like a good idea, so he did the same.

Twisting as he fell, Owen saw a streak of fire coming from the northwest, moving incredibly fast. It hit the capsule, producing a pressure wave that punched the front of his suit and a flash of brilliant light that caused the faceplate of his suit to automatically dim protectively. But he could still see the second missile come in, hitting higher up on the capsule, blowing away the tethers of the main parachutes.

No longer supported by the chutes, shattered pieces of wreckage spreading out from the impact explosions, the pieces of the lifeboat plummeted toward the ground below.

What the hell? What the hell? What the hell?

What is going on? This doesn't happen.

It is happening. Snap out of it, man. You're still falling. Thanks entirely to Selene Genji, you're still alive. Maybe it's time you started contributing more to the effort.

They were still pretty high up, high enough that the suits were welcome protection at this altitude against the cold, the thin air, and the lack of oxygen. In the brief moments before they'd had to bail out of the capsule, it had displayed a map of their position on Earth. He twisted again, looking northwest and seeing, as expected, the distant, familiar outlines of a very large spaceport set amid the sere landscape, a major city spreading out to the south. Albuquerque.

Spreading his arms, he slowed his fall and angled west.

Seeing his motion, Lieutenant Genji matched it.

Together, they arrowed down through the sky, heading west, away from the place where a cluster of small new craters soon marked the landing site of the lifeboat's remnants.

SELENE GENJI HAD BEEN OPERATING ON AUTOMATIC, FOLLOWING TRAINING AND instincts honed by battle to stay alive. But now she was falling toward what really seemed to be the Earth.

Impossible. But it was really there. The atmosphere she'd watched blown away as the planet died had just nearly killed her. The idea that everything since her awakening on that ship had been a simulation, a fake, had been hard to shake given the absurdity of thinking she might have actually traveled back in time to 2140.

But it sure seemed like the Earth was really there.

Knowing she couldn't give in to emotion, she watched Kayl slightly above and to the left of her. If what he'd described to her during their earlier conversations was accurate—a career in Earth Guard marked by routine, predictable events—he'd done a pretty good job of reacting and thinking in an emergency. Fate had thrown her together with someone who could help with the seemingly impossible mission she had assigned herself.

She already had the parachute ring in one hand, so when Kayl's chute bloomed she instantly followed suit. It didn't seem to slow her nearly enough, the ground still coming up uncomfortably fast for someone used to using impellers for this kind of thing, but by doing a rolling landing she made it down in one piece, which was more than could be said of the lifeboat.

Standing, she found and hit the quick-release buckle, letting the harness drop off her, a wind from the south catching the chute and sending it gliding away to the north.

Yanking off her suit helmet, she looked around.

And it hit her.

She was standing on Earth. She'd expected a lot of heat, forgetting that it was February. Genji could feel the wind, smell the living plants, hear the noises of a living world. It was really here. Kayl hadn't lied.

She could still save this world. Or die trying.

Lieutenant Owen walked up to her, dragging his own chute and fighting to try to keep it from inflating again. "Selene, are you okay?"

"Why wouldn't I be okay?" She realized that her cheeks were wet and wiped at the tears, still taking in the incredible beauty of this world. "We're going to save this planet, Kayl."

"I hope so. Why did someone shoot down the lifeboat?"

Snapping back to the present, she pushed the quick-release buckle on Kayl's parachute harness. "Let it go. We don't want the chute anywhere near us. That'll make it too easy to find us."

Genji started pulling off her suit, seeing Kayl giving her a perplexed look.

"We want it to be easy to find us. And we need to keep the suits on," Kayl said. "They've got homing beacons—"

"Which is why we need to shed them and get out of here, Lieutenant Owen!" She pointed upward. "Someone just tried to kill both of us twice. Do you really think whoever shows up looking for those beacons is going to be search and rescue?"

He was overwhelmed. Understandably so. The forces he counted on to protect him, the forces of which he was a part, had just tried to murder him. Kayl Owen hadn't experienced the slow collapse of Earth Guard that was to begin in not much more than another decade, hadn't experienced the brother-versus-sister battles that would be fought without mercy. He hadn't really believed her when she'd told him that was coming. But now early manifestations of that reality had tried to kill them both two times in quick succession.

Had there been deadly incidents involving anti-alien sentiments in 2140? It seemed unlikely with the Tramontine not even having made contact yet. Or had her arrival in this time triggered things that wouldn't have otherwise shown up until much later?

"Lieutenant Owen." He seemed to respond better in a crisis to the use of his rank. "If I'm right," Genji said, "we don't want to be here when whoever is coming gets here. If I'm wrong, all we have to do is attract the attention of the SAR team. But if I'm right, and we're here when they get here, we will not survive a third attempt on our lives today. We need to get out of here. Fast."

Kayl looked south, where the flat area they were on ran for several kilometers, interrupted by occasional short arroyos.

Genji shook her head. "Not that way. It's easier ground, so it's the first direction they'll look. We need to head off at an angle."

"Umm . . . okay." He pointed west. "There's some rougher terrain that way that will offer us cover. And it's in the direction of Albuquerque, which is where we want to go."

"All right. Let's go."

"Wait." Kayl knelt by the discarded suits. "These are the survival kits with emergency food and water." Popping off the kits, he tossed her one and started west at a trot.

She followed, their feet leaving no marks on the hard soil. The sun was partway up the sky. Midmorning or midafternoon? Genji hoped it was midafternoon, with night not far off. That would make it a little easier to avoid detection.

Kayl looked back at her. "You've had Survival, Evasion, Resistance, and Escape training, haven't you?"

"Yeah," Genji said. "SERE training was standard in the Unified Fleet. We were fighting a war. Do you believe me now?" He didn't answer, which seemed fair enough given her own doubts of him that had only vanished when she had stood on the surface of the Earth and drunk in its life.

Despite the bright sun and the desert landscape, the temperature was mild. Pretty good conditions for running and hiding, but it took a while to reach the rougher terrain. Genji gasped with relief when they finally entered an area of hills with jagged slopes rising above and narrow gulches winding between them. They'd be forced to slow down on this ground, but they wouldn't be easy to spot.

Kayl paused for a minute, breathing heavily, looking up at the hills.

"We could see better up there," Genji said, "but we'd also be a lot easier to spot. If we want to stay hidden, we need to stay low."

"Okay." Kayl didn't argue. From his expression, he was still trying to come to grips with what was happening. But until he did, he was listening to her advice.

It was easy to like Lieutenant Owen.

Getting through the brush lining the gulch wasn't fun, but her uniform had been made of a tough material that could handle far worse dangers, and Kayl's also seemed able to deal with sharp branches and thorns. They paused at one point to drink from the emergency water canteens, Kayl eyeing her. "You're not sweating nearly as much as I am from this running."

"No, I'm not," Genji said, wondering whether he would make a big deal of it. Alloys could handle both heat and cold extremes better than humans.

But all he said was "lucky you" before they started off again.

The gulch remained well below the hills ascending on either side but hadn't bent much and was rising slowly. Looking back,

Genji saw the area where they'd landed coming into view again as they got higher.

Two steps farther on, she stopped, grabbing Kayl's arm. "Hold it," she whispered, pointing upward with one hand while pointing to one of her ears with the other. Whatever was making that high-pitched whine seemed to be getting closer fast.

He stopped, puzzled, listening. It took several seconds before his ears caught the noise. "Aircraft."

"We need to hide," Genji urged him.

"But—"

"Lieutenant Owen, stay with me. If I'm wrong, we're still fine. If I'm right, you do not want to be seen."

With obvious reluctance, he lowered himself alongside Genji, concealed amid the brush but still able to see in the distance the place where they'd landed.

Two fair-sized aircraft tore into sight from the northwest, slowing and circling in a search pattern as they neared the spot where she and Kayl had landed, the beacons on their discarded suits still attracting "rescue."

Kayl pointed toward the aircraft, one of which was coming to a hover. "See those specks around them?" he breathed in as low a voice as possible. "Drones linked to the larger aircraft." He'd pulled out a monocular from the survival kit and raised it to one eye. "That's weird. Those don't look like search and rescue. They're combat birds."

Lowering the monocular for a moment, he looked over at her. "I don't want you to be right."

"I wouldn't either in your place," Genji said.

Raising the monocular again, Kayl squinted. "Maybe these were just the closest available rescue birds. There are people dropping out of the craft on hover. Six . . . eight . . . nine. What the hell?"

"What is it?" Genji asked, aching to grab the monocular from him and look herself.

"Why would a search and rescue team be carrying so many weapons?" Kayl said. "They've got rifles out. Looks like they're doing a search assisted by the drones. They're—"

Genji heard the distinctive low rumble of the thunder that accompanied the use of energy weapons, the bolts of charged particles tearing through the air and creating the same vacuums in their wake as lightning bolts did.

She watched Kayl lower the monocular, his expression reflecting shock and disbelief.

"They . . . they opened fire," he said. "There's a small arroyo just south of where we landed. Remember that arroyo? They must have picked up life signs amid the brush at the bottom, because they opened fire. They didn't try to see who or what it was. They opened fire."

"What was it?" Genji said, her voice still low but sharp. She had to snap Kayl out of his shock. "Lieutenant Owen, what did they shoot at?"

"Huh?" Kayl blinked, breathing fast. "Javelinas. Wild pigs. I saw some of them running. Why didn't they try to see who was in the arroyo? Why did they just try to kill them?"

"Welcome to my world," Genji said.

He stared at her. "I still didn't believe you, I guess. Not all the way. But this . . ." Kayl stared back at the aircraft, which were continuing their slow search, spreading out but trending south. "How could Earth Guard . . ."

"I'm part alien, Kayl."

"That shouldn't make any difference." He frowned, shaking his head as he watched the search. "There is no way Earth Guard authorities reached a decision to do this. Not this fast."

"Lieutenant Owen—"

"No. I know Earth Guard." He looked at her. "They don't move fast. They don't decide fast. To the people running Earth Guard, critical emergency means they need to hold a meeting to talk about what to do." Owen pointed toward the aircraft. "There is no way they would decide to take these kinds of steps this fast. These are unapproved actions being taken by someone with sufficient authority to order them. I'm absolutely certain of that."

She considered his words, not wanting to dismiss them as wishful thinking. He was, after all, the expert on 2140. "Okay. I can believe that. You've been at peace for a long time. From what I was told of the history of First Contact with the Tramontine, it took quite a while for humans to decide how to handle them. How to welcome them, whether to welcome them, how they fit in humanity's laws and practices. People argued a lot. The people running Earth Guard are probably arguing right now over those same issues. Which left room for those who knew what they wanted to do to act."

He seemed pleased that she'd accepted his argument. Beckoning, he backed carefully away through the brush, trying not to cause any stir that might be spotted from the search aircraft.

Unsaid was something she knew Kayl must realize, that just because these actions hadn't been officially approved didn't mean they weren't deadly, and they very likely hadn't seen the last of them.

IT DIDN'T TAKE LONG TO LEARN THAT IT WAS LATE AFTERNOON, THE SUN DROPPING toward the horizon. They kept moving, listening intently for any signs that drones were approaching. Most of the search had seemed to be aimed south of their landing site, along the easy ground where someone would be expected to flee, but Genji knew the search area would expand as the hunt found no prey.

The land they moved through had hard soil interrupted by patches of brown grasses, numerous low trees and bushes dotting the area. The heights around them differed from the level ground mainly in their slopes and ridges, their sides either nearly bare or covered with the same sparse fields of bushes and trees. Numerous exposed rocks and boulders pocked the landscape. The vegetation didn't offer perfect cover but was dense enough to always offer something to dive under to hide.

Twice she warned Kayl to take cover beneath bushes before drones hummed overhead. After the second time, he gave her an appraising look. "You've got really good ears, don't you?"

"Yeah," Genji said, trying to make it sound like no big deal. Full humans usually didn't like being told about ways in which alloys had better capabilities.

But all he said this time was "lucky for us." As the sound of the drone receded, they headed west again.

"Can I ask you something, Selene?"

"Sure."

"When we first landed on the ground, you seemed really happy. But now you're looking around as if you're at a wake viewing the remains of a beloved relative."

"It's nothing," Genji said.

Kayl barked a short, humorless laugh. "I know when 'nothing' means 'something.'"

She glanced at him before directing her gaze to the dirt beneath them. "It's beautiful out here."

"Yeah," Kayl replied. "Why is that making you unhappy?"

She had to talk to someone about it. "I watched it die," Genji said. "I watched it all be totally destroyed. I look at this now and it feels like I'm looking at a ghost, at something I know is dead and gone."

"Oh." Kayl took a while to say more. "I can't even imagine what it must have felt like, seeing that. Why? Why would anyone do that?"

"I've told you. The Spear of Humanity believed Earth had been polluted by the alien presence. They also believed that if they 'cleansed' the Earth, it would be reborn as a 'pure' world for them

54

to live on forever while everyone else stayed dead and went to their various hells."

Kayl shook his head. "You're telling me they were crazy."

"They believed in what they were doing. But, yes, I think so."

"How . . . how did they do it? How does someone destroy an entire planet?"

Should she tell him? One other person needed to know, because it was all too likely she wouldn't last long enough to get the mission done. If she told Kayl Owen, it would mean she was making a decision she couldn't easily revoke in choosing him as her partner in this mission. A mission whose elements he himself didn't yet understand. But she'd be committing him, committing his life, to it without his own knowledge of that.

I'm sorry, Kayl. I'm really sorry. I have to save the Earth.

Genji finally looked at him. "*You* have to know exactly what we want to stop. It was a Sigma bomb."

He missed her emphasis on the word "you." "Sigma bomb?"

Genji let her gaze return to the land around them. "Sigma being for the strong force. One of the four fundamental forces of nature, and the most powerful. Depending on how you measure it, six thousand trillion trillion trillion times more powerful than the force of gravity. The bomb was a device that triggered a self-sustaining reaction breaking the bonds holding subatomic particles together and liberating all that energy. As long as there's sufficient density of mass, solids, liquids, and the lower portions of the atmosphere, the reaction keeps spreading with terrible speed. Earth, and everything and everyone on it, both dissolved and exploded with unbelievable force in a matter of seconds."

"Oh my God." She looked his way again, seeing the horror in his expression. "How did they even design something like that? I thought the strong force holding quarks together into what makes up atoms can't be liberated that way."

"Hate can inspire an awful ingenuity," Genji said. "But it was also ironic. The Spear of Humanity hates . . . will hate . . . everything about the Tramontine and alloys like me. But they used hybrid Human-Tramontine technology to create that bomb."

"How did it come to that?" Kayl asked. "You told me while we were aboard *Vigilant* that institutions failed."

Genji sighed. "I don't know all of the details. Things stopped working. In the 2170s, I was dealing with the aftermath. I know the Earth Cooperation Council will hold its last meeting this year."

"What?" Kayl shook his head in disbelief. "The ECC has kept the peace and coordinated actions among nations ever since the United Nations disbanded. What about the Security Committee of the ECC that controls the mutual defense forces like Earth Guard?"

"The committee will meet every once in a while for a longer time, until 2169," Genji said.

"What happens in 2169?"

She stared ahead of them, reluctant to discuss events that still created strong emotions in her. "A lot. The important thing is, the council and the committee stop doing their jobs. Maybe they've already stopped doing them."

"How do we fix something like that?" Kayl asked.

"I have no idea. I do know how I can try to fix First Contact, if I can get to Mars. How do we do that?"

Kayl looked around as if seeking a spare spacecraft left lying about. "Do we assume people are going to keep trying to kill us?"

"Yes."

"Then the first thing we need is fake IDs so we can travel, and money. We're not that far from the eastern suburbs of Greater Albuquerque. My aunt Hokulani lives there. She can help us figure out how to get the IDs, and I can borrow some money from her."

Genji nodded. "And then we can tackle getting to Mars."

"Which will not be easy, not if people are hunting us."

"That's okay," Genji said. "I'm not giving up."

/////

"THIS WAY!"

They'd been moving slowly west through the night. They were hiking along the south edge of a narrow valley that Kayl had told her he was fairly sure divided the Ortiz Mountains to the north from the San Pedro Mountains to the south. Somewhere ahead of them were the Sandia Mountains.

And while the daytime temps were mild, at night they were dipping to or just below freezing. That didn't bother Genji because of her alloy metabolism, but it was important to keep Kayl moving.

Until Genji heard a faint whine.

The nearest cover was about a dozen meters to the left. She and Kayl bolted in that direction, hurling themselves against the base of a steep slope littered with fallen rocks and brush.

She knew her uniform would help conceal her from searchers using infrared. She didn't know if Kayl's forty-year-older design would do the same for him. "Get under me!"

"What?"

"Unless your uniform protects against IR searches, I need to lie over you so mine covers both of us!"

He didn't waste time on silly protests. He lay face down. She sprawled on top, her head near his, facing up so she could scan the sky, pulling her collar up to cover as much of her face as possible.

There. And there. Faint dark objects moving against the sky, occasionally framed by the stars filling the heavens. Moving in a steady search pattern.

None of them reacted as they moved past overhead nearly silently. Genji suspected only her ears could've picked up the faint whine of their motors, which had warned her. She waited as they vanished to the east. "We may be clear. How are you doing?"

"You're lying on my back," Kayl said.

"I know. It's not very comfortable," Genji said. "But you're warmer, right?"

"I guess."

"With your tech today, what are they searching for?"

Kayl took a moment to answer. "Movement and heat mostly. It's too hard to sort other indications out of all the background noise in the environment."

"Good." She paused. "I'm hearing something bigger coming. Do not move."

Genji held herself absolutely still as a larger aircraft swung slowly overhead, pivoting to ensure its sensors scanned as wide a range as possible.

As it moved on, the slight clicking noise of uneven rocks and gravel being stepped on sounded.

Kayl could hear that, too. He seemed to be trying to avoid breathing any more than absolutely necessary.

She saw a dark shape moving along the slope, making little noise, then another, then a third. They all had rifles, though Genji wasn't familiar enough with forty-year-old designs to identify the type of rifles in the dark.

She readied herself. If the nearest one spotted her, she'd roll off Kayl, evade, then charge, and . . .

The nearest one paused, scanning the slope above where Genji and Kayl lay.

After a long pause, the searcher moved on.

They lay still for another half hour before Genji was willing to risk moving.

She helped Kayl to his feet. "Sorry about that."

"It probably saved our butts," Kayl said. "Speaking of butts—"

"Do not go there."

She understood his high spirits after their latest escape. Genji felt it, too. But that could lead to overconfidence. "We can't assume there are no other searchers out tonight. Let's stay close to the bottom of the slope and stay alert. You say you hiked this area in the past? Any idea if there are fixed sensor grids we have to worry about?"

"There were back in the 2120s," Kayl said. "But they were allowed to deteriorate when funding fluctuated. My aunt Hokulani mentioned talk of installing new grids to monitor conditions and help hikers in need of assistance, but that hasn't happened yet. I don't think any of the old ones are still active."

Genji looked about them as they moved on, thinking about what would happen in 2176. "Where does your aunt live in Albuquerque?"

"Technically it's one of the far-eastern suburbs of Greater Albuquerque, near the south edge of Santa Fe County. I was going to take us south once we get around this mountain and head that way."

"She lives that far east?"

"Yeah. Why?"

"Nothing. It's nothing. We can talk about it later."

AFTER CIRCLING THE MOUNTAIN TO THE SOUTH, KAYL LED THEM PAST A SMALL TOWN named San Pedro and a ways east again through a pass before angling south once more. Over the next two days they hiked slowly closer to the eastern outskirts of the Albuquerque megalopolis, still moving mostly by night and keeping to cover whenever possible.

No more searches for them appeared. Kayl thought he knew the reason. "Whoever tried to kill us could do something small-scale and fast without many questions being asked," he said. "That kill team sent after us when we landed was probably told we were someone else, someone really dangerous. But the bigger the effort and the longer it lasted, the more people would be wondering what was happening and why. I doubt whoever they are wants to call attention to us. They made that effort when we were coming through the mountains, probably thinking we'd be heading directly for the spaceport. But I'll bet there were some hard questions raised about what was going on and they've probably had to back off."

Her mood kept shifting from wonder that this world still existed to depression that she'd seen it die. How could anyone change fate enough to stop that outcome?

Kayl Owen's moods also seemed to shift from one extreme to the next. Sometimes he seemed happy to be hiking through territory he'd visited before, and other times gloomy, clearly thinking about the attempts to murder the pair of them.

Which made her feel guilty, because obviously the attempts were linked to her.

"I'm sorry for all this," she said one morning as they rested beneath a low tree.

"It's not your fault," Kayl said.

"Of course it is. You were a well-respected officer in the Earth Guard—"

His bitter laugh cut her off. "Where the hell did you get that impression?"

"What—" Genji began, startled.

"It's nothing."

She wasn't the only one who could refuse to talk about things.

Another time, discussing the alloys, Kayl used the term "pure human," only to physically retreat from her as she directed a glare of intense anger his way. "What did I say?"

He wouldn't know, she told herself. "'Pure human' is the term used by the Spear of Humanity. Please use 'full human' instead. It's . . . important."

And so they gradually learned more about each other.

As they prepared for another hike through the night, one that should bring them into the area near Aunt Hokulani's home, Genji noticed Kayl looking at her. "What?"

He looked away hastily. "Nothing."

"I know when 'nothing' means 'something,'" she said, deliberately using his own words from a few days earlier. "You're acting a little different. Am I doing something that bothers you? Or is it . . ." She might as well address this head-on. "It's because I'm an alloy, isn't it?"

"What?" Kayl shook his head, looking at her in the twilight. "No."

"Kayl, you don't have to lie. I'm used to full humans not being comfortable around me. I won't push you on it. I'll keep my distance."

"I don't want you to keep your distance," Kayl said, scowling at the ground between them. "And I'm not bothered by you being an alloy."

"Then what is it? Something about me is bothering you. What is it?"

"Nothing!" Kayl insisted. "I . . . like being around you. Talking to you."

What was that about? Genji wondered. "You don't have to pretend you enjoy being around an alloy. I understand."

"This isn't about you being an alloy! It's about you being a person. A special person."

"A special person?" Genji asked. What was this? Why would he say that? Why wasn't he looking at her? "Kayl, I'm just me."

"And I'm saying you're pretty special and I . . . like you."

"You . . . ? Wait. Are you saying . . . ?"

The awkwardness she'd been sensing in Kayl had become obvious as he shuffled his feet, looking at the ground. Finally, he looked up at her. "I'm saying you're really special and I really like you."

Genji stared at him, momentarily lost for words. She'd just been herself around him. "Why?"

Kayl looked startled at the question. "You . . . umm . . . I like talking to you. And you have saved my life a few times."

"Oh. Okay." If it was just that . . .

"And . . . I like being with you," Kayl finished.

"What?" Full humans didn't say things like that to alloys. They always kept some emotional distance on top of the usual physical distance. She'd experienced that over and over again. And that was for the best, she'd come to realize. A close friendship that might be mistaken for something more would expose a full human to the same treatment alloys received. Or maybe worse. "Kayl . . . I'm an alloy. You can't . . . we can't . . ."

"Why not?" Kayl shook his head at her. "Before I learned about the DNA, the alloy thing, I didn't question that you were a person. And I didn't afterwards, because I already knew enough about you."

"You don't know nearly enough about me."

He looked stung by her words. "Are you saying you're like one of those alien monsters in the movies who comes to Earth to seduce and kill human men to harvest their DNA?"

Genji was momentarily wordless until she realized he really was mocking the idea and had no idea of the sort of things she'd heard thrown at her growing up. "I have been accused of being that." He stared at her. "But, no. I'm not that. Kayl, I'm an experiment. Every alloy like me is . . . was . . . will be an experiment. An attempt to combine the best in both species. But no one knows how it will turn out. Whether I'll have a normal life span or suddenly develop serious physical ailments and die young. Whether my mind will stay rational or grow unbalanced."

"You're not—" Kayl tried to object.

"*No one knows.* Including me. And that's not even talking about how . . . difficult life alongside an alloy would be for a full human." Genji finally looked away again into the growing night. "Just . . . forget it. Okay? For your sake. And for mine. I . . . appreciate the offer of friendship, but I've got an entire world and most of humanity to worry about. I don't want your happiness added to my burden."

Kayl shrugged as if indifferent. "I don't know what you think I meant, but it's not that serious."

"Of course not." Genji nodded in quick agreement. "Of course not."

They didn't speak again for quite a while as they trudged along, Genji occasionally glancing quickly at Kayl to try to judge his mood.

He'd surprised her. There had been guys interested in being with her before, but they'd always seemed far more intrigued by her physically than by who she was. *What's an alloy like?* Locker room gossip. She wasn't going to get burned by guys who were only looking for an alien experience in bed and something to boast about to their friends. Though there had also been plenty of those who'd been repulsed by the very idea, which hadn't done anything for her self-image.

Kayl seemed different. Did he really like talking with her? But that didn't change the basic reality of what she was. And the mission did have to take priority, had to be all she thought about.

"How could they do it?" Kayl said abruptly. "How could they create people as an experiment, not knowing what would happen? Not knowing what would happen to them? Maybe that wasn't illegal, but morally it just sucks."

She couldn't fault him for the question. She had wrestled with it as well. "I wasn't around when the decisions were made. Obviously. But my understanding is that the risks were judged worth the possible benefits."

He shook his head in anger. "*They* judged the risks were worth it. The risks to lives they were bringing into the world, who had no voice in it."

"That's right." Genji sighed. "I've asked myself that question a lot. And I found myself thinking how it's a roll of the dice every time anyone is conceived and born. No one choosing to have a kid knows what'll happen to them, whether they'll live a long, happy life or die very young from some accident or illness. Whether they'll be a great person who does great things or a monster who hurts and kills others for the fun of it. No one ever knows. Every single time, they're taking a chance. Every single time, they're hoping. Isn't that true?"

He frowned, but he was clearly thinking through her words instead of dismissing them. "You seem to be sort of an extreme case of that."

"Yeah." Genji shrugged. "I've had those 'I didn't ask to be born' moments. I had some very pointed arguments with my mother about it." She gave him a half smile. "Yeah, I would've liked to have had a say in that decision. But I am kind of glad that I'm here. Because I am, Earth has a chance."

They walked a little farther in silence before Kayl spoke again. "Sorry I made things awkward back there."

"That's okay," Genji said, meaning it. "For what it's worth, I think you're the first guy who ever looked at me and saw *me* right from the start, not an alloy."

"Umm . . . the first time we met, you told me I must know what you were, that I could see it." Kayl turned a puzzled look on her. "What is it that makes it obvious you're an alloy?"

"Eye size and shape," Genji said, wondering why she didn't feel as uncomfortable discussing her appearance as she usually did. Maybe because Owen very clearly wasn't judging her based on that. "But the biggest thing is my skin. You've seen how it glows under light. It's a lot easier to see in the sunlight, but you must have noticed it."

"I did," Kayl admitted. "I thought it was some kind of makeup."

"If only!" Genji laughed, hearing the edge of bitterness in it. "To think I could choose whether or not to look like this!"

"Can you use makeup to hide it?"

"Sort of." Genji winced at the memories that idea brought up. "It's pretty conspicuous. Makeup made for humans doesn't adhere well to the skin of alloys."

He didn't answer for a moment. "I wish you wouldn't say 'humans' as if you're not one."

"I'm not. Kayl, get used to it. I'm not full human by any definition."

"Maybe by any *physical* definition," Kayl insisted, giving her a quick, stubborn look. "Maybe that's not what really matters when deciding whether or not someone is human."

She couldn't help sighing at those words, the same futile argument that alloys and their families had made for more than two decades. "It's too bad everyone doesn't feel that way. It's too bad everyone won't feel that way. But thank you."

He'd come up with that sentiment on his own, though. Pretty quickly, too. It really was awfully hard not to like him.

THEY HAD FINALLY REACHED A MINOR ROAD LEADING TOWARD THE SUBURB THEY sought, only an occasional vehicle humming along it during the night. "I think I know exactly where we are," Kayl said. "There was a charity along this road a couple of years back, a place where they'd have donated clothes to give out. We need to get something to wear instead of these uniform coveralls. Those will stand out more and more as we get closer to the city."

His prediction proved accurate, as they found the building alongside the road in the early morning hours, well before dawn. Kayl found an unlocked side door, which to Genji screamed "trap," but he was inside before she could object.

The main room was filled with donated objects and clothing, enough light provided by the moon to allow them to see. She looked over the piles of women's clothing in dismay. "What are styles like right now?"

"Styles?" Kayl asked. He'd already chosen trousers and a shirt and jacket.

"Women's styles. In clothing."

"Umm . . ."

"Typical," Genji muttered, trying to remember what sorts of clothing she'd seen grandmothers wearing. "I don't like this. We're stealing."

"I'm not happy, either, but we don't have any money. As soon as we get some, I'll donate enough to this place to cover the clothes."

"That won't be necessary," a man said.

Genji, halfway out of her coverall, dodged behind a pile of clothing as Kayl turned to face the new arrival. She'd already worked out a way to approach the man using the cover provided by piles of clothing and take him down when he spoke again.

"It's all right," the man said, his voice calm. He stepped closer so he could be seen in the moonlight streaming through the windows. Tall, thin, a beard. "We're here to help those in need."

"We're not thieves," Kayl said. "Really."

"Of course not." The man gestured around him. "We've had a lot of donations recently. Because of the aliens, I think. People get worried and try to clear their karma."

Genji finished pulling on a long-sleeved shirt that would hide as much of her skin as possible. "The aliens are peaceful," she said, drawing a warning glance from Kayl. "They aren't a danger."

"I hope you're right! The world has troubles enough. Do you need any food?"

Half an hour later, they were trudging alongside the road toward the eastern suburbs of the Albuquerque megalopolis, munching on sandwiches. Kayl had a battered backpack holding both of their coveralls, a hat that would also help hide his face, and a pair of sunglasses. "Whenever I start to lose my faith in humanity, I run into someone like that," he said.

Genji repositioned the wide-brimmed floppy hat she'd picked to hide her face. In one pocket she also had a pair of sunglasses with oversized lenses to cover her eyes once the sun came up. "I wish there were more of them. Are you sure we can trust your aunt?"

"Absolutely."

"How long until we get there? I don't know how much time we have before the negotiators head to Mars to speak with the aliens. They haven't left yet because the Tramontine ship hasn't adjusted its vector to meet Mars in its orbit. Everyone on Earth still thinks the Tramontine ship is going to keep heading here. There are things I can tell the negotiators," Genji said, "to prevent the misunderstandings that caused trouble during First Contact."

Unable to use public transit without having their identities scanned, they had to hike the remaining distance, which took a frustratingly long time. But once at Aunt Hokulani's community, Kayl had all the codes he said his aunt had sent to him along with open invitations to drop in anytime, allowing them easy access to both the community and her home, a stand-alone in the ageless pueblo style.

Weary, Genji flopped down on the couch, thinking that the décor looked nice but badly dated. Either Aunt Hokulani or this era favored pastel colors in wall coverings and furniture, though the tables were of some exotic wood with beautiful graining. The walls held pictures that mostly showed beaches and oceans, but also what were clearly family portraits. Including a picture of a boy who looked a lot like Kayl, a girl older than the boy, a woman, and a man in Earth Guard uniform.

"Aunt Hokulani must be at work," Kayl said. "We'll have to wait until she gets home. Might as well get some rest."

"Sure," Genji mumbled, lying down on the couch.

GENJI BOLTED AWAKE AS SHE HEARD SOMEONE SPEAK, REALIZING SHE MUST HAVE fallen asleep.

"I said, who are you, and why are you in my house?"

Genji looked up, seeing a middle-aged woman eyeing her suspiciously. She jumped up from the couch. "Lieutenant Selene Genji."

"Lieutenant?" The woman's expression shifted. "Are you Kayl's friend? Is that how you got in?"

"Uh . . ." Friend? For a full human to publicly declare friendship with an alloy was a major thing. She had no right to presume that Kayl would want that. Where the hell was Kayl? "I'm . . . umm . . . we're . . ."

"Oh my God! You're his girlfriend? Isn't that just like Kayl, not telling us anything about you until he drops in from space!"

Genji stood frozen in shock as the woman wrapped her in a tight hug.

"I'm Hokulani," she said. "You can call me Aunt Hokulani like Kayl does. Where are you from? I love your makeup!"

"I . . . I . . ." Nothing in her life had prepared Genji for an effusive welcome from a full human she'd never met before.

"Aunt Hokulani?"

Genji breathed a sigh of relief as Kayl came down the stairs.

Hokulani ran over to Kayl, giving him a tight embrace as well. "Kayl Owen, what is the matter with you? You bring home a smart, pretty girl and you never even mentioned her before this? You are smart, aren't you, Selene? I can tell. Does your mother know you're on Earth, Kayl?"

"No," Kayl said. "She can't be told."

"What? Why not?"

Kayl looked at Genji, who nodded permission. "It's a long story, starting with three attempts to murder Selene and me."

Aunt Hokulani looked from Kayl to Genji. "Three? Not one? Three?"

"Three," Kayl said.

"Okay." Hokulani gestured to her and Kayl. "Come sit down. I'll make some coffee, and we'll talk."

"I can't drink coffee," Genji said apologetically. Alloy metabolism didn't agree with something in coffee.

"That's fine. How about tea? I've got pure green sencha!"

"Tea is . . . fine," Genji said. "I love sencha. My mother drank it."

"Wonderful. Are you going to visit her? Do you want to take some for her?"

Genji swallowed, trying to maintain control of her voice. "My mother was murdered several years ago by a Spear of Humanity Cleansing Team."

Aunt Hokulani instantly dialed down her exuberance. "I'm so sorry, my dear. Come sit. Let's talk."

An hour later, Hokulani set down her coffee cup and sighed. "Kayl, you believe all this about Selene? All this she says is going to happen?"

"Now I do," he said.

"It's a lot to accept. She being from the future, the Earth going to be destroyed . . ."

Kayl nodded. "There's no doubt she's got alien DNA in her genome. My ship's doctor was seriously scared by that. Where did it come from? And Selene predicted alien First Contact would happen in April."

"If she's part alien, maybe they told her," Aunt Hokulani said.

Genji waited for Kayl to reply, feeling that she should leave this up to him. Hokulani didn't seem hostile, just wanting to know more.

"But why have her show up like she did if she was supposed to be a spy?" Kayl said. "That wreckage I found her on, the way it appeared out of nowhere, none of it makes sense any other way. And . . . Aunt Hokulani, you watched her while she was talking about it. About watching Earth be destroyed. Did she seem to be acting to you?"

"No," Hokulani said, sighing. "What she says, about people, I've seen enough to know how that could happen. But, like you, it's those attempts to kill you that convince me. She's got some people seriously scared, but instead of dealing with it right, they're trying to hide everything. Instead of listening to what she says, they're trying to silence her. You can tell a lot about someone from who their enemies are. So they tried to kill her because she's this alien monster," Hokulani added, her tone making it clear what she thought of that. "But why you, too? What does killing you gain them? What did you do?"

Genji watched Kayl shrug in a way that seemed too well honed by practice. "I'm an Owen."

"Not another word about that!" Aunt Hokulani declared. "Have you told Selene about your father?"

"No."

"You have to. She's trusting you to help her save the entire world, and you're not even trusting her with family history?"

"It's . . . painful," Kayl mumbled, looking at his hands.

"You mean like watching-the-entire-world-be-destroyed painful?"

He looked at Hokulani. "It still hurts. Dad was my world."

"Listen to me. You still have your mother and your sister. You still have your aunt Hokulani. You two are taking on a big, big job. There has to be total trust."

Kayl nodded, but Genji averted her gaze, feeling guilty again.

"You can't go to the press," Hokulani said, looking as if she were thinking things through. "They'd laugh at you. Everyone would laugh at you if you tried to speak to the world."

"That's what I thought," Kayl said. "Selene telling everyone she's from the future, here to warn us that the world is going to be destroyed, would just sound like another scam or another crazy person. Earth Guard has officially declared that there was nothing unusual about that wreckage, and there was no survivor, so it'd be my word against Earth Guard's. Anyone who believed her part-alien DNA was authentic might do what someone has already tried to do—kill her because they think she's the danger."

"The press won't listen to me," Genji said. "I'm an alloy. We're not . . . trusted."

"And," Aunt Hokulani added, "the people already hunting you would hear of it and know how to find you. What can you do that might work?"

"We need to get to Mars," Genji said. "I need to be able to speak with the human negotiators who will communicate with the Tramontine. I know I can make a difference there."

"There are people who can probably help you," Hokulani said. "I need to check with some of them. An old family friend in particular who might be able to get you to Mars."

"Who's that?" Kayl asked.

"Rear Admiral Raven Tecumseh. She and your dad were friends."

Kayl stared at his aunt Hokulani. "Yes, but, why would Tecumseh get involved with this? Why would she give Selene a chance to explain who she is?"

"Because she and your dad were friends," Hokulani said again. "Let's see. You need better clothes. And you need some new identification and all that stuff in order to travel around."

"Any idea how to get that?" Kayl asked.

Aunt Hokulani grinned. "A lot of people know how to get that stuff."

Kayl shook his head. "This seems like a lot of things outside your normal range, Aunt Hokulani. We need fake IDs that can pass scans."

"Hey, I'm your auntie. I've got this." Hokulani made a sweeping gesture encompassing the world outside. "Governments want to know everything we say, everything we do, everything we buy, and everywhere we go. Corporations want that, too."

"The information collected by the government is rendered anonymous before storage and analysis," Kayl said.

"Yeah. Sure it is." Hokulani shook her head. "Who wants somebody else knowing everything about them? Did you tell Selene why hats with wide brims and large dark or mirrored glasses are so popular? Because they make it a lot harder for the public cameras to identify you and watch everywhere you go. Everyone wants to do things sometimes without letting the government know. Not that I'm complaining any more than usual about our government, but it's healthy to have a little distrust and to be able to keep personal secrets when you want to. I just need to check with some local friends for the right contacts. For now, let me throw together some dinner. Do you like Spam, sweetie?"

Genji nodded. "We ate something like it in the Unified Fleet."

"There you go. Nothing fake here. Real Spam musubi. Don't you two worry. Aunt Hokulani is on the job."

As Hokulani went to work in the kitchen, Genji gave Kayl a worried look. "How confident are you that she can handle this?"

"Aunt Hokulani says she can," Kayl pointed out. "And, from my experience, she can get things done. You know aunties."

"No," Genji said. "I don't."

"You don't have any aunts?" Kayl asked. "Even honorary ones?"

"No," Genji repeated, hearing usually buried emotions come into her voice. She never talked to anyone about family issues, including that no one from her extended family had ever wanted to acknowledge her. No one except her mother, and Okaasama, her mother's grandmother. In a world filled with people who saw only an alloy when they looked at her, Genji had precious, faded memories of herself as a little girl meeting Okaasama, the old, old woman smiling and speaking gently. Those memories had made her rejection by every other relative all the more painful.

Kayl must have read the feelings wrapped around the single word "no," eyeing her with a concerned expression for a moment. "Uh . . . well . . . aunties are special. They're keepers of traditions, family knowledge, sources of support and strength, all of those things. Sort of the Swiss Army knives of families. When something needs to be done, an auntie can do it. I guess not all cultures have that, though."

"I guess not," Genji said, trying to keep her voice flat this time. She felt a burst of resentment that Kayl had been able to experience such things, had such things, that she never could. And then hated herself a moment later for envying him. His good fortune had nothing to do with what her life had been.

And it wasn't as if Kayl's life had been perfect. Not when his father had died when Kayl was still a boy.

She looked toward the kitchen, watching Hokulani putting together a meal, wondering what a life such as Kayl's would have been like to live, and thinking about how many such lives would end on the twelfth of June 2180 if she failed.

CHAPTER 4

GENJI HAD INSISTED ON TAKING THE COUCH RATHER THAN THE GUEST ROOM BED. But after midnight, the ghosts who haunted her memories had come, as they always did, ghosts of dead comrades and friends, ghosts of battles, ghosts of enemies she had killed in the war, and she couldn't sleep. Her night vision was better than that of full humans, so she didn't turn on any lights. Genji walked softly into the darkened kitchen, stopping when she saw Aunt Hokulani sitting at the table. "I'm sorry."

"Sometimes late-night coffee is just the thing," Hokulani said, raising her cup.

"Not for me," Genji said.

"Oh, that's right. Have some more tea?"

"Thanks." At least self-heating tea hadn't altered appreciably since 2140.

"You look like someone with a lot on your mind," Aunt Hokulani said. "Have a seat."

"Okay." Genji sat down, feeling awkward.

After a moment, Aunt Hokulani spoke up in a softer voice. "You really watched it happen?"

It wasn't hard to guess what she meant. "Yes. I mean, it only took a few seconds, but . . ."

"Nightmares?"

"When I'm awake." Genji shook her head, frowning slightly. "I don't know why that doesn't trouble my sleep. It ought to."

"I know you're going to have other priorities," Hokulani said, gazing toward the nearest window, "but I hope you'll keep an eye on Kayl."

"I owe him," Genji said.

"Is that the only reason?"

Genji bent her head, staring down into her tea. "The mission comes first. And Kayl doesn't need . . ."

Aunt Hokulani sighed. "Let me tell you something about the Owen family. My side of the family, we're pretty laid-back. But the Owen side . . . I think from the moment they're born, every Owen starts looking for a hill to die on."

"'A hill to die on'? What does that mean?"

"It's a metaphor about choosing something, a person, a cause, an action, a belief, that you're willing to give everything for." Hokulani took a drink of coffee. "Kayl, his hill for a long time was redeeming his father's name. But he's learned, the hard way, that he can die on that hill a thousand times and not accomplish anything. I think he's been looking for another hill, maybe without even realizing it, something else to put his heart into."

"I hope he finds it," Genji said.

"He has."

Genji looked up quickly, seeing Aunt Hokulani watching her. "*No.* I've told him that."

"Oh, it's not just you, Selene. Kayl is looking at what you're trying to do. Changing the fate of the entire world! That's the biggest hill you can find, right?"

"That would be okay," Genji said, her eyes back on her tea. "If that's what is motivating him."

After a long moment, Hokulani spoke again. "Did you lose

someone special? In the future when Earth was destroyed? You said your mother was already gone. Was there anyone else?"

Genji frowned. "Special?"

"A partner, a spouse, a child?"

Genji let out a pained gasp before she could stop herself. "I'm an alloy."

Another pause. "How does that answer my question? You don't need to tell me, but I don't understand."

Genji hesitated, never having had to explain that before. "Alloys are not . . . accepted by full humans. Not completely. Even in the Unified Fleet there could be some awkwardness."

Hokulani sighed. "What about other alloys? None of them were close to you? No boyfriends or girlfriends?"

"There weren't any boys," Genji said. "None of the male embryos were viable. Only female alloys were successful. No one knows why. I had some friends among the girls, but not really close ones."

"I'm sorry," Hokulani said. "Kayl told me you were worried about what might happen to you as you got older."

"I'm first-generation alloy," Genji said. This was easier, because it was something alloys had often been asked by full humans. "There was never a second generation. In theory, first-generation alloys should be cross-fertile with full humans. But no one knows what the children would be like, whether they'd be viable, or whether they'd develop unforeseen problems. Not a single alloy was willing to test it, to see what our children in a second generation would be like. Others could decide if we in the first generation would be born. But they couldn't decide whether we'd have children. Only we could make that choice. And none of us wanted to. Especially with all the full humans who didn't want there to be a second generation. How could we think about bringing children into that? Now . . ." She shook her head. "The surviving alloys were in the Unified Fleet ships near Earth, or on the surface. I'm the last one."

And, no matter what, she'd stay the last, even though she didn't say that out loud. Hokulani didn't need to know about the long-term contraceptive implant that provided nearly perfect assurance of that.

Aunt Hokulani looked sad. "Damn, that's a hard burden to carry, Selene. Surviving alloys?"

"A lot of alloys had already died," Genji said. "Some of them murdered for being alloys, some fighting like I was, others . . . couldn't handle it anymore. Being an alien on our own world. Being treated like . . ."

"It was that bad?"

"It . . . I don't want to talk about that. He doesn't . . . Kayl likes me. He told me that. Even though I'm an alloy. I don't *understand*. I can tell he doesn't know what it'd be like," Genji said. "He doesn't know what it's like to walk down the street with everyone knowing you're an alloy, or with an alloy. Like you're . . . infected. That's all in the future. I lived that future. No matter how this works out, I lived that future. But I don't want anyone else to have to live it." She took a drink of tea, the warm liquid moving down her throat and into her stomach, feeling lighter for having emptied herself of those thoughts.

"Why do you want to save it?" Aunt Hokulani asked. "Why do you want to save Earth if that's been your life?"

Genji smiled slightly, looking back at Hokulani. "Because I've also seen how great people can be, how they'll stand up for one another, the amazing things humans can bring to any situation. Earth gave me my comrades in the Unified Fleet. Earth gave me my mother." She paused. "Have you ever read Marcus Aurelius?"

Hokulani paused to think before shaking her head. "I don't think so."

"My mother used to read to me from his *Meditations* when I was a little girl. She said his teachings could help me in life. Like, with this. Why do I want to save Earth? Aurelius says 'rational creatures are born for each other's sake . . . tolerance is a part of justice . . . wrongdoing is not deliberate.' He says we shouldn't hate others for their actions and should always act for the common good. I'm not perfect. But neither is anyone else. I am part of this world, even if there are a lot of people who don't think I should ever have been born. And I have to try to do what's right for the world."

"That sounds like the sort of thing Kayl would say," Aunt Hokulani noted, taking another drink of coffee. "No wonder he's helping you."

"I'm using him," Genji said. "You know that. I need his help."

"Uh-huh. You're one cold-blooded killer of the innocent, you are," Hokulani said sarcastically.

"I can kill," Genji said. "I have killed. We were fighting a war."

"This future of yours doesn't seem all that worth saving," Aunt Hokulani said. She leaned back, looking toward the window again. "But, then, you want to change it."

"We can. I know we can. I was given the opportunity and I will make the most of it."

"I hope you're right about that," Hokulani said. She smiled at Genji, surprising her. "Because if you were chosen for that opportunity, it must mean someone or something has a lot of faith in you."

Genji shook her head. "I've been trying to tell you what an awful person I am."

"Sorry, Selene. Big fail on that one. It seems like you've had a lot of dark thrown at you, but you still strive for the light." Aunt Hokulani fixed her with a look. "What are you not telling Kayl?"

"I . . . I'm not . . ."

"I can see. What is it?"

She had to confide in someone or she'd explode. "I'm going to be doing everything I can to change the future."

"Yeah, I got that."

"I won't be born for another eighteen years. As part of a special program created under special circumstances."

Aunt Hokulani sucked in her breath, staying silent for a while. "You want to change the future," she finally said, "but you're the future. You change it, and you might change the conditions that led to you being born."

"Right," Genji said, whispering the word.

"What happens then?"

"I don't know. If I never was, I guess I just . . . am not. I won't be anymore. I never would have been."

"Oh, girl." Aunt Hokulani surprised Genji by reaching across to grip her hand, just as if she were another full human. "To succeed, you have to do things that may cancel you completely."

"I think it's more of a *will* cancel," Genji said. "I don't see any way I can do this and . . . exist."

"I see why you don't want Kayl to know. But you have to tell him."

"No! I need Kayl's help! I don't know 2140! What if he won't help if he works out that what we're doing will surely make me vanish at some point? Do you believe that I'm using him now?"

"I think you're seriously underestimating Kayl."

"Hokulani, I cannot let his feelings of friendship get in the way of getting this mission done!"

"Is that how you see it?" Aunt Hokulani sat back, shaking her head. "You hear 'friend' and you think 'vampire.' Right? It's work, they drain you, they need you. But that's only one kind of relationship with someone else. There's another kind. That's the kind where, when you no longer have the strength to take one more step on your own, your friend is there, and they help you take that step, and the next, and the next. Because they know you'd do the same for them. Just like you said about rational creatures being there for each other." Hokulani took a drink of coffee. "I don't know how rational most humans are, but I do know that you owe it to Kayl to tell him."

"I can't."

"Is it okay with you if I do?"

It was the coward's way out, but Genji snatched at it. "Yes. He doesn't have to tell me if he decides not to help anymore. I'll know if I leave here alone. If that happens I'll have to find someone else, I guess."

"No, you won't. I told you, you're underestimating Kayl," Aunt Hokulani said.

"But don't tell him anything else we talked about. Anything personal."

"Not a word," Aunt Hokulani said.

"Thank you." Genji stood up, nodding to Hokulani. "I think I can sleep now." She walked out of the kitchen, feeling Hokulani's eyes on her.

OWEN DIDN'T FEEL PARTICULARLY RESTED OR REFRESHED THE NEXT MORNING. Small wonder given the worries riding him.

Aunt Hokulani had already prepared some breakfast, watching silently as he ate. When he was done, she pointed upstairs, where Genji was still showering. "Kayl, we have to talk about her."

"What about her?" Owen asked, instantly feeling defensive.

"You need to do some thinking before you take one more step with her."

His defensiveness shifted into outrage. "Aunt Hokulani, I can't believe you'd—"

"I'm going to stop you right there," Hokulani said, her eyes flashing a warning. "Because I think you're about to say something

I wouldn't like at all. Listen to me, Kayl. You and Selene want to try to change the future so the entire world isn't destroyed in forty years, and I am one hundred percent with you both on that. I'll do everything I can to help. But there's something you're going to confront, maybe more than once, and you need to think about it. The future you want to change includes Selene Genji, and whatever program it was that created her and others like her. At some point, you're going to make a change that could cause or would cause that program to never happen. Or maybe just change that program. And that means Selene Genji never gets born."

Owen stared at her, a sort of dark buzzing filling his head, no thoughts making their way through it.

"She knows that. She has decided what she must do. You will have to decide, too, Kayl. Can you make those kinds of changes if they seem necessary? That girl," Aunt Hokulani said, pointing upstairs again, "will do it. I have no doubt. But can you? Will you help her? Will you try to stop her? Knowing that next step might mean she vanishes, never having been? Sure, maybe you'll have saved the world. But she might be gone."

He managed to force some words out. "That shouldn't be . . . an issue. How could anyone in their right mind not make the only possible choice when it's between one life and the lives of everyone on Earth and the whole planet?"

Aunt Hokulani looked exasperated. "How did you get to be your age without learning that being in your right mind and being in love are not the same thing? In fact, they're pretty much opposites."

In love? "Aunt Hokulani, it's not like that."

Hokulani sighed. "It's not like that yet, but it could be. Things happen. But even if she stays a friend, that's one life you care about versus billions you don't know. And that can be a real hard choice." She leaned closer, her eyes intent. "You are going to face that choice. Maybe more than once. You owe it to yourself, and more than that, you owe it to that girl, to make up your mind about what you'll do when that time comes. Got it?"

"Got it," Owen said. He took a deep breath, feeling the answer inside him that he didn't want to admit to but knew he had to honor.

"And, just for the record, since you seemed about to imply I'd have a problem with Selene, I don't know much about her yet, but from what I do know I'd say she's a decent person trying to do what's right. That makes her good company as far as I'm concerned." She reached out, resting one hand on his shoulder, her gaze fixed on him. "Kayl, she has her reasons for keeping you at arm's length. If you care about her, you'll respect that. And you'll think about and make that decision—before you're faced with trying to decide on the spur of the moment if an Earth without Selene in it is worth saving."

"I've made it. I can't let her down. I won't. I'll do whatever she thinks we need to do." He hated saying it. He hated knowing he'd have to do it. But the alternative would be a completely selfish act, an utter betrayal of Selene. What kind of person would do that? What kind of friend would do that?

"That's my nephew," Aunt Hokulani said. "Your father would be proud."

Selene came down the stairs, passing through a shaft of morning sunlight. As she did, her skin glowed, giving her the aura of an elven queen, Kayl thought. It made the thought of her ceasing to exist even harder to think about. But it also made the idea of betraying her trust in him impossible to even consider.

"Wow," Hokulani said admiringly. "I wish I could make an entrance like that."

"If you figure out how to trade skins," Selene said, "I'll be happy to switch with you." She looked at Owen. "Is there anything I need to know?"

He shook his head, looking away from her. "Just that I will

follow your lead on this, no matter where that takes us. I understand the very likely cost of that."

She didn't say anything. He finally looked back at her, to see Selene gazing steadily at him. Owen had to avert his gaze again, wondering what he'd seen in her eyes. Surprise, certainly. But maybe something else?

"Thank you," she finally said.

Aunt Hokulani brought out some clothing and other items. "I ordered some fashionable clothes for you, Selene."

"Thank goodness," Selene said.

"You know about UV Aversives? They try to avoid any sun exposure? Do they still have those in 2180? You can wear these, cover almost all of your skin, and look like one of them without attracting much attention. Sun jacket, light gloves, hat with wide brim and neck flap in the back. Oh, and these glasses to hide your eyes. Looking good! Just find reasons to raise your hand near your mouth when you're around people to hide the skin around your chin.

"Now," Aunt Hokulani said, "next thing is you need new identities. I have a friend whose cousin needed to disappear for a while. You go here, tell this guy Uncle Jesus Romero sent you, and he'll fix you up. Also, here's cash cards he can convert into anonymous cash cards for you. That way no one can track your purchases."

"I'm a little surprised you know about all this," Owen said.

"I'm an auntie. We do things. And like I said, this isn't all that unusual. How do you think people get the medications they need for prices they can afford in places where it's unapproved or illegal? Or if they want to watch a certain movie or buy a certain book without worrying about someone knocking on their door and calling them a freak? Or they want to avoid stalkers? Or businesses wanting to know all your secrets? Without this stuff we'd all be living in a fishbowl, and a lot of fish want to be able to draw the curtains sometimes. Yeah, yeah, I know, you're technically law enforcement, so I shouldn't be talking about this because technically this sort of thing doesn't happen. Lucky for you, it does. Once you get your fake IDs, you need to go to LA."

"Los Angeles?"

"Right. This address. Actually Santa Barbara. Not too far from the Vandenberg Earth Guard Base. That's where Rear Admiral Raven Tecumseh lives now."

Owen looked at the address. "She's retired. Do you really think she'll help us?"

"Do you know why she retired?" Aunt Hokulani asked. "Because when the *Sentinel* exploded, she stood up for your dad while the rest of the Earth Guard brass wanted to blame him and protect themselves. It killed her chances of further promotion. She will listen to you. Maybe she can even get you to Mars," Hokulani added to Selene.

"How can I ever repay you?" Selene asked.

"Repay me? Our family owes the life of our boy Kayl to you. No matter what happens, you can always find a home here. Not because of the obligation, but because of your heart."

Selene seemed lost for words, as well as strangely baffled by Hokulani's attitude.

Aunt Hokulani turned to Owen. "Your mother pinged me this morning. Earth Guard notified her that you are 'missing in the course of routine training activity.' She's worried."

"Routine training activity?" Owen said. "Those—"

"Don't say it. I agree. Next, they'll tell her you're dead. Can I let her know you're okay? Using family code, you know."

Owen looked at Selene. "Is that okay?"

"Family code?" Selene said, running one hand through her hair. "How secure is that?"

"I won't say anything that would trigger any search terms," Aunt Hokulani said. "I don't know about 2180, but even here in the past we've figured out how to talk around automated snoop searches. I'll let her know you're okay, and, if it's all right with both of you, go to visit and 'comfort' her in a week or so and fill her in on things in person. Her and your sister, Malani, Kayl. I should tell Malani, too. She's going to be really upset because she loves you so much."

"Malani has funny ways of showing how much she loves me," Owen said.

"She's a big sister. Someday I should tell you about your mother and me growing up. So can I tell both of them?"

Once again, Owen had to look to Selene.

"It's okay," Selene said. "The more people who learn now that the Tramontine are peaceful and not a threat, the sooner we can start shifting the history of events around First Contact."

"Should I tell her about you? Everything about you?"

"Yes. I'm not ashamed of being an alloy."

"Tell Mom that I'll be okay. Selene is my friend," Owen said.

"She might not be comfortable with that," Selene cautioned.

"What is that?" Aunt Hokulani demanded, cupping one hand to an ear. "I thought I just heard something that didn't make any sense. Hey, Malani is a doctor. Genetic researcher. Maybe she'll get involved in that alloy project sometime in the future."

Selene looked uncertain. "I hadn't even thought about that end of things. Directly impacting the alloy program itself."

Aunt Hokulani nodded. "A little scary, huh? If you don't want—"

"No. This has to happen. The future has to change. Tell her."

Owen saw Selene look at him and realized that she was giving him input on the question even though this had hit their biggest fear head-on and would potentially have a far greater impact on her. She really did see them as partners in this, or maybe she was testing him to see if he had meant it when he said he would do what was needed regardless of the possible cost to her. Either way, his answer had to be the same. He nodded. "The future has to change."

They paused before slipping out the back door. "Aunt Hokulani,"

Owen said, "be careful. The people who tried to kill us might come after you."

"After me? A harmless auntie? Don't worry about me, Kayl. Go help this girl change the fate of the world."

Selene smiled at Hokulani. "Despite what you said about your side of the family, I think you sometimes choose hills as well."

"I'll take that as a compliment. Get going, you two."

EXPECTING TO ENCOUNTER A VILLAINOUS-LOOKING CHARACTER IN A RUN-DOWN part of Greater Albuquerque, Owen was surprised when the address given him by Aunt Hokulani led to a normal-looking office complex, and even more surprised by the man who greeted them. Far from appearing dangerous, the man looked like the stereotype of a retired librarian.

He worked with brisk efficiency, though. "Neither of you needs to remove any clothing. I can do my bioscans through them. Your new identity cards won't fool a DNA sampler, so avoid those. The standard ID package includes a couple of burner IDs. Use those only when necessary, when you want to throw off trackers. Here are your anonymous cash cards, minus my fee. And here are your new identities. Memorize your new names and be ready to respond to them. Any questions? Hasta la vista."

After they had left, Owen found himself gazing at their new IDs as they walked down a suburban side street shaded by the sturdy new species of drought-tolerant trees planted in the 2110s. "I had no idea that would be so easy. New IDs, burner IDs, burner phones, cash cards whose purchases can't be traced. And it didn't cost very much, meaning these things aren't rare, they're commonplace. I mean, I knew some of this went on. Everybody does. They even talked about it during my training, how as the ability to collect data about everything everywhere all at once expanded, eventually people started doing more and more things to hide what they were doing. But the official line is that sort of thing is really limited, and most people don't fight the data collection because they know it's to benefit everyone."

Selene didn't say anything.

"And no one in a position like mine does it because we'd get fired or court-martialed, and no one talks to us about doing it because they know we're supposed to report things like that. So it's easy to believe that just because we could easily get really good false IDs as kids or in college, it was something people grew out of. Instead it's like this whole world hidden from official view. I didn't want to believe you were right about what I wasn't seeing," Owen said. "But you were, weren't you? At least to this extent."

She nodded.

"What else am I not seeing, and why aren't you giving me the 'I told you so' treatment?"

Selene looked over at him. "Why would I try to hurt you? I imagine you're already feeling pretty bad about learning this."

"Yeah." He couldn't help smiling at her. "Thanks for not rubbing it in."

She didn't smile in return. "I'm pretty much an expert in how it feels to be hurt, Kayl. I try not to make others feel like that. Especially people who listen to me, and you do listen to me. Are we clear on . . . limits between us?"

Kayl nodded. "Aunt Hokulani reminded me I needed to respect the limits you had to set. I will."

That earned him a longer look. "Did you and Hokulani talk about anything else?"

Owen braced himself to get the words out. "Just the 'because of what we're doing you're going to cease to exist' thing."

"Hokulani told me I was underestimating you. She was right."

"Selene, you said I had guts." He gave her a serious, worried look. "Mine are nothing compared to yours. You're the one facing that. And you're not hesitating."

"You think that?" Selene laughed briefly. "I'm really good at hiding things, aren't I? Kayl, I'm trying as best I can to remember things that happened in 2140 that I can try to influence. I remember a lot about First Contact, of course. But beyond that? Imagine you're forty years in the past, in 2100, trying to remember enough history to know what you need to do."

"I don't know how well I'd do if I was retested on my college history courses," Owen said.

"College?" Selene shook her head, not looking at him. "That was a luxury the fighting left no time for. I joined the Unified Fleet right out of high school." She paused. "If I'm being honest, I didn't finish high school. Not after my mother was murdered."

"How did you qualify for officer training?"

"Believe it or not, Lieutenant Owen, in the future they'll be able to reliably test for ability." She shrugged. "But those weren't tests on my knowledge of history."

"There's not just one bad guy you can kill to change everything?" Owen said, seeing how talk of her personal life was bothering Selene. "It's usually like that in movies."

"There will be a lot of bad guys," Selene said. "Some of them will die from infighting and other causes, and their deaths won't derail things. I think we have to address the things that led too many people to listen to those bad guys."

"That sounds simple enough," Owen said. "Which means it's going to be really complicated and hard, right?"

"Right." Selene favored him with another serious look. "I wouldn't blame you if you were rethinking your commitment to this mission."

"Nope. That's not going to happen."

"I'm stuck with you?" She finally smiled again. "Lucky for me."

A nearby bus terminal linked them to the main maglev train station, where it proved surprisingly easy to purchase tickets to LA using an automated kiosk that accepted the fake IDs and anonymous cash cards without questions. The automated routines that were supposed to spot false identification and ensure purchases were linked to an individual didn't react at all, clearly demonstrating that people had found ways to fool or work around the safeguards. More proof, Owen thought, of what Selene Genji had told him about things that weren't being seen. Moving to the gate, Owen waited, tense, as he entered his new ID and ticket into the security gate.

After what seemed a very long moment, the security gate beeped green and let him through. A second later, Selene followed.

"So far, so good," Owen commented.

That earned him a glare sharp enough to be apparent through Selene's sunglasses. "Do you remember what happened the last time you said that?"

"Sorry."

At least this time no missiles materialized. Kayl did his best to look around as they boarded the train for LA but didn't spot anyone who seemed to be paying attention to a couple of nondescript travelers among the thousands crowding the busy station.

He'd paid for a private compartment, which wasn't big but did offer some protection from being overheard.

He saw Selene gazing out the window as they left the station, the spaceport sprawling off to the north. Beyond the spaceport could be seen the hulking shapes of the so-called Las Colinas Aireagua, great atmospheric water generators that drew moisture from the air to feed the needs of the megalopolis. Even though the UV Aversive clothing hid most of her face, he still had an impression of sadness. "Are you okay?"

"You can tell I'm not?"

"I think I can."

She shook her head. "It's just so strange, seeing it intact."

"The spaceport?"

"The spaceport. The city. In 2176, the Spear of Humanity got an attack through the Unified Fleet defenses and destroyed the space-port and most of the Albuquerque megalopolis. Everything we can see from here was turned into a field of craters. Millions died."

He stared at the view, trying to imagine it all being shattered. "Aunt Hokulani."

"If she doesn't move before then, her place is far enough east I'm pretty sure she'll be out of the zone of destruction." Selene turned her head to look at him. "But that will only buy her four more years of life, until 2180."

"We'll change things," Owen said.

The surrounding landscape blurred as the train smoothly accelerated to six hundred kilometers per hour. As the train dove into the tunnel drilled through the Zuni Mountains west of Albuquerque, the outside views were replaced with programming available on the windows. "It'll take about an hour and a half to reach LA," Owen said.

The news channels were full of information and speculation about the aliens. Even the most fervent skeptics now accepted that it was an alien ship entering the solar system. Observations had confirmed that the immense alien ship was rotating majestically, providing a sensation of gravity for those inside. Who or what was inside dominated the discussions, some commentators starry-eyed but most worried or frightened. "Most of them seem to be expecting the aliens to act like humans would," Owen said.

"Naturally," Selene said. "That's where a lot of the early misunderstandings came in. If I can get to Mars in time, I can help fix that."

THE TRAIN SLOWED TO A HALT IN THE MASSIVE REBUILT UNION STATION NEAR THE center of the sprawling LA megalopolis. Expecting to avoid detection here because of the huge number of travelers, Owen was shocked to instead see special security agents conducting out-of-

the-ordinary checks on everyone getting off the train from Albuquerque.

"Are those bulky things 2140 vintage DNA samplers?" Selene
asked.

"Yeah," Owen said. "We have to get past those." He looked
about him, but the temporary barriers channeling the passengers
toward the special security checkpoints looked effective enough to
prevent them from slipping through undetected. The passengers
around him were grumbling about the delays caused by the screening but didn't seem to be prepared to erupt into the kind of riot he'd
need to get them past those security guards.

"Lieutenant Owen?" Selene said in a low voice. "What are our
chances here?"

"I can't tell yet." A check of media sites revealed that there was
a block on postings from the station, so he couldn't get any details
on what was going on. Instead, he moved through the crowd
enough to be able to see the screeners at work. "They're waving
some through and checking others," Owen told Selene. "It looks
like everyone being 'randomly' selected for DNA sampling is a
young adult traveling alone. No, they just singled out a young
couple."

"They're looking for us," Selene said. "But they don't know if
we're traveling alone or with each other."

"That may be." Owen watched the screeners work, the crowd
moving past. "I think I know how to get past them."

"I trust your judgment."

It was the sort of thing that was nice to hear but also put a bigger burden on him. Owen scanned the crowd, searching for and
finding what he needed. An older woman was struggling through
the crowd while she tried to keep track of two toddlers and an automated luggage cart that was having trouble staying with her
amid all the people. "Follow me."

He pushed sideways and back through the crowd until he

reached the woman. "Hi. It looks like you've got your hands full. Can we help?"

The woman eyed him and Selene, clearly trying to evaluate their potential danger. "I'm all right."

"I can help handle the cart for you," Owen said. "It's not a problem. I'll stay right behind you."

She hesitated, looked about to see all the security personnel in sight who she could call on if needed, and finally nodded. "I'd be grateful. Thank you."

Owen went to the cart and switched it to manual guidance, Selene beside him, enigmatic in her UV Aversive clothing.

That didn't stop the elder toddler from running up and grabbing her hand. Owen saw Selene jerk with surprise.

"I'm Violetta," the little girl said. "Who are you?"

"Talia," Selene replied, giving her false ID name, her answering smile looking to Owen a little forced.

"We've been with Granny and now we're coming home to Madre and Papá," Violetta explained, walking along with Selene.

The grandmother smiled, relieved, and led the way toward the nearest screening station. Owen kept close behind her, Selene and Violetta walking beside her.

As they reached the screening station, the human guard took a quick glimpse at their apparent family group and waved them all through before singling out a young woman traveling alone and directing her to the DNA sampler.

Owen and Selene stayed with the family, wending through the station and the less dense crowds, until they reached the pickup zone just outside the building.

"Their parents will be here in a couple of minutes," the grandmother said, checking her phone. "Thank you so much. They can be a handful. Violetta, let go of Talia. I'm sure they have somewhere they need to go."

"I'm glad we could help," Owen said. "Take care."

He and Selene walked toward the ride stand. "Are you okay?" Owen asked.

"I'm fine," Selene said.

"You seemed a bit uncomfortable with Violetta."

"How did you know that would work?" she replied, changing the subject in a way that made it clear she didn't want to answer that statement.

"My roommate at officer training told me that when the police are looking for someone, they almost always think they know what that someone looks like," Owen explained. "If you don't look like that, they barely notice you. These screeners were looking for single young adults or couples. They didn't have any interest in a family group like we seemed to be."

"How did your roommate know that? Was he a former police officer?"

Owen laughed. "No. Edourd was a juvenile delinquent on Mars before he turned himself around, and liked to tell me stories about those days."

"Being a juvenile delinquent didn't prevent him from joining an officer program?" Selene asked.

"According to Ed, most kids on Mars are juvenile delinquents. He told me Mars isn't the kind of place to raise your kids. The colony isn't really set up for families, even though it's supposed to be. Since the officer training program had quotas for Mars-origin students, he got in. And he's a good officer," Owen added. "Win for him, win for Earth Guard, as far as that goes."

Selene nodded, changing the subject again. "DNA samplers. Singling out young adults arriving from Albuquerque. They were definitely looking for me. But why bother with DNA sampling when they could've just told people to remove hats and glasses and gloves? My eyes and skin would've given me away instantly."

"Personal privacy laws," Owen said, surprised by the question. "DNA sampling in transit hubs has been legal since the pandemics of the twenty-first century because of public health exceptions. But without probable cause, they can't just order people to take off articles of clothing like that, because people might have religious or personal reasons for wearing things."

"You recognize the need for DNA sampling in mass transit hubs but won't make someone take off their hat? You're joking." She looked at him, her eyes concealed behind the dark glasses. "Aren't you?"

"It's a matter of accommodation of differing religious and personal beliefs. Is that different in 2180?" Owen asked.

"Very different," Selene said. "After enough people die, personal privacy takes a back seat. How can you be so complacent?"

"We're not complacent," Owen said, hearing the resentment in his voice. "It works. It balances priorities."

"It's not working," Selene said, her voice flat. "You, your society, just thinks it does. I told you, it's all going to fail."

"Pardon me all to hell," Owen said. "You also said you don't know exactly why a lot of things failed. It doesn't sound to me like your society in 2180 will have a very solid handle on things. In 2140, we're not destroying cities."

Selene didn't answer for a moment. "I'm sorry. I shouldn't be so critical, so self-righteous. I know where things will end up, but I don't know everything about how they will get there."

"That's okay," Owen said, mollified. "You're living with the knowledge of what will happen. I can't imagine that's easy."

"You're living with it, too, now, aren't you?"

"I guess I am. But I didn't see it. I don't see the memories like you have to. I'm sorry I snapped at you for that." Owen frowned as a thought came to him. "If they knew what you looked like, they wouldn't have singled out women for screening who obviously are not alloys. Maybe the security screeners here haven't been given a description of your physical differences. If someone was trying to keep the whole alien thing quiet, maybe they're not alerting anyone to that yet."

"That's a good analysis," Selene said. "And you got us through that without attracting any notice. Kayl, you're obviously very competent. Why have you said you weren't well thought of in Earth Guard?"

"That's a long story," Owen said. "And here we are at the ride area." He could also change subjects when he didn't want to talk about something.

Owen used one of their burner IDs to order a ride to an area a few kilometers from Rear Admiral Tecumseh's home. It seemed important to both throw off possible tracking of them and reach a potential source of help as quickly as possible. Though given the distance to Santa Barbara, "as quickly as possible" meant about an hour and a half even using dedicated express lanes.

Selene sat silently for most of that time, her eyes and expression hidden behind the UV Aversive clothes and sunglasses. Despite that, Owen got a growing sense of moodiness. "Are you okay?" he finally asked.

She jerked slightly as if surprised to realize there was someone else in the car. "Memories," Selene said.

"You've been to LA before?"

She looked out the window at the night-shrouded landscape they were passing. "I'll be born near here."

Something about the way she said it warned Owen off asking any more about that. The longer he was with her, the more he realized that Selene had been absolutely truthful when she told him *you don't know nearly enough about me.* But, clearly, he would have to learn more at whatever pace Selene was willing to disclose more about her past. Pushing her to reveal more felt wrong.

Tecumseh's home was a stand-alone single-family house set on a small lot ringed with neatly trimmed bushes. A couple of eucalyptus trees framed the entry, their light, smooth bark pale against the night that had fallen before they reached the house. "We can't just go up and ring in," Owen said. "The door-sentry system will record us and send that to the local cops."

Cautiously circling the outside of the house amid the vegetation, Owen noted once again how surely Selene moved in the dark. "You have really good night vision."

She immediately stopped. "You caught me. Yes. I can see better in the dark than full humans."

"You didn't have to keep that from me."

"Sorry. Force of habit. Full humans never minded if I confessed to worries or weaknesses over the alien DNA, but most of them didn't like hearing about ways it made me better at anything."

He couldn't say much to that. They moved onward until Selene stopped again. "That ground-floor window isn't fully closed. It's either an invitation or a trap."

"And you think it's a trap?"

"Yes. But it's probably also a risk we have to take if this Tecumseh can help us."

"I should go first, since Tecumseh should be expecting me." The window opened smoothly when Owen tried it. He climbed inside, looking about the darkened room, then turned back to the window to help Selene in as well.

They'd barely straightened up when a cool voice sounded behind them. "Let me see your hands. Otherwise, don't move." The voice held the force and volume of someone used to giving commands.

Owen spread his arms, hands open. Selene did the same.

The lights in the room came on.

"Turn around so I can see you."

He turned, slowly, seeing a face he recognized from his Earth Guard duties. Raven Tecumseh was holding a high-powered stunner aimed at them, her expression making it clear she wouldn't hesitate to use it. Of medium height, she somehow felt taller, her dark hair graying, her dark eyes (that had been likened to death rays by those who had earned her wrath) still sharp. "Admiral Tecumseh."

The admiral studied his face. "You would be Kayl Owen. You're a lot like your father." She shifted her gaze to Selene. "And you?"

Selene straightened to attention, saluting. "Lieutenant Selene Genji."

"Earth Guard?"

"Unified Fleet."

Admiral Tecumseh eyed her a moment longer before putting away her weapon. "Your aunt told me it was important I speak with you, Lieutenant Owen. It wasn't hard to convince me because of who your father was. You might be interested to know you were officially declared dead an hour ago. Come along. There's a room where we can talk and nothing will be overheard."

The safe meeting room was comfortable, laid out like a library. Aside from physical books lining the walls, there were also models and pictures of various spacecraft. Selene stopped to stare at one of the models. "Is that an *Orion*-class ship?"

"Yes," Tecumseh said. "Why does that shock you?"

"They're . . . ancient."

"I see you're not here to flatter me," Admiral Tecumseh said. Her eyes fixed on Selene as she removed her sun jacket, hat, and glasses. "Unified Fleet, you said? When was that formed?"

"It will form in 2171," Selene replied, "after the final collapse of the remnants of Earth Guard."

Raven Tecumseh walked closer to Selene, studying her. "Lieutenant Genji, I may be retired, but I retain many ears inside Earth Guard. There are rumors flying of an 'alien monster' scouting out the Earth prior to an invasion. Are you human, Lieutenant?"

"No," Selene said at the same moment as Owen said "yes."

"Not entirely," Selene clarified. "But I am not an enemy. The aliens who have come here are not hostile."

"Then why are you here, Lieutenant?"

"To prevent the Earth from being destroyed on the twelfth of June 2180."

OWEN HAD HEARD NUMEROUS STORIES ABOUT HOW ROUGH ADMIRAL TECUMSEH HAD been on those who presented briefings to her. The reality proved to be tougher than he'd imagined, as Tecumseh probed every statement and sought more details on every detail.

Eventually, she sat back. "The bottom line, then, is that these Tramontine are coming here out of curiosity, not from any desire for wealth or conquest."

"Exactly," Selene said.

"And you say they have no practices that would cause humans to feel instinctive revulsion," the admiral said. "Do they have two sexes like humans do? Or three sexes or . . . more?"

"Two and a half," Selene said.

"Two and a *half*?" Tecumseh said. "You really need to explain that, Lieutenant."

"The Tramontine have one female but two types of males. The external differences aren't huge but are obvious to the Tramontine."

"Do the different males produce different outcomes?"

"No, Admiral," Selene said. "Regardless of whether the father is a onemale or a twomale, any child might be female, onemale, or twomale. That's why there's no discrimination along those lines. Anyone's child might be different than they are."

"That's certainly different, but it's not bizarre." Raven Tecumseh bent her head in thought. "We have your DNA as proof you are not the average lieutenant. What other physical proof exists to support your account?"

Owen held up the memory drive he'd brought. "Admiral, this contains all the files from the operating systems on the courier ship. The malware will be on there."

"Excellent. I know just who to send it to, an officer who will report the truth even when it displeases his superiors." Admiral Tecumseh let out a long breath. "You haven't yet realized why you were on that courier ship, Lieutenant Owen?"

"No, Admiral."

"I am certain that your death was to serve as a cover for the elimination of Lieutenant Genji. A ship is destroyed. An Owen is in command. What does everyone think?"

He felt his jaw tightening so much it hurt. "Another Owen screwup."

"Exactly. No need to probe too much. No need to wonder why he was even supposedly alone on that courier ship to begin with. Lieutenant Genji, why are you not as shocked as Lieutenant Owen to hear that he was deliberately targeted for death simply as a diversion?"

"Because I know what the Spear of Humanity is capable of, Admiral," Selene replied. "Even if it hasn't formed yet. Permission to ask a question, Admiral?"

"Go ahead."

"Why were you not surprised when I described the slow collapse of Earth Guard?"

Admiral Tecumseh slowly nodded toward Selene. "You notice things, Lieutenant Genji. That's a valuable trait. Earth Guard, today, is like a giant tree. From the outside it looks majestic, powerful, able to stand against any force. But the inside of the tree is hollow, worn away by corruption and self-dealing and careerism. I did what I could. It wasn't nearly enough. Yet if Earth Guard isn't somehow reformed, this future fate of Earth that you warn of will be much harder to avert. That will be something I will once again try to do. I admit to being tired, worn-out from apparently futile efforts to set things right. But this story of yours has a very strong ring of truth to it. I do wish you had more physical evidence to offer, though. You told me the alien ship will arrive at Mars for First Contact, but its vector is still aimed at Earth."

"They should have altered vector by now," Selene said. "If you have any way to check, Admiral . . ."

"As a matter of fact, I do. Don't say anything while I make this call." Admiral Tecumseh plugged in a phone, punched in a number, and waited. "Has the alien ship changed vector? When? Have you established its new intended objective? I see."

She unplugged the phone, eyeing Selene. "Lieutenant Genji, my source informs me that the alien ship is currently altering vector. The new track hasn't been firmly established yet, but initial assessments are that it appears to be aiming for Mars."

"The Tramontine were worried that coming to Earth first would cause too much concern about their motives," Selene said.

"In that much, they're right." Admiral Tecumseh sat back again, hands steepled in front of her. "There are many voices warning of impending invasion. It might be a good idea for an 'authoritative source' such as myself to contact a few media people I know to offer the information that the aliens have no hostile intent. In the history you know, Lieutenant Genji, how much did humanity learn about these aliens before they initiated First Contact?"

Selene shook her head. "As far as I know, we didn't know anything about the Tramontine prior to that."

Admiral Tecumseh regarded her with a thoughtful look. "You said 'we.'"

"Earth was my home. Earth *is* my home."

"I believe you. So, *anything* we get out now will change the history you knew. What is your next step, Lieutenant Genji?"

"I need, we need, to get to Mars, Admiral."

"Wouldn't it be wiser to stay on Earth where the First Contact negotiators are gathering?"

Selene shook her head once more. "As soon as it is confirmed the Tramontine ship is headed for Mars, the negotiators will be sent there by the fastest transport available to speak with the aliens."

Admiral Tecumseh nodded. "You make very detailed predictions about near-term events. Another question has occurred to me. This alloy program which created you. What was its intent?"

"To gain genetic benefits that could slowly spread through humanity," Selene said.

"Such as?"

"Primarily life span," Selene said. "The Tramontine live on average over two hundred standard human years. Even if the genetic sharing only increased the maximum human life span by fifty years, it would be a huge benefit."

"I can see that," Admiral Tecumseh said. "But I can also easily see how much resistance the idea of 'genetic sharing' would generate. Pardon me for being blunt, but if I was trying to find a bloody shirt to wave in the face of those worried about the aliens, your alloy program is exactly the sort of thing I'd want to point to."

"I can't deny that, Admiral," Selene said.

"Did the creators of the alloy program consider that?"

"I don't know. Almost of all of the records that would shed light on that were hidden by security classifications or medical privacy laws." Selene looked for a moment as if she were in pain. "A couple of my fellow alloys made it their work to try to unearth the answer to your question. They never found it."

"Why does that cause you distress?" Tecumseh asked.

"Because they're both dead. They were still on Earth."

Admiral Tecumseh nodded slowly. "Humans cannot figure out how to mourn for billions, but we can feel intense grief for individual deaths. I've yet to understand whether that's a strength or a weakness. My condolences, Lieutenant. You must have lost a lot of friends."

Owen saw Selene take a deep breath. "I lost a lot of friends before that. The war was intense. We lost. But I am going to change that outcome. No matter what it takes." She looked at him.

"No matter what it takes," Owen agreed.

Tecumseh smiled. "I'm suddenly feeling ready to fight a few more battles myself. There's a guest suite downstairs. Make yourselves at home while I check on a few things. Lieutenant Owen?"

"Yes, Admiral."

"It may not mean anything, but I offer my deepest regrets for the actions of some Earth Guard officers who treated your life as a simple means to their ends."

"Thank you, Admiral," Owen said. "It does mean something, coming from you."

SELENE WALKED RESTLESSLY AROUND THE GUEST ROOM, STOPPING TO VIEW THE pictures and documents on the walls. "She must have had quite a career. Did you ever work for Rear Admiral Tecumseh?"

Owen shook his head. "No. But she's still a legend inside Earth Guard."

"I don't remember ever hearing about her," Selene said. "She told us she was tired, worn-out from fighting battles. Maybe that's why."

"Tecumseh also said that after talking to you she's feeling motivated," Owen said. "It felt to me like she was getting ready to charge into battle again."

"I wonder if that'll make a difference," Selene said. She frowned. "I didn't come here hoping to make any changes to Earth Guard. I just wanted to get to Mars."

"But maybe you've set something else into motion?" Owen said.

"Do you think getting Rear Admiral Tecumseh back into the fight will help?"

"I can't think of anyone who could help more," Owen said. "But

I never would have had the nerve to ask her for help on fixing Earth Guard. Admiral Tecumseh isn't exactly approachable for the average lieutenant, you know?"

Selene glanced at him. "You're not exactly average, Kayl. In case you didn't see it, you impressed the admiral."

He shook his head. "I didn't see that."

"I did. I notice things, remember?"

After a few hours, Admiral Tecumseh came down to see them. "The fastest available transport to Mars is currently being arranged for the First Contact negotiators. Your perfect record of predictions stands, Lieutenant Genji. Ideally, I'd figure out a way to get you on the same ship. But, given the high level of security and the high level of public media coverage, there isn't any way to do that without you being identified by your unique physical characteristics. And, given other events, I think it highly likely that would result in your termination by some means or other as quickly as it could be arranged."

She turned to Kayl. "Lieutenant Owen, the preliminary results of examining that memory drive are that it contains a variation on the old Imperius malware designed to take over total control of systems without being detected. It appears to be a variation specifically designed to avoid detection by the latest Earth Guard electronic watchdogs. This will pretty much remove any doubt that the destruction of that courier ship and the attempted murder of both of you was an inside job.

"It's going to take a couple of days to set something up, but I have a promising lead to get you to Mars quickly and quietly. I'm starting to raise a fuss with my questions and that memory drive, so it wouldn't be wise for you to stay here while I'm attracting attention. Find a place to stay. One of those cheap no-tell hotels. Do you have any burner phones? Here. Take these. I'll contact you when I have things set up."

"Thank you, Admiral," Owen said.

"Thank *you*, Lieutenant Owen," Admiral Tecumseh said. "And to you, Lieutenant Genji, the best of luck in your mission. I'm happy to join, but my knowledge of history is that the ship of fate has a terrible momentum born of past events and current mistakes. Turning that ship onto a new vector will take more than courage."

"If it can be done," Selene said, "I will do it."

Admiral Tecumseh smiled for only the second time since they'd arrived. "If I were still on active duty, I'd have you on my staff in a heartbeat. Believe me when I say that as soon as the two of you are safely clear of here I will be telling everyone I can that the 'alien monster' needs to be listened to, not hunted down."

Selene insisted on leaving by a different window than the one they'd used to enter. "If there's anyone waiting for us out there, we don't need to make their job any easier."

It was nearly dawn, the sky to the east just beginning to grow a little brighter, as they left the admiral's home and headed down a busy side street. There wasn't a lot of foot traffic, but even this far from LA a steady stream of vehicles purred by them on the road.

"What exactly was your job on your ship?" Owen asked as they walked. "While you were talking to Admiral Tecumseh I found myself wondering."

"I was the assistant targeting officer."

"Is that all you did? You talked about leading assaults."

She didn't answer for a moment. "I have a primary specialty."

Owen thought Selene seemed reluctant to say more. "You don't have to tell me if—"

"Close combat," Selene suddenly said.

"Oh." Owen decided not to ask any more about that. "You definitely impressed Admiral Tecumseh. According to legend, that's only happened, like, one other time with one other person."

"I told you that you impressed her, too. So that makes two other times." She gave Owen a look from the sides of her eyes before speaking again, her tone not quite reproving. "I had to pretend I understood what you two were talking about when you were speaking about an Owen and a ship."

"That's, uh . . ." *Really hard to talk about.* He tried to deflect the question in her statement. "You've never talked about your father."

"I didn't have a father."

He looked at her, startled.

She was looking straight ahead now, speaking without emotion. "A man married to my mother contributed to my DNA. Mother said he had agreed to everything. But within moments of my being born, within moments of seeing me, he demanded that she choose between him or me. Mother chose me." Selene turned her head to meet his gaze. "He left. I never knew him. There was someone who contributed to my DNA, but I never had a father."

He couldn't keep looking at her, feeling ashamed over his own reticence and clumsy attempt to avoid sharing his own past. "I'm sorry. Sometimes I'm . . . I wish you could've met my father."

"He was a good father?"

She didn't sound envious or hurt. He glanced her way. Selene just appeared ready to listen. "He was a great father. Maybe if he'd still been alive when I was in my later teens we would've fought like most fathers and sons do, I guess, but that didn't happen. I still want to be like him."

"What happened? Something about a ship?"

"Yeah." Owen looked up at the slowly dimming stars, blinking when they blurred a bit. "The *Sentinel*." He started talking, and kept talking, and she listened as they walked along the street, the stars above fading as dawn overcame the night, and somehow a heavy weight that he'd been carrying for a long time felt less and less of a burden by the time the sun came up to herald a new day.

GENJI FOUND THE WAITING TO BE INCREASINGLY INTOLERABLE. ON ONE LEVEL, IT was ridiculous to chafe at every lost hour when the event she was trying to prevent was forty years in the future. But she knew how much First Contact had been hobbled by misunderstandings. "I need to be there!"

Kayl at least had the brains not to tell her to calm down. "You met the admiral. You can be sure she's getting something set up as fast as possible."

"That won't matter if I'm not there in time!"

They'd had the exact same discussion at least six times in the last six hours. It was getting more and more difficult not to lash out at Kayl in her frustration. She couldn't blame it on the accommodations, which if not great were at least tolerable for a place that rented rooms by the hour with no questions. She'd even sort of enjoyed fighting with Kayl over who got the bed and who got the floor, since they both tried to insist that the other get the bed.

"Hey," Kayl said. "Check this out."

"What?" She gave the media panel a dismissive glance, then focused her full attention on it.

"Authoritative sources report they have learned from reliable sources that the alien ship currently on course for Mars has no, repeat no, hostile intent," the bright-eyed host of the morning show proclaimed. "The aliens are curious and want to learn about other peoples. They are also reportedly humanoid in shape and appearance, though none of them could pass for humans."

The co-host, also bright-eyed but wary, broke in. "How could anyone know that at this time?"

The third co-host jumped on that. "Everybody's talking about them invading. What are they basing that on?"

Was that a fourth co-host or a program guest? "It's all speculation. But as long as Earth Guard is preparing to deal with any outcome, we should certainly consider the possibility that this is a peaceful mission."

"You're making a difference," Kayl said, giving her a happy

look. "You're already making a difference. You really did get Admiral Tecumseh back into the fight!"

Genji felt a funny sensation in her gut, as if a void was forming there.

"Selene? Are you okay?"

"I'm fine." Genji walked to the other side of the room, facing the wall, trying to control her breathing. She'd thought she'd faced this down, made her decision, and was at peace with the price she had to pay. She had long ago come to terms with the certainty that she would die young. Maybe because of malfunctions in her genome. Maybe by being murdered. Maybe, hopefully, while fighting to her last breath. But it wasn't going to be that easy. Contemplating death was one thing. She'd long sought comfort in what Marcus Aurelius had written. *"Even if you were destined to live three thousand years, or ten times that long, nevertheless remember that no one loses any life other than the one he lives . . . the longest and the shortest lives are brought to the same state."*

Thinking of being erased from ever existing was another matter, though, one harder to think about than even death. What guidance, what comfort, did she have to confront the growing probability that she would cease to have ever lived any life? *You're already making a difference.* When would that difference change the fate of the Earth enough to eliminate her from ever having lived on it? And how could she succeed in saving the Earth before that happened?

CHAPTER 5

NIGHT HAD FALLEN, THE VIEW FROM THE WINDOW OF THEIR FIFTH-FLOOR BY-the-hour, no-questions-asked room was of a colorful street-level display of cheap holograms, old simulated neon, and even extremely retro printed signs. Genji looked down at it, thinking how such districts changed with the times but also somehow stayed always the same.

Here she was, forty years in the past, but the red-light district looked a whole lot like the one outside the base where she'd received basic training. Some of the other trainees had been friendly enough with her to convince her to come along for a celebration just before graduation. The memory still made Genji wince, half of the people in the district staring at her as if she were one of the items for sale, the other half keeping arm's length away while assuring Genji's companions that of course they had nothing against alloys.

There had never been enough alloys for them to become an everyday sight for most people. Now there was only one.

Kayl hadn't turned on the lights, suggesting that would keep their room from standing out. Genji turned to gaze at him sitting in the room's one chair, looking worried. She'd turned his life inside out. There was nothing more important than the mission, but why did someone like Kayl have to suffer for it?

And why was she getting an antsy feeling, as if there was something important she was missing?

Genji looked down at the street again, seeing couples going into and out of the buildings and bars, many of them into hotels like this one, to emerge again within an hour or two. Over and over. How many times did a room like this turn over every night?

Oh, no.

"Kayl!" she called in an urgent, low tone.

His head came up, instantly focusing on her. "What is it?"

"We're obvious as hell in here. We're not blending into the environment at all."

"Why?"

One of the things she particularly liked about Kayl was that he listened to her and heard her out before interjecting his own opinions. "We've been in this room for fifteen hours now. How many of these rooms are occupied by the same clients for more than half a day?"

His eyes widened in alarm. "This room must be standing out like a flashing light to the automated city monitors." Kayl jumped up, grabbing one of their packs. "Let's go."

"Wait." She'd just looked down again, seeing several unmarked vehicles pulling to a halt in the street outside, figures in close-combat armor and carrying weapons spilling out of them as the crowd edged away, watching with all the excitement of an audience of Romans waiting to witness gladiators fight to the death. "They're already here. I see a lot of weapons."

"They'll be watching every way down," Kayl said.

"Did your juvenile delinquent friend ever tell you how to get out of something like this?"

To Genji's surprise, Kayl grinned. "Yeah. He did."

Grabbing their packs, they raced down the hall to the single elevator, where Kayl leaned on the ancient call button. "As long as we can get on first, we've got a chance. You said those police are heavily armed? Why? We've done nothing violent."

"Somebody must have told them we did," Genji said.

The doors of the elevator slid open, revealing the bad-smelling interior and the doors in the back that would only open on the ground floor to access the maintenance areas of the hotel. They were barely inside before the doors closed again in response to a call from another floor.

Kayl pointed up. "The top access. No matter what other changes they made to elevators, they had to leave that in as the only way to guarantee they could get people out if the elevator got stuck between floors." He bent to grab her legs and boosted her up so Genji could unlatch and move the access door aside.

She scrambled up, pivoting to reach down and help Kayl up as he jumped to grab the edge of the access. "Damn, you're heavy."

The moment he pulled himself up, she swung the access shut again, the two of them balancing on the top as the old magnetic-bar lift system kept lowering the elevator. Within a few seconds, the elevator thumped to a halt on the ground floor.

Genji heard several people getting on, moving with unusual quietness. As the doors were closing, some of them spoke in low voices.

"Check weapons." A chorus of muttered "ayes" followed.

"We don't get many lethal-force, shoot-on-sight orders," another commented. "What'd these guys do? It's not in the order."

"I heard they've killed a half-dozen cops."

"Don't give them time to kill you. The moment you see them, open up. Don't let them get their weapons out."

Another chorus of muttered "ayes."

"What's this stuff about don't be distracted by the woman's unusual appearance? Why aren't there details?"

"You can check out the details when she's down."

Genji looked over at Kayl, who was staring back at her.

The elevator thunked to a halt on the floor below where their room had been. It sounded like two of the police officers got off there. Then to their floor. Most of the rest. Then to the floor above. Two more off.

Was that all of them?

Genji cautiously moved the access enough to look down inside the elevator.

Empty.

Swinging the access open, she leaned down. "Hold my legs!" Reaching the control panel, she punched the ground floor command. "Pull me up!"

Back on top of the elevator, she waited, trying to control her breathing, as the elevator trundled down to the ground floor again, wondering how long the police would take to position themselves before entering the room ready to shoot to kill. The moment they saw their quarry had fled, they'd start looking nearby.

The elevator stopped, the front door opened, but no one came on. She dropped back through, followed by Kayl, and hit the control to open the back elevator doors to the maintenance area.

The lights were off here because the bots doing much of the work didn't need them and the few humans fixing and supervising them didn't work during the night. Genji had to slow down when she realized Kayl was having trouble making his way behind her without hitting something and making noise.

The back access door was unlocked from this side. Genji took two slow breaths, prepping herself, then swung through it as quickly as she could.

On the other side, two startled police officers were bringing up their weapons.

They were obviously trained to deal with criminals, but they weren't as fast and ruthless as Spear of Humanity shock troops. Genji had been trained to fight those shock troops. And Genji was an alloy. Even Kayl didn't know everything that meant.

Her first blow stunned the cop in front of her, the second knocked him down, and the third knocked him out. It had taken less than three seconds.

Spinning, she saw Kayl struggling with the second cop over her weapon as she prepared to shout an alarm.

Genji hit the police officer hard from the back, dropping the cop to her knees. She yanked out the officer's comms, slammed her to the ground, and grabbed her autocuffs. Within moments, the second officer was trussed up by her own equipment.

She was still conscious, though. Genji leaned down toward her. "We're not killers," she said. "You're being lied to."

Pinching the right pressure point rendered that officer unconscious, too.

Straightening, Genji nodded to Kayl. "Are you all right?"

"Yeah, I . . ." He looked down at the cops. "How did you—?"

"No time. Come on."

Once again, Kayl listened to her instead of wasting time arguing. He stopped talking and followed as she ran, the sound of alarms beginning to rise behind them.

THE AUTODRONES WERE THE HARDEST TO AVOID, SEARCHING EVERY ALLEY AND street. Genji had taken off her wide-brimmed hat and changed jackets with Kayl to alter her appearance a bit, but there wasn't much else they could do except move fast while trying to blend in with everyone else on the street. LA in 2140 was a lot like LA in 2180 had been, running at full tilt pretty much all day, every day, with only minor slowdowns at certain hours in the pace of entertainment and business activity. That gave them a lot of crowds to merge with. And the means to defeat or deceive drones and other security monitors that were everywhere, floating along the streets or sticking to buildings or balancing on the shoulders of pedestrians. As the ability of governments to monitor citizens had gotten better and better, citizens had responded with better and better ways to fool or block the monitors.

Unfortunately, removing her hat meant passersby occasionally noticed Genji's facial skin glowing from the nearby lights. The fact that this always generated gasps of admiration bewildered her. These people didn't know her skin marked her as different. As not fully human. She'd never encountered that before.

Kayl pretty much stayed silent as he walked with her. What was he thinking? He'd never seen her using her full capabilities.

She'd had friends who backed off after seeing that kind of thing. Most full humans didn't really want alloys to be any different from them.

They'd used up some of their remaining burner IDs on a couple of cabs to get more distance between themselves and the hotel they'd barely escaped from.

Stupid. Why hadn't she realized earlier how dangerous that location was?

You're not perfect, Selene. I don't need you to be.

How many times had her mother told her that? But her mother had died, and then the entire planet, and if Genji wasn't perfect now, it would still die in forty years.

They finally found refuge at a by-the-week apartment rental for low-wage laborers. Exhausted by a night spent fleeing, Genji wanted nothing but to sleep.

But Kayl was standing there, gazing at her with a troubled expression.

"All right." She sat down heavily on the bed. "Go ahead. Say it."

The sparsely furnished apartment also boasted a narrow couch that Kayl sat down on. "I'm not sure what to say."

"I'm an alloy. I never pretended otherwise."

"No, you didn't." He paused. "But just what does that mean?"

She sighed, looking at him. "My reflexes are really fast. I'm a bit stronger than a full human would be. I can see pretty well in the dark. I might live to be two hundred years old, or I might die next year. My hearing is really good. I can handle heat and cold extremes better than a full human. My bones are strong, but when they break they take longer to heal. Drugs, including stuff like alcohol, don't always have the same effects on me that they do on full humans. I can't drink coffee. I'm allergic to llamas. That's about it."

Except for one very big thing, about what could happen when an alloy developed a strong emotional tie to someone. But that had never happened to her; she'd been told by other alloys she could control it if she really wanted to, and it wouldn't be, couldn't be, an issue with Kayl.

He listened, his brow furrowing. "Llamas?"

That's what he'd keyed on? "Yes. Llamas."

"Every alloy?"

"Yes," Genji said. "Every alloy was allergic to llamas."

"Why?"

"I don't know! It doesn't matter! Can we drop the llamas?"

"Sure." He made a shrugging motion. "So, you're not superhuman, but a little better in some ways and a little different in others."

"Yeah." Why did his reaction matter so much to her?

"Okay."

"Okay?" Genji echoed in disbelief.

"Yeah," Kayl said. "Okay."

"What the hell does that mean?"

"It means okay," he shot back. "It means now I know, and that's . . . okay! What else would it mean?"

"I don't—" She waved a hand in frustration. "Why are you like this?"

"You're unhappy?"

"No! I'm just— I'm different."

"I knew that," Kayl said. "That's why I'm still alive. Again." He paused while Genji sought more words. "Selene, you really did do a lot of fighting, didn't you? In 2180?"

"Yeah," she said, "and the years before that. It was ugly."

"You could've killed those cops in less time than it took to knock them out, I bet."

"Probably," Genji said.

"Thanks."

"For what?" Why did Kayl have to be so exasperating?

"For getting us out of there. For caring about lives. For trying to change the future so Earth isn't destroyed even though—" He broke off, swallowing. "Despite the price."

She looked away, for some reason unable to keep looking at him. "Yeah, well, don't start thinking I'm great or anything. I mess up a lot. I messed up your life."

"My life was already messed up, Selene," he said. "You gave me a reason to try again."

"I am not your hill!"

"What?"

"Nothing! I'm tired! Are we done? Can you keep watch while I get some sleep?"

"Sure," Kayl said.

Despite her exhaustion, it took her a few moments to fall asleep, wondering why she felt simultaneously happy and despairing, but knowing she felt safe with Kayl keeping watch.

CAPTAIN ERNESTO HERNANDEZ HAD DEALT WITH HIS SHARE OF TOUGH, DANGEROUS situations. This had seemed like just one more of them, with sufficient force deployed and well-trained officers carrying it out, every exit guarded.

Which was why he was having trouble understanding why two of his officers were on stretchers and the objects of this operation had apparently managed a clean escape.

He bent down over Officer Maloney, who had regained consciousness first. "What happened?"

Maloney shook her head. "It was so fast. I'd just started struggling with one of them when the other hit me."

"Any idea why they didn't kill you?"

"She, the woman, told me they weren't killers and we were being lied to," Maloney said. "Right before she knocked me out."

"Explain to me how two civilians took out two of my best cops so quickly," Hernandez said.

Sergeant Chang answered, also having just recovered enough to talk. "Those weren't civilians, Captain. We *were* lied to. That woman came at me so fast I couldn't even see her hands moving. She hit me exactly where it'd be the most effective. Yeah, if she'd wanted to kill me, I'd be dead."

"Are you saying they're military?" Hernandez asked.

"Sure felt like it, Captain," Chang said. "I admit it, we were outclassed."

Officer Maloney nodded in agreement.

Hernandez put in a call to his superior. "We almost lost some officers because somebody lied in that takedown order. It looks like our civilian cop killers are actually military special forces of some kind. Maybe they've gone rogue and the military wants to keep it quiet. But they used us for their dirty work. This has to go all the way to the top. We need to know who put our cops in that kind of situation with bad threat information.

"I've got an expanding search underway but I'm not getting any hits yet. I'm going to be honest with you. I don't want to be the cop who finds them and tries to take them. If the military wants their mess cleaned up, they should open up on what's really happening and what we're dealing with. That's my opinion."

Hernandez was relieved when orders soon came in restricting the search and ordering surveillance but no pursuit if the two were spotted. He wasn't surprised to learn later the next day that the assistant chief who'd supposedly sent the takedown order hadn't actually done so and had no idea who had done it.

An investigation began, trying to find out how the police system had been compromised, and who within the ranks might have deliberately falsified a takedown order. If not for this incident, Hernandez later thought, that investigation would not have happened, a rat's nest of internal problems wouldn't have been uncovered, and fixes wouldn't have been set in motion.

/////

JUST BEFORE DAWN, AS KAYL SLEPT WHILE GENJI KEPT WATCH, THE BURNER PHONE they'd been given by Rear Admiral Tecumseh finally chirped. Genji almost flew across the room to view the text on it.

Chess Restaurant, 0745, today.

She roused Kayl. "Where is that?" he asked, blinking himself to full awareness.

Genji reached over to tap a line, bringing up the address of the restaurant. "That's in a pretty high-rent part of LA. Isn't it like that in 2140, too?"

"I think so," Kayl said. "Can we get there by 0745? That doesn't leave much time."

Genji nodded. "Yeah, but we should leave within the next half hour."

"There's something else we should check," Kayl added, calling up some commands on the room's cracked media panel. "Publicly accessible police alerts."

Genji looked over the scrolling data, including that from last night. "Not a word about us. Not a citywide search order, not an alert, not anything about the operation at the hotel."

"Maybe they're keeping that all classified and they are still looking for us."

"We need to act like that's true," she said. "Go ahead and shower."

"No, you go first," Kayl said hastily.

She gave him a suspicious look. "I guess I didn't mention that alloys can also stink a bit after certain kinds of exertion."

"You, umm, didn't need to."

"Thanks."

"It's not *that* bad . . ."

"Shut up!" Genji slammed the door to the bathroom.

WITHOUT ANY BURNER IDS LEFT FOR CABS OR OTHER PUBLIC TRANSIT, THEY HAD TO walk. Genji was pleasantly surprised to discover that some creaky remnants of the late 2000s vintage moving sidewalks that had once offered access to much of the city still existed in 2140. And enough people were moving about to blend in with. She'd swapped her sun hat for a scarf that covered her hair, neck, and part of her face and had picked up a different set of large sunglasses, but she still felt far too easy to spot.

They reached the building with CHESS emblazoned on it in massive gold letters just before 0745. "It's not open," Kayl said, peering inside. "It won't open until noon."

Genji looked about uneasily, seeing high-end stores and apartment buildings. The crowd of pedestrians was thinner here, most of them wearing service uniforms for various luxury businesses that flaunted their status by using exclusively human staff. "Is this a setup?"

"Maybe. But if it was, why haven't they hit us already?"

The door to the restaurant slid open suddenly and silently, surprising them both. Genji cocked one arm, prepared to either fight or run, as a figure appeared.

It was a robot, designed to look humanoid but obviously not human, with an exaggeratedly male physique and a costume apparently meant to evoke a knight in the game of chess. "Your table is ready, Lord and Lady," the robot said in a deep, melodious voice.

Oh, give me strength, Genji thought.

Kayl was staring at the knight/waiter. "It's one of those places for people with lots of money and not much sense."

"Let's get this over with," Genji said. As soon as she started moving, the knight/waiter moved back as if holding the door, waiting until they were both inside before walking smoothly ahead toward one of the tables. Standing rigidly around the room were other robotic waitstaff, all with similarly exaggerated female or male bodies and outfits designed to emphasize those features. "Never take me to a place like this."

"I wasn't thinking of this as a date," Kayl said. "And I wouldn't. If it was."

"I'm sorry," Genji said as the robot stopped at a table set for three. "I'm really not trying to keep saying things as if we have a relationship."

"We sort of do, don't we?"

"No. We can't." Leave it at that. Had the events of yesterday, her opening up to Kayl and his surprising acceptance of her revelations, led her to fantasize such a relationship would be possible? She owed it to him not to give in to such delusions.

They sat down, the waiter retreated, and they waited.

After about ten minutes, Genji spotted another figure moving through the restaurant with a brisk step. As he got closer, it was apparent he was a young man, maybe mid- to late twenties, with a beaming smile and confident attitude.

"Hey!" he called out as he walked up to the table. He stuck out a hand in greeting. "Tom Dorcas," he said in the manner of someone who didn't think he really needed to introduce himself but was going to modestly pretend he did.

"Dorcas?" Kayl said, giving Genji a look as he shook the offered hand. "As in Dorcas Funds?"

"Yeah, that's me." Tom Dorcas sat down in the third seat, looking over Genji, who had kept her scarf on despite being indoors. "UV Aversive? It's safe in here."

"I prefer to stay covered," Genji said.

"Suit yourself." Dorcas switched his smile back to Kayl. "My father and your father were together in Earth Guard! The same ship as lieutenants. Wild, huh? But my father saw some opportunities in business, so he got out. Made a lot of money."

"Didn't he die in an accident a couple of years ago?" Kayl said.

"Yeah. Terrible thing. Left me the whole company! So, for old time's sake, because our fathers were friends, I'm told you need a quiet lift to Mars." His smile shifted a bit. "And there might be some profit out of it? Advance information on important matters?"

Genji answered. "There might be." She didn't like this Dorcas. But at the moment she couldn't afford to turn down the opportunity he provided. "The alien technology is more advanced than ours. Knowing exactly what to ask for could give you a big leg up."

"Oh, I like you! You're saying all the right things. When do you want to take off?"

"Yesterday," Kayl said. "And the police are looking for us."

Tom Dorcas laughed. "It'd be awkward if you got arrested, huh?"

"They have shoot-on-sight orders for us," Genji said.

"Is that so?" Dorcas's expression finally shifted from exaggerated friendliness to calculation. "Did you kill somebody?"

"Not yet," Genji said, thinking that statement was true as far as 2140 went.

Dorcas laughed again. "I really like you! Are you two a couple? Because, if not, I'm interested, okay?"

"Thank you," Genji said, trying to keep her voice smooth, "but we are together." Hopefully Kayl would understand why she'd said that. Though they were together, weren't they?

"All the good ones are taken," Dorcas said with mock sorrow. "Say no more. Wait here. You'll be on your way pretty quick." Tom Dorcas got up, flashed his smile again, and walked away.

Genji looked at Kayl, meeting his eyes.

He nodded in agreement with the message in hers. "But we don't have any choice, do we?" he muttered.

"We stay on guard."

"We stay on guard," Kayl agreed.

The robot knight/waiter reappeared several minutes later, leading them toward the back of the restaurant, through some office areas, and to an enclosed parking lot. "Expensive antiques," Genji commented, looking at the vehicles parked there.

"They're the latest models," Kayl said. "But, yeah, expensive."

The doors on a large sedan with one-way window coverings opened invitingly.

Kayl led the way to it, getting in first and looking about.

She got in as well. The back seats were more like a well-padded sofa, before them various controls to bring up desks, a bar, and other amenities. The doors slid closed, locking with firm clicks that felt ominous.

"Destination, Greater Los Angeles Area Interplanetary Access Spaceport," the car announced, using a woman's voice with a strong Irish accent. "Relax and enjoy your journey."

The sedan rose and slid forward. "Impellers," Genji said.

"You can't use these as parachutes," Kayl said.

"You can once you figure out how." She looked out as the sedan left the garage and merged seamlessly with the slowly moving automated traffic flow. "I heard once that LA doesn't have traffic jams. It just has one traffic jam that has never ended."

"It's still like this in 2180?" Kayl said.

"Yes."

"It's like that story about Jorge and Linda."

"What?"

"You never heard that urban legend?" Kayl smiled. "Supposedly this couple got stuck in a traffic jam and fell asleep while their car was trying to get them home in LA. The car woke them up when they got there, but everything was different. That's when they realized they'd been stuck in the traffic jam for a century." He also looked out at the traffic. "LA never changes."

Genji's mind suddenly brought up her memory of watching the West Coast of North America vanishing in a blaze of eerie light.

She must have made a sound, because Kayl switched his gaze back to her, looking worried. "Are you okay?"

"I . . ." Her voice caught. "I'm okay. It's just . . ."

"You saw it all destroyed."

"Yeah." She closed her eyes, trying to control her breathing, trying to block out the vision from her memory.

"You're going to keep it from happening," Kayl said.

Genji opened her eyes, looking at him. "We're going to keep it from happening." She reached to grasp his hand, surprising him and surprising herself. "We can't have a relationship. But we are together, just like I told Dorcas. I can't do this alone. Is that okay with you?"

His hand tightened a bit on hers. "Yes."

AFTER ABOUT HALF AN HOUR, THE SEDAN MANAGED TO REACH AN ACCESS TO THE officially named Priority Lanes that Kayl told her were unofficially called the Plutocrat Lanes. Pay enough, and your car could drive on them. But the price was set so high—and kept there to keep the traffic in the lanes low—that only the wealthiest got to use them. Thereafter the sedan soared along at a good clip for kilometer after kilometer.

They passed the usual security scanners watching the traffic, and occasionally also police vehicles. But none reacted to the sedan.

"The negotiators' ship has left Earth orbit for Mars," Kayl said as he read the news feed on one of the sedan's panels.

"Can we still get there before First Contact?" Genji asked.

"It depends on how fast the ship is that Dorcas is planning on using for us," Kayl said. "A normal fuel-efficient trajectory wouldn't make it before the alien ship reaches Mars, but one burning more fuel could do it. Did you say the aliens won't contact us until they reach Mars?"

"Right. Not until the Tramontine reach orbit about Mars," Genji said.

"Then we've still got a chance."

She nodded, glaring out the window. "Can we make this car go any faster?"

The Irishwoman's voice answered her. "We're traveling at the maximum safe speed for this road. May I offer you a mild sedative?"

"No," Genji said.

"I sense that you and your partner would like some privacy."

"Yes."

"Would you like to view a selection of aids and contraceptives?"

"No!" Genji shot a glance at Kayl, who was pretending to be looking out his own window as if unaware of the conversation. "Are all AIs in 2140 this stupid?"

"I am a state-of-the-art conversational AI," the car responded. "If you have any complaints—"

"I said I wanted *privacy*, you witch!"

The car stopped talking.

After a moment, Kayl spread his hands. "Yeah, they're still pretty much all like that. They're better at reading tones of voice than they used to be, but they still don't get a lot of the nonverbal signals humans use. If it's just ordering tasks, okay. But if it's social interactions, let's just say that's a common trope in comedies."

The sedan finally veered smoothly onto a special exit, the expanse of LA Interplanetary spreading out before them. Genji tensed as the sedan approached one of the security checkpoints leading to the port, but the vehicle slid into another special lane and rolled through security without a pause.

"I guess it's good to be rich," Kayl said.

"I guess." Sloppy security bothered her, even when she was benefiting from it. She had lived with wartime security measures for so long that this sort of thing literally made her itch with worry.

Another checkpoint, another special lane, another smooth passage.

And another.

The sedan had left the main routes, heading to the far right of the landing field, where a cluster of private surface-to-orbit lifters sat around a special terminal. "Request permission to resume conversational and monitoring status," the car said.

"Go ahead," Kayl said.

"In five minutes, we will reach the *Golden Bolt*. Do you wish to debark directly into the *Golden Bolt* or visit the Restricted Access Terminal first?"

"Is the *Golden Bolt* our lift vehicle?" Kayl asked.

"That is correct, sir."

"We want to go direct to the *Golden Bolt*."

"Proceeding direct to the *Golden Bolt*," the sedan acknowledged. "I must inform you that Tom is not yet aboard the *Golden Bolt* but expects to join you within the hour."

"Tom," Genji mimicked. "I'll bet he's one of those who loves hearing their name said by their favorite AIs."

"A lot of people are like that," Kayl said.

"Oh?"

"Not me!" he added quickly.

The boarding ramp of the lifter they were approaching began extending as the sedan came to a smooth halt. When the doors swung open, it was only one step outside before entering the boarding ramp.

After all the exaggerated luxury they'd already seen, the heavily padded chairs in the main passenger area didn't surprise her. "I hope we can trust the pilots," Genji muttered.

Another woman's voice with an Irish accent answered her. "The *Golden Bolt* is operated on fully automated flight controls. It has a one hundred percent safety record and has never required human intervention."

"Can we access the pilot deck?" Kayl asked.

"Access to the pilot deck is normally restricted for safety reasons. If you wish to tour the pilot deck, I will require access approval from Tom."

"Never mind," Kayl said. He sat down in the seat next to Genji's. "How are you doing?"

"Feeling like a duck sitting in a barrel," she said.

"Don't you mean a sitting duck or fish in a barrel?"

"Why would fish be in a barrel?" Genji shook her head. "I guess the saying changed. You know what I mean. If this is a trap, we're in trouble."

"There's no way to get to Mars that doesn't run that kind of risk," Kayl said. "Unless we owned our own ship. Which we don't."

She was looking around and now produced one of the burner phones, which could also be used to display texts. I can get through that door to the pilot deck. If I do, can you drive this lifter?

Kayl typed a reply. Yes. I'm sure I can.

Good. That means we've got at least one option if this goes bad.

"Tom has reached LAI and will be at the *Golden Bolt* in three minutes," the Irishwoman's voice said. "However, Launch Control has just imposed a hold on launches."

"Why?" Kayl asked. "What's the reason for the hold?"

"No reason was given."

"Someone knows we're trying to get off the planet," Genji muttered.

"We should wait for Dorcas to get here," Kayl said. "This lifter alone can't get us to Mars, and if we leave it we'll stand out clearly to anyone looking for unusual activity on the field."

"Okay," Genji said. "Let's see how this plays out in the next couple of minutes. We might have to use this lifter to hop to some-where else on the planet."

"Every orbital and suborbital tracking system will key on us if we do that," Kayl said.

"Launch Control has reaffirmed the hold on launches," the *Golden Bolt* informed them. "It has also requested updated lists of all passengers and crew members aboard every vehicle waiting to lift, using full ID verification scans."

"Yeah," Kayl said. "They know we're here."

CHAPTER 6

"HEY, HEY!" A FAMILIAR VOICE CALLED OUT.

Tom Dorcas came bounding onto the passenger deck. "You're here?" he asked Genji and Kayl. "Great."

"Welcome aboard, Tom," the *Golden Bolt* said.

"Let's go," Dorcas said, fastening his seat harness.

"Launch Control has requested an updated passenger list."

"Tell them I'm the only one aboard."

"Yes, Tom."

"Let's go," Dorcas added.

"Launch Control has imposed a hold on all launches."

"Did I hear right?" Dorcas said. "So what? We have a preapproved launch window. Launch."

"Launching during a hold period will result in a fine and possible suspension of launch privileges," the Irishwoman's voice reminded him.

"Yeah, a fine. Big deal. They can't suspend the launching privileges of Dorcas Fund–linked ships. I've got plenty of officials in my pocket who'll stop that. Take us up."

"Yes, Tom. Initiating launch."

Thirty seconds later acceleration pressed Genji down in her seat as the *Golden Bolt* leapt skyward. She hadn't really believed they'd take off until they did, and now waited, tense, for the lifter to be engaged by landing field and suborbital defensive systems. No one could just lift off like this and survive.

But no warnings sounded, no weapons struck the lifter.

It's not the 2170s or 2180, Genji realized. There haven't been attacks and strikes and counterstrikes, and infiltrations and assaults. These people are so complacent they'll let an unauthorized launch take place and do nothing except threaten a fine.

What must it have been like to live in such a time? Feeling so secure, so oblivious to what was about to go all wrong?

No wonder Kayl was so shocked when someone tried to kill us repeatedly those first times. That's not what his world is like.

You fools. If I can't stop where things are going, this will all blow up in your faces and you won't even see it coming.

"Launch Control is ordering us to return to LAI," the *Golden Bolt* announced.

"Ignore," Dorcas said. He was relaxed in his seat, paging through documents on a couple of displays positioned near his hands.

"Orbital Control is ordering us to return to LAI."

"Ignore. How long until we reach the *Quasar*?"

"Forty-six minutes on our current trajectory, Tom."

"Is the *Quasar* fully stocked and fueled?"

"Yes, Tom."

"Don't bother me with any more of those warnings. Just forward them to the legal staff and tell them to deal with it."

"Yes, Tom."

Genji looked over at Kayl in disbelief, but he returned a look of weary resignation. Apparently he was used to the wealthy ignoring the rules and doing what they wanted. Earth Guard should be enforcing the rules, but it obviously wasn't. Maybe this was part of the corruption of Earth Guard that Admiral Tecumseh had spoken of. How many high-ranking officers in Earth Guard were looking forward to jobs with the Dorcas Fund or similar places when they retired?

She really wanted to get up, go over to Tom Dorcas, and slap him around until her arms got tired.

From the way Kayl was looking at her, he could tell what she was thinking.

Had anyone other than her mother ever been that good at reading her? Scary.

Genji closed her eyes, willing herself to relax as the lifter angled up past the atmosphere and to the orbit where Tom Dorcas's interplanetary yacht awaited them.

TO SOMEONE USED TO THE ACCOMMODATIONS ON A WARSHIP, THE LIVING SPACES on the *Quasar* were not simply lavish but ridiculous.

"No human crew," Tom Dorcas announced proudly. "Don't have to pay them, and that leaves more room for important people like us!" He led them through an atrium where display panels made it look like the vaulted overhead was lined with windows giving direct views to space. "You guys are sharing a room, right? Together, as the lady says?"

The "room" was a suite with a series of interconnected compartments. Genji looked at the bedroom, the bed itself more than two meters wide, the overhead made of panels currently set to mirror mode.

Kayl was having the good grace, or the good sense, not to look at her.

"Thanks," he told Dorcas. "We really appreciate this."

"No problem," Dorcas said, waving it off. "We're doing a high-fuel transit to Mars to get there quickly, so this is costing me. I assume your information on the alien tech will be more than worth all that."

"How fast is quickly?" Genji asked.

"Eighteen days," Dorcas said with a grin.

Kayl shook his head. "An Earth Guard cruiser boosting on a quick transit would take three weeks given this orbital configuration."

"This is first class," Dorcas said, spreading his arms. "Oh, if you want some new outfits, the printers there can churn out anything you want. Latest styles, any fabrics. No need to stay bundled up. As little as you want to wear. Catch you later!"

After the door closed, Kayl's expression turned hostile. "First he tries to get you to take off things at that restaurant and now this. His hints that he wants to see you in more revealing clothing are getting a little hard to take."

"He's going to be disappointed," Genji said. "These days my idea of revealing clothing is coveralls with the neck seal open."

"Eighteen days," Kayl said as he activated a display to get a news update. "The ships carrying the negotiators should arrive on Mars in sixteen days. We won't beat them there, but we'll be close."

"When will the Tramontine achieve Mars orbit?" Genji asked.

"Twenty-one days."

"I've got forty years but I'm worrying about every hour."

Kayl looked around them meaningfully, tapping one ear. She nodded in agreement. Dorcas would surely have his ship monitoring their conversations. They'd have to watch everything they said.

Were there hidden cams everywhere as well, watching everything? Probably in the bedroom, too. Dorcas would be disappointed if he planned on watching anything but sleeping in there. But she couldn't keep her clothes on for eighteen days. She'd just have to try to spot every cam in the bathroom.

Would he have IR cams in the bathroom? Probably not. Maybe low-light ones, but she didn't need any light to get clean.

Kayl was looking about, clearly thinking the same thing she was about their lack of privacy. "Eighteen days," he said.

/////

NORMALLY, SHIPS MAKING A LONG TRANSIT WOULD BOOST TO WHATEVER SPEED they needed, coast for most of the transit, then brake velocity at the end. Efficiency mattered when traveling across millions of kilometers. But the *Quasar* kept accelerating at a steady rate, clearly intending to maintain that until the midway point of the transit before turning and braking velocity at the same rate for the rest of the trip. That would make the journey faster and also provide a sensation of gravity for the entire trip. It would also cost a lot more than a normal transit, but when Kayl mentioned that to Tom Dorcas it was laughed off.

"It's a business expense tax write-off," Tom Dorcas said. "I can deduct so much I end up making money by doing it this way."

"Why'd they write the tax laws like that?" Kayl asked, clearly stunned by the admission.

"Because people like me told them that's what we wanted," Dorcas said, laughing again as he walked away.

Genji's first shower attempt ended about how she'd thought it would. Genji memorized the locations of objects and controls, turned off every light in the bathroom, waited five minutes without removing any clothing, started the shower, and ten seconds later saw all the lights come back on.

Ordering an old-fashioned nail file from one of the printers to use as a punch, she went through the bathroom methodically breaking everything that looked like it might be a light or a camera lens.

Repair bots started showing up while she was still working, replacing and fixing every broken light.

Tired of fooling around, Genji ordered one of the printers to produce a voluminous garment that might be accurately described as a tent, making sure the fabric it was made from contained numerous strands of metal thread and other materials that would mess with sensors designed to look through cloth. Draping the tent dress over the shower, she undressed and cleaned herself inside it.

Since the bed was so wide that both could lie on opposite sides and not touch the outstretched arm of the other, Genji suggested they both sleep in it to support their claim of being together, but without doing anything except sleeping.

It worked really well. Too well, she thought the next "morning," looking ruefully at the other side of the bed. If their hands had touched, it wouldn't have hurt anything, would it?

They were invited to one "formal dinner" with Tom Dorcas, which consisted mostly of Dorcas flipping through multiple work pads in front of him while various courses were served that Dorcas wolfed down without apparently paying any attention to the taste.

Afterwards, Kayl and Genji went to the "library," which actually had a few real books in it as well as comfortable chairs that appeared designed to hold more than one occupant. "None of these books are less than three years old," Kayl commented before taking a seat near Genji. "Tom didn't seem too happy with you, Selene."

"I noticed," Genji said. Dorcas had exchanged occasional words with Kayl but said nothing to her. "I'm fine with that."

"He's probably disappointed that he hasn't gotten to see you naked."

She grinned. "I'll add him to the list of disappointed men I've encountered."

"Long list?" Kayl asked.

"Not really. It's not like I've spent my life with a line of admirers following me around." Make a joke of it. Don't let even Kayl see the truth behind it, that the full human men who'd wanted her had only done so for bragging rights or because they were drunk. "So what's the story with the sort of thing we saw while lifting off from LA?" Genji asked.

Kayl answered with one of his trademark shrugs. "Enforcement of rules is what you might call selective."

"Based on what?"

"Money, mainly."

"Are you comfortable with that?" Genji pressed.

"No," Kayl said. "Did you think I would be?"

"No," she said. "That's one of the things that led to the collapses of authorities responsible for overseeing things, and those left vacuums that the Spear of Humanity exploited. When corruption gets bad enough, people start being willing to give extra powers to someone claiming to fight it and are willing to look the other way as long as the 'right' people get hammered."

"Which leads to a different form of corruption?" Kayl said, leaning back in his chair.

Genji hauled out one of her phones. It will in the 2160s and 2170s, she typed.

What about Dorcas Funds? Kayl typed in reply. What happens to them?

That's not really something I followed. I know Dorcas was really big on exploiting Tramontine technology. They even tried to get patents on some pure Tramontine tech even though they hadn't developed it and couldn't use it.

So your telling Tom about Tramontine tech is just continuing what happened in the history you know? Kayl typed. It's not a change?

I don't think so, Genji typed in reply. Not if it leads to the same outcome.

Kayl paused before typing again. Was Dorcas still around in 2180?

I don't know about Dorcas himself, but the company was still a major defense contractor. The wars, defending against the Spear, made Dorcas Funds a whole lot of money. There were claims the company was also selling weapon components to the Spear, but those could never be proved.

And then the Earth was destroyed, Kayl wrote. But before that they made a whole lot of money.

Yeah that pretty much sums it up.

/////

AS THE DAYS WENT BY, TOM DORCAS GREW EVEN LESS SOCIABLE. A SERIES OF TEXTS invited Genji to private meetings with Dorcas that were described in increasingly explicit terms, as if she would surely agree if she were smart enough to understand exactly what activities were on the agenda. She ignored all of them.

Under the guise of being restless, Genji roamed the ship, familiarizing herself with the layout and getting a feel for places inside the ship that weren't on the openly available deck plans and in fact didn't appear to exist.

As part of that, she had a growing feeling that someone was watching her. It wasn't the usual sense of automated surveillance following her movements, but of someone who was never there when she was. Part of her wondered if she was nervous, but another part had learned not to discount her feelings and instincts about such things.

Finally, she and Kayl sat down to type messages to each other.

There's someone else aboard this ship.

Not just bots? Kayl replied.

No. This feels like a person who's always around but never in sight. I can't explain it. But I'm sure someone else is on this ship with us.

Danger?

Maybe.

Under the guise of worrying about a food allergy, Genji acquired a broad-spectrum food tester from the *Quasar*'s one-room hospital, checking her food before eating any. It didn't surprise her when on day twelve of the trip a hallucinogenic drug turned up in her meal.

After that, Kayl started checking his meals as well.

It was a luxury yacht, but the *Quasar* felt increasingly like an extremely well-appointed prison.

It would have been a lot harder to get through without Kayl. Genji had stopped telling herself that she only socialized with Kayl because they were working together, admitting that she enjoyed talking to him and being around him. He also kept his word not to push her physically or emotionally, respecting her, maintaining the slight distance Kayl knew she wanted.

She did want that, right?

Genji found herself awake one "night," looking across the expanse of the bed to the other side, where Kayl slept. It felt very strange to feel safe around him even though they were in bed together. Sort of together, anyway, given how wide the bed was, and that they were both mostly dressed. Why wasn't she worried that he'd try something, even if it was just "accidentally" grabbing her while pretending to be asleep?

If it was any other guy, she'd assume that he'd make a move, and she'd have to make it clear how unwelcome that was.

But not Kayl.

What if she made a move?

What would happen if she reached out, if he then reached out . . .

No. Stop it.

What would it feel like to . . .

Stop it!

You can't do that to him and you can't do that to yourself. You're an alloy, he's a full human, and you've both got a world to save.

And any instant I could never have existed. Just dealing with that is almost more than anyone could bear. How long can I hold up facing that?

Aunt Hokulani's voice echoed in her memory. *When you no longer have the strength to take one more step on your own, your friend is there, and they help you take that step.*

There hadn't been anyone in her life like that since her mother's death. Could Kayl help her through it? But then she'd really be using him in the worst way.

Genji turned to her other side so she couldn't see Kayl anymore. But she could still sense his presence, still feel that odd combination of comfort and anxiety.

TWO DAYS OUT FROM MARS, TOM DORCAS, WHO HAD BEEN INCREASINGLY OBVIOUS in his appraisal of Genji whenever they were in the same room, maneuvered himself so he could give her an apparently comradely slap on the shoulder.

Had she felt a tiny sting? Genji checked the site.

I'm pretty sure he took a genetic sample off me, she typed to Kayl.

He'll know you have alien DNA?

No way he'd miss that.

Do you think he'll freak out like the doctor aboard Vigilant did? Kayl wondered.

I'm more worried about him realizing that I have unique DNA. That could be worth a lot of money, I think.

Should I confront him about it?

He'll just deny it.

Illegal, Kayl typed. My sister told me. Some people try to traffic in DNA w/o proper payment and licensing. If Dorcas tries to sell your DNA w/o your approval, he'd be breaking laws.

She looked at him before typing her reply. Why do you think that would slow him down?

Kayl had no response to that.

Genji realized that she'd have to do something about the DNA sample Dorcas had stolen from her before she left the ship. Exactly what to do was the question.

But Dorcas surprised her. She'd underestimated just how ruthless Dorcas was and how little he cared about the rules that others had to follow.

/////

GENJI CAME BACK TO AWARENESS, HEARING VOICES SPEAKING. SHE KEPT HER EYES closed. Two men who must have been standing close to her were talking. Her last memory had been of lying in the bed. Right now it felt like she was lying on the deck, probably in the main room of the ship, from the way the voices sounded.

"How much longer are they going to be out?"

That was Tom Dorcas, but not the Tom Dorcas they'd always interacted with. This Tom Dorcas sounded brisk and businesslike and almost emotionless.

"At least another half hour. But not more than an hour longer. I didn't want to risk oversedating them."

Who was that? He sounded older than Dorcas, speaking like someone who knew their job and did it without investing any feelings in the task. So she'd been right and there had been another person aboard the ship.

Genji felt the toe of a shoe nudge her. "Hit this one again," Dorcas said. "Make sure she stays out until I can get her down to my labs on the planet."

"If I give her that much without a doc on hand she might suffer some brain damage," the other man warned.

"Did I say I was worried about brain damage? Do it. I don't need her brain. She's some kind of freak. When I mass harvest her DNA it's going to make me the richest man in the solar system."

"Whatever you say. How about this guy?"

"Oh, yeah," Dorcas said. "Owen. You know, my father might be a little upset with me for this, but business is business. This guy is in the way. Get him out of the way."

"Sure thing. Won't be the first time I handled that kind of job. I'll make sure nothing is left for anyone to trace. Are you sure you don't want to have some fun with the girl after I dose her again before I take her down to the lab?"

"Now that you mention it—"

Genji had gotten a pretty good idea of where both men were standing.

She opened her eyes as she swung both of her legs together in an arc just above the deck, catching the legs of the older man and knocking them out from under him. As he slammed down to the deck, she drove stiffened fingers into his windpipe before the dazed man could react. His jacket had fallen open, revealing a holstered weapon.

Still in a crouch, Genji reached and grabbed the weapon, pivoting to face Tom Dorcas, who was watching her in shock, one hand beginning to reach beneath his own coat. She didn't have time to see exactly what kind of hand weapon she'd seized, but a private citizen should only be carrying a nonlethal stunner. Aiming the weapon at Dorcas's forehead for maximum stun effect, she triggered it.

Instead of the snap of a stunner charge, she felt the hum of an ultrapower capacitor discharging into an electromagnetic rail, accelerating a metal slug to around seven hundred meters per second.

A hole appeared in Tom Dorcas's forehead.

He fell backward.

Unable to give in to her shock at killing Dorcas, Genji swung back to check on the older man. Struggling to breathe, he was fumbling for another weapon, starting to bring it out.

Remembering his words about her, his offhand discussion of other deaths, his plans to dispose of Kayl, Genji straightened, lined up her weapon on the man's forehead, and fired again.

She paused, breathing deeply from her sudden bout of exertion. *Clear the area.* Genji began searching for any more opponents.

She'd done this before, on Spear of Humanity warships.

A security bot burst out of a nearby passageway, stunner arms extended. It swung around toward her with barely any pause.

Genji spaced three shots into the bot, aiming for locations commonly used for vital functions.

It shuddered to a halt, breakdown lights blinking.

Using the quick releases, she pried loose both stunners and discharged them at full power into the interior of the bot.

The lights stopped blinking.

Only after ensuring there was no one else nearby and no more security bots responding did she kneel by Kayl to check him. He was breathing deeply, still completely out, but seemed okay. Both Dorcas and his helper were most thoroughly dead.

A medical bot had appeared, heading toward Dorcas's body. Instead, Genji directed it to check on Kayl.

"The subject is sedated," the bot reported in an Irish-accented woman's voice. "There do not appear to be any adverse reactions underway. Recommend monitoring until the sedation wears off. I must check on other people in this area who may be injured."

Could she trust this thing? What sort of subroutines might Dorcas have installed in it? "Deactivate yourself," Genji said.

"I'm sorry. You are not authorized to give that command."

Walking to the medical bot, Genji yanked out the external emergency cutoffs.

After ensuring the medical bot was completely deactivated, Genji did a more exhaustive search, breaking locks on any sealed doors to see what was inside. She found the living area Dorcas's secret assistant had occupied, far smaller and less lavish than the quarters for Dorcas and his guests. And a sort of lair that Dorcas must have used for private entertainment that made Genji curl her lip in disgust. But no one else and no other threats.

Returning to the bodies, she searched Dorcas, finding a variety of anonymous cash cards, some of the cards with extremely large sums on them, a few burner phones, and what looked a whole lot like a DNA sampler case. It wasn't hard to guess what that held. Genji pocketed everything.

She also found the weapon Dorcas must have been reaching for, something labeled a "Tormentor." It looked like some form of stunner, though from the name Genji suspected it didn't simply knock out its targets.

The assistant proved to have on him not only another mag pistol that he'd been trying to get out when she shot him, but also a pair of stunners. That and a couple of cash cards and yet another burner phone. He wasn't carrying any ID.

Kayl was still out, sleeping peacefully.

She searched the assistant's rooms, looking for hidden storage areas, and found a variety of fake IDs as well as more cash cards. Dorcas's private rooms yielded what looked like very high-end fake IDs, more high-value anonymous cash cards, and more burner phones. Genji spotted a comm panel on his desk and tapped it with one knuckle. A partly drafted message popped up. . . . dropped them off safely. They should be okay. I don't know why they haven't contacted you . . .

Genji was feeling less and less bad about killing Dorcas.

She went back to the bridge to check on the progress of the ship. If she was reading these old data displays right, they were three hours from reaching a Mars orbit that they must have been assigned. There seemed to be a lot of other ships out there, but she couldn't properly read the antiquated displays and their symbology.

Kayl was finally stirring when she went back to him this time. "Hey, Lieutenant Owen." She'd kept a lid on her feelings, but with the need for immediate action subsiding, it finally hit her. And the thing that hit hardest was remembering the casual discussion about getting Kayl "out of the way." Genji fought off a wave of anger, focusing on the fact that he was alive because her alloy metabolism had allowed her to recover a lot faster than the assistant had thought possible.

"Wha—?" Kayl had his eyes open and was looking about as if trying to focus. "Wha-t?"

"Relax," Genji said, kneeling by him. "It's under control."

He rolled onto his back, staring up at her.

"What . . . happened?"

"Our buddy Dorcas had us knocked out. His friend over there was going to kill you and transport me to one of Dorcas's labs to mass harvest my DNA."

Kayl struggled to rise. "I . . . I'll kill him."

"I already took care of that," Genji said.

"You—?" He looked about, seeing the bodies. "Oh, man."

"Yeah. We're on a ship owned by a dead man that's about to make Mars orbit. Can you help me read the bridge status displays so we can get a handle on what else is out there?"

"I can do that." She supported Kayl as he struggled to his feet and stared again at Dorcas's body. "You really killed him."

What was that in his voice? Was he criticizing her? "I didn't have a choice!" Genji snapped at Kayl. "And, by the way, you're welcome for saving your life for at least the fifth time since I've gotten to know you!"

He stared at her. "Umm . . . thanks."

She stalked off toward the bridge, leaving a bewildered Kayl to follow on his own.

KAYL CONFIRMED WHAT SHE'D WORRIED ABOUT. MARS ORBIT WAS CRAWLING WITH Earth Guard warships. Looming only a few more days' travel away was the huge Tramontine ship, still headed for Mars orbit. The ship that had carried the negotiators to Mars was already in orbit, meaning they were probably on the surface.

"How do we get to the surface?" Genji wondered.

Kayl shook his head as he studied the Earth Guard ships as well as the regular Mars patrol craft orbiting the planet. "We can get down there. Getting down without being arrested or killed the moment we get there is going to be the hard part."

"You talked to Dorcas about the boats docked to *Quasar*, right? The *Golden Bolt* was left in Earth orbit, but we've got other options."

"We do," Kayl said. He called up some data, studying it. "The gig. This one."

Genji leaned closer to look. "Seems small."

"Small, fast, and able to operate in the Martian atmosphere as a runabout," Kayl said. "This is what someone would use to smuggle stuff that isn't high volume and has a high unit value."

"Drugs?"

"And other things." Kayl grinned. "I never thought my Earth Guard training on smugglers would prove useful in quite this way. But even the sport gig only works for smugglers in areas that aren't well patrolled, where they can drop off their load and run before anyone can intercept them. That's not the case here."

Genji looked through the screens, seeing images of Mars below them. "That's the main colony?"

"Yeah," Kayl said. "Pretty big, huh?"

"I was thinking tiny."

"Tiny?"

"In 2180," Genji said, "the Martian colonies held about a million and a half people, and terraforming had made a lot of progress."

"Terraforming?" Kayl said, startled.

"Yeah. Using Tramontine technology," Genji said. "Have they built the Commons yet?" The large open area near the center of the colony, an extravagance given the need to keep it sealed and maintained with life support, had been a symbol of Mars in her time. In the center of the Commons was a platform that anyone could mount to speak on anything they wanted.

"The Commons? Sure they did. During the big expansion fifteen years ago."

"It's strange to think that's one thing I'd recognize, unchanged in 2180." She looked down at the planet, suddenly depressed, thinking about the final battles that must have raged about Mars after 12 June 2180. If anyone had been left alive anywhere in the solar system.

"A million and a half, you said?" Kayl shook his head, pointing down toward the surface, unaware of the dark place her thoughts had gone. "Right now it's about fifty thousand people, and we're kind of proud of that."

"Is fifty thousand enough to hide among?" Genji asked, trying to shake the horrible images her imagination had conjured up.

"I think we've got a chance," Kayl said. "I've got one more trick Edourd told me about."

"I really should have gotten to know more Martian juvenile delinquents, I guess," Genji said. "Kayl, Dorcas is on me. My fault. I should give you a statement admitting my guilt just in case you get caught."

"No," Kayl said. He seemed to be intently studying the data readouts.

"I may be able to start making significant changes," Genji said. "Even if I'm not killed, I may not be around for much longer. You need to—"

"I need to focus on getting the mission done," Kayl said. "Not on you . . . not being here."

"You need to plan for when I'm gone."

He lowered his head, not answering for a while. "I know it's not easy for you to contemplate that. It's not easy on this end, either. How about I figure out how to get us down on the surface without us being killed right away? Then I can worry about . . . losing you."

Genji sighed. "Kayl, you're . . . my friend, in ways I never imagined a full human could be. I want to spend more time with you.

But you've always known it was going to be this way. We were going to be doing things that would make me cease to have ever existed. When that happens, I don't want to leave you with any more problems than I have to."

He kept his eyes averted as he replied. "Selene, I've never . . . had a friend like you, either. Don't worry. I'll keep trying to get the mission done . . . for you."

"Kayl, I told you from the start—" She turned away. "I need to deal with some things before we leave this ship. Can you handle getting that gig ready on your own?"

"Yeah."

"Thanks."

She needed something to keep her busy instead of brooding over Kayl or worrying about when her last moment of existence might be, and leaving a pile of evidence didn't seem like a good idea. While Kayl worked on getting the gig ready to go, Genji hauled first Dorcas's body and then that of the assistant to the large-mass incinerator/recycler in the kitchen area. Setting the incinerator to its highest level, she waited as it cycled through its routine, thinking about the assistant and his "no traces" comment. This was probably what people called poetic justice.

And yet . . .

She was trying to prevent the destruction of Earth, which had been the outcome of the Universal War. All of the killing hadn't, in the end, prevented that from happening. Now she had a chance to redo things, to try to avoid the mistakes of the past. But how could she change what would happen if she did things the same way? Kill or be killed. And, in the end, everyone had died.

She'd been startled when Kayl thanked her for respecting life. That wasn't who she'd been in the Universal War, focused on vengeance for the murder of her mother, returning hate for hate. Things had gone so badly wrong by then that she couldn't see any other way forward. Maybe there hadn't been any other way at that point.

But she could be different now, right? Try to set things on a new path by using different tactics, thinking in a different way. Get the mission done, without the merciless killing she'd lived with in the future.

Show everyone there was a different way to do things, to think about things. Be the example for the future the world needed, instead of leading history down the same road toward the same awful fate she knew waited on 12 June 2180.

"The best revenge is not to be like your enemy." As usual, Marcus Aurelius should have been her guide. How many times had her mother cited those words to her?

All right, Mom. I'll finally listen. Let's see if I can get this done without causing any more deaths.

When she got back to where the bodies had been, cleaning bots had just finished removing all signs that they had been there. The security bot and the medic bot had both also been hauled away, presumably to the automated repair shop.

The next stop was the "hospital," a small but very nicely appointed robotic medical facility that could handle every minor emergency and most major ones.

Another medical robot greeted Genji. "May I help you?"

"No." After yanking out the bot's power connections, Genji went methodically through the medical equipment, finding every biosample and possible DNA sample and tossing all of them into the medical incinerator. It was a lot smaller than the big one in the kitchen, but plenty big enough for this job. At the end, she tossed in the DNA sampler she'd pulled off Dorcas.

After that she went back to Dorcas's rooms and started destroying all possible data drives and workstations and phones registered to Dorcas, tossing them into a convenient "black hole" data eliminator that Dorcas had in one corner of his office. Cracking the safe in one wall took a little work, but it produced more data drives that went into the hole. In the back of the safe were a couple of files of actual paper records. Genji looked them over, seeing dates all more than two years before this. On top was a crumpled receipt.

Tom Dorcas had sold his father's Earth Guard ring for what must have been for him a totally insignificant sum of money.

She looked at the receipt, wondering. What had happened to Tom Dorcas in her history after 2140? Had he lived a long, dissolute, ugly, privileged life, doing whatever he wanted? Had he still been alive in 2180?

What would happen to Dorcas Funds with its leader gone? Would it still grow in power and influence, strongly impacting human policy toward the Tramontine in ways that profited Dorcas?

How much had Dorcas been involved with the rise of the Spear of Humanity? Would this positively affect the future, or would it create more chaos, more uncertainty, aiding the rise of the Spear of Humanity?

Genji had no idea. She had no fixed observer in 2180 telling her what her changes had wrought.

But, somehow, she suspected a solar system without rich, powerful Tom Dorcas in it might just be a little better than one with him.

Without planning to, she'd changed this as well.

"I have been unable to contact Tom for an extended period," the ship said.

"He's been busy," Genji said.

"If I cannot contact Tom within another half hour, I will need to notify authorities of a possible emergency. Please inform Tom of this."

"I'll be happy to," Genji said.

She checked on Kayl. "How's the gig coming?"

"About ready," he said. "What have you been doing?"

"Housecleaning. Is the gig independent of the ship at this point?"

"It can be."

"Good. There may be a serious malfunction occurring very soon."

"Oh." Kayl indicated the braces holding the gig in place. "I'd better make sure I can pop those from inside the gig."

"Are there suits in the gig?"

"Yeah." Kayl went inside, coming out with a decent space suit emblazoned with Dorcas corporate logos. "Should I put one on as well?"

"Yes, you should."

Once that was done, and she'd put on and sealed the suit, Genji went to the main computer room. The AI was actually distributed throughout the ship, which wasn't a bad design. But all the sub-components and memory units were linked either by wire or wirelessly, and all were physically linked to the power system.

"Access to this room is restricted," the Irish-accented woman's voice admonished Genji. "I will have to inform Tom that you have broken the lock and gained unauthorized access."

"You do that," Genji said, working on the links she'd already set up at the power control station, which had bypassed the normal safety measures. Her training at sabotaging Spear of Humanity ships had made this job fairly easy. And systems in 2140 were so primitive.

"I have notified the security robot of your unauthorized activity. I must insist that you cease your actions."

"The security robot is busy," Genji said. She'd already shut down the bot repair workshop. "Kayl," she called on her phone. "Are we ready to go?"

"We're ready. What are you about to do?"

"Take care of any remaining evidence and any files Dorcas might have on you and me. Hang on." Genji double-checked her work.

"I am sensing unauthorized configuration work," the ship said.

"Yeah, about that," Genji said. "I'm sorry. Say hi to Tom for me."

"I do not know where Tom is."

"You're about to go meet him." Genji activated the links.

All through the ship, massive power surges rolled through every computer component, literally frying the electronics and other parts, the power system itself failing as distribution hubs and lines melted.

Battery-powered emergency lights came on.

The main power source shut down automatically as its control links failed.

Genji walked quickly through the ship, sensing the unnatural stillness with life support dead. All the "windows" that had provided fake views of the outside were also out, so her path was lined with empty screens that seemed to suck up the light from her suit.

Kayl was just outside the gig, looking around. "You killed the ship?"

"It's one of the things I do," Genji said. "Usually I also blow it up, but I thought doing that here might attract too much attention."

"Orbital Control will notice the data feed from the ship is gone. It'll try to contact the ship, and when it gets no answer it will alert Earth Guard to a possible emergency on board."

"Then we'd better get going," Genji said. "What do you need from me?"

He gestured for her to get inside the gig. "Strap in and be ready to bail out the drop hatch when I say so."

"The drop hatch?" Genji looked back at the roughly meter-square hatch in the deck of the gig. "Are we bailing out?"

"No, they'd track us down," Kayl said. "We're going to play rat in the warehouse district."

"I'm going to need a better briefing on our planned course of action, Lieutenant Owen." And yet, she was liking this, her spirits rising with Kayl's confidence.

"We're going to make a fast, hot atmospheric entry," Kayl said, checking a few more readings as he strapped in to the gig's pilot seat. "Once near the surface, we're going to head for the warehouse district just outside the sealed colony. Do you know what that's like? Half-buried warehouses holding bulk supplies that don't need to be maintained in life-support conditions. Rows and rows of them, with streets between them."

"And what are we going to do there?" Genji asked.

"We're going to play rat," Kayl said, grinning. "The Martian aerospace cops will be all over us while I drive this little rocket just over the surface through those streets, until we bail out and leave them chasing the empty gig."

"Won't they see us bail out?" Genji said.

"Nope. Trust me." He winked at her. "Edourd told me this works."

"We're basing the fate of the planet Earth on stories you were told by a former Martian juvenile delinquent." Genji grinned. "All right, then. Let's go, Lieutenant Owen."

"Thank you, Lieutenant Genji." He sealed the top hatch of the gig and hit the controls to release the gig from the brackets holding it firmly to the *Quasar*. "Are you ready for an express trip to the surface of Mars, Selene?"

"Ready whenever you are, Kayl," she said, smiling despite her worries. "This shouldn't be as bad as our last atmospheric entry together, right?"

"Hopefully not." Kayl hit the thrusters and the primary propulsion, sending the gig on a sweeping curve toward the red planet below them.

CHAPTER 7

OWEN KEPT A LOOSE GRIP ON THE CONTROLS AS THE GIG TORE DOWN THROUGH the thin Martian atmosphere. The air couldn't be discounted, but it wasn't nearly as deadly to entry as the much thicker air in Earth's sky. He felt a surge of excitement mingled with worry. Even though he'd acted fully confident with Selene, this wasn't exactly risk-free.

"The orbits of the Earth Guard ships near Mars are all optimized for the expected arrival of the alien ship," Owen told Selene. "That means they're not positioned to intercept us on the way down."

Selene nodded. She looked as if she was in what he thought of as "action mode," outwardly calm and ready to react. That was comforting, even though Selene's skills shouldn't be called on until they were on the surface.

She'd given him a quick report on what had happened with Dorcas, speaking with crisp, dispassionate military terminology that left him wondering how many times Selene had delivered similar reports after encounters with enemy forces. He'd wanted to ask for more details but hadn't because of a feeling that Selene might think he was judging her and her actions. Since he'd been unconscious while she was saving both of their lives, he didn't want her thinking he wanted to do that. Owen didn't question what she'd told him about Dorcas's plans, though. It fit what he'd seen of Dorcas, and Selene had told it to him.

He'd realized when preparing the gig for flight that he no longer questioned anything she told him. That was trust, right? Because Selene had proven herself to be trustworthy.

She'd literally saved his life at least five times.

She might disappear at any instant, leaving him to carry on alone.

Why did that thought have to appear to torment him?

The attempt on their lives had forced him to confront something he'd been trying to ignore.

Be honest with yourself, Kayl. You've fallen hard for her. I need to remember what Aunt Hokulani said, that Selene has good reasons for keeping me at a distance. I won't try to push my way inside that distance. But it's so good to be with her, and it's going to hurt so badly when she's gone. Why the hell did the universe have to do this? Am I just dreaming that Selene likes being around me a lot?

The gig's communications system beeped. "*Quasar Nebula*, this is Planetary Orbital Control. Your flight is not authorized. Landings on Mars are currently prohibited except for high-priority official flights. Return to your ship."

Selene looked at him. "Should we answer?"

"No," Owen said.

She grinned. Damn, Selene looked good when she did that.

Is she hot? Sabita had asked him back on the *Vigilant*. He honestly hadn't thought so at the time. Now, though . . .

Focus, dude.

"*Quasar Nebula*, this is Planetary Orbital Control. Return to your ship immediately. Earth Guard ships are enforcing landing prohibitions and will use force to compel your compliance with this order."

Selene was squinting at the displays the way she did when

viewing the "antique" equipment in 2140. "None of them are in position to fire on us, are they?"

"No," Owen said. "What we'll need to worry about are the aerospace cops."

"*Quasar Nebula*, this is Planetary Orbital Control. Reply immediately. Failure to do so will result in authorization for pursuit and confiscation."

"It's not our gig anyway," Selene said.

"And Dorcas doesn't need it anymore," Owen said. "How long will it take them to figure out what happened to Dorcas?"

She shrugged. "They may have a whole lot of trouble with that. Though maybe I should have blown up the ship."

"I'm not complaining." He altered the entry vector, easing up a bit as atmosphere began screaming past the outside of the gig. "This is really a nice little boat. Did you ever drive boats in 2180?"

"Assault boats for boarding actions," Selene said. "I could drive others but I never did."

Boarding actions. Selene said it in that "don't ask me about this" way she had sometimes. Usually when it involved her wartime service. Maybe someday he'd earn the right to hear about those things.

"*Quasar Nebula*, you are under arrest. Atmospheric police are en route to escort you to a landing pad. Compliance is required."

"Now we've done it," Owen said. He could see the planetary surface coming up quickly, the warehouse district outside the sealed colony, row on row of large buildings separated by geometrically laid-out streets.

"The ground is getting closer pretty fast," Selene said.

"Backseat driving?"

"Sorry."

Owen altered their descent again, seeing two new craft about the size of the gig rising to meet them. "There are the air cops."

"I could probably take them once we're on the surface," Selene said.

That didn't sound good. "Selene, we shouldn't kill cops."

"I wasn't talking about killing them! Disarm, disable, defeat. I can do that, you know. Like I did in LA." She paused. "Is that what you think of me?"

He'd hit another nerve. "No. I was thinking of what just happened on the ship and forgetting LA, which was kind of stupid of me." The air cops, expecting the gig to have slowed a lot more, shot past before starting to come around to resume their pursuit.

"Your worry that I might kill cops here reinforces something I decided earlier. I've sometimes thought you're naïve. But maybe you remember important things that the future I experienced had forgotten. You reminded me of those things. So don't call yourself stupid, Kayl." Her eyes were on the view ahead, which was showing the surface of Mars growing very fast as the gig tore toward it. "I have confidence in you."

"Thanks." It was amazing how good hearing that from her felt to him. He moved the controls, swinging the gig about, thrusters firing on maximum, the primary propulsion also slowing the gig rapidly, pressure building very fast, the structure of the gig groaning and vibrating as it slowed. When he had the velocity low enough to avoid slamming into the surface, Owen swung the gig about again, one landing strut screaming as it briefly touched the surface. He whipped the gig around, heading for the "streets" of the warehouse district just ahead, flying at extremely low altitude, clouds of Martian dust billowing up behind the gig.

"They're above, behind, and to either side," Selene reported.

"Got it. Thanks." Owen swung the gig between warehouses, slowing it again just enough to whip about in a turn almost too tight for the gig to make, alarms wailing as the side of the gig came within a centimeter of one warehouse.

Selene laughed. "Woooo! Kayl, you can really drive a boat! Skills of a master!"

He grinned, watching the next turn point and preparing the maneuver. "Is this the first time that I've impressed you?"

"Oh, Kayl, this is far from the first time that you've impressed me."

Really?

Cool.

Owen brought the gig screaming through another course change onto a different "street," the Martian surface less than a meter below the gig, Martian dust flying up in their wake.

"They're having trouble maintaining chase positions on us," Selene said. "They've gained a little altitude."

"Yeah," Owen said. "Because of the dust we're throwing up. It's interfering some with their navigation and will get into their ship systems. Edourd told me the dust gets everywhere no matter how well you seal things." He yawed the gig through another tight turn. Visibility was down drastically. "This is getting a little unsafe. Get ready to drop out of the hatch."

They were on a straight stretch, so Owen quickly entered some commands into the autopilot. Selene unstrapped and went back to the hatch. "Should I pop it?"

The next turn was coming up, visibility so low that only Owen's instruments gave him any view of the outside. "Go ahead."

The hatch opened, the sound inside the gig suddenly a lot louder, dust surging past the fans trying to keep it out.

Owen swung the gig into its tightest turn yet, the velocity over ground dropping fast as the gig swung about. "When you hit the ground, keep rolling until you come up against a warehouse wall!"

"Got it!

He popped his own seat harness loose. "Go! Now!"

Leaping out of the pilot seat, Owen dove through the drop hatch in Selene's wake.

He'd lowered the speed over ground as much as he could, and the suit had decent padding, but it still hurt when Owen hit and rolled. He kept rolling, shedding speed, until he came up hard against something that didn't feel like a warehouse

No alerts were sounding, so he hadn't ripped the suit.

The gig had vanished, following its autopilot as it tore through some more turns before heading out across the Martian landscape. He couldn't see the air cops, but they were surely still in pursuit, not having been able to spot Owen and Selene making their exits from the gig.

He couldn't see a thing. The Martian dust formed a murky fog that limited his sight to less than arm's length.

"Do you mind?" Selene said.

The thing that didn't feel like a warehouse that he'd rolled into hard had been Selene, who was currently pinned between him and the warehouse side that she'd reached. "Sorry." He moved a little away from her but stayed close to avoid losing sight of her. "Looks like it worked. So far."

"What's next?" Selene muttered some curses as she stood up, holding on to Owen's arm to avoid losing contact. "That's going to leave some bruises."

"Stay with me." Owen began working his way around the side of the warehouse, feeling for a door. He was lucky, finding one within about ten meters along the wall. It was locked, of course. "Can you get us through this?"

She bent to examine it. "It's ancient. Piece of cake."

Since Selene's definition of "ancient" included anything from 2140, that didn't necessarily mean the Mars colony had been neglecting their warehouses, Owen thought.

Inside the warehouse, Selene took time to play with a panel inside the door. "The security cameras watching the inside have been redirected to stare at the ceiling. What are we looking for in here?"

Owen looked out across the warehouse, seeing piles and stacks of materials in the light from his suit. "That. Emergency station. It should have a temporary tent and some spare suits for emergencies."

It did. Owen inflated the tent so they could change suits inside. "We'll need to shed these high-profile Dorcas suits and put on these emergency spare maintenance worker suits."

She didn't protest until she was out of her suit and starting to put on the spare suit. "This thing stinks," Selene complained.

Owen pulled on his spare suit as well, wrinkling his nose. "They're obviously not using their best suits as emergency standbys. These must be old ones not worth using for any other purposes. Ow!" The suit had done a literally painful job of adjusting to him. "I guess the last occupant of this suit was female."

Selene appeared amused. "That happened to a guy in my unit. I hope nothing important on you got damaged."

"What happened to him?" Owen asked, surprised that she was sharing one of her wartime experiences with him.

"He walked funny for a while." Selene paused, her expression shifting. "And then a few months later he lost both legs in action against the Spear. The last time I saw him he was in the hospital getting the legs regrown. Uh, sorry. What do we do with the Dorcas suits?"

"It's okay," Owen assured her. "As for the suits, we hide them." Deflating the tent and returning it to the emergency station, Owen looked for somewhere to hide the Dorcas suits. A far corner of the warehouse looked like it hadn't been touched for years, so he buried the Dorcas suits under some boxes there.

"What's going to happen when they finally catch that gig?" Selene asked.

"They probably won't," Owen said. "After building speed in a dash near the surface, the autopilot is set to go into a climb, maintaining full acceleration until fuel is exhausted. Odds are it's going to sail off into space and never get caught. Unless one of the Earth Guard ships can hit it before it gets too far beyond Mars orbit."

"Even that won't leave much evidence. How are we going to sneak inside the colony?" Selene asked.

"We're not," Owen said. "We're going to walk right in one of the maintenance air locks."

She didn't question him, following as they left the warehouse, Selene resetting the lock, and then the pair of them trudging through the slowly falling dust toward the colony.

Their "new" suits were on the colony frequencies, so both Owen and Selene stayed quiet as they neared the closest maintenance air lock. They could hear chatter among the maintenance workers, though.

"Stupid kids. This dust is going to be everywhere."

"They oughta make them clean it up. With hand brooms."

"Yeah. Hope the cops nailed 'em."

"Didja see what they were flying? Big money. Nothing's gonna happen to them!"

"Yeah, if it was you and me we'd be sent to Phobos, but those rich scum will just walk away and leave us to clean up the mess."

"Typical."

Owen looked over at Selene. Much of her face was concealed by the helmet and the worn old faceplate, but what he could see looked grim. This was more of the corruption she worried about. The loss of confidence in institutions that would leave room for the Spear of Humanity to rise.

He cycled them through the maintenance air lock, trying to make his movements look tired and stiff. With bruises forming as a result of their exit from the gig, that didn't require much acting.

Inside, Owen started walking steadily into the colony. They

both had backpacks on over their suits, holding their few possessions, but as Owen had recalled, a lot of the maintenance workers had personal backpacks to haul around their work supplies, lunches, and other items. He and Selene shouldn't stand out.

"Hey! You two!"

Owen turned to look, pointing to himself as if asking whether he was the one being called out. He'd seen plenty of sailors play this "who, me?" game.

"Yeah, you! You didn't leave by this lock, did you?" The supervisor seemed like someone who didn't need much to make her unhappy.

"This one's closer," Owen mumbled.

"You know the rules! In and out, same air lock. What's your number?" she asked, checking his suit and Selene's. "I got your numbers. Pull this again, and you'll be on leach-field duties for the next Martian year. Got it?"

"Got it."

"Get the hell out of here and get back to work!"

Owen started walking again, Selene with him.

He needed a maintenance locker. Where—? There was one.

They both crowded inside, opening their helmets once the door was closed.

Selene was actually laughing. "Everywhere you go, Lieutenant Owen. Everywhere you go, you're trouble."

"I think you deserve some of the credit." He gratefully peeled off the old suit. "There should be disposable overalls in here."

"Yeah. Right here," Selene said, sighing as she got her own suit off. "We put on overalls and continue pretending to be maintenance workers?"

"Right," Owen said. "Who pays attention to low-level workers on their way to their next job? Are those masks?"

"Yes!" Selene grabbed one. "Hazard work masks. This will cover my eyes and face. Do you see any gloves?"

"Disposable ones. Here."

"You should take a mask, too. Just in case you need to hide your face. Do you know anyone on Mars?"

Owen paused to consider that. "I'll have to check the colony directory. There should be at least a few people I served with in Earth Guard assigned to the colony right now."

"Do we want to run into them?" Selene asked, pulling on the gloves.

"I don't know," Owen said, watching her. "I'm sorry you have to hide your skin and eyes so much."

Selene gave him a surprised look. "I've been doing that all my life whenever I could, Kayl."

"Why?"

She appeared aggravated. "Alloy. Okay?"

"Umm . . . okay." Owen, knowing that he'd stepped in it again, hauled out one of their burner phones, checking the colony ads. "We need a short-term apartment. Someplace catering to temp workers. What do you think?"

"Sure. Check the ratings, though. I'm glad to be out of the absurd luxury of the *Quasar*, but I'd like accommodations that won't be too horrible."

"There's not a lot free right now," Owen said worriedly. "Hardly anything. Wait. How about this one? It looks like just the sort of low-profile place we need. Oh. One bedroom, one bed."

"That's okay," Selene said. "If they're looking for an alien and a rogue Earth Guard officer, they won't expect us to be in a one-bed place. I'll take the floor."

"I'll take the floor," Owen insisted.

"The bed is probably really uncomfortable," Selene insisted. "I'll take the floor."

"No, I'll— Let's argue about it once we get the room."

She pulled on the mask, Owen carried his, and they went out onto the Martian street.

He hadn't been to Mars in a while, and then only for brief liberty on the surface. The bar district probably hadn't changed all that much, but they were nowhere near that.

Along here the standard housing and other buildings were slowly being modified to meet personal preferences. The roof running between buildings, sealing off the street from the Martian environment outside, looked reassuringly solid.

He could hear a lot of excited chatter. The alien ship would reach orbit about Mars soon. It still hadn't responded to any attempts to contact it. "People are worried," Owen said. "Scared."

"That's what the histories reported," Selene said. "But they don't have to be! Kayl, we can't waste any time. We get this room, we call the contact Admiral Tecumseh gave us, and we get this rolling."

"We should rest," Owen argued.

"No time. I can power through this. Can you?"

"Sure," Owen said.

The automated kiosk handling the apartment rental accepted without any protest a couple of the false IDs Selene had found aboard the *Quasar* and didn't balk at the anonymous cash card Owen used to pay two weeks of rent the way a higher-end apartment complex might have. *Or would it?* Owen wondered. From the number of anonymous cash cards and the amounts on them that Tom Dorcas had lying around, it seemed as if the wealthy routinely used them to avoid letting anyone know what they were spending money on.

Inside the apartment, he looked around. Martian concrete, sealed on the inside but otherwise unfinished. Minimal, rugged furnishings. The apartment was fairly small, the living area about three meters across and including a food prep/storage area against one wall as well as a small table with two chairs. A doorway led to the bedroom and bathroom. It would do.

Selene pulled off her overall, leaving her in shorts and a short-sleeved shirt for one of the few times Owen had seen her like that. He paused for a moment, watching her skin gleam in the lights of the apartment.

She noticed him and turned away as if embarrassed.

Owen also pulled off his disposable coverall before hauling out the burner phone Admiral Tecumseh had provided. "Ready?"

"I already said I was ready," Selene said. She seemed to be on edge again, but that was understandable.

"How much should I tell this person?"

Selene paused. "As little as possible. I'm worried about telling all of the negotiators where I came from and exactly what I am. They're far less likely to believe me and far more likely to leak that information."

"We did tell Admiral Tecumseh," Owen pointed out.

"One person at a time, privately, we can decide to do that," Selene said. "But not to this group. My instincts are telling me not to make the time-travel thing the public focus of who I am. Not yet. The focus has to be on making First Contact work, not on me." She must have seen the uncertainty in him. "Kayl, how many people in authority are ready to hear about the Universal War, about how everything they're doing is leading toward collapse, about the Earth being destroyed in 2180? They won't believe me. Not yet. I need to prove what I know."

He paused, thinking about that. "It took me a long time to believe you. It took them trying to kill us more than once. I guess we do need more proof before we try to convince a lot of people that you are what you are."

"If I fix First Contact, that will be the start of the proof we need," Selene said. "Make the call."

Owen hit the contact call button.

"Yesenski," a gruff voice said.

"Admiral Tecumseh sends her regards, sir," Owen said. "We need to see you, sir, right away."

"Why can't you come here to my office?" Yesenski paused, probably checking the number that had called him. "I see. This is urgent? I've got an alien ship close to making Mars orbit."

"It's very urgent," Owen said. "Admiral Tecumseh told us you were the one we needed to talk to."

Owen heard a heavy sigh. "If you're wasting my time, Admiral Tecumseh will be hearing from me. Where are you at?"

ON THE OFFICIAL EARTH GUARD SITE, CAPTAIN YUSUKE YESENSKI HAD THE LOOK OF a man who didn't bear fools lightly. In fact, he looked exactly like the sort of officer Rear Admiral Tecumseh would have reached out to. Owen was still worried, though, knowing how thin the ice was that they were walking on. The fact that he and Selene were both in civilian clothing, she with her alloy characteristics plainly visible, wouldn't make dealing with Yesenski any easier.

"Are you sure?" Owen asked her. "If you want to cover up again before he gets here—"

"At the moment, I'm tired of covering up."

He nodded, not wanting to get into an argument with the both of them so worn-out, even though Selene appeared to be oddly fatalistic. Owen still wished they'd taken a few hours to sleep, hoping his fatigue would not show or cause him to say the wrong thing when Yesenski got here.

The bell sounded and Owen let him in.

Their surroundings clearly did not impress the Earth Guard captain. "Who the hell are you?" he demanded of Owen.

Even though he was in civilian clothing, Owen came to attention and saluted. "Lieutenant Kayl Owen, sir."

"Kayl Owen." Yesenski looked him over slowly. "Are you aware that you're dead?"

"I have been so informed, sir."

Captain Yesenski shifted his gaze to Selene, his frown of disapproval making clear what he thought of her physical appearance. "And you?"

She also came to attention, saluting. "Lieutenant Selene Genji, sir."

"You're a lieutenant?" Yesenski slowly shook his head at her before looking back at Owen. "I was told you would have a very important package for me. What is it?"

"Information about the aliens," Selene said, her voice composed and professional. "Who they are, what they want, why they came here."

"You know that? All of that?"

"All of that, Captain," Selene said. "And a lot more."

His frown of disapproval at her appearance shifted to a look of reluctant admiration. "That's what all that's about, huh? Someone actually got an agent in place to learn that stuff, and back here to report on it before the aliens actually got here?"

"We aren't permitted to discuss the details," Owen said, quickly playing along with what Yesenski seemed to have concluded.

"I understand operational security, Lieutenant. Especially about something like this. Admiral Tecumseh said I should listen when you called. She's involved with this?"

"Yes, Captain," Owen said.

Yesenski eyed Selene. "Lieutenant Genji, I assume we need to keep you under wraps." His tone of voice, his attitude toward her, had undergone a complete shift.

"That's correct, Captain," she said. "But I can speak directly through voice-only circuits. I need to make contact with some of the negotiators so I can provide them with critical advance information."

"Such as what?" Captain Yesenski said, in a "show me" sort of voice.

"Such as why the Tramontine, the aliens, have not yet responded to our communications, and exactly when they will send their first message."

Yesenski looked impressed. Very impressed. "When? Tell me that first."

"The moment the Tramontine ship enters Mars orbit."

"Tramontine? That's what they call themselves?"

"Yes, Captain."

"I need to— Wait." Yesenski faced her again. "Their purpose. You know that?"

"Absolutely, Captain," Selene said. "They are here because they are curious."

"Curious?"

"Yes, Captain," Selene said. "Even more curious than humans. They want to know things. They don't want to fight, they want to learn."

Yesenski eyed her, rubbing the back of his neck. "Admiral Tecumseh told me the same thing. If you're wrong . . ."

"Captain, I am right. I will be proven right. I can tell our negotiators exactly what will be in the first message they receive from the Tramontine."

"Damn. This is hotter than the sun's surface. Why isn't it being filtered through Earth Guard Intelligence?"

"As you noted, Captain," Owen said, "this is very hot information."

"Special channels. Got it. Lieutenant Owen, are you Lieutenant Genji's handler?"

"And assistant," Owen said.

"Good. Good. The death thing is a cover story, huh? I want to hear the details on this someday. You want minimum action around here to avoid drawing attention, right? Naturally. I'm going to get some special communications gear delivered here. Plug and use. Video capability deactivated or removed?"

"We'd prefer removed, Captain," Owen said. Hackers and government investigators were always finding new ways to secretly activate video capabilities that had supposedly been safely deactivated.

"Then you'll get that. I know at least two of the negotiators who will want to talk to you and will keep quiet about where they got their information. Am I considered trustworthy in that regard?"

"Yes, sir," Owen said.

"Good. Good. Let's get this going. Damn good job, you two." Captain Yesenski stopped to look at Selene. "Lieutenant Genji, is that, uh, reversible?"

"No, Captain," Selene said.

"You're one damned amazing officer, Lieutenant Genji. Stand by to get that gear."

"Yes, sir," Owen said.

After the captain had left, Owen couldn't help grinning at Selene. "That couldn't have gone better. You really impressed him."

She nodded, looking worried. "We're close to something big. There's not a lot of time."

"What can I do?"

"I don't know."

Owen paused, watching her. He didn't recognize this kind of behavior in Selene, this sudden passivity, and didn't know what it meant. "If I read Captain Yusuke Yesenski right, we'll have that communications gear delivered within a couple of hours and be speaking to some of those negotiators soon afterwards."

"That's great," Selene said.

Something was wrong. What? "I can order some food. Tea. Should I have some tea delivered?"

"Yeah. Thanks." She sat down in one of the two chairs, her eyes on the floor. She was probably worn out, he decided. After all, she'd dealt with Dorcas and his assistant while Owen himself had still slumbered away under sedation. Owen ordered some food as well as essentials like tea and coffee before hauling around the single table the main room boasted so that it faced Selene's chair. "Do you want to get some sleep? I can wake you when—"

"No."

"Umm . . . so, you'll get the bed. I'll take the floor." That old debate should rouse her.

"Fine."

She wasn't arguing over that? They always argued over that. What was wrong?

The food arrived, providing a welcome diversion. Selene only picked at her food.

Then the communications gear arrived, just as Owen had predicted. It was in a nondescript package, delivered by someone who looked a lot like an Earth Guard officer pretending to be a civilian package handler.

Selene sat and watched as he got out the panel and the backup that Captain Yesenski had sent. For security reasons, these plugged into connections built into the walls, linking through them to special conduits.

The primary lit up. "I'm seeing this line active and secure," Captain Yesenski's voice said.

"It's active and secure on our end, sir," Owen said.

"Are you ready to talk, uh, Lieutenant?" Yesenski said. "I have some of the negotiators standing by right here."

Selene finally roused herself by what appeared to be an effort of will. "I am here and ready to answer."

Another voice came on. "Hello? What do I call you?"

"Genji, please."

"Genji. All right. You told Captain Yesenski the aliens, you called them the Tramontine, will send their first message when they enter Mars orbit. Why then? Why have they waited and not responded to our messages?"

Owen saw Selene smile slightly. "The Tramontine want to avoid misunderstandings."

"What did you say?"

"They want to avoid misunderstandings. The Tramontine only conduct negotiations when real-time communications are possible. To them, any discussion that has time lags and delays of any length between the back-and-forth breeds confusion and miscommunication."

There was a pause before another voice came on. "Uh, Genji, why didn't they tell us that when they arrived? That they would conduct negotiations when they reach Mars?"

"Because that would be initiating a discussion," Selene said, "at a time when large time lags between messages and responses were impossible to avoid. And because they can't communicate that well with us yet. Their first message will be an attempt to clarify the meanings of words."

"You know what the first message will contain?" The new voice held disbelief and hope mingled.

"It will be pictograms paired with Tramontine words. They want us to send the message back with the human words that we think match the images and Tramontine words," Selene said, speaking slowly and clearly. "The very first pictogram will show a Tramontine and a human standing side by side on a planet. This will be— This could be misinterpreted as a wish, or a demand, for them to settle on Earth or Mars. In fact, it is simply to illustrate the word 'share.'"

"'Share'?" the first negotiator asked. "Why 'share' instead of 'peace' or 'friend'?"

"Because to the Tramontine, 'share' means both of those things. You share with your friends. You share with those you are at peace with. The opposite to the Tramontine is 'take.' You take from enemies. Enemies take from you. The second pictogram will show what appears to be one person taking an object from another person. This will— This could be misinterpreted as a positive symbol, showing an exchange of gifts or giving. In fact, it is meant to illustrate the Tramontine concept of taking, a bad thing."

Another pause. "How can you know this? It's priceless, if true. I can't imagine how hard it would have been to figure out those meanings. But how did you learn them?"

"I can't disclose that," Genji said. "But you will see. The First Contact message will be sent the moment the Tramontine ship enters Mars orbit, the first pictogram on it will show that image, and the second the other image. I repeat what I told Captain Yesenski. The Tramontine are an intensely curious species. Curious enough to build ships capable of interstellar journeys so they can learn who or what lives around other stars. They do not seek anything from us except permission to settle in part of the asteroid belt so they can mine resources to refit and resupply their ship and travel on to another star."

An even longer pause.

"Genji, if this is all accurate, it changes everything."

Owen, watching closely, was shocked to see Selene shudder.

"Genji, we need to share this and get back with you. Certainly some of it can quickly be confirmed when the aliens reach orbit. One other thing. What about their technology? There is a lot of concern about that."

Selene visibly steadied herself before answering. "The Tramontine technology is somewhat in advance of human technology. They are willing to share it. Sharing is what friends do. Sharing means peace."

"What about weapons? Do they have weapons well in advance of ours?"

"The Tramontine ship has only defensive weapons. They have no offensive weapons," Selene said.

A new voice came on, a woman speaking loudly. "Genji, this is the sort of interpretation and understanding that would have required months of learning each other's languages and meaning. It could end the fears of invasion and conquest overnight. But how could you possibly have acquired this knowledge?"

Selene closed her eyes and surprised Owen by suddenly speaking three words in a fluid language that he didn't recognize. "Rowlerria basssanri tythosei. Those are the Tramontine words for 'Greeting let us share.'"

"*You already know the language?* Are you—?"

"Kararii fessandri etheria," Selene said. "My words are truth."

A long silence followed. "That . . . is remarkable," one of the negotiators finally said. "Who are you?"

"Selene Genji. I am my mother's daughter. I will say no more on that, but I will answer more questions about the Tramontine."

Owen, increasingly worried by Selene's strange attitude, wondered if he should step in. Fortunately, the negotiators had apparently been stunned by what they'd heard. "We need to discuss this. We can speak tomorrow, yes? Eight Earth hours. Is that acceptable, Genji?"

"That's acceptable. If . . . I am unavailable, it is because I am no longer able to share information with you."

The call ended, Selene gazed at the table. She didn't seem to be looking at anything except perhaps her own memories.

"Selene? Selene? Lieutenant Genji?"

She finally looked up at him, her eyes dark. "What is it?"

"This is big, right? This should change everything about First Contact, just like that guy said."

"Yeah. It should."

"It could be enough to change the fate of the Earth."

"I doubt it. But maybe."

What was wrong? They'd made a breakthrough. Surely this would change the future. Why was Selene upset? If he didn't know her better, he'd think she was . . .

She was scared. She was terrified. He hadn't thought he'd ever seen Selene scared, but of course she was now. Because if this would surely change the future, it might well cancel her as those changes rippled through time. She might vanish at any instant. *If I am unavailable, it is because I am no longer able to share information with you.* How must she feel right now? Waiting for something worse than oblivion, for a never-was?

"Selene, I . . . what do you need from me? Name it. Anything."

She refused to look at him again. "Just leave me alone."

"But . . . but . . . you're . . . you might . . ."

"Leave. Me. Alone!"

"Okay." He'd never felt so helpless.

In the small apartment, there were only two places for him to go. The bathroom was too small, so he went into the bedroom. It lacked chairs, so he lay down even though he'd resolved to give her the bed. He might as well rest as best he could, though that seemed unlikely given how his mind and heart were churning.

How would he know? Would Selene just not be there anymore?

The idea of that happening made him feel empty.

He couldn't imagine what was going on inside her.

Waiting for the sudden . . . never-was. Ceasing to have ever been.

Maybe it was lingering effects of the sedation used on Dorcas's ship. Maybe it was just exhaustion. When had he last slept? Despite the turmoil filling him, Owen passed out into deep sleep.

He woke suddenly in the darkened room, still lying on his back, trying to place where he was and what had happened. Gradually realizing that Selene was lying close to him in the bed, one of her arms resting on his chest. "Selene?"

"Who am I?" she whispered, her lips near his ear, her breath warm against his skin.

It took a major effort of will to hold himself still and answer her in a calm voice. "Lieutenant Selene Genji."

"What am I?" she asked, her lips lightly brushing his ear this time.

"An . . . an alloy." Did Selene have any idea how this was making him feel? How much he wanted to roll toward her and pull her next to him? Why was she doing this?

"Do you want me?" Selene whispered, her breathing noticeably faster.

"Hell yes," Kayl said, his own breathing speeding up despite his efforts to remain in control. Was this a dream? How could she really be doing this?

"I want you," Selene breathed. Before he realized what was happening, Selene was on top of him, her mouth seeking his with desperate urgency.

CHAPTER 8

WHEN OWEN AWOKE AGAIN WITH MEMORIES OF FALLING ASLEEP WITH SELENE, their arms still about each other, the first thing he noticed was the lack of any sign of her. Pulling on a pair of shorts, he raced to the bedroom door, his heart filled with fear.

She was sitting at the table, drinking tea. As Owen sagged with relief against the doorframe, Selene looked up at him. "Are you okay?" she asked, as if nothing unusual had happened.

"Umm . . . yeah," Owen said. What was this? What had happened to the fey Selene he'd seen before and the tigress who'd been in bed with him? "Are you okay?"

"Yeah. I'm okay." Selene looked back down at her tea.

Feeling awkward, Owen sat down opposite her. "Selene?"

"What?"

She wasn't going to make this easy, was she? "Where exactly are we? What happened?"

"That's a fair question." Selene let out a long, slow breath. "I'm still working through it. I'm not saying I regret anything. But I sort of sprung it on you by surprise."

"Yeah," Owen said. "You might say that."

She paused, staring down at her tea. "In the cold light of morning, how do you feel about it?"

"About last night? It was every dream come true for me."

"You must have some very interesting dreams." Selene hesitated again. "No regrets?"

"No. Are you saying you *do* have regrets?" He didn't like asking that, but avoiding the issue wouldn't be doing him or her any favors.

"No," Selene said. "No regrets at all. Except, I . . . I may cease to exist at any moment. I've resolved not to waste any more of those moments. I want you to be with me, but I can't promise you anything. I could be gone before I finish speaking this. I needed you, so I used you, knowing I couldn't offer any assurance of anything beyond the next moment. That's not fair to you. Can you live with that?"

"You're worried about what's fair to me?" Owen asked.

"Yes." She raised her gaze to meet his eyes. "Because I don't want you to doubt for even one moment that if it had been anyone other than you, last night wouldn't have happened."

"I hadn't even thought of that." Would he have, though? At some point wondering if her fear had driven Selene to seek comfort with anyone she could? "I understand the limits on what you can promise. I'm happy with every moment we can be together."

"Good."

"Uh . . . Selene, you were . . . umm . . . different, last night."

She eyed him, her expression hard to read. "I had a lot of tension to burn off. Did you like it?"

Owen quickly held up his hands. "Yes. It was . . . incredible. It was just, like you said, a surprise."

"And you're wondering if I'll be like that next time?"

"I . . . there's going to be a next time? I wasn't sure at this point whether that was a onetime thing."

"I want there to be a next time," she said. "A lot of next times. I want us to share the bed from now on. Not just because of the physical thing . . . which was really . . . great . . . but because . . .

because it's you. I know it could end at any moment, but I want . . . something special. With you. For as long as it can last, even though that probably won't be . . . all that long. If that's okay with you."

Owen nodded. "Yeah. That's okay with me. That's what I want, too. For as long as it can last."

She smiled, but a moment later, the smile vanished. "However, even though some things have changed between us, I am still not your hill."

"What?"

"I am not your hill. Our mission is the hill. That hasn't changed."

"What are you talking about?"

"The hill you're ready to die on, Kayl Owen!"

"Oh." He remembered that she'd talked to Aunt Hokulani. "All right."

"Do you agree?" Selene pressed.

"You're not my hill," Owen said. "Our mission is the hill."

"Good. Now, can you do something for me?" Selene paused, looking toward the door. "I need to be able to focus on what else I'm going to tell the negotiators and how I'm going to tell it. But it's only a matter of time before problems develop here. Maybe the people who tried to kill us track us down. Maybe Captain Yesenski decides I'm not really a supersecret Earth Guard spy who infiltrated the alien ship. Maybe something else. We need to prepare for that. I know every plan is a challenge thrown in the face of chance, but—"

"What?" Owen interrupted.

"Every plan is a challenge thrown in the face of chance," Selene repeated. "You must have heard that saying."

"No, I never have."

"How could you not have heard that? It's stressed at officer training! It's . . ." She closed her eyes for a moment, looking pained. "In the 2170s. Everyone knows that saying in the 2170s."

"Sorry."

"Anyway," Selene continued, "can you handle that? I won't

174

worry about escape routes or detecting surveillance of us or any-thing else if I know you're working it."

"Of course I can do that," Owen said, grateful to realize that he had something important to do. "I'll try to cover all the contingen-cies and have enough slack built in to cover contingencies I didn't think of."

"Great." She sighed. "I know you can take care of everything."

"I will. Are you really okay, Selene?"

"Part of me is scared out of my mind," she said. "But I've . . . found a safe place. As long as I hold on to that, I think I'll be okay."

"Tell me if there's anything else I can do," Owen said.

She looked thoughtful. "I think we've still got about half an hour before we need to kick into gear on our respective tasks."

"All right."

Selene took another drink of tea, looking at him over the top of the cup. "Remember what I said about not wasting any moments? Are you ready to find out what I'm like this morning?"

He stood up and vaulted over the small table, making her laugh as their arms went about each other.

SEEING SELENE ONCE AGAIN EMOTIONALLY CENTERED MADE OWEN FEEL IMMENSELY better. As did knowing that they were now . . . What exactly were they?

Though there was no telling how much longer they'd have to-gether.

He didn't have much trouble imagining how a lot of people might respond to knowing he had a physical relationship with a partly alien, mostly human woman. All of the movies he could think of involving alien or partly alien women coming to Earth were either horror stories or pornography or some weird combina-tion of both. Which said a lot more about humans than it did about alien or partly alien women.

"Selene?" She had settled herself in front of the communications device, ready to be on the moment the negotiators called. "What do I call you now? Are you my—"

"Selene," she said.

"But how do I describe—"

"Selene. Or, in formal settings, Lieutenant Genji. You're still Kayl, right?"

"I'm still Kayl. Or, in formal settings, Lieutenant Owen."

Selene smiled. "So what's the question?"

"I can't remember," Owen said. "You smiled and my brain went blank."

"That must be one of my mysterious alien powers."

"I don't think that's an alien thing," Owen said.

"Kayl, you understand, you have to think of this as temporary. If you think of it as permanent, start coming up with special names, things like that, it'll just make it harder when . . ."

He didn't want to say it, either. "Are you going to be okay? I need to go out looking for some things they don't sell in legitimate markets."

"I'm a big girl. I'll be fine. Have fun making your black market purchases."

The comm panel lit up. "Genji? Are you available?"

She waved a quick farewell to him. "Yes. I'm here."

Would she still be here when he got back? Or would she have vanished from ever existing? If he let that fear dominate his life, it wouldn't help anything, but it would ruin Selene's chance to grasp some happiness before what seemed to be her inevitable fate. Owen willed himself to leave with a smile, determined not to let her down in whatever time was left to them.

THERE WERE A NUMBER OF TASKS HE NEEDED TO CARRY OUT CAUTIOUSLY TO PREpare for them having to flee that apartment, possibly with a lot of danger in pursuit. Being able to watch for trouble independent of the city camera network was one of them. The ability of the authorities to control what the cameras showed meant they couldn't be used by the average citizen as a reliable form of warning.

And there were discreet devices that would help fool the cameras for those who didn't want the authorities to easily track them.

But, of course, all such things were illegal. As a stranger to Mars, Owen didn't know how to find the contacts who could get them for him. He did have a substantial number of anonymous cash cards thanks to what they'd brought from the *Quasar*, but he needed to know where to spend them.

Which brought him back to Edourd Guyon.

Whether you were on Mars or Earth, Owen thought, certain groups of teenagers always looked like trouble.

This particular group looked like particular trouble. But at least a few of them seemed to resemble his old friend in terms of similar ethnic background. "Hey," Owen said, walking up to them.

To call the looks he received cold would be to understate things.

"Do any of you know Edourd Guyon?"

One of the young men cocked an eyebrow at Owen. "Ed's my cousin. Why you looking for him?"

"I know he's not here," Owen said. "He's back on Earth. He told me if I got to Mars I should look up his friends."

"Friends, huh?"

"I'm looking for a little, umm . . ."

"No drugs here, man," Edourd's cousin said, generating some snickers from the other teens. "Find yourself someone else."

"I need electronics," Owen said. "Stuff that's not on the market."

"So? Why you coming here?"

"Because Ed Guyon told me some of the things he did as a teen on Mars," Owen said.

That at least earned him some grins.

Ed's cousin looked him over. "You haven't been here long. I can tell by your walk. How'd you get down with all the landings shut off? You one of them people who came to talk to the aliens?"

"Not me," Owen said.

"Somebody being a rat around the warehouses really recent," another teen spoke up. "You the rat?"

"Why would I be the rat?" Owen said, moving both hands as if he were controlling the gig.

"Huh." Ed's cousin pulled out a ragged piece of paper and wrote something on it. Even on Mars, people wanting to write messages that couldn't be traced or tracked fell back on small pieces of paper. "Talk to one of these guys, rat. Maybe they can help you."

"Thanks." Owen looked at the contact info, wondering if he dared use it. He turned to go, resolved to try another tack.

"Who should I tell Ed was looking for him?" Ed's cousin asked.

He couldn't give his real name. But he could pass on a nickname. "Duke. Ed called me Duke after Duke Kahanamoku."

"Duke?"

"Yeah. It's a surfing thing. Ed loves surfing."

The young man's attitude underwent a sudden shift. "Surfing? That's the thing with waves and lots of water, eh?"

"Yes," Owen said. "Edourd got orders back to Earth so he could keep doing it."

"You do know Ed. You been surfing with him?"

Owen grinned. "A couple of times. I'm the native Earth guy but he's a lot better at it than I am." Once again turning to go, he spread his little finger and thumb, the other three fingers curled in, in the ancient gesture. "Hang loose."

"Hey, I seen that! Ed told me that was a surfer sign. Duke, wait." The young man took the paper from him. "You don't want to see these guys. Here. She'll fix you up. Anything you need. What's it like, man? That much water?"

He gazed at the teens, their faces suddenly alight with interest.

"It's . . . so cool. It can be scary. It's so powerful. But amazing. Beautiful."

"Wish we had oceans," one of the girls muttered.

"You will," Owen said. Selene would approve of this, wouldn't she? "Mars will be terraformed."

"Yeah, in a few centuries," another teen scoffed.

"Another few decades," Owen said. He pointed up. "The Tramontine, the aliens, they have tech that can do it. They'll share it with us."

"Share it with us? Why would they do that? People don't just share stuff like that."

Owen shook his head, smiling. "They're not people."

"You know this, man?" Ed's cousin asked. "Not a guess? This is something you know?"

"This is something I know," Owen said.

"But they're dangerous, right?" another girl asked. "Scary."

"They're not dangerous," Owen said. "There's no reason to be scared of them."

"Then why's everybody telling us to be scared of them?"

Owen shrugged. "You've all been around, right? Why do people tell you to be scared of something?"

"Because they don't want us to know anything about it," Edourd's cousin said. "They want to tell us what to think."

"You said it," Owen said. "I've got to go. Thanks again."

He'd planted another small seed of change. What would grow from it? Hopefully, Selene would approve.

Thinking about Selene resurfaced his worries. Whether she would still exist when he got back. If he wasn't there, would he be able to sense it when Selene ceased to exist? Or would he instead suddenly look around, finding himself on Mars, wondering why he was there and how he'd gotten there? Or, if everything was canceled out, would he find himself back aboard the *Vigilant*, waiting nervously for the arrival of the alien ship in Mars orbit, with memories of a mysterious piece of wreckage that hadn't had any living survivor aboard it?

Owen paused to breathe deeply a few times. It was one thing to think about the pain of losing Selene, of spending the rest of his life remembering these few days together and trying to carry on with her mission. It was another to imagine all memory of her vanishing from him, no trace that she had ever existed or influenced his life or anyone else's. He desperately hoped that he'd remember as much as possible, preferring the thought of that pain to the thought of losing all his memories of her.

This was the closest he could come to feeling what she must feel at the thought of being erased. And it was horrible. How much harder must it be for her?

He had to assume he would remember, had to assume that Selene would be in existence long enough for his efforts to ensure their safety would matter. And he had to do his best with those efforts. Because he wasn't going to let her down.

The woman the contact info led to proved to be remarkably resourceful when shown one of the larger cash cards. She was also able to provide some more burner phones and a classified diagram of the colony that included things regular citizens weren't supposed to be aware of, and was able to point Owen to someone who could provide authentic full-time maintenance worker overalls and full hazard work masks and gloves to go with them. Disposable overalls and masks could do the job, but avoiding attention would be easier if they looked like full-time workers, Owen thought.

He discreetly stuck his tiny new minicams into place on the side street outside the apartment, as well as a few more locations.

A collection of surveillance-confusing devices went into the bag with the maintenance worker uniforms.

Owen studied the diagram of the colony, keying on the maintenance tunnels running beneath all the dwellings. Few of the tunnels were very big, though all were large enough for a worker to squeeze into when things needed to be fixed or replaced. The accesses were all locked to prevent unauthorized entry, but one of the devices he'd acquired could handle that problem.

There were other potential escape routes, depending on how much warning they got. And various unoccupied places to hide. The problem was, the sealed colony monitored oxygen consumption in every building. If a supposedly empty place suddenly started showing oxygen consumption consistent with two people, it would be like sending up a flare.

Far better would be finding an occupied place to hide while any searches died down.

Owen went through the colony directory, searching for familiar names, anyone who might be willing to help him out even if Earth Guard had issued orders to bring him in. As far as he knew, that wasn't yet a problem. Earth Guard had officially declared him dead and hopefully thought that was indeed the case. But that could change very quickly, and based on what had happened in LA and at the LA spaceport, someone sure seemed to still be trying to make sure both he and Selene were at least caught and perhaps killed. So he found a few addresses and figured out routes and prepared for a very quick departure from the apartment.

In the midst of this, the Tramontine ship reached orbit about Mars, and almost immediately news sites began blaring reports that the aliens had finally sent a message. He saw visuals of the negotiators, recognizing some of their voices as they confidently described the intended meanings of the Tramontine images. While a few of the negotiators expressed ongoing concerns, most appeared relaxed, saying the aliens were indeed peaceful. More than one commentator wondered at how quickly understanding was developing between the aliens and the human negotiators.

Four days after their arrival, Owen came back from a mission scouting out an escape path to find Selene dozing in front of the comm panel. Opening the door to the apartment was always accompanied by a tight knot in his gut as he wondered if he'd find an empty place with no sign anyone but him had ever been in it.

The apartment's entertainment panel flared to life. "Important public safety announcement! A warrant has been issued for the arrest of this individual for questioning in the disappearance and possible murder of famous money manager Thomas Dorcas."

The report woke up Selene, who gazed at the panel. "That looks like you."

"That is me," Kayl said.

"Kayl Owen, an Earth Guard officer, has been absent without leave and declared a deserter. Anyone seeing him should notify public security immediately. A substantial reward may be available in exchange for useful information."

"I thought I was officially dead," Owen said, sitting down and bringing out the meal he'd brought back.

"Substantial reward," Selene said. "It's a good thing for you I like you so much. How do you suppose Earth Guard will explain you being officially dead and also a deserter?"

"They'll probably declare the whole thing is classified and refuse to provide any explanation," Owen said.

"I guess we'll have to order all our meals on delivery now," Selene said. "How are we doing on escape plans?"

"We can roll whenever we need to," Owen said.

Half an hour later, Captain Yesenski showed up. "You're alive again, Lieutenant Owen."

"So I understand, sir," Owen said.

"And wanted for murder. Questioning in relation to a possible murder, that is. I am officially required to arrest you if I know where you are. Fortunately for you, I'm going to remain unsure of this address for another twenty-four hours while you get your superiors to contact me and assure me this murder thing isn't real. You didn't kill Dorcas, did you?"

"No, sir, I did not kill Dorcas."

"I'm not saying you might not have been justified from all I've heard of Dorcas, but I'm still glad to hear that, Lieutenant Owen." Fortunately, Captain Yesenski didn't pose the same question to Selene, probably because she wasn't mentioned in the arrest warrant. "Lieutenant Genji, your information has made a huge difference. But even though the negotiators can't get enough of you, I'm getting pushback from some quarters. Any idea why?"

"Some people don't want First Contact to go smoothly," Selene said.

"I'm getting that same message from Admiral Tecumseh. She thinks you're something special, Lieutenant. And you've done an immense service with your information. You two get me that reassurance from your superiors. I can't delay acting too long without that, given the orders I have."

"Thank you, Captain," Owen said.

When Yesenski was gone, Selene leaned back and sighed. "Twenty-four hours. It was nice while it lasted. Captain Yesenski doesn't seem like the sort to be put off."

"No," Owen said. "The only superior officer we could contact is Rear Admiral Tecumseh, and Captain Yesenski clearly wants to hear from someone else. We need to get ready to go. When's your next contact with the negotiators?"

"Four hours."

"I'm going to recheck our escape bags. We need to think about getting out of here in about twelve hours."

GENJI WASN'T LOOKING FORWARD TO "MOVING." SHE'D GOTTEN USED TO THIS PLACE and the ability to speak with the negotiators. This move would seriously disrupt those contacts.

Everything seemed to be going right otherwise. She'd definitely changed First Contact. A huge amount. All of the misinterpretations, all of the misunderstandings, all of the misreadings and miscommunications. She seemed to have fixed all of that before it happened. And this cheap apartment would always be the place where she and Kayl had become something more than friends. Just what they'd become she still wasn't certain of, but she was grateful for whatever it was, for however much longer it lasted. It was strange to think how this small, grungy place would occupy such a fond place in her memories.

For as long as such memories existed. For as long as she existed.

She should already be gone.

Why was she still here?

Why was the universe playing games with her?

One of the devices Kayl carried chattered urgently. He checked it. "The video feed from the cameras on our street is being edited."

"That's not good," Genji said.

Kayl was checking something else. He showed her a screen. "The public cameras show nothing unusual on our street. The usual number of people walking past. This is what my minicams show."

Genji looked, seeing a street empty of foot traffic. They'd gotten used to the number of pedestrians on the street, which always seemed to be busy, day or night. "That's really not good."

Another alert. Kayl put one finger to his lips to urge silence before pointing around and then to his ear.

Somebody had activated listening devices in the apartment.

Clearly, it was time to go. The next meeting with the negotiators in about three hours wasn't going to happen.

He tossed her a maintenance overall. After Genji pulled it on, she swept the apartment to make sure everything important was in her pack.

Kayl was also in his overall. Crouching on one side of the apartment, he used a device that caused a meter-square panel to pop up from the floor.

He gestured her to go first, pointing in the direction he wanted her to take.

Genji slid down into a claustrophobic horizontal shaft, tubes of various sizes carrying water, waste, and other things lining the sides and top. Pushing her pack before her, she wriggled in the direction Kayl had indicated, hearing Kayl drop down behind her, the light being cut off as he lowered the panel back into place and a lock clicked.

Genji stopped moving, waiting for her eyes to adjust, but there was too little light for even her to be able to see. Moving with difficulty in the confined space, she got her arm under her to pull out the minilight that was part of the overalls, clicking it on and moving again.

Kayl was right behind her. Even if his attitude didn't convey urgency, she still would have kept moving as fast as possible.

"Right," he said in a very low voice.

Genji wriggled her way around that junction, thinking that this must be even harder for Kayl.

Move, move, move . . .

"Left."

Move, move, move. How many meters had they traveled? At least a hundred, she thought. Probably more.

"There should be a panel above you soon."

Genji used her light to search above her. "Yeah. Right there."

"You should be able to open it from this side."

She manipulated the lock, moving carefully. The panel sprang up, revealing a darkened room above.

Genji turned off her light and came up as quietly as possible, listening for any sign of danger. Light was leaking in around a closed door, giving her enough to see by. This was another maintenance locker, bigger than the earlier one they'd used.

Kayl had dragged himself to the panel. She reached down to help him up.

He sat for a moment, breathing hard. "That wasn't any fun. We're still too close, but we should be past any surveillance of the street our apartment was on. They probably think we're still unaware of anything being off."

"They won't hear anything from the apartment," Genji said. "That'll tip them off."

Kayl grinned. "I left behind an occupied noisemaker. Do you know what those are? They generate sounds as if a room is occupied. It's supposed to scare off criminals, but it comes in handy for us for other reasons. It should take them a while to realize we're gone, at least until they get a camera or a person inside and see there's no one home. How does it sound outside?"

Genji got close to the door, listening. "Sounds like normal foot traffic. This is another side street?"

"Yeah. Okay. Hazard work masks on both of us. I've got stuff that should confuse surveillance cameras, but we should use the masks, too. You got your gloves on? I know someplace we might be able to hide for a while."

"Someone you know?"

"An old friend. Hopefully one who'll listen to me. This is the top of my list for hopeful places to hide."

They walked out of the maintenance closet with the slow gait of workers at the end of a shift, striding down the side street, Genji trying to observe everything around them without obviously doing so.

A couple of thumps sounded, echoing from the direction where their former apartment lay. Genji and Kayl pretended to act like everyone else, turning to look that way, then moving on.

She saw him check the device that showed the views from their hidden minicams. He turned it to her so Genji could see the blank screen with a notation of "interference." "Get rid of it," Genji advised. "They might be able to track it through the minicam link."

"It's gone." Kayl yanked out the power supply to deactivate it, then tossed the device into the next waste disposal chute they passed.

She really wanted to run, to put as much distance as possible between them and whoever was hunting them. But that would be stupid. They needed to act in ways that wouldn't stand out.

Genji followed Kayl as he walked at a steady pace, wishing she'd been able to get detailed briefings on his escape plans. She trusted him, but she didn't like totally depending on him, not knowing where they were going.

She watched Kayl as they walked, thinking that she was doing this for him, not for herself. Any moment might be her last moment of having existed, so why struggle to survive? She was starting to think at times that it might be a relief when it happened, to no longer have that sword hanging over her.

But she treasured every moment right now. Every moment with Kayl. Every moment she had a chance to alter the fate of the Earth.

They'd gone quite a ways, altering their path several times, before they finally stopped before an apartment door with a large SHIFT WORKER—DO NOT DISTURB notice posted beside it.

Kayl leaned on the buzzer.

After a minute, the door slid open and a slightly disheveled young woman stuck her head out. "Are you stupid or just illiterate? Read the damn sign!"

Instead of answering, Kayl pulled off his mask.

She stared at him for a long moment. "Wait a minute." She ducked back and reappeared a few moments later. "Get inside. I've shut down all the listeners in here."

Genji followed Kayl inside.

"Hi, Jeyssi," he said as the door closed.

"That's all?" the woman asked, spreading her hands. "Hi? Do you know there's an arrest order out for you? For murder?"

"Yeah, I know that," Kayl said.

"Did you do it?"

"No. Jeyssi, we need a place to lie low for at least several hours. Can you give us that?"

"We?" Jeyssi looked over at Genji, who was shedding her own mask and head covering so her eyes and skin were visible. "Nice look," she said, in that cutting way only another woman could.

"It's not a look," Genji said, tired and not particularly liking this Jeyssi at the moment. "I was born with it."

"You were—?" Jeyssi physically recoiled a couple of steps, her wide eyes fixed on Genji. "You're— Oh my God, you're— Kayl, do you have any idea what that is?"

"I know *who* that is," Kayl said, his voice sharpening.

"Lieutenant Selene Genji," Genji said. "Pleased to meet you."

"You're not human!" Jeyssi said.

"Yes, she is!" Kayl said. "Okay, not full human. But most of her DNA is human."

"*Most* of her DNA? Is that supposed to be reassuring? Because it's not!"

"Jeyssi, Selene is not an enemy."

"Is Selene an alien?"

Kayl hesitated.

"Partly," Genji said.

Jeyssi stared at Genji as if startled by the admission. "You probably don't know this, Kayl, but there's a classified annex to that arrest order. It says you may be in the company of, and under the control of, an alien advance scout preparing the way for their invasion."

Genji wasn't able to stop herself from rolling her eyes. "I'm not a scout and there is no invasion."

"And I'm not under her control," Kayl insisted.

"Look," Jeyssi said, "you're my friend. I'll let you stay while we decide what to do. But not . . . that. It has to go."

"We're a package deal," Kayl said, his voice hardening. "*She* and I either stay together or go together."

"A package deal? What are you saying, Kayl? What exactly is your relationship with this alien spy?"

Kayl shook his head. "I can't believe you'd think that I'd sell out humanity for a pretty face."

"I don't think it's her face that she's using to manipulate you!"

Genji felt her hands clench in anger, but before she could move, Kayl spoke in a rough voice.

"Jeyssi, you can say anything you want about me. But Selene Genji is a veteran who has suffered and fought for *Earth* in ways you and I can't even imagine. Do not ever speak like that about her again." Kayl nodded to Genji. "Let's go, Selene. Jeyssi, for old time's sake, please don't tell anyone we were here." He started to move past Jeyssi, but she put a hand out.

"Wait." Jeyssi looked from Genji to Kayl. "Kayl, unless you've changed a whole lot, none of this makes sense to me. Which means maybe I don't know enough. Including about . . ." She looked at Genji again. "Her. Are you saying she's an Earth Guard officer?"

"No," Genji said, barely controlling her impulse to punch out Jeyssi. "I'm not. But I am trying to protect the Earth, and everyone who lives on it."

Jeyssi rubbed her forehead, looking uncertain. "Look, the orders say I'm not supposed to talk to . . . the alien. But I think it's my duty to figure out what's going on here. I need to know what's really happening. Am I safe, Kayl? With her in here?"

"Yes, you're safe," Kayl said. "My word of honor."

"Mine, too," Genji said. "If that matters to you."

Jeyssi gazed at her fixedly for a long moment. "Kayl, I honestly think you would never lie to me. But I need a few minutes to get my head straight before we talk about this. Sit down. I'm going to go in the bedroom and center my head, okay? I promise not to call anyone or alert anyone or sound any alarms."

Kayl nodded to her. "Sure thing. I trust you."

"You are still such an idiot, Kayl Owen." Jeyssi walked into the bedroom, leaving them alone in the living area.

Genji finished pulling off the maintenance coverall and sat

down on the couch, cooling her temper. It was entirely possible that Jeyssi was actually leaving them alone in the hope they'd reveal something incriminating while speaking to each other. But Kayl was willing to trust that she wasn't calling authorities, so Genji sat and waited. After a moment, Kayl joined her.

"I'm really sorry for what Jeyssi said about you," he said. "She's not really a bad person."

"I've had worse things said to my face," Genji said. "Is she an old girlfriend?"

"Umm . . . no."

"You asked her out and she turned you down."

"Yeah," Kayl said. "The old 'I like you as a friend' bit."

"At least she was honest with you." Genji looked down at her hands. "I should be, too."

"How have you not been honest with me?"

"I have been manipulating you, in a way," Genji said. "Entangling myself in your emotions."

"Entangling yourself?"

"It's a common expression in the 2170s!" She grimaced, trying to find words. "I tried to say this before. When . . . I cease to exist . . . there'll be nothing remaining of me. But you'll be left. Left with all the memories, all the regrets, all the might-have-beens. For all the rest of your life. I had no right to do that to you. I needed you, so I used you. I hope someday you can find it in your heart to forgive me."

He didn't answer for a long moment. "Are you serious?"

"Of course I'm serious."

"Selene, I'd trade one day with you for everything. You do really care about me, don't you?"

"I used you."

"You're not answering the question. You told me if I'd been anyone else nothing would have happened."

She looked him in the eyes. "And I meant it. Kayl, you're not any port in a storm for me. You're my safe harbor. I couldn't have made it this far alone. I couldn't keep going alone. Knowing every instant might be my last. Yes, you big idiot, I do care about you."

He smiled. "That's all I need to know, then."

Genji felt tears starting and blinked them away. Why did hearing him say that matter so much? "Does every woman who knows you end up calling you an idiot?"

"I can't think of any who haven't," Kayl admitted. "We're not beaten yet."

"No. We're not. But regardless of what happens to me, keep trying. Billions of human lives depend on it. You have to keep trying to change what will be."

"I'll never stop trying," he promised.

Looking past him, Genji noticed Jeyssi standing awkwardly in the bedroom doorway. *Oh, great. That witch has been listening while I spilled my emotional guts. I wonder how much she heard?*

Enough apparently that Jeyssi averted her gaze as she walked to the chair and sat down facing them. "Uh, so, I am ready to listen. No promises, but I will listen. Because I believe it is my duty to learn everything I can about . . . your companion, Kayl." She looked at Genji. "We weren't actually introduced. I'm Lieutenant Jeyssi Arronax, Earth Guard. Kayl and I served together as ensigns. Who exactly are you?"

"Lieutenant Selene Genji." How much should she tell this person? There wasn't any way to be sure. But her gut told her that this time she needed to be totally open. "Unified Fleet."

"Unified Fleet? That's an alien force?"

"The Unified Fleet will be a human force, formed in 2171 from the remnants of Earth Guard and various independent forces created by powers on Earth in response to the slow collapse and eventual dissolution of Earth Guard in the late 2150s and through the 2160s," Genji said. She saw Kayl giving her a surprised look that he quickly smoothed over without any warning glance or gesture to her. Knowing that he'd accepted her judgment on this, and agreed that Jeyssi should be told, Genji decided to provide more detail. "The primary task of the Unified Fleet will be to counter and defend against forces of the Spear of Humanity backed by other powers on Earth and throughout the solar system. They will not have to defend against any aliens because the Tramontine will pose no threat."

Jeyssi stared at her silently for almost a minute before blinking and looking at Kayl. "Twenty-one seventy-one? She's from the future?"

Kayl nodded. "From 2180."

"How can you know that's true?"

"She's accurately predicted exact actions by the aliens and when those actions would occur," Kayl explained. "Selene convinced Rear Admiral Tecumseh she was the real deal."

"She convinced Tecumseh? That's why Admiral Tecumseh has been pushing back on our assessments of the intentions of the aliens?"

"That's why," Kayl said.

"Holy crap." Jeyssi focused back on Selene. "So, you're actually one of those time travelers sent back to . . . fix something?"

"I wasn't sent back," Genji said, deciding to let Jeyssi know what was at stake. "It seems to have been an accidental by-product of the weapon the Spear of Humanity will use to destroy Earth on the twelfth of June 2180."

Jeyssi's mouth fell open as she stared at Genji. "Earth is going to be destroyed?"

"Unless I can change things," Genji said.

"That's the mission she's given herself," Kayl said. "That I've signed on to as well. To try to change what happened in her history so that our future doesn't come out that way."

"Okay," Jeyssi said. "I can see why you'd be on board with that. Why did this Spear want to destroy Earth?"

"To cleanse it of alien contamination," Genji said. "Including alloys like me."

"You really are part alien? So humans and these aliens can—"

"No," Genji said. "I'm the product of genetic engineering, not natural reproduction."

"How can you say that so calmly?"

"It's what I am."

Jeyssi looked at her silently for another few seconds. "I'm starting to understand what Kayl sees in you. You saw Earth being destroyed?"

"My ship was in near lunar orbit when it happened."

"How . . . how long did it take?" Jeyssi asked, looking like someone afraid of the answer but unable to avoid asking.

"Seconds."

"*Seconds?* What kind of weapon could destroy an entire planet in seconds?"

Genji shook her head. "I wouldn't tell Admiral Tecumseh that, and I won't tell you. I can't risk what I say somehow guiding research in that direction. No one in this time can know what the weapon was like. I have told one person since arriving in 2140, and only that one person. Because if I die or cease to exist before my mission is done, he will need to carry on and somehow prevent Earth's fate from happening. That's an awful burden to pass down, but I had to." Kayl had never called her on that, never brought up that she had shared that burden with him when she hardly knew him. *But he knows that I chose even then to use him for my own purposes. I hate myself for having done that.*

Jeyssi looked from her to Kayl and back again. "Oh. No wonder— Cease to exist?"

"She's changing the future," Kayl said. "She's from that future."

"Jeez." Jeyssi took a long breath, looking down before raising her gaze to them again. "I heard you say you cared about her. But you're helping her do something that'll make her cease ever having existed."

"To save the Earth," Genji said.

Jeyssi stared at her. "You're either crazy or a far better and braver woman than I'll ever be."

"I'm just desperate. I have to save the Earth. If you'd seen it . . ."

"There have been a lot of movies," Jeyssi said. "But those are all fake. Everyone knows that. Mass-disaster porn. The real thing . . . how do you sleep?"

"I don't know," Genji said.

Jeyssi paused again, looking at her. "I'm talking to you. I'm sitting here talking to an alien."

"Part alien," Kayl said.

"I mean, that's prohibited. The orders say, don't give her a chance."

Kayl shook his head. "Why do you think they don't want you to give her a chance to talk?"

"You were always good with questions, Kayl," Jeyssi said. "Maybe that's why senior officers don't like you." She sighed. "I believe this. I can't believe I believe it, but I do. That's partly because of other things that made me willing to listen to you. Like the 'accident' that supposedly killed you, Kayl. A couple of weeks ago a report came out from the safety lab reporting that your courier ship was totally infected with malware, that it wasn't an accident but deliberate sabotage. Likely *internal* sabotage from within Earth Guard. You can imagine how that news landed. Except two hours later another message from Earth Guard headquarters canceled the safety lab message and ordered all copies destroyed."

Genji grasped Kayl's hand. "Admiral Tecumseh thought he'd been targeted as a scapegoat so no one would look too closely into the loss of the ship."

"And Tecumseh was right!" Jeyssi said, pointing at Genji. "In the weeks after that so-called accident, I heard a lot of 'what do you expect from an Owen?' talk. I stood up for you, Kayl! I told everyone you'd been a competent, capable officer, and this didn't smell right. For that I got labeled a discarded girlfriend who was still mooning over you. Oh, hey! And that ties into the wreckage thing."

"The wreckage we encountered on the *Vigilant*?" Kayl said. "You read that report?"

"Nope. Guess why? After the courier ship was destroyed and you were declared missing and probably dead, a friend of mine on another watch shift told me about the report he'd read from *Vigilant* about that wreckage. But when he tried to pull it up to show me, it was gone from the system, along with everything that might've referenced that report."

Kayl shook his head, looking grim. "I wonder just how much information is disappearing from Earth Guard systems."

"A lot more than anyone realized, I think," Jeyssi said. "Survivor." She pointed at Genji again. "My friend said he thought the wreckage report had referenced a survivor, but when he brought that up to the shift commander he got his ears pinned back. You're the survivor, aren't you?"

"That's right," Genji said.

"So, Kayl has gone from dead to wanted for murder, and you've gone from doesn't exist to alien advance scout."

"Why is the alien invasion narrative still being pushed?" Kayl asked. "Selene has spoken directly with the negotiators talking to the Tramontine. She's told them the aliens are here for exploration and out of curiosity. Their ship doesn't have any offensive weapons."

Jeyssi shook her head. "I haven't heard a word of that. News reports, yes, but nothing like that is coming through Earth Guard intelligence channels."

"She told the negotiators exactly when the First Contact message would arrive and exactly what would be in it!"

"Nope. We haven't seen any of that. Has anyone else been told?"

"Captain Yesenski."

"There's no way Yesenski wouldn't have submitted reports of that," Jeyssi said. "But we're not seeing it. It's all 'alien intentions remain unconfirmed but presumed hostile,' based partly on how long it took them to talk to us."

"I told the negotiators and Captain Yesenski exactly why the Tramontine took so long to communicate," Genji said.

Jeyssi slapped the end table near her. "This stuff isn't just not getting to us. It's being deliberately suppressed. That's not only unprofessional, it's criminal. Why are people doing that?"

"What was your reaction when you learned I was part alien?" Genji said.

"Fair point," Jeyssi admitted. "But I did listen. I was willing to hear you out."

"Because you knew and trusted Kayl?"

"Yes," Jeyssi said. "Honestly, if not for that, I wouldn't have listened to you."

"Some people won't listen," Genji said. "Never. Their minds are closed."

Jeyssi made a face. "I managed to talk to Sabita Awerdin, Kayl. You know *Vigilant* is among the Earth Guard ships here at Mars, right? Sabita still thinks you're dead, by the way. Were you two dating?"

"No," Kayl said quickly. "We never dated."

"Did she ever ask you out?"

"No," Kayl said, glancing at Genji and shaking his head to emphasize his reply.

"Well, she was pretty torn up about you being dead."

"I wasn't too happy to hear about it myself," Kayl said.

"Oh, yeah, you're still Kayl Owen," Jeyssi said. "Sabita said Earth Guard had just about beaten you, though."

"It had," Kayl said. "I found something to fight for again."

Genji made a frustrated noise. "I am not your hill."

"Our mission, I mean," Kayl said.

"Right," Jeyssi said. "Anyway, you had a ship's doctor? Davis?"

"Darius."

"Yeah. Sabita said he went totally off the rails, freaking out about alien contamination of the ship and ordering quarantines of compartments and isolation of half the crew and demanding sterilization of the entire ship and all that. When the commanding officer relieved him of duty, the doc got a message out through medical channels accusing the captain and the executive officer of colluding with the aliens."

Genji looked at Kayl, who seemed uncertain whether or not to laugh. "It may sound funny to you, but that kind of thing is going to get worse. People are going to start dying if it isn't countered. And to me, there's nothing funny about my presence being considered a horrible contamination."

He had the sense to look ashamed. "I'm sorry."

Jeyssi was watching her. "I hadn't thought about that, how the 'alien monster' would feel about being seen that way. We've done that so many times to other humans, and now we're transferring it to another species."

"Not everyone," Genji emphasized. "The Unified Fleet, all of the people and countries supporting it, will be . . . all right, not always perfect, but willing to die to protect someone like me. Maybe a lot of them wouldn't have wanted their sons to bring me home, but they didn't want me and people like me or the Tramontine to be treated that way. Everything to come is because of humans like that ship's doctor, but also because a lot of humans will push back against people like him and will not be willing to see that kind of thing done to another species, to those who are different. People like you."

"The one who called you a thing?" Jeyssi said.

"The one who decided to listen and learn who I really was."

After a long moment of quiet, Kayl spoke up again. "What happened to Darius?"

"He's on the *Yamanaka* being shipped back to Earth along with some other nonessential personnel. So is Captain Garos."

"Garos got relieved of command?" Kayl said.

"Yup. About a week ago. On the grounds he'd lost control of his ship. I'm sure being tied to that 'accident' with the courier ship didn't help him. Really, he embarrassed the brass so he became the fall guy."

Kayl shook his head. "Can I enjoy this one a little, Selene? Garos was a total jerk, and unsuited for command, but he had punched all the right tickets and knew all the right people. After command of the *Vigilant*, he was going to punch another high-profile ticket and then probably be lined up for promotion to rear admiral. In another few years he would have been calling a lot of shots in Earth Guard. But now his career is over in disgrace."

His eyes widened and he stared at her. "Selene, Garos is exactly the kind of person who must have helped along the slow collapse of Earth Guard. And if your wreckage and you hadn't shown up, he would have. But now he won't."

"Looks like you already changed something else," Jeyssi said. "How much do you need to change?"

"I don't know," Genji said. "There's no way to know. I have to keep doing all I can to fix mistakes and try to forestall things that had bad results, and hope they're enough by the time I . . . am dead or gone."

"You never get to say to yourself 'I won,'" Jeyssi said. "You signed on to this with her, Kayl? Knowing all that?"

"I did," Kayl said.

"Man, I hope I find a guy like you someday."

"You did," Kayl said.

"And I wouldn't go out with him," Jeyssi said. "Nice job rubbing that in. And really, Kayl, I like you as a friend, but there's still no chemistry. I mean, you're sitting there, and I have zero desire to kiss you."

"That's very fortunate for you," Genji said.

Something in her voice made Jeyssi and Kayl stare at her.

"You're the type who wouldn't react well to another woman trying to move in on your man, aren't you, Lieutenant Genji?" Jeyssi said.

"You have no idea, Lieutenant Arronax. My primary specialty is close combat, by the way."

"Right. Did I mention there's no chemistry between Kayl and me? None." Jeyssi frowned as her phone sounded an alert. "That's strange. I'm being asked to report in to the Earth Guard command center two hours early."

"How often has that happened?" Kayl asked.

"Never."

Genji inhaled slowly. "It's us. Something has started moving."

Kayl gave her a worried glance. "Jeyssi, has there been anything else unusual going on the last couple of days?"

"You mean besides all the First Contact stuff with the aliens?" Jeyssi said. "Yes. Unusual maneuvers by the Planetary Defense Forces, and call-ups of all their soldiers. The Martian PDF is mostly part-timers with a professional core. People in the Earth Guard command center were saying the MPDF has never activated their entire force at once before this. Supposedly it's to maintain order if there's panic over the aliens arriving, but there haven't been any reports of impending panic despite the best efforts of some people to whip up fear of the alien invasion."

She looked at her phone as another alert came in. "What the hell? Reports have been confirmed that MPDF soldiers are being posted at critical locations throughout the colony. Supposedly that's to protect them from sabotage by the—" Jeyssi grimaced. "By the alien scout who has been reliably reported to be operating within the colony. There's a description of . . . of 'it.'" Jeyssi glanced at Genji. "No one reading this is going to recognize you, except for the skin thing. You're also . . . oh, for pity's sake. You're a particular danger to young males, who might be distracted by your appearance."

Genji looked down, feeling depressed. "People have been warning about the danger I am to young male full humans ever since I was little."

"Not funny, huh?" Jeyssi murmured.

"No."

Another alert. "Soldiers have shown up near the negotiator offices. Do you know the layout? We've got the Earth Guard command center and intelligence center adjacent to each other, then a couple of hundred meters away is an office complex that was repurposed for the negotiators with the aliens. I'm being called in *now*, guys. Stay here. You should be safe in here until—" She broke off speaking, staring at her phone.

CHAPTER 9

"JEYSSI?" OWEN ASKED. EVERYTHING ABOUT THIS SITUATION WAS FEELING BAD. Selene was sitting next to him, suddenly seeming very calm, as if ready to leap into action. But what action should they carry out?

"No way," Jeyssi said. "The Planetary Defense Forces have taken control of the negotiators' offices and placed all of the negotiators under arrest. They're supposedly in protective custody, but it's arrest. The MPDF commander is declaring martial law and claiming that all Earth Guard assets on the surface should report to him."

"What are your orders?" Owen asked.

"Get to the command center by any means possible, and do not respond to any orders from within the MPDF command structure," Jeyssi said.

Owen looked at Selene, who was listening with apparent disbelief. "Selene, why didn't you warn us this was going to happen?"

Selene shook her head. "Because it didn't. This did not happen during the First Contact negotiations."

"Maybe they sanitized history," Owen suggested.

"No! This did not happen! There's no way I wouldn't have known if martial law was declared on Mars within days of the Tramontine arrival!"

Jeyssi ran one hand through her hair. "Well, girl, you wanted to change history. Congratulations."

"Is this a good thing?" Owen asked Selene.

"How do I know?" Selene said. "No. I know this. I know that martial law is not good, especially when it's motivated by anti-alien hysteria. Somehow me being in 2140 has triggered this sort of thing far earlier than happened in the history I know."

"What do we do?" Owen asked her.

"We have to shut it down. We have to counter this attempt to impose martial law."

"You and me?" Owen asked.

Selene met his eyes. "You and me. What's the status of the negotiators, Lieutenant Arronax?"

"Umm . . . like I said, they're being 'protected' by MPDF soldiers."

"Can you get through to Captain Yesenski?" Owen asked her.

"I can try."

As Jeyssi worked her phone, Owen turned to Selene. "Should we let Yesenski in on the truth about you?"

"No," Selene said. "Not while all of this is happening. Not unless we absolutely have to. We keep the focus on First Contact."

"Jeyssi! Please do not tell anyone else about Selene having come from 2180!" He turned back to Selene. "What can we do to counter the martial law?"

"Find out enough to answer that question." Selene had called up news reports on her phone. "The press hasn't been shut down. They're bypassing military attempts to cut off their access to planetary nets. Here's a live view of the Commons."

Owen looked, seeing a large open space, in the center of which stood an elevated platform that could be used by anyone speaking to the people of the colony. "Yeah. It looks like the soldiers are trying to seal off access to it."

His own phone chirped to reveal an official statement. "All

citizens are to remain in their homes," Owen read. "Access to public areas is temporarily suspended. So much for that idea."

"We can still do it," Selene said, pointing at the images. "Only two soldiers are blocking each entrance to the Commons."

"Do it? Do what?" Owen asked.

"I've got Captain Yesenski," Jeyssi said. "Yes, sir. Sir, Owen and Genji are with me. Both of them. I did not report their presence in my apartment. I hereby surrender myself for arrest for— Yes, sir. I'll shut up, sir. Lieutenant Genji was asking about the status of the negotiators." Jeyssi looked at Selene. "He confirms the negotiators are effectively all under arrest. Captain Yesenski wants to get them out, into the command center, but there are too many soldiers blocking access. He wants you both to get to the command center as fast as possible."

"We have to get the negotiators freed," Selene said.

"Captain Yesenski says there are just too many soldiers."

Owen saw Selene breathing slowly in a way he recognized. She was getting ready to do something. "Selene? What are you planning?"

"Lieutenant Arronax," Selene suddenly said, "ask Captain Yesenski if he can get to the negotiators if a substantial number of soldiers are drawn off by a diversion."

Jeyssi stared at her but relayed the message. "He says if enough can be drawn off he can do it. No one will expect Earth Guard's people to sortie out and bring the negotiators in. But he wants to know what kind of diversion I'm talking about."

"Me," Selene said. "Tell him Lieutenant Selene Genji will provide the diversion."

Owen, momentarily shocked into silence, hastily spoke up. "And Lieutenant Kayl Owen. I'll be with her."

"Yes, sir," Jeyssi said, her eyes fixed on Selene and Owen. "Genji and Owen. They say they'll provide the diversion. Captain Yesenski says no. He is ordering both of you to fall back with me to the command center. There are shoot-to-kill orders out for you. He thought you were both dead. There were . . . holy crap . . . there were reports of a special forces kill team sent to the apartment you were in."

Selene shook her head. "Tell the captain we're unable to comply. We will provide that diversion. I can't let the negotiations be short-circuited this way. It would be disastrous. Tell Captain Yesenski to be ready to move when enough soldiers are drawn off."

"Captain Yesenski repeats that you are not to do that, you are to accompany me to the command center, and if you do not he will throw your asses in the brig."

Selene smiled. "He can do that once we reach the command center after we cause the diversion and the negotiators are safe."

"Captain, I'm telling them. They're not listening. I don't know." Jeyssi looked at them again. "Just what is this diversion you're planning?"

"A public appearance," Selene said. "Kayl, can you get our uniforms out?"

"Yeah." Owen went to their packs and pulled out the uniform coveralls they'd last worn in the desert outside Albuquerque. "Are you sure, Selene?"

"I'm doing this right," she said, pulling on the uniform.

Owen was surprised that despite the tension, he could feel himself smiling as he looked at her. "It's been a while since I've seen you in that."

Selene grinned at him as she sealed the last fitting. "The gold trim sets off my skin real well, doesn't it? Alloys in the Unified Fleet used to joke about that." Her smile faded into determination. "I'm the last of them. I'm doing this for them. I caused this, Kayl. I'm going to fix it."

"We're going to fix it," Owen said.

Selene nodded to Jeyssi. "We'll see you in the command center,

Lieutenant Arronax. Tell Captain Yesenski that we're moving out and he'd better be ready to liberate the negotiators."

"Why don't you tell him? Can you hear him shouting at you?"

Selene shook her head. "My hearing isn't very good. Let's go, Kayl."

"Kayl!" Jeyssi said. "Take this spare phone! I'll call! Where are you going?"

"The Commons," Selene said.

As they left the apartment, Owen glanced at Selene. "Your hearing isn't very good? Since when?"

"It's a sudden problem," Selene said. "It'll probably clear up in another minute or so."

"You're nuts, Lieutenant Genji. You know that, right?"

"Who's walking beside me, Lieutenant Owen?"

"Another nut," Owen said.

Jeyssi's apartment was just off one of the main roads into the center of the colony. Like it, the other "streets" and sidewalks of the colony were full of scattered groups, speaking anxiously to each other, defying the orders to stay in their living spaces. "It's to the right from here, isn't it, Lieutenant Owen?" Selene asked him.

"The Commons are to the right, Lieutenant Genji."

"Good. Let's show them how Unified Fleet and the right people in Earth Guard do things." She started walking, him keeping step with her. They immediately drew attention, at first for the uniforms, Selene's in particular evoking puzzled comments, but then eyes went to her face.

"People of Mars, we're going to the Commons!" Selene called out. "Who's with me?"

People started following. More and more. Glancing back, Owen saw the street behind them filling, those people ahead watching and gawking as Selene and he walked steadily toward them, then joining the crowd following as they passed.

Owen heard the anxious conversations behind him, excited sentences spilling over each other.

"Who is she?"

"What is she?"

"She's got Earth Guard escorting her."

"They're heading for the Commons."

"She wants us there, too!"

"Yeah, to the Commons!"

A squad of police, standing around uncertainly, pulled aside the barricades they were guarding and joined the march.

"People of Mars, we're going to the Commons! Who's with me?"

The roar from behind them that answered Selene's call this time nearly unnerved Owen. He hoped Selene knew what she was doing. Because what was gathering behind them could do a lot of damage if it ran amok.

A woman ran up beside them, holding up a press broadcaster. "Why are you here?"

"To fight for you," Selene called. "To protect the Earth."

"But aren't you an alien?"

"I was born on Earth."

One of the gates into the Commons had come into view, the two soldiers guarding it staring at Selene and Owen and the crowd behind them. Owen saw one of the soldiers speaking frantically into a comm device. The other waved her rifle, calling commands to "disperse" that were lost in the rumble of the crowd.

They were about two meters from the soldiers when both started to level their weapons at Selene in response to some order they must have received.

Owen went for the soldier nearest him, gaining an impression of Selene almost blurring as she went straight at the soldier facing her. He heard two rapid blows as he struggled with the other soldier for his gun, then Selene's hand came over to also grab the weapon before her free hand hit that soldier and dropped him. Owen found himself holding the rifle, the two soldiers sprawled unconscious.

Selene turned to call to the suddenly hushed crowd. "They're okay. I am not here to harm anyone! Come on! To the Commons! They can't keep us out of the Commons!"

"To the Commons!" the crowd roared.

Owen decided to keep the rifle, cradling it as he walked beside Selene. She kept moving at a steady pace, the crowd pouring into the Commons, ahead of her and out to either side, but a clear path was kept free for her as Selene marched toward the platform in the center. Looking about, Owen saw the soldiers at the other entrances to the Commons being swamped by civilians as they called for help. "Selene, you do know what you're doing, right?"

She smiled. "Making it up as I go along, Kayl."

"I was really hoping you'd have a different answer."

Selene looked at him. "If these are my last instants, I will live them trying to fix things, not cowering in a hole."

He nodded to her. "I'll be right there with you."

"Your job is not to die. You need to make sure this gets done after I'm gone."

Owen took a moment to reply. "You know, my fitness reports have often noted my special need for extra supervision. If you want to be sure I do the job right, you really ought to be here to keep an eye on me."

"That is one of the most desperate excuses I have ever heard, Lieutenant Owen." Selene smiled at him for a moment. "I'll keep it in mind."

She started up the platform, walking up the two lower levels toward the third, highest one.

A hush fell over the crowd, thousands of eyes staring at them. The cameras and microphones focused on the platform were active, as they always were for anyone who wanted to speak, showing them both. Owen fingered the rifle, looking about him, wondering how long it would be before a lot more soldiers got here.

Selene gave him another look, letting her anxiousness show. He nodded to her again. "You got this."

"I got this," she said.

Raising her gaze, she stepped onto the speaking platform, looking about her. "I am Lieutenant Selene Genji," she said, her voice echoing from the loudspeakers, being repeated on channels all over the colony. "I am here to defend you. I am here to defend Earth, which is the most beautiful and precious planet in the universe.

"Some of you may have heard of an 'alien monster' here to threaten you, here to invade." Selene spread her arms. "I am that monster. I am not your enemy." She rolled up a sleeve so the skin of her arm shone in the lights of the Common. "I do have alien DNA as part of my genetic code. You can see that. I am not full human."

Baffled murmurs filled the crowd.

"But while my genetic code contains some alien DNA," Selene shouted, "my spirit is one hundred percent human! My heart is human! My home is Earth! It is you, my fellow humans, that I will defend to my dying breath!"

A wild roar followed her words, Owen feeling as if the noise was physically battering him. He saw soldiers appearing at two of the entrances, their numbers growing rapidly.

"Kayl!" his phone sounded. It was Jeyssi. "Captain Yesenski says you've drawn off enough soldiers. We're going in to free the negotiators. He wants you two to get out of there. Run!"

Owen looked at Selene.

"Not yet, Jeyssi."

"You are free people with the right to decide your own fates! Every person has that right! Yet you are being told you must surrender your rights because there are monsters you must be protected from! Monsters like me!" Selene pressed her hands against her chest. "My mother told me the only monsters in this universe are those inside us, and it is our responsibility to those we love to keep those monsters from harming anyone. The aliens are not your enemies, any more than the living creatures of any world are your enemies. They want to be friends, they come in peace. Anyone who tells you otherwise is lying."

The soldiers at the two entrances, their numbers swelling, charged into the Commons, forcing their way toward the central platform.

"Selene," Owen called urgently. He stepped closer to her, putting himself between Selene and the nearest soldiers.

"Who is carrying weapons?" Selene demanded, ignoring him. "Who is threatening you? Who wants to tell you what you must do? It is not the aliens. It is not me. Don't let anyone tell you that you have to be afraid. I am on your side! I am here to protect the Earth and every one of you!"

The roar this time shook the Commons. The crowd was compressing to block the charging masses of soldiers, some of the listeners climbing onto the lower levels of the platform to link arms in a defensive wall.

Kayl heard the low thunder of energy weapons. "Selene, please get down! They're shooting!"

Instead of jumping down immediately, she raised one arm high, fist clenched. Only then did she yield to Kayl's tugging.

"Are you out of your mind?" he called to her as he tried to force a path away from the oncoming soldiers.

She grinned at him, clearly riding an adrenaline high. "I've been shot at before. It's no big deal."

"I haven't," Owen said.

"Sure you have. Missiles over Albuquerque. I was there, too, remember? Kayl, if I'm going to go in the next instant, I will make this instant a good one."

"Yeah, well, I want you around for a few more instants, okay?"

"Kayl, where the hell are you?" Jeyssi demanded from the phone.

"Making our way toward, uh, Exit D from the Commons. That's Exit Delta."

"We've got the negotiators. The MPDF stripped just about every soldier to send to the Commons. They want you guys dead."

"Nothing new there," Owen said, surprised he could hear that without feeling a jolt of fear. A lot had happened since he and Selene had been targeted near Albuquerque.

The people in the crowd had realized the two of them were trying to leave and were helping him and Selene toward the exit while the soldiers still strove to reach the platform. "We're almost to the exit."

"Everybody's forting up in the command center and intelligence spaces. Go left out of the exit. Can you see the map guidance I'm sending you?"

"Uh . . . yeah."

"Follow it. Once the soldiers realize you're out of the Commons they can try to cut you off from getting here. Kayl, Captain Yesenski wants me to emphasize that they have shoot-to-kill orders on you and Lieutenant Genji. Just in case you weren't listening to him the first three times he told you that."

"I understand. Oh, hell." There was a clear route to the exit, only three meters away, but several soldiers had suddenly appeared at the exit, looking about in confusion.

He heard a yell and realized that Selene was sprinting into the center of the soldiers, shouting. He ran after her, still carrying the rifle.

It was his first chance to really see what "close combat specialist" meant when it came to Selene Genji. These soldiers weren't professionals. They were clearly among the part-timers, and clearly not ready to deal with a veteran of vicious combat. He couldn't see many details, just bodies dropping and weapons flying through the air.

With the soldiers concentrating on Selene, Owen was able to

charge in unnoticed. He reached the unit as one soldier was trying to find a clean shot at Selene. He swung the rifle like a bat, slamming into the back of the soldier's head and losing his own grip on the weapon. A second soldier was lining her rifle up on Owen, who was realizing he didn't have a lot of chances this time, when suddenly Selene was pressing a pistol barrel against the soldier's head. "Drop it."

The soldier let go of her weapon.

The other soldiers were down, surrounded by jubilant citizens.

"There are more coming! Go!" someone called to Owen and Selene.

She tossed the pistol to a nearby citizen and ran, Owen racing to keep up. "You didn't kill any of them?" he called.

"Not a one," Selene called back. "Nice work back there for an Earth Guard antique."

"I did receive a little training. But I don't want to ever fight you. We need to turn left up here."

This street felt dangerously empty, only a few individuals peering out of doors and windows as they ran down it.

Right. Left. Right.

A half-dozen individuals in light-blue-and-silver uniforms appeared at the entry to a side passage. "Lieutenant Owen? This way!"

Owen and Selene veered to follow, the combined group racing past three improvised barricades and a security post all occupied by grim-faced Earth Guard personnel before coming to a gasping halt in what Owen recognized from briefings as the Mars Planetary Command Center.

A familiar figure came walking up to them. "Lieutenant Genji. Lieutenant Owen."

They both straightened to attention, saluting. "Captain Yesenski," Owen said.

Yesenski looked them over, his gaze lingering on Selene's Unified Fleet uniform. "I'm going to recommend both of you for medals, and then I'm going to recommend both of you be court-martialed, and then I'm going to recommend you both be promoted. Are you okay?"

"No serious injuries," Selene said. She held up her left hand, showing a vicious burn on the back from a near miss from an energy bolt. "I could use a little help with this."

"Medic!" Yesenski called before gazing intently at her. "Lieutenant Genji, what uniform is that?"

"The uniform of a fleet that may never exist, sir."

"Is that supposed to make sense?"

"Yes, sir."

"Has this fleet got any more like you in it? Because if so, I want some of them."

A commander had run up along with the medic, who had begun treating Selene's hand. "Captain, that . . . umm . . . that . . . is an alien."

"Really?" Yesenski pretended to study Selene closely. "All I'm seeing is a damned fine officer. One we're lucky to have with us. Without her, the negotiators would still be confined by a bunch of amateur soldiers with twitchy fingers on their triggers."

"Captain, we have very clear orders concerning this . . . this . . . And Lieutenant Owen has an arrest warrant out for him!"

"Operational necessity," Yesenski said. "That overrides a warrant that is only for questioning."

"Captain, we can't—"

"Don't you have something important you should be doing?" Yesenski interrupted the commander. "Get going." As the commander walked off quickly, Captain Yesenski pointed to Owen. "Stay with Lieutenant Genji. I don't care what other orders you have. The operational necessity of you safeguarding Genji is why no one is going to act on the arrest warrant, Owen. Lieutenant Genji, as of this moment you are officially in the custody of Lieutenant Owen. Is that clear?"

"Yes, Captain," Selene said, breathing deeply as the medic finished applying rapid heal to her hand.

"If I see an alien monster, I have orders to confine, quarantine, and if necessary kill that alien monster. I don't see any alien monsters around. Other Earth Guard officers may not have as clear a vision of things as I do, though. You're not entirely safe here even though you've officially been taken into custody." Yesenski gestured to one side. "You're probably safest among the negotiators. Over that way."

"All done, uh, Lieutenant," the medic said. "I gave you a mild sedative to help you cope as the rapid heal works."

Selene had been sitting while her hand was worked on. "A mild sedative? That might . . . Okay, thanks." She stood up carefully. "Kayl, that sedative may hit me differently. I'm . . ." Selene staggered, looking like someone who was at least slightly drunk and trying to maintain their balance.

Owen stepped up, supporting her, draping one of Selene's arms over his shoulders. "Let's get you over there where you can lie down."

"Okay." Selene took wobbly steps, Owen trying to keep her from falling. "You're helping me make the next step," she told him, laughing. "Just like Aunt Hoku— Hokulani said."

"Selene, what's the matter?" Owen asked.

"Sedative. I'm an alloy!"

Owen caught Selene as she nearly staggered off to the right. "Are you drunk?"

"Feels like it!" Selene laughed again.

"What happened?" Yesenski said, staring.

"Her metabolism is different," Owen said. "The sedative the medic gave her has made her, uh . . ."

"Happy," Selene said, smiling broadly. "Like reaaalliy drunk." She looked over at him. "Hi, handsome."

"Hi. Look, here's a couch. Can you lie down here?"

"Sure." Selene flopped down, laughing again. "Lie down here with me," she told Owen.

"I don't think I should do that," Owen said.

"Come here, then. I need to whisper something to you."

Concerned, Owen leaned close to her face.

Selene raised up suddenly, her lips meeting his, holding the kiss until finally she broke it. "I wanted to do that," she said, still smiling.

Owen was abruptly aware that everyone within eyeshot was either staring or pretending not to stare at him and Selene.

They'd just seen an alien kiss him. A "monster."

It felt strange to wonder what they might be thinking.

But he realized he really didn't care what they were thinking.

He leaned down, kissing her back for a moment. "I'm glad that you did."

"Knock off the public displays of affection, Lieutenant Owen," Captain Yesenski said. "You're in uniform."

Owen straightened up. "Yes, sir."

Yesenski shook his head. "If you'd asked me a month ago what I'd do if I saw something like that, I honestly don't know what I would've answered. Keep a close eye on her until she's, uh, sober, Lieutenant Owen."

"Yes, sir."

He sat down on the narrow part of the couch that was still free, looking anxiously at Selene. Owen wasn't sure how much time passed. People were leaving them alone, hopefully out of respect rather than fear of contamination. Or maybe in keeping with Yesenski's orders that Selene was in custody and Kayl was carrying out an urgent task.

Selene's eyes had closed, her head had fallen back, and her mouth was hanging open. She had started snoring softly.

"Your alien girl looks pretty human right now," a familiar voice said.

Owen looked up. "Hi, Jeyssi. Thanks for guiding us here."

"No problem." She walked around and perched on the end of the sofa, looking down at Selene.

"What are people talking about, Jeyssi?" Owen asked.

"You mean aside from you sucking face with an alien?"

Owen winced.

Jeyssi grinned. "Kayl, these aren't normal humans. They're sailors. Some are grossed out, sure. But most are like, 'I sure wish I knew where I could try some of that for myself.' Sorry if I'm assuming too much, but the way you two act makes me think you're doing a lot more than kissing each other good night."

Owen felt his face warming. "That's . . . umm . . ."

She laughed. "You just answered that question. I told you that someday you'd find the right girl."

"You did," Owen said. "And I did. What do the people in here think of her, Jeyssi?"

That question drew a long silence while Jeyssi looked out across the command center. "That's a mixed bag. I mean, there's a big majority looking at what Selene did to draw off the soldiers, and how she's helped the negotiators—which, by the way, they are hearing about now—and everything else, and saying, 'Wait a minute, why is this a monster, and why aren't we at least listening to her instead of trying to kill her?'"

"That's good," Owen said.

"And she said all the right things in that little speech. Lieutenant Genji didn't try to pretend she wasn't different, but she said she was the same where it counted. Did she already have those words ready?"

"I don't think so," Owen said. "I think they came straight from the heart."

"Good. Really." Jeyssi made a face. "So, among the Earth Guard here, who know what she's done and maybe met her, Lieutenant Genji is almost one of us to a lot of people. Especially compared to the soldiers who seem to have lost their primary stabilizers. I don't know about the rest of Mars colony, though. Or among the Earth Guard ships in orbit. And I don't know how any of this is playing on Earth. You know how people can be. Some of them would've heard Lieutenant Genji say 'alien' and their minds would've shut off. So I can't say. I think you've still got a lot of work, a lot of danger, ahead of you."

"I thought that'd be the case," Kayl said. "But at least some people are hearing us."

"You still don't want me telling anyone about the 2180 thing?"

"How many people who haven't met her are going to believe that? Selene thinks it would turn into a circus focused on whether she was really from the future, and that would hurt her ability to make changes in First Contact and other issues. She wants to accomplish as much as she can before that becomes widespread knowledge."

"Yeah. I can't disagree with that." Jeyssi gave him a contemplative look. "You know what else they're talking about a lot? This Owen guy."

"Really?" Owen said.

"You've heard of him, right? The screwup who most of the senior officers treat as if he's radioactive?"

"I think I've heard of him," Owen said, wondering where Jeyssi was going with this.

"Turns out he survived that sabotaged courier ship, and atmospheric entry, both of which should have killed him. You couldn't see when, uh, your monster here was giving her speech on the Commons. But it's been everywhere. And while she was declaring her heart is one hundred percent human, there was that Owen guy, right with her, holding a rifle and looking seriously badass. Suddenly people are asking themselves, why does the brass hate this guy? Maybe because he's running rings around them? Maybe because he's got more guts in his little finger than Earth Guard brass has in their collective gold-braid-and-medals-bedecked bodies?"

"Give me a break, Jeyssi," Owen said.

"I am not kidding, Kayl. They're also wondering about that arrest warrant coming out while you were still officially dead, meaning someone knew all along you weren't really dead. And the canceled safety message. And then we find out the MPDF has issued shoot-to-kill orders on you as well as Genji. Since when is it open season on Earth Guard officers? Why are they so worried about you?" She spread her hands at him. "Put it all together, and your rep has undergone a big change."

"That's nuts," Owen said. "Huh. I wonder what they think of me back on the *Vigilant*?"

"I don't know what everyone thinks, but Sabita Awerdin is happy you're alive and really unhappy with you for not letting her know you were alive." Jeyssi eyed him. "Are you sure you never dated Sabita? Because she seems seriously unhappy with your alien girl."

"We never dated," Owen said.

"Well, I told her to give it up, because we human women cannot compete with somebody like Selene Genji in your eyes. And that got me a lot of 'Selene? Selene? Even you're calling the alien Selene? We have to rescue Kayl from the alien!' Seriously, Kayl, be glad you're not on the *Vigilant* right now."

Selene emitted a loud groan as she sat up, clutching at her head. "What happened?"

"Drug reaction," Owen said.

"My head. Help me, Kayl."

"Does regular aspirin work for you?" Jeyssi asked.

"Yes!" Selene opened her eyes, staring at her. "Lieutenant Arronax."

"You can call me Jeyssi."

"Can you bring me aspirin, Jeyssi? Just aspirin. No added drugs. Pure aspirin."

"Hang on." Jeyssi hopped down from the end of the couch and dashed off.

Selene massaged her head, leaning over. "It's not fair to feel like this when I didn't have a fun drinking binge to compensate." She paused, looking over at him. "There was something. What did I do?"

"Not much," Owen said.

"There was kissing, wasn't there?"

"Yes."

"Why didn't you stop me?"

Jeyssi reappeared. "Aspirin and water, Lieutenant Genji."

"I love you, Jeyssi. Call me Selene." Selene swallowed the aspirin and drank all the water, sighing. "Is there food?"

"Over there with the negotiators," Jeyssi said, pointing farther back in the command center. "They've been chomping at the bit to talk to you but were told you were recovering from an injury."

"I was." Selene held up her hand.

"Look, I've got to go. Are you two okay?"

"We're good," Owen said. "Thanks."

"Kayl, I'm going to try to stand up." Selene rose cautiously, her eyes mostly closed. "Okay. Which way?"

"Over here." Owen helped guide her to the large table where the civilian negotiators who had been gathered from all over the Earth quickly made room for Selene and for him. "What do you want, Selene?"

"Do I smell French fries?"

Before Owen could pass on the request, a big plate of fries was in front of Selene.

"What sort of thing does she drink?" an anxious woman asked. "We have a chemist who can try to compound different substances."

"Tea," Owen said. "Green sencha if you have it."

The request seemed to astound everyone within earshot.

"Is there any ketchup?" Selene mumbled, her head bent over the plate of fries.

"She eats ketchup? Is it safe for her? Get her some ketchup!"

Owen watched her eat, feeling his own stomach rumble.

Selene looked over at him. "Don't you want any?"

"Sure." He dug in as well, eating off the same plate, acutely aware of people watching him as if he and Selene were exhibits in a zoo.

"That one was mine," Selene complained. "Stop trying to take all the good ones. I think I'm going to live."

"Good. There are some people who want to talk to you."

She raised her head and shifted her gaze to finally look around her. "Why didn't you tell me?" Straightening her shoulders, Selene took a deep breath, running both hands through her hair, her hangover persona suddenly shifting into the professional Owen had grown used to seeing in these types of situations. "I'm sorry," she told those watching. "I'm Lieutenant Selene Genji."

Someone deposited a cup of green tea in front of her. Selene picked it up in both hands, breathing deeply of the steam rising from the tea. "Thank you."

"You like sencha?" a man asked.

"My mother drank it," Selene said, taking a sip.

"Your mother? She was . . ."

"Full human," Selene said.

"And your father?"

"Also full human." Selene looked around the table. "I'm the product of genetic engineering."

"By whom?" a woman asked. Owen recognized her voice from the conferences with the negotiators. "Who did this genetic engineering?"

"I can't tell you that," Selene said.

"It was the Tramontine aliens, wasn't it?"

"No," Selene said. "Humans."

"How—?" Another man spread his hands in frustration. "Lieutenant Selene Genji, everything you have told us has checked out.

One hundred percent accurate as far as we can tell. Your input has provided us with priceless insights and saved literally months of trying to parse meanings and interpret intent. But, *how*? How do you know these things?"

"I'm sorry, but I can't explain that yet. I assure you my intentions are to assist you. I want to help in any way I can. But I can't tell you the source of my knowledge."

"Your alien DNA," another woman asked. "Is it Tramontine?"

"Yes," Selene said.

A third woman, studying Selene's uniform closely: "What exactly are you a lieutenant in? What organization? My database can't get a match for your uniform."

Selene looked over at Owen. "Lieutenant Owen knows the answer to that. He can assure you that I am not an agent of any hostile force."

"You're Earth Guard, Lieutenant Owen. Sworn to defend. Is she?"

Owen shook his head. "Lieutenant Genji is not part of any force posing any danger to Earth, or to humanity."

"Why can't you tell us what it is?"

"I'm sorry," Owen said. "I can't."

"What is your relationship with Lieutenant Genji?" another person asked. "Were you assigned by Earth Guard to her?"

"Not exactly," Owen said. "I am committed to assisting her, though."

Yet another negotiator spoke up, eyeing him and Selene in a not-very-friendly way. "You have been seen engaging in . . . physical interactions with Lieutenant Genji, Lieutenant Owen. Does your relationship with her go beyond professional boundaries?"

Owen glanced at Selene. She looked back at him, something about her making him think she expected him to minimize or deny their relationship. "Absolutely," he said. "I love her."

A ripple of reaction ran around the table.

220

Was it his imagination that another sort of ripple ran through the room, as if something fundamental had shifted, something that wouldn't have been confronted for decades in the history that Selene knew?

Selene stared at him, startled by his admission. But then her hand reached out and grasped his.

"This is wrong," the questioner said. "This is wrong. Humans and aliens? Together?"

"She has said her heart is human," another interjected.

"Look at her! Why are these aliens here? One of their . . . creations . . . is already worming her way into a human family—"

"What exactly are you saying?" the woman who'd first spoken demanded.

"You have a son! Is this what you'd want for him?"

The woman looked at Selene, uncertain. "I hadn't thought about it."

Owen glanced at Selene, who was sitting erect, her face expressionless.

She'd heard this before, hadn't she? How many times, growing up? *You know what I am. You can tell by looking at me.* Selene had expected to be judged by that the first time that he'd encountered her.

"With all due respect," Owen called out over the rising roar of conversation, "it's none of your business. This is between Lieutenant Genji and me. I am *not* asking your approval."

Selene squeezed his hand. "Are there questions regarding the Tramontine?"

A pause, people exchanging looks, major issues that had suddenly arisen left unresolved.

"The Tramontine are not a threat?" one of those who'd spoken earlier asked Selene.

"No, they are not."

"You keep talking about defending Earth. If the aliens aren't a threat, what are you defending it from?"

Owen saw Selene look along the table. "You're all familiar with human history. If you had to guess where the greatest danger to Earth would come from, where would you think it would originate?"

An old man smiled in a way that held no humor. "From Earth. From us, Earth's children. Is that what you're trying to tell us, Lieutenant Genji?"

"That is something we all have to decide for ourselves," Selene said.

CHAPTER 10

"DON'T YOU NEED SOME SLEEP?"

The voice was vaguely familiar. Owen stifled a yawn. Selene was deeply asleep once more, trying to recover from the sedative high she'd suffered earlier. He'd been watching over Selene, not willing to sleep himself when he didn't know how all the Earth Guard personnel were reacting to her, how much danger one or more of them might pose for her. Of course, he was also in danger, subject to arrest for that warrant and for desertion and who knew what else. "Hector?"

"Yeah. The hero of the Magsaysay bar crawl." Hector Thanh sat down near Owen, his impressive height and width undiminished from the days when they'd been at the same training school. "I wasn't sure you'd remember me."

"We weren't exactly friends," Owen said.

"We weren't enemies," Hector said. "What do you need, hero?"

"You're right. I could use some sleep. But . . ." Owen looked to where Selene was slumbering again.

"You can trust me," Hector said. "What's rule one of the Magsaysay bar crawls?"

"Never try to move in on someone else's girl, or guy, or whatever," Owen said.

"See, you do remember. That's your girl, right? She's safe while I'm around. No one's getting to her."

Owen looked at him, remembering nights when he was barely acquainted with Hector, but they hung out in the same group. "Why?"

Hector shrugged. "You weren't exactly a hit with the girls back then."

"True."

"But you never tried to break rule one, even though I could see you wanted to chat up Yolanda. And, frankly, my relationship with her got a little rocky at one point, you remember, and I knew during that period she was a little interested in knowing more about you. But you kept your distance. You honored rule one."

Owen couldn't help a short laugh. "Yeah. Yolanda was one heck of a woman. Best mathematician in our group, too. But she was with you. You hadn't broken up. Whatever happened to her?"

"She married me," Hector said. "Best thing that ever happened to me. I'll say hi to her for you next time I send her a call. She'll want to know I helped out the guy who was on the Commons." He looked around with a pensive expression. "There are some people in here who are wondering why you and your girl aren't either dead or in handcuffs and leg irons. I'm not one of them. Get some sleep."

"Are you sure, Hector? You know Selene is—"

"Too good for you? Of course she is. Were you going to say something else?"

"No. Nothing else."

Owen settled himself down an arm's length from Selene on the floor, looking across the flat surface to her face, relaxed with sleep. He didn't really feel himself fall asleep, still gazing at her.

BACK ON EARTH, ROUGHLY TWO HUNDRED TWENTY-FIVE MILLION KILOMETERS FROM where Kayl Owen and Selene Genji slept, Dr. Malani Owen yawned and stood up from her desk. AIs kept getting "better," but that still meant they were better at doing things humans had already thought of. They could easily miss something that no one had told them to look for. Which was why junior researchers in genetic engineering like her got to double-check the work of the AIs, which was why she needed more coffee.

There was an unusual amount of fuss in the break room, but Malani kept her priorities straight and got coffee before paying attention to it. It looked like just about everybody was out of their offices, watching news reports together. "What's going on?"

"You don't know what's happening on Mars?" one of her colleagues said. "The Planetary Defense Forces there have tried to declare martial law, but Earth Guard is pushing back on that."

Mars. Where the aliens had arrived. And where Kayl was trying to get to, along with that alien woman. Malani had been worrying about Mars way too much lately.

"Look! She says she has alien DNA as part of her genome!"

She? Malani craned her head to see someone on the famous Commons platform in the Mars colony who looked a whole lot like someone she'd had described to her by Aunt Hokulani.

The room was buzzing with back-and-forth. "What's with her eyes?" "Has anyone seen that anywhere before?" "What's the functionality tie-in?" "What about her skin? She's showing it." "Is it stiff?" "Looks flexible." "Is that a protective feature or ornamental?"

Then the view pulled back slightly, showing a young man standing next to the woman, a man who Malani had no trouble recognizing at all.

What was with the way Kayl was standing with the alien? Protectively, but not only like a guard. Too close. More like . . . No. No way.

The room erupted in more commentary. "That's the Earth Guard officer!" "What's he doing there?" "It looks like he's guarding her." "Who is he?"

"I know who he is." Malani hadn't spoken loudly, but suddenly she was the center of everyone's attention. She smiled. "He's my brother." Everyone stared at her. "Excuse me. I need to call my mother."

She went back to her office. After the last, in-person meeting, when Aunt Hokulani had filled in Malani and her mom on what was going on, she and her mother and aunt had invested in the latest and supposedly best encrypted personal phones. "Hi, Mom. Yeah, I saw the news."

"Your aunt Hokulani is on the line, too. Let me link her in. Hokulani?"

Aunt Hokulani's familiar face appeared, showing excitement rather than the fear Malani felt. "Hey! Hi, Malani! Did you see her? What did I tell you? Some girl, huh?"

"Some something," Malani said. "I thought you said she and Kayl weren't involved."

"They weren't supposed to be. Maybe that changed. I told you he liked her."

"Malani, is she really an alien?" Malani's mother asked anxiously.

"I don't know, Mom. What does an alien look like? I heard a lot of comments about her eyes. Nobody's seen anything like those."

"Did you see her skin?" Aunt Hokulani asked. "That's something, isn't it?"

"That's natural for her?" Malani asked. "Did you get a chance to see how it felt?"

"Yeah. It felt like skin. Maybe . . . maybe a little smoother?"

"Or slicker?" Malani asked.

"No. No. Not slick. Smooth."

Malani looked over at the nearest news feed. The view had pulled out, showing soldiers pushing their way toward the platform where Kayl and the alien were. "Those soldiers were shooting," she said, feeling a jolt of fear. "Either Kayl is being a great bodyguard or he's really into her. He's putting his body between her and the shots."

"Is that romantic or what?" Aunt Hokulani said.

"I was thinking stupid, but okay," Malani said. "I wonder if they . . . ? Aunt Hokulani, did you talk with her about reproduction issues?"

"Reproduction issues?" Aunt Hokulani asked as if she'd never before heard of such a thing. "What about reproduction issues?"

When Aunt Hokulani dodged a question, it usually meant she had a big reason for not wanting to answer it. "Do you know something?"

"No."

"Auntie, this is important."

"So are confidences, young lady. I don't know anything."

"What are you two saying?" Kayl's mother broke in. "Are you thinking she might be . . . ?"

"Pregnant with Kayl's child?" Malani said. "I don't think so. She doesn't look pregnant." Though, come to think of it, what would a pregnant alien look like?

How could that even be possible? A human and an alien? But then what was Aunt Hokulani being so reticent about?

And how had she suddenly, matter-of-factly, started talking about possibly having a half-alien niece or nephew?

"Kayl could not do better," Aunt Hokulani said. "That's my opinion."

"He is not *your* son!" Malani's mother declared. "That's not something you should be weighing in on."

"Leilani, I am his auntie! Look at them! If I were you, sister, I would be opening my heart to her."

"I'm a little more worried about how much longer they'll be alive," Malani said, watching the footage of soldiers and reports of more shots being fired. "There was that nonsense about him being wanted for questioning, and now this. Aunt Hokulani, do you really think Kayl would be a big enough fool to get himself killed protecting that alien?"

"I think, when it comes to the right girl, that Kayl is just as big a fool as his father was."

"Oh, no," Malani's mother groaned. "That means he'll do anything for her. People are trying to kill them! Why did he choose someone that people are trying to kill? Why an alien? Malani, you have to do something."

"What am I supposed to do, Mom?"

"You're his big sister. Find out more about her! Talk to him!"

"About a girl? Why do you think Kayl pays any attention to what I tell him about girls? Or aliens, for that matter? Or alien girls?"

"Part alien," Aunt Hokulani said.

"Fine," Malani said. "Part-alien girls. I don't know anything about that woman! Except what I can see now and what you've told me, Auntie. And if there's anything else you can tell me, you should."

"There's nothing else I can tell you."

"Kayl's life is in danger, Auntie. For real. He can be a real pain, but I don't want to see him die."

"Do you want to see everyone die, Malani?" Aunt Hokulani asked, her expression totally serious. "Do you want to see the entire world die? Forty years, Malani. That's how long we've got. And that girl is the only one who has any idea how it might be stopped."

"I'm still not sure I believe any of that." Malani looked at the news from Mars again, seeing close-ups of the soldiers, their faces, the fear and excitement visible on some of them as they tried to kill her brother and the alien he'd linked himself to. "Maybe I do believe it. But what can we do?"

"People are going to know it's Kayl," Aunt Hokulani said. "They're going to come talk to us. Maybe we can't do anything else, but we can decide what we're going to say."

"That's easy," Malani's mother said. "I love my son, and I know he would never do anything to help anyone who was a danger to Earth, or who wanted to hurt people. If he's helping her, it's for a good reason. I will tell anyone that."

"Some people might not like hearing that," Malani warned.

"This family stands up for each other, Malani. You're his big sister."

"This isn't like when Kayl was bullied in elementary school, Mom!"

"Look what she was saying," Aunt Hokulani said. "What Genji said on Mars. What in there isn't worthy of support?"

"What if she's lying?" Malani said.

"I have talked to that woman," Aunt Hokulani said. "Heart to heart. Genji's words are 'oia'i'o. Truthful and genuine. I am certain of it."

Malani sighed. "Okay. Okay. He's my brother. I love him. Whatever he's doing must be the right thing. I'll tell that to anyone who asks. And if he wants to marry her, I'll be her maid of honor if she asks me, if aliens have maids of honor, and if that doesn't involve anything really weird in alien weddings."

"Nobody said anything about marrying!" her mother said. "I haven't even met this girl yet! Do aliens marry?"

"I don't know, Mom. Ask Aunt Hokulani."

"We didn't talk about marriage," Aunt Hokulani said. "Did I tell you she likes Spam and green tea?"

"See?" Leilani said. "These are the things I need to know. I can see for myself how brave she is. Hokulani says she's smart. Are there any negatives?"

"You mean aside from her being part alien?" Malani asked. "Look, Mom, I've got to go. Someone here needs to talk to me. Later, Auntie." Malani ended the call. "What is it?"

The middle manager who'd come to her office gave Malani a measuring look. "You're that guy's sister?"

And so it begins, Malani thought. "Yes. I am. I love him. What-ever he's doing must be the right thing."

"The top office doesn't care about that. They want to talk to you about genetic samples and whether you can get any."

At least the heads of this lab would know her name now.

OWEN WOKE UP, BLINKING AT THE CEILING IN THE COMMAND CENTER, FEELING SUD-den panic that he'd slept while Selene needed to be guarded. He sat up, looking about, immediately seeing Selene sitting nearby, watch-ing him. "You're okay?"

"Fully recovered, yeah," Selene said. "Your friend Hector had to head off, but not until he was sure I could handle any threats that might show up. I don't think he entirely believed me that I could, but then he saw a video of you and me encountering those soldiers at the exit from the Commons, and after that Hector was okay with the idea."

"He wasn't really my friend before," Owen said, stifling a yawn.

"Really? He seems like a nice guy. He acted like I was just your average woman."

"Nothing about you is average, Selene," Owen said.

"I'm not used to encountering full humans who treat me like one of them, Kayl. It's weird. Anyway, Hector seems like a decent friend. You need more friends, don't you? I checked out your escape list while you were still out. Three names. Fifty thousand people on Mars, about five hundred of them Earth Guard, and you could only find three. That's sad, Kayl."

He looked about for food. "Lieutenant Owen hasn't been the most popular guy in Earth Guard."

"Once we save the Earth, we'll work on that." Selene produced a tray. "I figured you'd be hungry. I already ate. They brought cof-fee that I couldn't drink. Sorry it's cold."

"Earth Guard coffee is notoriously bad," Owen said, taking a gulp. "Hot or cold. I can swallow it quicker this way. Do you have any idea what's going on right now?"

"People running around. No one's talking to me. With most of them it doesn't feel like the usual isolation. More like they don't know if they should. There are a few who looked like they'd toss me out the nearest air lock if they had the chance. The negotiators are all asleep, except for that one guy who seems to be trying to drink every drop of coffee on Mars. How are the eggs?"

"Rubbery," Kayl said.

"Mine were, too. Sometimes it's like I'm back in the Unified Fleet."

He caught the wistfulness in that. "How does that feel, Selene? Knowing that the Unified Fleet was the . . . I mean, will be the product of a history we're trying to alter. Knowing it might never happen if we're successful?"

"It feels strange." She smiled slightly. "But maybe that'll mean some people, some friends, won't die in the battles that won't be fought. If we succeed, they'll never know their lives would've ended in blood and fire, their efforts ultimately futile when the Spear of Humanity managed to destroy the Earth. And I guess that means they wouldn't know me if we met, even in 2180 again, though I don't see how I'll exist that long. But all that's good, right?"

"I guess so." A question had occurred to him that he'd been reluctant to bring up, but Selene seemed in the mood for it. "Selene, your mother is alive right now, isn't she?"

"Yeah. She's alive."

"Have you thought about . . . ?"

Selene laughed. "Seeing her? Kayl, in 2140 my mother is twelve years old. How do you think that twelve-year-old girl would react if I showed up at her door and said, 'Hi, I'm your fully grown, part-alien daughter from the future'? Do you think she'd want to hang out with me?"

Owen laughed briefly at himself, embarrassed. "I didn't think of that. I guess you already had."

"Sure I did." Selene looked out across the command center. "But I can't link myself to her. Especially now with so many people hunting us."

"Someone might search for Genjis."

"My mother's last name wasn't—isn't—Genji. That's an alloy name."

"Huh? You've never mentioned that before."

"My mother gave me the name Selene," she said. "And she told me to be proud of the Genji. So I am."

Owen shook his head, his feelings an odd mix. "I keep thinking I know everything about you, but then there's something else big. You're like a bottomless well, always something more hidden down inside."

"Yeah, that's me," Selene said, smiling. "A bottomless well. Do you always say such sweet things to your lovers? Is that my new special name? Your bottomless well?"

"I thought we weren't going to do special names."

"I changed my mind," she said. "I may change it again."

"You really are crazy, aren't you?" Owen said.

"You're the one who likes being with me." She looked around, her smile fading. "Kayl, this siege of the Earth Guard command center. The martial law. This didn't happen. I told you that, didn't I? All of this didn't happen. There are major changes going on to the history I know. Not just the changes I was trying to make. All sorts of things, just because I'm here in 2140."

"You're kind of rampaging through the history you knew, I think," he said.

"Why am I still here, Kayl? Why haven't I ceased to exist?" She looked at her hand as if wondering why it was solid. "The only reason I came back in time was because Earth was destroyed. Does me still being here mean we haven't done enough, that Earth will still be destroyed on the twelfth of June 2180?"

Owen shrugged helplessly. "How can we know?"

"We can't. We just have to keep trying, even though we can't know even the short-term consequences of our actions. Why am I still here?"

There wasn't any good way to answer that.

"You two ready for a serious talk?" Captain Yesenski walked up, looking very tired.

"Yes, sir," Owen said, getting to his feet as Selene did the same.

"Sit down. This won't be easy to say." Captain Yesenski rubbed his face, looking unhappy. "Here's the drill. I don't run the universe. We have firm orders from Earth Guard headquarters about the alien monster. Despite those orders, there are a few hundred Earth Guard officers and sailors in here who would be willing to form a living wall to protect that monster, no matter the consequences. There are also a few score who think the few hundred are nuts. But that living wall will not stop the force that's going to be brought against us. After a really long night of discussions and some very pointed messages from authorities on Earth, we've got an agreement to get the soldiers back in their barracks and the negotiators free to act again . . . but the alien monster is a no-go. If she isn't turned over, if we are still protecting her, this turns into an assault on this command center, and we will lose."

"I can't ask that of you," Selene said.

"Lieutenant Owen is also a no-go," Yesenski said, looking at him. "Earth Guard brass never managed to make charges stick against your father, but now they see a chance to nail you to the wall. My duty is to protect the negotiators. I cannot protect the two of you. If there was a way, I swear I would do it. You two aren't who I first thought you were, but it's obvious you've run some tremendous personal risks to get vital information to where it needed to be, and to protect the negotiators and their mission."

"Thank you, Captain," Owen said. "We'll have to make a break for it."

"Easier said than done." Yesenski gestured around him. "I'm supposed to have you both under heavy guard, but if you happen to escape while I'm looking elsewhere, that'd just be too bad. However, I don't know where you'd go." He called up a diagram of their surroundings. "The soldiers have had time to lock things down a lot better. Accesses out of here are all covered. If you stay on the surface, you're going to get nailed."

"What about off the surface?" Owen said.

"You know how many Earth Guard ships are here, Lieutenant. There's no safe place in space for you, either."

Selene pointed upward. "There's one safe place."

"Where is that, Lieutenant Genji?"

"The Tramontine ship."

Owen realized that he and Captain Yesenski were both staring at Selene.

"They'd take you in?" Yesenski asked. "Is that where you came from?"

"It's not where I came from, but I speak their language," Selene said. "The Tramontine will be mad with curiosity over that. They'll let Kayl and me onto their ship. I'm sure of it."

"Lieutenant Owen would be safe with them?" Yesenski asked.

"Yes, Captain." Selene smiled at Owen. "I wouldn't take him anywhere that wasn't safe."

"You mean aside from Mars?" Yesenski said dryly. "Getting up there isn't going to be easy. You can see the lifters out there on the field. They're not under tight guard because the soldiers know you've got no place to run. But if you go out there and board one, they'll see it and they'll be on you before you can activate the systems, prep the reaction mass, and lift."

Owen looked toward the landing field, trying to figure out ways to escape from what was feeling like a trap with no exits. "There are shortcuts to readying a lifter."

"There are," Captain Yesenski said. "All prohibited, but that sort of thing doesn't seem to slow you down, Lieutenant Owen. However, those shortcuts are not short enough. You need more time than you'll have."

"What if the attention of the soldiers is elsewhere?" Selene said, her eyes on the diagram of the area around them.

"Another diversion?" Yesenski said.

"We'd still need too much time once we got to the lifter," Owen said.

"Not if I was diverting their attention while you got to the lifter and started prepping it," Selene said, looking up to meet his eyes.

"No," Owen said. "I am not lifting from Mars without you."

"We can do this! Look," Selene said, her eyes back on the diagram, "I go out this way. I can break past them easily at this juncture. Every soldier is going to be looking that way, toward where I am, while I head into this section. That means you can get out to a lifter without being noticed and start preparing it." Her finger moved, tracing a path. "While I'm going this way. Or this. Then here."

"That's a dead end," Captain Yesenski said before Owen could. "See these warning symbols? You can't get through the accesses at the end of that passage in a suit. They're too tight."

"I can if I'm not wearing a suit and am just in my uniform," Selene said. "I can get to this outside access once I'm past the passage. They won't expect me to head for that access."

"What good does that do?" Owen demanded. "You won't have a suit."

"I won't need it," Selene said. "I can make it from that access to the nearest lifter without a suit."

Owen stared at her, aware that Captain Yesenski was doing the same. "Without a suit?" Owen finally said. "On the surface of Mars?"

"I'm an alloy. I can do it."

"It's nearly two hundred meters from that access to the nearest lifter," Yesenski objected.

"I can do it," Selene said.

"How?" Owen said. "You are not superhuman. You told me that yourself."

"Do you trust me or not?" Selene said, looking down at the diagram. "We can build in backups so you'll be safe, Kayl. I can record announcements for the Tramontine so they'll still let you aboard even if I'm not there."

"You're not planning on making it, are you?" Owen said. "You're planning on creating a diversion so I can get free while you die on the surface."

"That's ridiculous, Kayl," Selene said. But she kept her eyes on the diagram. "Captain, can Lieutenant Owen and I speak in private?"

"Sure," Yesenski said, his expression troubled. He got up. "Let me know what you decide. We don't have a lot of time."

"I understand, Captain. Thank you." She waited until Yesenski was several steps away before speaking to Owen in a low voice. "Kayl, we don't have any other options."

"What good is an option that kills you?" Owen demanded.

"It won't kill me. I can do this."

"Nobody can go that far on the Martian surface without a suit," Owen said.

"I can," Selene said. But she still wasn't looking at him.

"Promise me," Owen said. "Promise me you can make that distance."

"I can make that distance," Selene said. "I promise."

"Because if you don't, I will not lift that ship."

Her head finally came up, her gaze fixing on him, her eyes

flashing with anger. "Kayl, you promised! It's not me! It's the mission! No matter what happens to me, you have to keep on with it."

"I just discovered I'm not strong enough to do that," Owen said. "Not like this. I will go to the absolute end to help you achieve the mission, but not to help you kill yourself. If you don't make it to the lifter, I will come out and get you."

"If I don't make it to the lifter, it'll be because I'm dead, Kayl!"

"Then I'll die beside you."

She stared at him as if uncertain whether to still be angry. "You can't do that. You know any second could be my last."

"That hasn't happened yet."

"Is that about what you said to the negotiators?" Selene demanded. "I . . . appreciated the support, but you don't have to pretend you really meant it."

He'd been wondering why she hadn't brought up his saying "I love her" before this. "I did really mean it."

She stared at him for a long moment without speaking. "You can't— Kayl, this can't be about me."

"I could not live if I left you on the surface," Owen said. "I told you. I'm not that strong."

"It's the entire *Earth*, Kayl! That's so much more important than me!"

"I've backed you on that over and over again. But not like this. Selene, you have to make that lifter."

She gazed at him steadily. "I'll make the lifter. If somehow I don't, you're going to need some recordings in the Tramontine language—"

"No recordings," Owen said. "No 'what if you don't make it.' No ifs at all."

"Fine. No ifs. I'll make the lifter." Selene wrapped her arms about him, holding Owen tightly. "Make sure you're ready to lift when I get there."

"I will be." He held her, wondering how it would feel if Selene ceased to exist while she was in his arms. He'd been haunted with worry that Selene would vanish when he was sleeping or looking away, leaving him always wondering. But what if she went this instant? Left him holding nothing? Somehow that felt even more horrible. "I'm sorry. I will keep my promise to put the mission first. After you reach the lifter."

"You're not very reliable, Kayl Owen," she said. "Putting new conditions on your promises like that. But I guess you're the best I can get." She pulled back a little, searching his eyes. "There's something I should have told you. It probably doesn't matter, there's no way it should matter, but there shouldn't be any secrets. Not anymore. But now is not the right time."

"You can tell me once we reach the Tramontine ship," Kayl said.

"Sure. If for whatever reason I never make it back to Earth, tell your aunt Hokulani thanks, and she can tell you everything, and I wish . . . I don't know anymore."

"What is this about, Selene?"

"Something I never wanted, which is impossible now." She leaned in and kissed him. "I know people are watching. Our next kiss will be on the Tramontine ship."

"I'M GOING TO BE PERSONALLY GUARDING THIS ALIEN," CAPTAIN YESENSKI SAID IN a loud voice, "as I take her over somewhere to a place she'll be absolutely secure. The fewer people who know where she's locked up, the lower the risk, so nobody follow us."

Owen held her hand tightly. "Selene . . ."

She smiled reassuringly at him. "See you in a little while, Kayl."

Her hand slipped from his. Owen watched Captain Yesenski and Selene heading toward a darkened area of the command center, where they were quickly hidden from sight behind consoles and security barriers.

"Where's she going?" Jeyssi asked. She'd come to stand beside him.

"To risk her life again for people who think she's a monster," Owen said.

"Kayl, when I first saw you with her I thought you needed to get away from Selene as fast as you could. Now I think you'd be crazy to leave her."

"When you're right," Owen said, "you're right. Be careful, Jeyssi."

"Where are you going?"

"I'm just taking a little walk," Owen said.

"A little walk?" Jeyssi had never embraced him, as far as he could recall, but she did so now, a quick, fervent gesture. "Good luck. I'll do what I can to make things right inside Earth Guard even though I'm not exactly a big voice."

"Thanks, Jeyssi. Every voice matters. See you around." He walked toward the exit that would give access to an air lock leading onto the landing field.

To his surprise, he saw Hector Thanh along with several others waiting. The others, like Hector, either were large or carried themselves like martial artists. "What's going on?"

Hector shrugged. "Captain Yesenski talked to us about checking out an air lock for possible equipment problems. We thought we would do that while things are a little quiet. Don't mind us."

"Sure," Owen said. He started walking again, Hector and the others around him. "Are you guys sure about this? You could end up facing charges."

A chief spoke up with a grin. "It wouldn't be the first time I got in trouble for fighting with ground apes."

"You're worried about us?" Hector said. "What about your girl? Is she going to be okay?"

"If she isn't, I won't be, either."

"I never got you, Kayl. You were ready to take stands when the rest of us were ready to say that's just how things are. And you were pretty toxic as far as the brass were concerned, even though you did your job fine. But, now, man, if you're ever looking to make up a crew, give me a call."

"I'm just trying to get through today in one piece," Kayl said. "You know?"

Hector laughed. "That is literally true for you, isn't it? Maybe you won't get blown up."

"That'd be nice." They came around a corner, seeing a pair of soldiers at the air lock watching them.

An alert sounded.

"They're making a break!" someone shouted. "The alien is at building 356!"

"All available reaction forces converge on sectors three and four," an announcement ordered.

Owen felt a nearly overwhelming urge to run back that way, to where Selene was facing those soldiers alone. *Keep walking. Do your part.*

The soldiers had stopped paying attention to the unarmed Earth Guard personnel and were excitedly checking their status readouts. "They're going to get it this time!" one declared excitedly. "It's not getting away this time!"

"That's no way to talk about an officer," Hector said reprovingly.

A moment later both soldiers were on the ground, their communications gear being methodically broken by some of the Earth Guard. Hector tossed an energy rifle to Owen as Owen finished pulling on and sealing his suit. "You might need this."

"Thanks," Owen said. "Keep them quiet as long as you can, okay?"

He cycled the air lock and walked out on the Martian surface. Owen breathed the air in his suit, thinking of Selene out on the surface without that air, felt the protective suit keeping in pressure. Selene's skin, even if it only matched human skin, could hold in her pressure for a while. As long as she didn't breathe.

They'd found a maintenance mask that would protect her eyes and ears for a little while, but nothing bulkier than that would get through the accesses Selene needed to use.

Why had he agreed to this?

Trying to block out the fear he felt for Selene, Owen focused so intently on what he was doing, what he was thinking, that he felt like an outside observer of his own thoughts and actions.

Walk along the concrete, his feet stirring up small puffs of Martian dust, move steady, slow, nothing to see here, nobody to ask what he's doing. Wondering about the alerts sounding inside the colony. About Selene dodging fire and escaping down unexpected routes, the soldiers trying to kill her or trap her.

"Sector three! Where is the alien? Send extra forces to sector two."

He reached the lifter nearest the access Selene would use. Owen depressurized the interior, allowing him to leave the air lock's inner and outer doors open. He made his way up to the flight deck, sat down, and started preparations for takeoff. The checklist popped up as soon as he powered up the instruments, allowing Owen to work quickly. *Skip that. Do that. That doesn't need five minutes. Set it for three. Do that. Do that. Skip that.*

The communications system on his suit lit up. "The alien is trapped within sector two. Shoot to kill. Repeat, orders are shoot to kill."

Owen had to pause for a few seconds, trying to breathe.

He scanned the controls, checking the preps.

It would be ready.

Owen went back down the ladder. There was an emergency air hood in a first aid locker. He got it out, resting it on the deck, ready to use. Picking up the rifle again, he stood just inside the air lock door.

There. Selene would be coming out there.

Three soldiers came running out of the air lock Owen had left by, looking around.

He waited, wondering why his heart sounded so loud.

Selene burst into view, her medium-blue-and-gold uniform bright against the dull Martian soil and the concrete of the landing field. The mask obscured her face and head, and she had gloves on, but otherwise she was ridiculously exposed to the extremely thin Martian atmosphere and the cold.

She sprinted toward the lifter as soldiers came boiling out of the colony behind her, their suits protecting them, their weapons glinting in the weak sunlight as they leveled them to fire.

Owen stepped into the outer door of the air lock, aiming, and fired at the nearest soldiers. He probably wouldn't score a hit, but their suits would report the incoming fire, distract the soldiers, give them another target in the form of Owen.

How long did it take for someone to run two hundred meters?

A very, very long time when soldiers were lining up to shoot from two directions, when the oxygen in Selene's lungs must be long since used up, she drawing on her body's reserves, trying to keep moving while her lungs screamed at her to take a breath, a breath that would be fatal as Mars emptied and froze her lungs.

Some of the soldiers had shifted their aim to him. Owen stood there, seeing the outer hull of the lifter bubble in places as energy bolts hit. There were at least a dozen soldiers in sight, some still aiming at Selene as she ran, others aiming at him now.

Owen braced himself against one side of the air lock, steadying his aim, cursing the way his helmet got in the way, firing again, seeing one of the soldiers aiming at Selene stagger as his shot hit their armor.

She was close now, her run starting to lose its pace, her feet wobbling slightly. Selene was slowing down.

"Come on, Selene!" Owen shouted, taking a step onto the

boarding ramp, firing at the soldiers again, hearing an alarm sound inside the lifter as one of the shots aimed at him struck inside the ship.

So close, even through the mask he could see her face twisted with effort, reaching . . .

Dropping the rifle, he took three more steps down, grabbing her outstretched arm, seeing a slice of the top of the suit on his arm vaporize as a shot narrowly missed both of them, pulling Selene into the lifter with a single titanic effort using strength he didn't know he had, a pull that tossed her into the deck inside while he reeled back to the controls and hit the air-lock-close and emergency-pressurize commands.

Owen knelt by her, tugging the emergency oxygen hood onto her head and activating it so the hood filled instantly, hearing the energy bolts hitting the closing inner and outer air lock doors, knowing the soldiers were running this way. He had to lift now.

But Selene was lying still. Was she breathing? Her eyes were closed.

If she was still alive, the only way to save her was by lifting this bird immediately.

It might have been the hardest thing he'd ever done, tearing himself away from the passive form of Selene lying on the deck and racing up the access to the pilot deck, strapping himself in, scanning the readouts—critical systems still good, hull damage registered but not critical, ready to lift—hitting the command, seeing the soldiers on the external screens so close, running fast, the propulsion ramping up, dust flying, soldiers frantically scampering backward, acceleration pressing him down, the lifter jumping skyward, the Martian sky rapidly shading to the dark blue of space . . .

There were a lot of ships up here. Some of them, Earth Guard warships, were already altering vector to pursue and intercept him.

To hell with them. Owen yanked off his helmet, twisting his seat around to jump out and check on Selene.

She was sitting in the co-pilot seat, oxygen hood and mask discarded, her eyes on him large and dark.

"Selene?"

"Hi."

"You're okay?"

"I guess. I saw you standing there in the door, waiting for me. I had to reach you." Selene seemed to have trouble looking away from him, her gaze coming back to his face as if fascinated. "The Tramontine ship," she said.

"Right." Selene seemed to be oddly off, but given the physical stress her body had just endured, that wasn't surprising. Owen swung back to face his controls, sizing up the situation, feeling Selene's eyes still watching him. "The Earth Guard doesn't know we're heading to intercept the Tramontine. Are you sure the aliens will let us reach their ship?"

"They will." Selene kept her eyes on him as she reached toward the communications controls, triggering a transmission. She started speaking in that strange language, the fluid syllables and words forming a stream of sound almost like a spoken song.

Selene paused as the lifter neared orbit.

Owen saw an open vector and swung the lifter onto it, tapping on the primary drive to boost the speed slightly and raise the lifter in its orbit.

Words sounded on the speaker, the voice slightly off, as if the speaker weren't human. Which they weren't, Owen realized. But despite that, the amazement and interest in the Tramontine voice could be recognized by a human.

Selene answered.

Another speaker came to life. "Stolen lifter, this is Earth Guard. Steady on your current vector and await boarding. Failure to comply will result in use of lethal force."

Owen ignored it, studying the slew of orbital traffic for safe paths, dozens of spacecraft on dozens of orbits and vectors, interweaving.

There. If he headed toward that freighter, its path would block the Earth Guard ships coming in on intercept from above and his right. Owen activated the thrusters, pivoting the lifter, hitting the primary propulsion again for a moment to slightly brake the lifter's velocity and kick the lifter onto the new vector.

"Oooooh."

Alarmed, he looked at Selene, to see her still staring at him, her chest rising and falling with deep breaths. "Are you okay?"

"Yeah," Selene said. "The Tramontine are madly curious about who could be talking to them in their own language from this lifter. I told them the only way they can learn the explanation is to let us land on their ship. I'm waiting for the answer, but they'll say yes. Get us over there."

"Okay." Three more Earth Guard ships were homing in on him, assuming the lifter would either stay on its current vector or break away from the Tramontine ship's orbit.

The autopilot was blinking suggested courses but Owen shut off that function, waiting for the right moment. *Now.* More thrusters, primary propulsion, propulsion again, the lifter slewing under the kicks onto a vector bringing it well above the Tramontine ship, as if Owen was aiming to break free of the blockade by running through it.

"Aaaaah."

He spared another quick look at Selene. "Are you sure you're okay?"

"Yes. Have you ever . . . realized how hot you are when you're driving a ship like that?"

Another split-second glance at Selene, her eyes still fixed on him, then Owen tried to focus back on the controls and the situation in space around them. "What the hell are you talking about?"

"Your hands . . . on the controls . . . so firm . . . so precise . . ."

"Selene, what the hell? I need to concentrate here!"

"I know." The main speaker broke into more alien speech. "The Tramontine have given us clearance to land on one of their platforms."

An alert began frantically beeping. Owen saw two specks of light leaping away from the Earth Guard ship *Pathfinder*. "They've fired missiles at us."

"Get close to the Tramontine. Their defenses will handle it."

He judged possible vectors, his hands hitting thruster controls and then holding the primary propulsion for a long moment to shed velocity, the lifter veering over and down, its track now heading along an arc for an intercept with the center of the huge Tramontine ship.

"Oooooh. That was amazing."

"Selene! Knock it off!"

She called out a few more words in the Tramontine language, receiving a quick reply. "They'll take care of the missiles. See that blinking light? That's the landing stage they want us to use."

"Got it." The missiles were closing fast. If the Tramontine defenses weren't as good as Selene had promised, this lifter had less than a minute left before it turned into a big ball of wreckage. "I've got to brake velocity to land. Lining up." *More thrusters, hit the primary harder this time, hold it, try to ignore another long, excited exhale from Selene . . .*

The alarm was beeping frantically. Ten seconds to impact of the missiles. Eight. Seven.

Both missiles disappeared.

"Pocket disruptors," Selene gasped.

Owen lined up the lifter's autopilot with the landing stage on the outside of the Tramontine ship and activated the automatic controls. Even though the alien ship was rotating, the autopilot could easily match it. "That's it. We're on autolanding."

"We're on auto?" Selene cried. "We're on auto?"

"Yeah, we're—" Turning to look at her, Owen was shocked to see that Selene had shed both her seat harness and her uniform and was launching herself at him. "What—"

She hit him full body, her hands popping open quick releases and ripping loose his seat harness.

Two Tramontine words came over the main speaker.

Selene turned her head long enough to call a single word in reply before directing all of her attention to Owen.

"Selene, what— Hey— Are— Ow— Ah— Selene!"

CHAPTER 11

TWENTY-FIVE MINUTES LATER, GENJI SAT IN THE CO-PILOT SEAT AGAIN, HER UNI-
form on once more, watching the instruments and displays
showing the lifter making its final drop onto the Tramontine landing platform, her face pleasantly warm, her body very pleasantly
relaxed, knowing that Kayl was still staring at her with a stunned
expression. "Stop looking at me like that."

"What . . . what . . . ?"

"I needed you. What's so strange about that?"

"What's so . . . ? Selene, what just happened?" Kayl asked.

"Extreme stress can trigger a . . . physical response in alloys,"
Genji said.

"Is that what you call that?" Kayl said.

"I'm sure you enjoyed it."

"Did my enjoying it have anything to do with it?" Kayl asked.
"Did I have anything to do with that?"

She swung her seat to face him, her face now hot with anger.
"How can you say that? It had everything to do with you! My pas-
sion, my need, was for you. Only you could satisfy it. Yes, it was
physical, but the trigger is purely emotional. I can only have that
kind of reaction with someone I care very deeply about, someone I
am willing to share my total self with. No one else could have made

me feel that. Yes, Kayl Owen, it was all about you! What the hell does that look on your face mean?"

"It means I'm not sure whether I should be very flattered or very frightened," Kayl said.

"You didn't have any complaints the first time this happened."

"There was a first time?"

"The first time we slept together!" Genji said.

"That's what that was?"

"That's what that was." She looked back at the displays as the lifter settled onto the landing stage. "I'd been trying to hold you off both emotionally and physically, but facing . . . oblivion, I finally let it go. Don't worry. It won't happen very often. Just, you know, sometimes in reaction to life-threatening stress. *If* I am willing to go along with it. Oh, and one more thing. If I ever hear that you have shared even one word about this to any of your male friends, I will hurt you in ways that will make you wish I had killed you. Do you understand?"

"Yes. I understand." He looked down at his clothes. "You ripped—"

"Aren't there any spares aboard? Don't you have any in your pack?"

"Yeah." A few minutes later, Kayl was settled back in his seat. "I skipped some steps getting us ready to lift. I should check everything for damage, assuming we're going to need this lifter again."

"I'm assuming we will," Genji said. "The systems on this lifter seem even more antiquated than usual, but I'll try to help."

"Okay." He looked at her. "This seems strange, just business as usual."

"It is business as usual right now. Don't make it weird."

"I'm not the one who made it weird."

"If you want to go back to a nonphysical relationship," Genji began.

"No!" Kayl looked back to the controls. "Initiating system checks. What's happening outside?"

"The Tramontine have automated landing platform systems. They're adapting to the lifter's configuration and locking us securely to the landing platform. Then they'll configure an air lock to match the one on the lifter. I'm guessing twenty or thirty minutes."

"That's pretty quick work," Kayl said.

"Yeah. What's going on among the rest of the orbital traffic?" Genji asked, trying to sort out the information on the unfamiliar displays.

"All of the Earth Guard ships backed off," Kayl said. "They're still forming a screen around the Tramontine ship, but they're not trying to get any closer. I think seeing those missiles vanish rattled them. What did you call that?"

"Pocket disruptors," Genji said. "We had them on my ship, *Pyrenees*."

He glanced at her. "That's the first time you told me the name of your ship."

"It is?"

"'Lieutenant Selene Genji, Unified Fleet. That's all you'll get out of me,'" Kayl quoted.

Genji nodded. "I had to assume you were hostile. I mean, that Earth Guard story was so obviously fake. But Spear of Humanity shouldn't have even wanted me aboard their ship, contaminating it. And I was a little shook up. I had to figure out what was going on." She paused. "Thanks for being there when I arrived in 2140. If it had been anyone else . . . I don't know. The chances of saving Earth might have been zero. I don't know what they are now, but they're better than that."

"You know I'm happy to help with the mission," Kayl said, checking some of the readings the system checks were producing.

"And you know when I say thanks for being there I'm not just talking about the mission," Genji said. "I don't . . . I'm going to be honest, Kayl. I don't think I could've made that lifter. Not for anyone else."

He didn't say anything.

She looked over to see him gazing at her, smiling slightly. "What?"

"Nothing." Kayl checked another reading. "I could say I knew that. But I won't. We've got a minor air leak. At least one of the shots that hit us on the ground penetrated the hull."

"It's fixable, right?" Somehow this routine felt calming.

"I think so. Let me take care of it." Kayl looked about him to unstrap himself, looked at his seat harness still lying in a corner of the flight deck where Selene had flung it, shook his head, and went down the ladder.

She sat there, watching the orbital traffic, wondering what was happening back on the surface of Mars.

The speaker came to life, a Tramontine woman calling her, speaking the alien language. "One who shares, are you well?"

"I am well," Genji replied in Tramontine. "Are you well, One who shares?" She couldn't forget her manners.

"The humans are upset. Possibly? They ask that we return you and the other, or just the other. Do we understand?"

"Yes," Genji said.

"Have you taken?"

To the Tramontine, that would mean had she committed a crime. "No," Selene said. "I have not taken. My words are truth. I request again that you share your ship with me and . . . and the one who shares my life." How would Kayl feel if he understood that she'd told the Tramontine he was her life partner? But she didn't want to risk the Tramontine thinking she and Kayl could be treated as separate matters.

"The other with you shares your life?" the Tramontine woman asked.

"Yes. Some of the humans wish to take him from me. Only some."

"There are always some," the Tramontine said. "We will share our ship with your sharer of life. How did the humans learn our meanings so quickly? Was this you?"

"I have shared," Genji said.

"Please. Tell us more."

"Later," Genji said.

She heard Tramontine laughter, an enjoyable sound. "Pleasant anticipation. What do we call you, One who shares?"

"Lieutenant Selene Genji."

"Lieutenant is status? Yes? Selene is . . . ?"

"The name my mother shared to me."

"Ah. And Genji?"

"This means . . . I come from two origins."

A long pause. "Wait and be safe, Lieutenant Selene Genji, One who shares."

Genji heard a noise and turned to see Kayl was heading back to the pilot seat. "What's up?" he asked. "That seemed like a long conversation. Are we still okay here?"

He was tense from overhearing that. Naturally. To him, the Tramontine were a totally unknown element. "We're okay. The authorities on Mars have asked the Tramontine to turn us over, or if not both of us, just you. The Tramontine just told me they won't turn over either of us."

Kayl nodded slowly, his brow furrowed with worry. "Will they hold to that? They're curious about what you can tell them, but I'm nothing special in the eyes of the aliens."

She had no right not to tell him. "They know you're special. I told the Tramontine you're my husband."

His head spun to look at her. "Your husband?"

Genji smiled reassuringly. "The most important bond to the Tramontine is sharing of a life. What humans call marriage. I told them you're that to me. They will *not* separate us."

"But . . . we're not. We're not married."

Her clever idea didn't seem to have produced the results she wanted. Genji felt a tightness in her gut and tried to keep her voice calm. What did that tone of voice mean? Why did Kayl look unhappy? Was that what she was seeing? He was full human, after all. Maybe, despite his earlier words, being linked to an alloy wasn't something he really wanted to even consider. "Is that . . . is that something . . . that upsets you? I'm an alloy and I know that is not easy—"

"Selene, I'm sorry." Kayl looked and sounded sincere. "I was surprised. But it's not about that."

"You don't have to have them thinking I'm married to you, Kayl. If you would rather not be identified with me that way, I understand. They might tell other humans, and then people would think it was true, and I know that's not—"

"Selene!" He gazed at her. "Would you?"

"Would I what?"

"Marry me."

She stared at him. "Are you out of your mind?"

"According to Aunt Hokulani, yes," Kayl said. "Would you?"

"Would I marry you? Kayl, it is not that easy. Why did you even bring that up now?"

"You're the one who told the aliens that we were married," he pointed out.

"I had a good reason for that!" Genji sat back, gazing at the controls, her mind whirling. "Tell me you're not serious."

"I am serious."

"Any instant, Kayl. Any instant I could vanish. And the mission is still the only priority that matters. Is that what this is? An attempt to make me the hill? I will not be the hill, Kayl!"

"If we're married," Kayl said, "the mission will still be the hill."

"I don't believe you." She stared at him, her emotions a tangled knot that would not unravel. "Please take it back."

"My proposal? No. You don't have to answer me, but I won't take it back."

"Why not?" Genji demanded.

"Because taking it back would mean I didn't want to marry you, and I do."

Why was he doing this? "Haven't we had this conversation, Kayl? You don't know what you're asking. Even if I don't disappear, my genetically engineered DNA might malfunction at any time."

He stared at the deck unhappily before raising his gaze to hers again. "You don't want to waste any moments. Neither do I."

She leaned back again, glaring at the overhead. "Fine. Leave it there. I'm not giving you an answer."

"Why don't you just say no, then?" Kayl asked.

I can't tell him. "Because! Reasons! Stop pressing me!"

"Okay."

"Stop saying okay!" Genji slapped the controls in front of her. "Did you fix the air leak?"

"Yes, I fixed the air leak."

"Are there any other problems we need to worry about?"

"No," Kayl said. "It looks like the lifter systems came through all right. We are down twenty percent on our reaction mass, though, after the maneuvers to get up here. Otherwise, we're good to go, Lieutenant Genji."

"Kayl . . . dammit." Genji slumped over the controls. Now he'd be moody for a while. Just because he was too crazy to see how big a mistake it would be for them to get married. Next he'd be wanting to talk about . . .

That thing she'd still kept secret from him.

Kayl, you really do not want this big bag of sharp rocks named Selene tied to you. Why can't you see that? And why can't you admit that sooner or later you're going to do what everyone else does? Though when I cease to exist you won't ever have to admit to it. Maybe it's better that way. You can keep pretending this could have been forever.

But I have to tell you that thing when I can. I owe it to you.

"You saved my life, back there on Mars," Genji said in a soft voice. "I just want to clearly say that."

He didn't answer.

She lowered her head onto her arms, wondering why saving the entire planet Earth couldn't be just a little easier.

The next ten minutes, waiting for the Tramontine to adapt an air lock to mate with the human lifter, went by very, very slowly. The silence on the flight deck started to feel like a physical thing, smothering Genji.

Kayl finally spoke. "Are you okay?"

"Yeah," she said. "You?"

"I'm okay." A pause. "I don't get this. But I'm going to back off. You've made it clear that's what you want."

"I don't *want* it, Kayl. You are incredibly important to me. I—"

Further conversation was halted by another call from the Tramontine. "Lieutenant Selene Genji? The air lock is tested. Our air is good, yes? For you and the other?"

"Your air is good," Genji replied. Tramontine atmosphere didn't match Earth standard, but it was close enough in every way that mattered.

"We are ready to share our ship."

"Thank you, One who shares." Genji got up from the co-pilot's seat. "Are you ready to meet some fully alien aliens?"

Kayl looked at her anxiously. "I hope I am."

"It's okay. They're not that strange. And you'll be in the histories now, the first full human to physically meet a Tramontine. Instead of, uh, who was that? Somebody . . . I can't remember the name."

"Glory is fleeting, I guess," Kayl said, getting up, his nervousness still clear.

"You trust me, right?" Genji said.

He met her gaze, nodding. "Of course."

"Then don't worry."

Despite all of the recent friction between them, Kayl nodded again and followed her without hesitation.

Genji paused at the air lock, reading the outside data, getting confirmation there was an air lock with safe air mated to that of the lifter.

Kayl activated the controls to open the lifter air lock, inner and outer doors.

There were three Tramontine waiting for them, a female, a one-male, and a twomale, the usual composition of a formal delegation. They all wore the slightly baggy trousers and tunic-like tops that were common among the Tramontine, the cut of the clothing similar for all three, but different muted colors on each. The garments also had elaborate designs woven into them, the colors of those reaching into shades full human eyes couldn't see but Genji could. All had their lips pressed tightly together in a flat line, expressing joy at the meeting. Realizing that Kayl would not understand the expression, Genji leaned toward him. "Those faces mean they're happy."

The Tramontine offered her a device she recognized, as well as one for Kayl. "This is a quarantine barrier," she told Kayl. "It creates a zone around us that kills anything our bodies give off. Bacteria, viruses, anything."

"You're kidding." Kayl looked at the small device in wonder. "My sister told me people are working on something like that, but she thinks we're still decades away from any useful prototypes."

"Once the Tramontine share this technology, we'll have it within a couple of years," Genji said. "It'll make a huge difference in controlling disease outbreaks. Except for among those people who refuse to use them."

"Why would anyone refuse to use them?" Kayl wondered.

"It's alien technology." Genji sighed heavily. "Whole countries end up banning them."

"How do we help keep that kind of mindset from taking over?"

"I don't know. We have to try."

Kayl hadn't openly reacted to the appearance of the Tramontine, which pleased her a lot. Not that the Tramontine were horrible or ugly in appearance. They had two arms, two legs, and a head with two ears, two eyes, a nose, and a mouth. They had no visible hair on their heads except for a long fringe growing along an arc on the lower back and extending down past their necks. The features on the head were notably off from those of a human, some too large, some too small, all placed "wrong," but not fundamentally different enough to appear grotesque to a human. It took getting used to, though. Kayl seemed to have come through with flying colors.

The Tramontine twomale and female led, the onemale behind, as they walked through the ship, the rotation of the huge ship providing a sense of gravity. The passage was lined with nooks and shelves, many holding living plants, others with artifacts from a variety of worlds, and even books similar to human printed matter, though they opened down and were read bottom to top. Genji could smell the scents of the plants and their flowers, conjuring up happy memories of a few weeks spent aboard this ship in the 2160s.

They passed only a few other Tramontine, who watched them with intense curiosity that somehow didn't feel rude. Occasional doorways led into rooms and offices, as well as a large garden with a soaring ceiling where vegetation similar to trees grew. A display board held a collection of awkwardly done, colorful drawings. "Children?" Kayl asked. "Those are children's drawings, right?"

"Yes," Genji said. "This ship is meant to travel for many generations."

"This is so cool. I wouldn't mind spending a long time traveling to another star if it was in a ship like this," Kayl said.

One of the Tramontine looked at Genji. "Your other has question?"

"My other is admiring your ship, One who shares."

"Ah! Your other knows much of ships of space?"

"He does," Genji said. "Master of flight, his skills unmatched. You saw?"

"It was your other who controlled your ship coming to us? Master of flight, indeed."

"What are you talking about?" Kayl asked.

"I'm bragging about you," Genji said. "They're impressed by how well you can drive ships."

"You're not really, are you? They are?"

"Yes, I am, and yes, they are. Are you doing okay?"

"Yeah, fine." Kayl grinned at her. "None of this is what I expected."

"And now you're famous, first full human to meet Tramontine."

His smile faded as he looked around again. "I wonder how they're reacting back on Mars. And in the Earth Guard ships. If only they could see this."

"They will eventually. But for now we're safe here."

Their destination proved to be a small series of connected rooms, the functions mostly matching the same ones humans used. A sleeping room, an area for eating and working and relaxing that, disconcertingly for humans, also contained an open shower, and a small room for a toilet that looked enough like its human counterpart to be comforting.

Food was already laid out on the table, a nice collection of Tramontine dishes that Genji knew were safe for humans. All but one, that is. "Many thanks for the food, but this one, the duurinaan, would upset the digestion of my companion and other humans. It would not be fatal, only unpleasant."

"Forgive us!" the twomale cried. "Our analysis was flawed."

"How," the female Tramontine asked, "do you know this? You recognize our food?"

"Yes," Genji said. "I will explain when I share the answers with all who wish to hear."

"The wait will be difficult," the Tramontine replied. "But courtesy cannot be overlooked, and for us this is the time of sleep. Rest before sharing, sleep before sharing. Acceptable?"

"Acceptable," Genji said. "Grateful."

She sat down at the table after the Tramontine had left. "We're off the hook until after a sleep period. Relax."

"This is all safe?" Kayl asked, sitting down as well.

"Yes. Except for that one dish they took. Oh, chatturiami! I haven't had that in ages!"

Meal done, they cleaned themselves in the highly efficient Tramontine shower, Genji grateful that she and Kayl were now comfortable around each other unclothed. Showering would have been extremely awkward otherwise.

That finished, she sat down on the bed. As she remembered, Tramontine beds were amazingly good at conforming to anyone lying or sitting on them. Instead of joining her, though, Kayl hesitated. "Don't you want to share the bed?" she asked.

"Yes," he said. "I just . . . I was pushing you."

"Oh, hell, Kayl, we just showered in front of each other. Come here." She waited as he sat next to her. "Closer. Okay. I know one of the reasons we've had a few . . . difficult discussions lately is because . . . well, because there's something hugely important I have kept from you. And that has made me feel increasingly guilty. With our relationship having . . . evolved, you deserve to know this."

He waited, watching her, plainly worried by whatever she was planning to say.

Genji slid a little closer to him, looking at her hands. "There shouldn't be secrets like this between us. This is the last one, I think. You've earned the right to know about . . . Wow. This is hard. Please don't interrupt or ask any questions. Just let me explain."

She did, going over the worries about the second-generation alloys and the reluctance of the first generation to have a second, and her own thoughts.

"And I thought that was it," Genji said. "It would never change. Even when you and I started sleeping together I didn't think it mattered. I still have the contraceptive implant. There's still only a very, very, very small chance that something might happen, and with me likely ceasing to exist at any instant, it wasn't like I had to worry about what might happen nine months down the line. But as long as we keep doing it, there's still that very, very, very small chance. Okay. You can ask questions now."

"That was your first time?" Kayl asked. "With me on Mars?"

"Yeah. So?"

"Umm . . . I . . . uh . . . didn't . . . know."

"You did fine," Genji said. "Believe me, I have no complaints about that night."

He smiled as if embarrassed before getting serious again. "You and I can be cross-fertile?" Kayl asked. "I just assumed we weren't, because you said it wasn't a concern."

"Bad assumption, because I wasn't being fully honest with you. Listen. If I don't vanish soon, if no one succeeds in killing me, I could be here a little longer. In which case, there's a very, very, very small chance that you and I could, umm . . ." Why was it so hard to say?

But he knew what she was trying to say. "You just said you've never wanted to even consider that," Kayl said.

"I didn't! Never! And I still don't want to try! But . . ." She gave him a troubled look. "That wasn't with . . . I mean . . . if it was you . . . and me . . . ours. If it was ours. I thought of 'ours' and suddenly . . . suddenly everything I'd thought before wasn't so certain anymore."

He stared at her wordlessly for several seconds. "That may be the nicest thing you ever said to me."

"Don't make this about you," Genji said.

"It is about me. About us."

"No, it's about our child."

"Our chil—" His eyes grew huge. "Are you saying—"

"No! No, no, no. It has not happened. Very, very, very small chance. But if, I think, it did, I would, maybe, there's a chance . . . want. Which would make it . . . harder."

He nodded, looking serious. "I understand. I know you're not asking my permission."

"I'm not," Genji said. "Totally not. If you don't like our deal, you don't have to keep participating in chances that might happen."

"I kind of like participating. So if, maybe, will you tell me? Let me tell you how I feel?"

She sighed. "Yes. I'd owe you that."

"Okay, then."

"Good." Could it be this easy to finally address the topic?

"And, Selene, I really would like to . . . I mean, I understand the concerns, the second generation and all. But," Kayl said, "like you said, 'our.' That would be . . . great. To me."

"Stop. Please. I am so not there yet," Genji said. "The fact that I'm even willing to consider it if there's that accident is more huge than you can imagine. Maybe . . . I don't know. Because you are seriously messing with my mind, Kayl Owen. But there are no more secrets. I have roped you into my mission and turned your life upside down and generally been a chaotic force as far as you're concerned, but I will not lie to you or withhold any secrets. Not ever again."

"All right," Kayl said.

Genji took a deep, relieved breath. "I'm glad I finally talked about it. I felt so bad keeping that from you." She laughed with relief. "Can you believe this? We're talking about potentially having a child and I haven't even met your mother yet."

So easy after all.

Because you're still lying to him and you're lying to yourself. You're still afraid to tell him everything.

He wouldn't understand. He couldn't understand.

And sooner or later, despite his declarations of love, he'll leave.

I'll cease to have ever existed before he can do that. I hope.

The mission. The mission is what matters. I can do this. I can prove that alloys belong here. If he goes, I can still do this, on my own. That's how alloys have to do things. On our own. Always. I'll be fine.

Liar.

Kayl chose that moment to say the wrong thing.

"Meeting my mother hasn't exactly been an option," Kayl said, smiling, oblivious to the huge land mine he was stepping on. "But that should be the least of your worries. I'm sure my mother would love to have you in the family."

"What?" Genji stared at him. "In the family? Are you proposing to me again? How could you do that?"

"By accident," Kayl said, taken aback. "Apparently."

"This isn't a joke," Genji insisted, her emotions churning. "I thought I'd made it clear—"

"Selene, I was not bringing that up! We can drop it."

"Then withdraw your proposal!"

"No! If you don't want to, just say no."

How had they gotten back here? Because they hadn't actually resolved anything earlier, that was why. "You can't tell me what to say, Kayl Owen!"

He sat back, his hands in the air. "I give up. What's going on?"

Something inside her that had been under increasing strain finally gave way. "You did not grow up with this, Kayl!" Genji held her hand out, the skin glowing in the light. "You did not grow up being told that your DNA might go haywire at any time, and that even if it worked, no one really knew how that might work. You did not grow up with people watching you on the street, and talking about you, and refusing to touch anything that you'd touched, and making sure they never brushed up against you, and warning their kids not to play with me or go out with me or invite me to parties because who knew what I might do or what might happen, and the ones who were all 'sure, we accept you completely' but got worried if their sons seemed too friendly with me. You did not grow up with two older sisters who treated you like a monster and made it clear you would never be *their* sister. You did not have a father who took one look at you and left forever. Your mother wasn't murdered because she was your mother! *You did not live that, Kayl!*"

She subsided, looking at him. "And I don't want you to. I care for you too much to tie you to that. All right? That's the truth at last. I won't say no, because I do want to marry you. But I won't say yes, because I . . . I care for you too much to make your life like that."

He gazed at her, his distress clear, his mouth working. "Selene . . ."

"Drop it, Kayl. I cannot change what I am."

"I don't care—"

"Drop it."

His eyes stayed on her for a long moment. "All right. Because I love you too much to keep pressuring you on something that . . . hurts."

"Thank you."

They sat together for a long time, neither one of them saying anything.

Had she ever confessed her pain to anyone like that? Really admitted to everything she'd held inside?

Genji felt moisture hitting her hands and looked down, seeing her tears fall. *No, no. I'm not going to cry. Stop. Crying just lets them know they got to you. You can hold this in. Hold it in as long as it takes. Another forty years if necessary. Long enough to win.*

Long enough to save a world that never wanted me. Long enough to prove I belonged on that world.

But the tears kept coming.

Kayl didn't say anything, but his arm came out to hold her and draw her in, and she let him, leaning into him, her tears falling onto him as she finally let go some of the long-accumulated pain.

/////

GENJI AWOKE THE NEXT MORNING TO FIND HERSELF STILL WRAPPED CLOSE TO KAYL, holding on to him as if he were an anchor protecting her from being swept out into space. She felt drained.

But he was still here. Maybe . . . he really wouldn't go?

Kayl only exchanged brief, awkward greetings with her as they got up.

The door chimed. Genji answered to find a Tramontine there with a tray of food, the Tramontine's lips pressed together in the Tramontine smile.

Genji brought the tray to the room's table. "Breakfast."

He sat down opposite her, gazing at the tray. "Meat?"

"Mostly. This is taratarabis. Sort of a rabbit," Genji explained. "This is all vat-grown, of course. No real taratarabis were harmed in the making of this meal."

He looked at her, apparently surprised that she'd attempted humor. "Selene?"

Don't talk about it. Don't talk about it. Please don't talk about it. "What?"

"You'd told me before I didn't understand, and I didn't. I'm sorry."

"That's okay." She bent over her food, trying to convey how little she wanted to rehash anything from the night before.

"I really hurt you."

"Other people hurt me. Can we let this go? Please?"

"Sure. I promise not to ever bring it up again."

She took a few bites, not really tasting them. "I still want to be with you. I may care for you more than I did before."

264

"Sometimes I wonder why," Kayl said. "Uh . . . this is sweet."

"Yeah. The Tramontine like sweet meat dishes. Their vegetables tend to be sharply seasoned. Their desserts are . . . I guess the word is 'savory.'"

"Wow. It's like they're aliens or something."

He was trying to make a joke. She looked up at him and forced a smile. "Weird, huh?"

"Seriously weird." Kayl looked down at his food. "What's going to happen now? With the Tramontine, I mean. What's next?"

"They'll gather some of their councils. That's what humans call them even though they're not exactly that. Different specialists in different fields of questioning, which is what they call science and research. I'll be called in and I'll make a statement and then they'll ask questions. It'll probably take a while."

His eyes were worried. "What are you going to tell them?"

"Everything. Kayl, the Tramontine won't accept 'I can't tell you that.' They want answers, answers that make sense. It's possible they'll have some answers for me. And I owe it to them to be as truthful as I can. They also need to know what will happen."

He didn't look happy. "What's my role in all this?"

"To be honest, you can either come with me and sit there while there are long conversations in Tramontine that you don't understand, or you can stay here and . . . rest, I guess."

He shook his head. "That's . . . Hey, would the Tramontine let me back on the lifter?"

"I don't see why not," Genji said. "Why? This room is a lot more comfortable."

"I can use the communications systems on the lifter to see what I can find out about what's happening on Mars and in orbit, maybe figure out how to get in contact with someone."

"That's a great idea," Genji said. "I'll ask the Tramontine. Hey."

"What?"

"You really are the one who shares my life."

He looked up again, and this time his smile seemed to be real. "Thank you for letting me do that. But you don't make it easy."

"I know."

/////

THE DISCUSSIONS WITH THE TRAMONTINE WENT VERY SMOOTHLY. *OF COURSE THE one who shares your life can return to your ship. One will wait there for when the Master of Flight needs to return to your room.* "The Tramontine have given you the name Master of Flight. I'll teach you how to recognize it later so you'll know when they're talking about you."

Kayl gaped at her. "Master of Flight? That's my Tramontine name?"

"I told you I was bragging on you."

Are you ready to speak with us, One who shares? There are so many questions.

And so, after seeing Kayl heading back to the lifter, Genji found herself seated in the center of a back wall facing a large semicircular room filled with row after row of eager Tramontine. Every other Tramontine on the ship was probably watching and listening remotely, excited to learn something that promised to be unique.

"Proceed?" a female Tramontine asked. "How should you share?"

Genji chose her words with care. "Share all first. Give you all I know. After, if questions exist, try to explain."

"Questions always exist," the Tramontine speaker said, generating soft Tramontine laughter in the room.

"I cannot answer *all* questions," Genji said, earning another round of laughs. They were pleased that she understood Tramontine humor.

"Proceed. Share. Anticipation is strong. We have all noticed, your command of our speech is very good. Tell first, please, how and when you learned our words. How long in the past?"

"I first learned Tramontine words twenty-five human years from now," Genji said.

Stunned silence answered her.

"Twenty-five years . . . from now?" the Tramontine woman finally said. "Was this said correctly?"

"Yes. In human reckoning, it is May month of year 2140. I share what will happen in June month of 2180, forty human years from now, how I came here, and who I am." She certainly had their attention. Genji began speaking.

It was lucky the Tramontine had provided her with water. She needed it several times as her throat went dry. But, finally, she finished.

And waited, as the Tramontine talked among themselves, their excitement easy to see.

But the first words spoken to her were tinged with sorrow. "This we will cause?"

"No," Genji said. "You shared. Other humans will cause. I will stop them. It will not happen."

"Sharing technology will lead to this. Should technology not be shared?" That question also held sorrow. Sharing, after all, was one of the Tramontine's highest virtues.

"Some can be shared. Most can be shared."

"What will be the nature of the weapon?" another asked. "What should be withheld?"

"That is not easily answered," Genji said. "Sharing anything about the weapon might lead to the weapon."

They understood that. More debate.

"You are part Tramontine?" a twomale said, his voice filled with wonder. "You carry part of us inside you?"

"Yes. Some of my genetic code is Tramontine."

"You are part sister to us, then."

"I . . . like to think so," Genji said. "Some humans fear this in me, though."

"The one who shares your life does not fear?"

"No." She made a Tramontine smile, pressing her lips together tightly. "He does not fear. He is beside me, sharing our task to try to save our world."

Another Tramontine spoke, a onemale. "Your task intrigues. Changing time may be very hard. Experiments show time may be . . . not elastic. Wants to hold to what was."

"It has not happened yet," Genji said.

"*Was*," the Tramontine emphasized. "You observed the event. The event has not yet been but already *was* because you observed."

"Do I . . ." Genji hesitated, terrified at the implications. "Does that mean I must cease before the event can be stopped?"

"No. No. If experiments show what we think we see, if theories correct, once observed, fate of observer not relevant."

Great. "Why am I still here?" Genji said, forgetting to form her words in Tramontine grammar. "Can you explain that? I've changed so many things already. Major events have happened which did not happen in the history I know. My birth was, will be, based on a large number of very specific things, some of which must have already been changed. Why do I still exist?"

CHAPTER 12

HERE WAS A PAUSE FOLLOWING HER ANGUISHED QUESTION, FOLLOWED BY more discussion as Genji waited and tried not to show the tension filling her. "Two primary possibilities," another Tramontine woman finally said. "First, your changes are not enough. More must change to result in you not to exist. This seems . . . unlikely, if major events already changing. Second possibility, stronger possibility, to make change, cause must exist. Universe, time, needs you to explain, justify, these changes, events happening in this time. There is a circle. Cause. Effect. You are inside. You *must* be inside. You are cause."

"I must exist?" Genji said, unable to believe her ears.

"You can die. But not never-was. This is theory. Not certain."

"But how can I exist if I was never born?"

"Must exist now to explain events you cause. Being born is different matter."

"I don't . . ." Genji looked around her at the intent, sympathetic faces of the Tramontine. "What about 2180? The only reason I'm here is because events in 2180 hurled me back in time. How does the time travel work if I never get born in 2158 and am not there watching Earth die on the twelfth of June 2180?"

A twomale answered, his voice soft. "Lieutenant Selene Genji, if you not born in 2158, then you need not travel in time to be in 2140. You are here already in 2140 human year. Here in 2140 human year is only place you have been. Paradox is resolved because time travel no longer required."

"What?"

They could see her distress.

"You are here in time. You must be here in time. This is theory. Still you might be never-was," another Tramontine said. "This is beyond what we certain know. But it offers strong answer, why you still exist."

She might not cease to have ever been? Genji felt her universe reel. She'd braced herself for extinction, worked assuming it would all end at any moment.

What if it wouldn't? What if, unless she died, she'd continue on, living a life until at least 2180 even if she wouldn't be born in 2158?

She had been wondering if Kayl Owen really meant what he said about wanting to stay with her. She would have to tell him this, and finally learn the answer.

OWEN SETTLED INTO THE PILOT SEAT, REACTIVATING THE SYSTEMS ON THE LIFTER. Everything still looked good.

He called up the channels offering news broadcasts from Mars.

The soldiers were back in their barracks. The commander of the Martian Planetary Defense Forces had retired effective immediately. The negotiators had resumed discussions with the Tramontine, though for unknown reasons, progress seemed to have slowed a great deal. Rumors were flying of a secret source who had aided the negotiators. More than one person suggested that the only possible source on Mars of information about the aliens was the alien who'd been pursued by the MPDF, had made a speech on the Commons declaring her fundamental humanity and support for their

270

freedom (loops shown on apparently endless repeat), and then had disappeared.

This was accompanied by much speculation concerning the Earth Guard officer who had been with and defended the alien. The officer had been identified as the formerly officially dead Lieutenant Kayl Owen. Why was he working with the alien? Why had he been officially declared dead in the absence of evidence? An Earth Guard safety report linking the destruction of the ship he'd supposedly died on to internal sabotage had been leaked and officially denied. Why was Owen being sought in connection with the disappearance of Thomas Dorcas when no evidence had been cited linking him to that?

Earth Guard was responding to the questions by declaring the answers were classified and reassuring everyone that everything was fine.

A lifter had been stolen, right about the time the alien and the rogue officer, Lieutenant Owen, had somehow escaped from the Mars command center despite being heavily guarded. Earth Guard had declared there was no connection between those events. Earth Guard refused to comment on why missiles had been fired from an Earth Guard warship in orbit about Mars.

Observers on the planet had seen the lifter on a landing platform on the outside of the huge alien ship. Earth Guard refused to comment on that, as well.

After remaining mostly passive, the populace of Mars was asking when the negotiations would be publicized. There had been a large demonstration in the Commons, citizens hoisting an effigy in a medium-blue-and-gold outfit onto the speaking platform and demanding to have a voice in the negotiations. "If there really is danger, tell us why!" one man was shown yelling. "If there really isn't danger, tell us that!"

Was that Edourd's cousin and his gang among the demonstrators? Strange to think they could have been motivated to get involved in the demonstrations by his talk with them, a talk that wouldn't have happened if he hadn't come to Mars, which he wouldn't have done if Selene Genji hadn't entered his life.

Selene seemed to be knocking over things everywhere, simply by existing in a time when she hadn't existed.

How much did all of this mean? Owen wondered. Were he and Selene really making a difference? Or were these alterations in the history that Selene knew just surface scratches on a reality that didn't want to fundamentally change?

He'd never realized how much she was holding inside. What she'd endured in life. How could he have been so blind?

How much strength did it take for someone to keep going after all that? More than he'd ever have. But he would give her all he could, for as long as he could, until . . .

How much longer did they have?

What could he do now?

Could he get through to the command center? Let everyone know he and Selene were all right, and the Tramontine as peaceful as advertised?

Master of Flight. He felt absurdly proud of his Tramontine name, though he expected he'd be widely mocked in Earth Guard if it became common knowledge.

To Owen's surprise, the incoming-call alert started blinking. Someone was calling this lifter.

Might as well see what that was about.

A startled-appearing commander looked back at him. Apparently they hadn't expected him to respond. "Lieutenant Owen. Stand by for Admiral Meng."

Rear Admiral Meng? Hadn't someone mentioned that Meng was in command of the Earth Guard ships near Mars?

Owen tried to remember everything he'd heard about Meng. He couldn't recall anything particularly horrible but also couldn't remember anything that stood out as good. Just the usual ticket puncher making his way up the Earth Guard promotion ladder. Meng had apparently remained passive, avoiding any involvement, as Captain Yesenski had confronted and resolved the martial law situation on the surface of Mars. That wasn't too surprising, since ticket-punching careerists tended to avoid sticking their necks out when it was possible such actions could imperil their next promotion. Meng would surely try to claim credit for what Yesenski had done, but that might be hard to do given the amount of publicity Yesenski's actions had generated.

The image of Meng appeared on Owen's screen, looking coolly professional. "Lieutenant Owen."

It was the most minimal possible greeting. That didn't bode well. "Rear Admiral Meng," Owen said, using the same form in reply.

"Earth Guard is prepared to offer you a deal."

There wasn't any harm in listening. If calmer heads had prevailed, it might even be a deal that would help things. "What is it, sir?"

"Safe passage back to Mars, the murder charges dropped."

That was it? "There are murder charges? I thought I was being sought for questioning regarding a possible murder."

"I may have misstated that," Admiral Meng said in a way that left Owen unsure whether he had or not.

Had somebody filed murder charges against him? Based on what? "So, just the charges involving questioning?"

"Are there other charges against you, Lieutenant?" Meng challenged him.

"I don't know, Admiral. I can well imagine charges pertaining to not reporting for duty and being absent from my ship without authorization, among other things. I've been identified in the press as a deserter. Given my father's example, I can even imagine being charged with the destruction of that courier ship that I was supposed to die aboard."

The admiral's prolonged silence was not reassuring. "You're not in a position to make demands, Lieutenant," Meng finally said. "This is not a negotiation. It is an offer. One that could determine whether you survive this experience."

"What about Lieutenant Genji, sir?" Owen asked. "What about safe passage for her?"

"Who?"

"Lieutenant Genji. Lieutenant Selene Genji."

Another few seconds of silence. "The alien is not part of our discussion."

"Lieutenant Genji is not a threat to Earth or to humanity," Owen said.

"Whether the alien is or is not a threat awaits reasoned and informed evaluation, Lieutenant Owen."

"Earth Guard has been trying to kill her," Owen said. "The MPDF tried to kill her. Is this reasoned and informed evaluation going to take place after she's dead?"

"You need to get your head on straight, Lieutenant. You need to think about your loyalties, and your own future."

He tried to keep his temper under control. Not entirely successfully. "With all due respect, Admiral, what about protecting the Earth? What about the future of humanity? Why won't Earth Guard listen to what Lieutenant Genji has to say?"

Meng did not look happy. "I see your reputation as a difficult officer is well-earned. You spend too much time questioning orders and too little time obeying them."

"If the admiral is aware of any incidents prior to the courier ship's destruction in which I failed to obey orders, I'd be interested in hearing them," Owen said. He had been forced to passively listen to dressing-downs many times. He wasn't in the mood to put up with that now. Maybe Selene had also changed him.

Admiral Meng instantly changed the topic rather than provide any examples, which didn't really surprise Kayl. "Lieutenant Owen, you are the primary example of why we have no desire to give the alien a forum. The alien clearly has the ability to cloud the minds of humans and bend them to the alien's will. You also have no idea what sort of actions that alien has been committing, the sabotage, the espionage, laying the groundwork for invasion. Or have you simply blinded yourself to those things?"

"Admiral," Kayl said, "the first part of that is nonsense. Her arguments are persuasive. That's not clouding of minds. And the second part is even more absurd. I've been with Lieutenant Genji almost full-time since she encountered Earth Guard. I know what she's been doing. Whatever you've been told is wrong. She has committed no espionage, no sabotage, and there is no invasion."

"How do you explain the destruction of the courier ship the alien and you were both aboard, Lieutenant?"

"My understanding is that incident has already been explained, Admiral. By Earth Guard's own safety office. That report has become public knowledge." He had the ear of a senior officer. Owen told himself he had to try to get through to him. "Admiral, Lieutenant Genji's actions have been focused on helping Earth, helping humanity, and staying alive while people who won't even listen to her try to kill her. I can prove this. She wants to help us."

Meng shook his head. "Lieutenant Owen, you're either a fool or a traitor. If you are so deluded you have stopped thinking about yourself, you might want to consider the safety of your family."

"My family?" Owen breathed slowly in and out, trying not to yell. "Are you threatening my family?"

"Earth Guard would never threaten anyone's family," Meng stated. "But there are people on Earth who have legitimate concerns, and there is no telling what they might do if your actions continue to reflect submission to the alien agenda."

His temper went out, replaced by ice. "Rear Admiral Meng, I want to make something very clear. If anything happens to my sister, my mother, or my aunt, or any other relations, I will hold you personally responsible, and I will ensure you personally pay the price for it. And, if you're planning on hiding from me behind your walls of warships, I will remind you that so far Earth Guard has not been able to stop me from getting where I want to go and doing what I want to do."

Meng glared in reply. "How dare you threaten me!"

"How dare you threaten my family. Sir. You heard me."

"This is the only offer you're going to get, Owen!"

"In that case, with all due respect, go to hell." Owen ended the call.

That hadn't gone well. He'd let his temper get the better of him after Meng indirectly threatened his family. But at least he knew Earth Guard's leadership wasn't ready yet to change its vector regarding either him or, more importantly, Selene Genji.

Making a decision, Owen set the lifter's transmitter to broadcast to the planet below. "To the people of Mars, and to the Earth Guard and other defenders of Mars and Earth. This is Lieutenant Owen of Earth Guard." They hadn't taken his official status from him yet. "I wanted to ensure that everyone knew Lieutenant Selene Genji and I are safely on the Tramontine ship. The alien ship. They are humanoid; they are friendly. Lieutenant Genji is continuing her efforts to assist in a peaceful First Contact between humanity and the Tramontine. She is willing to do anything necessary to help ensure the safety of Earth and the security of all humans. I will continue to assist her in that. If—"

A loud, pulsing tone cut across the lifter's transmitter, drowning out Owen's words.

Earth Guard had taken longer to start jamming his message than he'd expected. Hopefully enough had gotten out for people to question the official statements of Earth Guard's leaders.

OWEN HAD WAITED FOR A COUPLE OF HOURS AFTER BEING ESCORTED BACK TO THEIR rooms before Selene returned. "How'd it go?"

She looked at him, her expression flitting through emotions too quickly to read. "We need to talk."

"Okay. There's food—"

"Right now." Selene sat down, facing him. "I may not cease to exist."

Owen stared at her, feeling his heart leap. "That's . . . that's wonderful."

"Is it?"

"Of course it is. Why wouldn't it be?"

She was watching him with what seemed an unhappy sort of anticipation. "I may not cease to exist, Kayl. I may be here for a long time. Even if I'm not born in 2158, the universe needs me to be in 2140."

"Really? But . . . if you won't be born, where did you come from?"

"Apparently," Selene said, "the universe doesn't care about how I got here. All it cares about is that I'm here."

"Okay," Owen said, still elated. "I have to tell you, Selene, the universe and I are in total agreement when it comes to that."

"Stop it! I may need to exist in this time."

"I got that," Owen said. "Why do you seem to think that is a problem?"

"You can't—" Now Selene seemed to be frustrated. "Why don't you stop deluding yourself?"

His elation fell into a pool of wariness and worry. "What am I deluding myself about?"

"I may not vanish, Kayl! You got into this relationship expecting it would end at any moment and could not possibly last. But now I'm here and I may stay here!"

"Good!"

"Stop pretending!" Selene shouted. "Just go ahead and let me know."

"Let you know what?"

"You don't have to stay."

Owen stared at her again, trying to understand what this was about. "Maybe I want to. I was pretty sure I told you I wanted to stay with you as long as possible."

Selene shook her head at him. "I'm an alloy."

"Yeah, I'm pretty clear on that now."

"What is the matter with you? Is it because of your father?"

"My father?" Owen gave her a look combining bafflement and a trace of anger. "What would my father have to do with you and me?"

"He was taken from you. Just like my mother was taken from me. Maybe you . . ." Selene appeared to be searching for words. "Maybe you just don't want to lose someone again."

"Are you saying my staying is about my father, not about you?" Owen shook his head firmly this time. "No. I'll admit to imagining how he would have reacted to meeting you, and what my father would have done about what Earth Guard is doing if he was still alive. But, in terms you have used more than once, my staying is all about you, Selene. Not my father."

Instead of answering, Selene looked about her as if seeking a reply she couldn't find. "Let's go ahead and eat."

Despite the chill in the air when they ate that made Owen barely taste his food, when they went to bed Selene cuddled up against him, one arm reaching across him. "I don't want to do anything tonight except hold each other."

"All right. Same old question, Selene. What do you need from me?"

"I need you to hold me."

She wouldn't say anything else.

Owen lay there with her, trying to figure this out. Hadn't they brought out all the things that haunted Selene, that burdened her?

Maybe not all the things. He had a sense, based on exactly what, he couldn't say, that there was one more large thing hidden in the dark of Selene's bottomless well. Something that would explain her odd insistence that her not ceasing to exist might be a problem for him.

Sooner or later, whatever it was would reach the light.

OWEN FOUND HIMSELF GETTING INCREASINGLY FRUSTRATED AS THE NEXT FEW DAYS passed. There was only so much he could do aboard the lifter. Earth Guard would now jam his transmissions before he could get more than a single word out.

The excited news reports from Mars, talking about how "Genji and Owen" were helping First Contact to the benefit of the human species, countered by those insisting Genji was an alien and couldn't be trusted so obviously neither could Owen, were a particular source of frustration since he couldn't actually do anything more than he already had. His "helping" consisted of scanning news reports, searching for any further attempts to send a message to him, and making futile efforts to send any messages of his own.

His only other option was to sit in their room, which was comfortable but felt more and more confining. He'd figured out how to activate an entertainment system, but the shows on it were baffling, in a language he didn't understand, the Tramontine on them acting in ways he couldn't interpret. He'd grown used to their appearance, but aside from the flat-mouth "smile," Owen couldn't yet understand their expressions.

It was strange to remember days on the *Vigilant* when he'd had far too little time to sleep. Now he had all the time to sleep he could possibly want, and it was driving him crazy.

But he couldn't show it, because Selene was spending long days talking to the Tramontine, explaining what the humans meant and how they would perceive various messages and actions. She had a lot to do. He had to make sure he gave her the room to do it.

On the sixth day after their arrival, though, Selene came back early from working with the Tramontine, flopping down in a chair and waiting stoically as it accommodated itself to her shape. "So much for negotiations."

"There's a problem?" Owen said.

"Me. I'm the problem." Selene looked at him. "I don't want you to feel unimportant. You're a problem, too."

"I'm so happy to hear that."

At least that got a brief smile out of her. "The negotiators want access to me. But Earth Guard jams the message channel whenever I get on it, while claiming they're not doing it and it must be some glitch in the system. The negotiators are frustrated, the Tramontine are frustrated, I'm frustrated. How are you doing?"

"Frustrated," Owen said.

"Give me your honest assessment, Kayl. What does this feel like to you?"

"All I know about what's going on with the Tramontine is what you've told me," he said. "But based on what's happening when I try to use the lifter's communications, I get a sense of a big brick wall. We've been bricked in by people trying to keep you from having any more influence on events."

Selene slumped back in her chair and nodded to him. "Yes. This ship is safe for us. We could live on it for years, eating taratarabis. But it's also sort of a cage, and there are people who want us to stay in it so they can prevent us from doing anything else. And their attempts to block me are also blocking more progress in the First Contact negotiations." She sat silent for a moment. "Tactically, if we're being penned in, that means we have to reposition."

"Operationally," Kayl said, "we need to come up with actions that put us back in control of what's happening to us. Back in control of what we can do. Oh, speaking of what we can do, there was a new item on the Mars news channels today. Dorcas Funds is disintegrating as various shareholders fight over the carcass and try to rip off pieces for themselves."

"Disintegrating?" Selene sighed, her eyes gazing somewhere into her past. "Another change. That means Dorcas won't dominate the trade in Tramontine technology in coming decades. Who will? We didn't try to make that change, but events forced it on us. Tom Dorcas forced it on us. Speaking of which, is there anything new on that questioning-about-murder arrest warrant that's out on you?"

"It's still out," Owen said. "There's a public interest group that's filed a lawsuit demanding to know what evidence exists tying me to the disappearance of Tom Dorcas, but that could be tied up in the courts for decades. Do you think there is evidence linking me to it?"

"I doubt it," Selene said. "I did some pretty thorough house-cleaning, and the gig got up enough speed before running out of fuel to keep heading up and out of the solar system fast enough no one will ever catch it. Anything they do find should link the killing to me, not you. Me, the alien saboteur, spy, and clouder of the minds of human males."

"I wish Jeyssi hadn't told you about that," Owen said. "I recognize the whole mocking-it thing. I did the same bit for a long time about the things Earth Guard brass said about me. Like it didn't matter, even though it did."

She looked at him for nearly half a minute without saying anything. "We need to get back to Earth. Mars is too hot for us, and Mars orbit is even hotter. Earth has room to hide, and room to do things without being blocked."

"All we've got is the lifter. Not exactly an interplanetary craft."

"It could be. The Tramontine could make modifications to the lifter that would allow it to make the trip to Earth. But that might not be our best bet."

Selene leaned forward, pressing the side of the room's table. To Owen's astonishment, a three-dimensional orbital display appeared above it, the vast bulk of the Tramontine ship dominating the image. "There are a few interplanetary ships in orbit about Mars that either have skeleton crews or have been put on automatic while travel to and from Earth is still banned except for Earth Guard ships. If we could get to one of those and boost out of orbit without warning . . ."

Owen shook his head. "They'd know as soon as we started activating systems. None of those ships are particularly fast. Even if Earth Guard didn't spot us preparing to run, their nearest ships could run us down easily once we started moving."

"So, we need another diversion, right?"

"Maybe," Owen said, concerned now. Selene was acting too assured, too certain. This felt too familiar.

"The Tramontine can give you an individual maneuvering pack that'll let you reach one of the ships on automated standby," Selene said.

"I'll be noticed."

"Not if attention is elsewhere! I'll take the lifter and distract them, get the Earth Guard ships out of position, and then boost to an intercept with you and join you as our new ship heads out on a vector for Earth."

Owen took his time to answer, studying the orbital movements.

"What do you think?" Selene pressed him.

"I think it makes the plan to get us off the Martian surface look extremely safe by comparison. Selene, there's no way you can maneuver that lifter through all the Earth Guard ships like that. There are too many of them, covering too many vectors, and they'll be able to predict where you want to go to meet up with the ship I'm on."

"I can loop completely around the planet," Selene insisted. "They won't be prepared for that."

"Maybe not," Owen said, "but they'll have plenty of time to react to it and set up an inescapable kill zone for you when you try to intercept whatever ship I'm trying to escape with."

"You have to have confidence in me, Kayl. I'm an alloy. I can do this."

He shook his head firmly, looking at her. "Where have I heard that argument before? What are you doing, Selene? This is just like on the surface of Mars. 'Don't worry. I can do this.' While you run head-on into a situation very likely to kill you."

She looked away from him. "You're just trying to avoid confronting the issue. I'm not. Our mission remains the priority. You need to get back to Earth. Whatever we have to do, we have to do."

"That is not what you're doing here."

"Yes, it is!" Selene spun to face him, visibly angry. "You want to keep finding excuses to avoid these tough choices. 'We need another way, Genji. You can't do this, Genji.' Well, sometimes there aren't other ways, and you have to try to do it even if it seems impossible."

"That's not what this is about," Owen insisted.

"It's not?" Selene got angrier. "You keep doing this. Trying to make me the priority. I am not your hill! Our mission is the hill! And I am ready to—"

Her voice cut off, Selene staring at him.

Something crystallized inside Owen, a realization of something he'd only suspected before. "Why don't you finish saying it, Selene?"

"I don't have to."

"You were about to say that you're ready to die on that hill. For real," Owen said. "Weren't you?"

Selene looked away, her face working. "I . . . it's important."

"You rushing to your death isn't going to help the mission."

"I'm not . . ." She took deep breaths, her gaze directed away from him. "You have no idea what it's like."

"I can't pretend I do," Owen said. "I thought the Tramontine said the chances of you never existing are getting smaller all the time, instead of stronger."

"That's a theory. They don't know."

"We're making changes," Owen added.

"We'll never know if they're enough."

What could he say to her? "I thought you said you'd found a safe harbor."

"I did." Selene finally looked back at him. "And, despite occasional problems, he has been everything I could hope for. But it's still been getting to me. I haven't been admitting it even to myself. When did you get so good at reading me?"

It didn't sound like praise. More as if Selene was worried that he could do that. "There's stuff I'm still not getting. Why did you think I'd even consider wanting to leave you when the Tramontine suggested you might not cease to exist at any moment?"

She gazed at him, her eyes steady on his. "Because everybody leaves, Kayl Owen. Everybody leaves. Everybody except my mother, and she was taken from me."

There it was. Finally. "I'm not leaving," Owen said. "You can tell me to go, but I won't leave on my own. Never."

"Yes, you will. I'm an alloy."

"Stop saying that! That's always your answer!" He glared at her, trying to come up with words, his hands working in front of him. "I know now how much being an alloy has defined your life. Defined it in often terrible ways. I can't fix that. But I can tell you that as far as I am concerned, the greatest day of my life is when you came into it, and the worst day will be when you leave it. I wish for just one moment you could see yourself through my eyes, and you'd see how amazing you are, and that no man in his right mind would ever leave you." Owen lowered his hands. "You wouldn't just see an alloy. Because I see a lot more than that. I see you. All of you. And it's . . . it's awesome."

She stared at him, silent for a long moment. "You . . . you . . . what is wrong with you?"

"Nothing that you haven't made right." He looked steadily at her. "I love you."

She gave him that stare again, the one that mingled disbelief and wonderment. "Why do you keep saying that?"

"Because it's true."

"I can't . . . Kayl . . . you do mean it, don't you?" Selene's eyes stayed on him as if trying to look inside him. "Why don't you see that it's impossible?"

Owen shook his head. "Time travel is impossible. Changing the past is impossible. Falling in love with you was easy. Look, you don't have to return the feeling. It's not conditional. I will stay with you as long as you need me, regardless. I will do everything I can to carry out the mission, regardless. But I need to be honest with you about how I feel."

"'All's right that happens in the world,'" Selene murmured. "Oh my God. I love you, too. I never expected to be able to say that to anyone, but I'm pretty sure that's what this feeling is. What have you done to me?"

Owen couldn't breathe for a moment. "Seriously? You mean that?"

"Yes. I do. I want you to stay with me for as long as you're willing." She shook her head, looking away. "But your delusions don't change things, Kayl. Just because you . . . see me that way . . . doesn't mean anyone else will. I've told you what life is like for an alloy. It would be like that for both of us."

"We're trying to change everything else," Owen said. "Why not change that, too?"

"What?" She stared at him again in disbelief. "Change what?"

"How people see alloys."

"That is irrational, Kayl. That *is* impossible. You're serious, aren't you? Kayl, we don't need that hill. We've already got a really big hill, trying to save the Earth."

"Maybe," Owen said, "that hill and the trying-to-save-the-Earth hill are the same hill. You've told me how things spin out of control in the future, because no one knows who to trust. You're already trying to change that. Look at the speech you gave in the Martian Commons."

"That wasn't . . . I was just responding to events, Kayl."

"You told them to trust you!" Owen said.

"No, I didn't! I told them I would fight for them, and protect the Earth, and was no danger to them." She hesitated. "All right. That might be sort of similar."

"If they realize they can trust you, it will change how they see alloys." He paused, his gaze on her worried. "So, since we . . . love each other, can we plan for the long term, Selene? Can we come up with another plan for right now?"

She watched him for several seconds, not saying anything, as if still trying to absorb what had just happened. "Yes. We should do that. Go ahead."

He could feel in her voice that her words weren't a challenge, but a genuine invitation. Which meant he'd been an idiot. "Is that what part of this is, Selene? I've been waiting for you to tell me what you wanted to do next. Have you been waiting for me to suggest something?"

"Maybe."

"Damn," Owen said. "I've been deferring to you, thinking this was your mission and you needed to be able to direct it as you wanted, but what you wanted was for me to stop dumping the responsibility for decisions like that on you."

After a few moments, Selene nodded. "I don't want you making decisions without me, Kayl, or trying to tell me what we have to do. But I do want you to actively express your feelings and your opinions. We're equals in this, right?"

"No," Owen said. "Not when it comes to the mission. This is your mission to command. I'm supporting it. I'm supporting you. But I'm going to start being more proactive."

"That . . . would be welcome, Kayl. It would take some of the pressure off of me," Selene said.

"I've got an idea. Let me know what you think. Can this orbital imagery pull back?"

"Yeah." Selene manipulated some controls that Kayl couldn't see, the image of Mars shrinking to a speck, the tiny dot of Earth appearing. "How's that?"

He looked at the orbital dynamics, thinking. "You said the Tramontine can modify the lifter?"

"Yeah. Roughly doubling the efficiency of the reaction mass conversion."

"Doubling it?" Owen blew out a breath. "Yeah, that could get us to Earth with some room to spare. How about this? On the lifter, we break free of the Tramontine ship. Earth Guard will assume we're aiming to land on Mars, because anything else would be nuts. Instead, as they alter vectors to intercept any landing attempt, we boost out on a vector for Earth. If the Tramontine can give us that much extra capability, we can get a good velocity up in time to prevent Earth Guard from intercepting us."

Selene shrugged. "What prevents the Earth Guard ships still near Earth from intercepting us when we get close enough? Why wouldn't Earth Guard intercept us well short of the planet?"

"Because I'll give them an easy target," Owen said. "Make it look like we've got no maneuvering mass left, which would be the case if we didn't have those Tramontine modifications you talked about. Can you zoom this in on the Moon?"

"Sure." The globe of the Moon suddenly grew, details visible.

"When they think we're in the bag," Owen announced, "unable to run, we shift vector and do a quick dash to here." He pointed to a sector of the Moon.

She leaned her head to look. "Why would we go to the Dead Zone?"

Owen stared at her, rattled by her casual statement. "That's the Free Zone."

"No, it's—" Selene took another look. "Oh. I forgot it's 2140. It's not the Dead Zone yet."

"When does it become the Dead Zone?"

"Twenty-one sixty-nine."

He waited, but she didn't seem to feel any need to elaborate. "What happened? I mean, what will happen?"

Selene's expression bore the marks of old anger. "Basically, some people did really bad things, then took refuge in the Free Zone. A lot of other people told the Free Zone to cough up the people who did the bad things. The Free Zone said, *No way, we're the Free Zone, we're neutral, and you can't do anything to us.* Then lots of other people did lots of things, and when they were done, it was the Dead Zone." She pointed to parts of the Moon. "These areas had a lot of lunar topography reworked. A whole bunch of big new craters."

"But—" Owen looked at the image of the Moon in dismay. "Why are you so casual about this? A lot of people must have died."

"Yeah," Selene said. "Because they were stupid, and they were protecting scum. My sympathies alter a bit when people bring things like that on themselves."

"But—"

"Have you ever visited Karachi, Kayl? If you want to, make sure it's before 2169." She pointed. "You see those Free Zone defenses on that image, Kayl? Guess how many of those defenses were working in 2169? None. Zero. Because everybody in the Free Zone thought somebody else would pay to keep them working, and even when hell was about to fall down on them, they still wouldn't pay. I remember seeing the news reports, Kayl. *You can't take my money to reactivate those defenses! That would be theft!* They were protecting scum, and they were stupid, so they died."

"But—"

"Kayl, in 2169, the world will be conducting grief triage. There won't be enough tears left. And the worst will be yet to come. No one wanted to shed any tears for the Dead Zone. They were cried out over Karachi. Remember what's going to happen to Albuquerque, Kayl? We'll cry over that, too." She looked at the image. "Where's the main settlement in the Dead Zone? I mean the Free Zone."

"Here," Owen said, pointing.

"Utopia Crater?"

"It's not a crater, Selene."

"It will be."

All Owen could do for several seconds was gaze at her silently. "This future you're trying to change, that we're trying to change. I knew it was bad. I didn't know how bad."

She kept her eyes on the image of the Moon. "Earth is going to die on the twelfth of June 2180. Do you need more details than that to motivate you?"

"No."

"This may be the best plan available to us, Kayl. It could work. But what happens once we get to the Dead Zone? I mean the Free Zone?"

"There's a tremendous amount of space traffic on and around the Moon," Owen said. "The Free Zone has smugglers who have perfected the art of getting people and things past Earth Guard and various police forces. If we make it to the Free Zone, they'll get us to Earth."

"How do they feel about aliens?" Selene asked.

"I don't know. We still have a whole lot of money on our anonymous cash cards. That should be enough for them to not worry about anything else from us."

"Even people who can be bought can turn around and betray you," Selene said. "All right. Let's do this."

"Seriously?" Owen said. "You like it?"

"It's doable," Selene said. "In a perfect world, I'd try something else, but we have to work in this far-from-perfect world with what we've got. This sort of thing is what I need from you, Kayl. When I'm wrapped up with the Tramontine or other things, for you to step back and see the big picture and tell me what you think we should do. We're a good team when we remember to talk to each other. I'll speak to the Tramontine about this plan and the modifications to the lifter. I think they'll be fine with it all. They haven't said so openly, but I think the Tramontine also recognize that as much as I did to ease First Contact, I've become a roadblock to further progress as long as I'm here on their ship."

She paused to look at him. "You're a roadblock, too, Kayl. I don't want to minimize your importance."

"Thank you. I think. Selene?"

"What?"

"No more suicidal plans. Are we agreed on that?"

A slow smile appeared on her face. "You keep making unreasonable demands of me. All right. Fine. If it's that important to you."

"There's nothing more important to me," Owen said.

"Kayl, I am not—"

"The hill. Right." He felt something loosen between them, a tension that had been born of unresolved issues. Was he seeing the bottom of that well? The last secret standing between them? "Are we good on the leaving thing, too? That it is not going to happen unless you tell me to go?"

"I'm still trying to accept that could be true," Selene told him. "That what we've said to each other today could be true."

"Tell you what, Selene. In twenty or thirty years, when we are still totally together, I'm going to tell you I told you so, and I expect you to admit you were wrong."

Her full smile was back at last. "That's a deal, Kayl."

"I do have one more question. Do the Tramontine make rations we could take on the lifter that have taratarabis in them? That stuff has really grown on me."

"It's good, right? Best alien rabbit ever. I'll ask along with all of the other things we need from the Tramontine. It's a good thing they like to share."

/////

"DR. OWEN! DR. OWEN! WHAT DO YOU THINK OF YOUR BROTHER'S ACTIONS WITH THE alien, Dr. Owen? Is he betraying the human species, Dr. Owen?"

That last finally made Malani Owen turn and confront the scrum of reporters who had ambushed her outside the company's offices as she arrived for work. "My brother's actions? What about Earth Guard's actions? They tried to kill my brother. I've seen that leaked report. You must have seen it, too. Why aren't you asking Earth Guard about its actions?"

"The leaked report has been officially denied—"

"They tried to kill him! But you're hounding me about the alien and what she's done? How many people has the alien tried to kill? Your own reports said those soldiers were shooting at her, and my brother, shoot to kill, but not one soldier got killed."

"Some were injured," a reporter said.

"Oh, excuse me! Some got injured while the alien was trying to stop them from killing her! *Her* name, by the way, is Lieutenant Selene Genji."

"She's . . . the alien isn't human."

"She told us some of her DNA isn't human," Malani said. "I'm a genetics researcher. Every single one of us here has Neanderthal DNA in us. Neanderthal. That's not *Homo sapiens sapiens*. Every single one of us has nonhuman, 'alien' DNA in our makeup. Does that make any of us less 'human' than anyone else?"

That shut them up for maybe two seconds. "You're saying you support your brother's actions?"

"I love my brother. I'm sure whatever he is doing is for the right reasons. Yes, I support him." *Even though he didn't have to make my life this difficult!*

"Are you comfortable with the idea of an alien as your sister-in-law?"

Malani almost didn't answer the provocation, but she was, after all, part Owen. "I'd much rather have that alien as a sister than some of the humans I've met."

She turned away, but before she could enter the building, a final question stopped her.

"Dr. Owen, Jim Tregarth, *Style Nova*. Do you know how she treats her skin to get that look?"

Malani spun to look at the questioner in bafflement.

"The glow," Tregarth continued breathlessly. "How does she do it? Millions of people want to know."

"It's . . . natural. As far as I know. That's how her skin naturally looks."

"Major cosmetics corporations are reportedly making big investments in trying to create products that will allow others to have that glow. Are you assisting them in that research?"

"I . . . I'm a doctor, Jim, not a cosmetician."

"Is there any chance you can answer some questions about her secrets? About how she maintains her appearance? About how she handles makeup around those eyes?"

"I don't know anything about her, uh, beauty secrets," Malani said. "I have to go."

She went into the building, confused. From what Aunt Hokulani had said, Genji had been unhappy with her skin, seeing it as some sort of banner proclaiming her difference. But now "millions of people" wanted that same look?

Granted, it did look really good on the videos she'd seen.

One of the lab's leaders was waiting for her inside the building.

"Good morning, Dr. Jerez." *Am I going to be fired or just put on long-term leave for the good of the company?*

"Dr. Owen." Jerez reached out to lightly touch her shoulder. "The lab's leadership has been discussing what's going on. We want you to know that you have our full support. These aliens, the Tramontine, appear to offer unmatched opportunities for the human species. We can't afford to give in to hysteria. Keep up the good work, Dr. Owen."

"Umm . . . uh . . . thank you."

Most, though not all, of those within earshot applauded.

Applauded her.

She'd have to share this story with Kayl the next time she saw him. Assuming that he didn't get himself killed before she could see him again.

Malani's high lasted until she sat down at her desk and logged in, to find her message files clogged with a wide variety of often crude death threats.

Her mother had been urging her to hire a bodyguard. Not easily done on a researcher's salary, but maybe a good idea.

GENJI PAUSED TO CHECK SOME POWER COUPLINGS. THE TRAMONTINE HAD DIVED into modifying the lifter, going beyond her requests. She'd been able to answer most of the Tramontine questions about the lifter systems but sometimes had run into something so old she'd had to ask Kayl about it. After the changes to a number of systems, including life support, it would safely make the run to Earth.

"How's it look?" Kayl asked her.

She looked up at him and smiled. "It's looking good, Master of Flight."

"Do you realize how much grief I'll catch if you call me that around other humans?"

"Of course I do. We've got everything ready to go, and supplies aboard, including your taratarabis packets. We can take off at any time. What do you think?"

"I think . . ." Kayl looked around as if he could see through the lifter to all of the ships in orbit about Mars. "Earth Guard has gotten complacent with us just sitting here. And they've got too many ships running at once because of the 'emergency' of First Contact, so there must be equipment problems piling up and personnel being run ragged."

Genji stood up and stretched. "In the Unified Fleet, personnel being run ragged was the normal order of business."

"I guess that's true of Earth Guard as well. Would you mind stretching again?"

"Keep your mind on our task, Lieutenant Owen. So, when?"

"About ten hours," Kayl said. "If they stick to the pattern they've been developing, three or four of the Earth Guard ships that will still be in orbit at that time will be in degraded status while they work on critical systems. That'll make our escape easier."

"Okay. Ten hours. I'll tell the Tramontine. They'll be happy to see you demonstrate your flight skills again.'

Kayl gave her a weary look. "Is that Master of Flight thing going to follow me around forever?"

"Only as long as you're with me," Genji said.

"So, forever."

She'd stopped questioning such statements. Why not believe along with Kayl that it could last? "If we survive this latest thing," she said.

The Tramontine were indeed both sad and understanding of her need to depart their ship. "Impossible to calculate value of knowledge you have shared," one told her. "Impossible to offer adequate thanks for assistance in First Contact. Very concerned for safety of you and the one who shares your life."

"I have to keep moving, keep trying," Genji said. "The one who shares my life will do so as well. We will save the Earth."

"Amazing experiment. Our theorists wonder if possible."

"I'll prove it is. And we will have learned something very important. Is that not what gives meaning to life?"

Genji saw Tramontine smiles. "This is Tramontine in you! Seeking answers to such questions! Permit us to be proud?"

"But also," another Tramontine said, "permit us to remind you, meaning in life is not only seeking answers, but finding answers in those you share life with."

"I think I am finally learning that," Genji said.

"Will you permit us one more thing?" a Tramontine woman asked. "To share with you a Tramontine name?"

"A Tramontine name?" Genji said, startled.

"For us to speak of you. Is this acceptable to you?"

"I . . . yes."

Genji saw the flat-lipped Tramontine smiles all about her. "We wish to share this name for Lieutenant Selene Genji. To us, also, now, Sister."

"Sister?" Genji felt further words freeze in her throat and had to take in a long, trembling breath. "You share this name, with me? I am not Tramontine."

"You ask questions, you seek answers, you attempt to learn things no one has ever discovered," another Tramontine said. "You are Sister to us."

"Thank you," Genji said, trying desperately not to cry.

SEVERAL HOURS LATER, GENJI AND KAYL SAT IN THE LIFTER. THE LOWER LEVEL WAS packed with extra supplies. Kayl was running final system checks. "I've been doing this every day," he said, "so if the Earth Guard ships pick up any indications of activity from the lifter, they should discount it as a routine thing that hasn't been followed by any actions. Are you okay?"

"Why wouldn't I be okay?" Genji said, reviewing her own

knowledge of the antiquated status displays on the lifter so she could read them as well as Kayl could.

"Ever since you came back from saying goodbye to the Tramontine you've been sort of out there. What happened?"

"I just received a Tramontine name," Genji said. "I'll tell you about it later. I'm focusing, okay? I've learned to read these displays. I'll be ready when we lift."

"All right," Kayl said. "Can I ask you something else?"

"More questions. Business or personal? We're getting ready to run a gauntlet here."

"Business, I guess," Kayl said. "Just something I realized I never got an answer to. On the wreckage of your ship I saw sort of a motto written on one bulkhead. *We Are One.* I never got to ask you about that."

"That is, or will be, the motto of the Unified Fleet," Genji said. "If there ever is a Unified Fleet."

"It's a really good motto," Kayl said, clicking through some more system checks. "I guess that was a response to all of the divisiveness?"

"Yes," Genji said, watching the orbital movements of ships displayed on the panels before her. "That was our ideal. A lot of people died fighting for that sentiment. *We Are One.*" She fought off a wave of sadness, thinking of friends who'd perished in the years before Earth itself died.

"That's still what's motivating you, isn't it?" Kayl asked. "*We Are One.* Full humans, alloys, everybody."

"Yeah, I'm kind of stupid that way."

"I'm proud to be stupid that same way with you," he said. "We're ready to roll, Selene. The Tramontine can release the lifter."

Genji called over the transmitter. "Please separate this craft from the landing platform. It is time to sever."

"Understand. Commands sent. Ships may sever, but spirits remain connected. May you find difficult questions, Sister, and your Master of Flight."

It was a very Tramontine form of well-wishing. "May you all also find difficult questions," Genji said. "Thank all of you for all you have shared, including a name I will forever treasure." She ended the call. "They're releasing the lifter, Kayl." This was a tense moment. If Earth Guard had optical sensors closely focused on the lifter, they might see the tie-downs being opened and the air lock pulling back.

"Got it. Yeah. We're loose."

Kayl moved some controls, the primary propulsion lit, and the lifter bolted away from the Tramontine landing platform.

CHAPTER 13

O WEN KNEW THERE WOULD BE ALARMS SOUNDING ON THE EARTH GUARD SHIPS in orbit about Mars, crews suddenly jolted out of the boredom and routine of their days. Automated systems would be estimating the track of the lifter, deciding the most likely paths it would take on its way back down to the surface and making recommendations for maneuvers to ensure the lifter was trapped and couldn't rise again without being destroyed.

Owen held the lifter on a vector for a reentry near Olympus Mons, a vast volcano whose interior was a maze of lava tubes. They weren't really suitable for humans to hide in, but legend said they were, and it seemed a good decoy site. Earth Guard senior officers would surely assume the disreputable Lieutenant Owen would be dumb enough to try to seek refuge there. He kept the thrust from the lifter at a normal level for the ship, not wanting to reveal yet how its capabilities had been enhanced by the Tramontine modifications.

He watched the movements of the Earth Guard ships. As he'd hoped, three of them weren't reacting, having been temporarily disabled by repair work in orbit. That had the remaining ships scrambling to cover the gaps.

One of those ships was *Vigilant*. His former ship, the officers and crew well-known to him. Garos was no longer in command, but Owen had no reason to believe Commander Kovitch would be any less willing to target a ship he was on. How would the others in the crew feel about that? Would anyone hesitate? Surely Joe, his former roommate, would. Surely Sabita would. What about Lieutenant Commander Singh? No telling. He couldn't risk his life and, more importantly, Selene's life on the chance that one of them would be able to impact the outcome of an attack on him. He'd have to assume *Vigilant* was just as dangerous as every other Earth Guard ship out here, something that left him not so much sad as bitter, thinking of the bonds that should have restrained more of his former shipmates.

"We're now outside the range of the Tramontine defenses," Selene said, her voice calm. "We're about to enter firing range for the nearest Earth Guard ship."

Owen did his best to shove his thoughts about *Vigilant* to the back of his mind, looking carefully at the movements of all of the ships and the lifter, feeling their relative motion, judging the right moment. Having Selene able to back him up fully meant he could focus on the maneuvering of the ship. "Is anyone attempting to contact us?" Would there be a last-moment attempt to get him to surrender himself and Selene?

"No," Selene said. "The nearest Earth Guard ship is positioning for a firing solution. I give it ten seconds before they engage us."

He didn't question her assessment. Earth Guard knew he was trapped, knew the lifter couldn't escape, but was preparing to kill him and Selene before they could reach the surface. He wondered why. Maybe Earth Guard brass was worried about the reception Selene might receive on the surface by the Martians who saw her as the hero of the Commons during the short-lived period of martial law?

It was time.

Owen used thrusters to swing the lifter about, angling it for the dash away from Mars.

"We've got a new problem!" Selene called out.

One of the "disabled" Earth Guard ships had been playing possum or had been able to get critical systems back online, and had suddenly begun accelerating at maximum for an intercept of the lifter.

"They're going to cut too close to our planned vector," Owen said. "Hell. Okay." He used the thrusters to pivot the lifter again, cutting in the primary to push the lifter along a vector as if planning to head for the colony.

"You're going to skim atmosphere?" Selene said.

"Sure am." He wasn't surprised she'd been able to read the vector so fast.

"That's going to take us within firing range of four Earth Guard ships and the orbital defenses near the colony."

"Their firing solutions will assume the lifter can't exceed its normal thrust and acceleration," Owen said. "Let me know if you see any Earth Guard ships on more distant vectors moving to block us if we head away from Mars."

"Not so far," Selene said. "Except for the one that sprung that surprise, they're all heading to hit us as we enter atmosphere."

"What's that one doing?"

"Coming about and down. Closing our path if we tried to cut back again."

"We're good, then." Owen used the thrusters and primary to alter his vector, diving toward the surface of Mars, watching the tracks of the four Earth Guard ships ahead converging toward him.

"The closest two ahead and above us are getting ready to fire," Selene said.

"Hang on." Owen used the thrusters again, not aiming for a vector toward Earth, just one out and away from Mars. He hit the primary again.

"We've got four missiles inbound," Selene said.

"Got it." Owen held down the primary propulsion command,

feeling the lifter leaping higher away from Mars, alarms suddenly sounding as the lifter's systems warned of overstress. Under normal circumstances, the lifter was a bit cumbersome, designed to reach orbit and return to the surface efficiently rather than quickly.

The modified lifter could accelerate at twice the rate of normal lifters.

Owen grunted as the g-forces built, pressing him back into his seat.

"Missiles still inbound," Selene reported. She sounded totally unaffected by the pressure of acceleration. "I'm seeing one of them outside of engagement parameters. But the other three are locked on and are still closing."

"Understood." Owen fought against the pressure as he reached for the thruster controls. He shifted the heading of the lifter again, aiming for a vector not only away from Mars but headed toward Earth.

"We need another boost," Selene said. "Two of those missiles are a little too close."

"Understood." Owen twisted the primary control, activating more thrust from the Tramontine-modified system, alarms jangling, the structure of the lifter emitting a frightening, prolonged groan. "Can't hold this long."

"Five more seconds," Selene said.

Another alarm began clanging harshly. A warning suddenly blared, the lifter's "voice" sounding frantic. "Reduce acceleration! Reduce acceleration! Main structural failure imminent!"

"We're good," Selene called.

Owen released the primary propulsion control, causing immediate relief from the acceleration pressure. He checked the track of the missiles, seeing the last two had expended their propellant and ceased closing on the lifter. They'd reach their built-in engagement limits soon and self-destruct.

All of the Earth Guard ships had been caught flat-footed by the lifter's sudden dash into space. They were swinging onto intercept vectors, but Owen knew they'd abandon those soon, knowing how much reaction mass they'd have to burn to try to catch the lifter. "How are we doing on the vector to Earth?" he asked.

"Just about dead-on," Selene said, sounding amused. "Show-off."

"Really?" How had he managed that?

"Good work, Master of Flight."

Owen took a deep breath, trying to calm his heart rate. "That was a little more intense than I counted on."

"Every plan is a challenge thrown in the face of chance," Selene said. "Hey, we've got a message alert. Someone is trying to call."

"Let's see who it is," Owen said.

The panel lit up with the face of Rear Admiral Meng. "Owen, your actions are futile. That lifter can't get you to Earth. You'll die on the way."

"Admiral, you just tried to kill me. Why this sudden concern for my life?"

"You should have just enough reaction mass to get back on a vector to pass close to Mars. Agree to surrender, and one of our ships will intercept that lifter and take you off."

Owen reached to pan out the message view so Selene was visible. "There are two of us in this lifter," he said.

Meng kept looking at Owen as if he were the only person in view. "This is your last chance, Owen. Do you want to die slowly, alone?"

"I'm not alone, Admiral."

Selene leaned forward. "Admiral, this is Lieutenant Selene Genji. I just wanted you to know that your missiles suck, and your battle maneuvers are slow and clumsy. Your ships really need to work on their combat training. I'm willing to help you with that since you don't seem to have any personal combat experience."

Despite his efforts to avoid looking at her, Meng couldn't help directing a glare at Selene. "You can't defeat Earth Guard."

"I'm not trying to defeat Earth Guard, you incompetent hack. If I was, you'd all be toast. But I'm on your side. I'm trying to help you. Please stop trying to kill me."

"Owen! This is your last—!"

Owen killed the communications link. "Really, Selene?"

"What?" she said, projecting innocent surprise at his reaction.

"That message was probably being monitored by a lot of other Earth Guard ships."

"Good," Selene said. "I know it's not easy on you having your life threatened, but being ignored by the same people trying to kill me is getting old. Besides, there's this person really close to me who's been telling me I shouldn't hold things in where they can eat at me on the inside."

"What idiot told you that?" Owen said, wondering if he should have given Selene that advice, and watching the Earth Guard ships breaking off their pursuit. "You know, anyone running the maneuvers would see that Admiral Meng's offer to me was nonsense. Without the Tramontine modifications, I might have been able to get the lifter back on a vector close enough to Mars for Earth Guard ships to fire on it again, but they couldn't have managed an intercept and rescue."

"That guy lied?" Selene said. "I'm so shocked."

"The thing is, everybody else can tell he lied. Why did he hang that out there where so many people can see it?"

She sighed. "Having dealt with some ruthless opponents, I'd say it was because he wanted credit for killing us. Then he'd be a hero. Instead, he's the guy who let us escape. Twice. Within about half an hour, his superiors in Earth Guard are going to be preparing the altar they're going to sacrifice him on."

"That's a persuasive argument," Owen said. "We still need to do a short burn to get us on the exact vector to Earth, and after that we'll have about five weeks of nothing happening except Mars getting smaller and Earth getting bigger."

"We'll have a lot of personal time together," Selene said, "but even with that, five weeks will be a while in something this small."

"We can take bets on which Earth Guard ships near Earth are going to be vectored to intercept us short of the planet," Owen said.

"I'd rather get started on the personal time," Selene said, unbuckling her seat harness. "We were too tense to do anything last night."

"I'm not going to get attacked this time?" Owen said.

"Oh, you wish."

THE LIFTER HAD MINIMAL ENTERTAINMENT OPTIONS, AND MOST OF THOSE SEEMED to have been devoted to pornography that (like most porn) was boring, repetitive, and unimaginative. With limited space aboard, neither one of them could ever feel like they had privacy, which proved harder to bear than Genji had expected. An epic fight on the eighth day, over exactly what she wasn't sure (and apparently Kayl also didn't know exactly what they'd been arguing about), led to a mostly silent ninth day, followed by apologies by both of them on the tenth, and a growing sense of closeness.

They increasingly spent long periods sitting together on the flight deck, not talking much, something Genji had thought would grow intolerable but that instead felt increasingly comfortable. Because, she realized, there was no longer anything lurking in the silence between them, waiting to pounce. "All right, your turn to choose a topic."

Kayl squinted at the images of the stars outside. "I can't really think of anything else."

She could hear it in his voice. "Except?"

"Well, things you don't want to talk about."

Genji laughed. "That doesn't narrow things down much, does it? Toss it out, and if I throw it back you'll know not to bring it up again."

Kayl paused before speaking a single word. "Sisters."

"Do we have to?" Genji sighed, leaning back to look at the overhead, wishing she had never mentioned them. "I had two older sisters. Both full human. Both of them were horrified to discover they had a new sibling who was an alloy, and decided to deny it. Neither one of them ever spoke a word to me."

"Not a single word? Ever?" Kayl said in disbelief.

"Not a single word. Ever," Genji said. "They told everyone they knew that they were the only children in the family and left 'notes' around the house attesting that no one else lived there but our mother. They both eventually left for college, and I've never seen either one since, even at Mother's memorial service. They're both dead now, of course, along with everyone else on Earth."

He didn't say anything for a while. "But if you save the Earth, you'll save them, too."

"I know. Can't be helped. But I think about how incredibly upset they'd be to owe their lives to me, and that's some compensation." Genji looked over at him. "Mother told me I shouldn't hate them. And I try not to. I really try. To honor my mother's wish. But it's really hard, Kayl."

"Is it okay if I hate them?"

"Be my guest."

"And now you have that Tramontine name?" Kayl asked.

"Yeah." She heard her voice catch slightly. "I can't tell you how much that means to me. Sister. They claimed me. I can be human in my heart, but also be accepted by the Tramontine. Two origins, and now, I guess, two families. I know I don't have any real right to claim your family as mine, but it sort of feels like that to me."

"I heard Aunt Hokulani say you'd have a home with her," Kayl said, smiling. "As long as we're sharing our lives, I don't think anyone in my family would object. There's something I don't understand, though. This Tramontine name sharing really seemed to hit you hard. Didn't you . . . won't you have a Tramontine name in the 2160s or '70s?"

Genji shook her head. "No. None of the alloys did." She felt a sad smile form. "Do you know why? Because all of these people who were trying to help us, help all of us alloys, advised us and the Tramontine not to get too close to each other. Because they thought if we spent too much time with the Tramontine, people who were worried about the alloys would focus on that as a reason to call us aliens, too. We were supposed to emphasize our human sides to help all other humans accept us."

Kayl sighed. "From what you've told me, that didn't work very well."

"It didn't work at all," Genji said. "The people who were uncertain about us didn't see how much we were isolated, and those who were afraid of us weren't going to be less afraid no matter what we did. All we ended up doing was cutting ourselves off from a source of support and . . . and love. Because of people who thought they were helping us, thought they were giving us the best advice."

"I'm sorry, Selene." Kayl shook his head, staring out at the stars. "My father once told me that the more sure I was that my intentions were good, the more important it was for me to question what I was doing. Because people tend to think that if their intentions are fine, then whatever they do must be fine, too."

"I wish I'd met your father," Genji said. "Permit me to be envious?" she added, using Tramontine grammar. Time to turn the topic around. "Enough about me. What about you? One big sister, right?"

"Yeah," Kayl said. "Malani."

"Her name is not enough. I spilled my guts, you spill yours."

"There's not much spilling to do," Kayl said, spreading his hands. "Mal is a big sister. Not too prone to ceding her authority as the eldest. We've butted heads a lot, probably because we're so much alike we can't live together without fighting, though neither one of us would ever admit that to the other's face. But when I was little she always stood up for me and looked out for me. And when . . ." He paused, clearly struggling to keep speaking. "When our father died, and I thought the universe had broken and could never be fixed, Mal was there with me, helping me through it. Her heart was broken, too, but she helped me through it."

Genji smiled, surprised she could be happy for Kayl and not at all jealous. "She sounds like a good person."

"Yeah, for a big sister. I still wish she was easier to live with."

"As priorities go, would you really make 'easy to live with' your highest one?"

He looked at her, grinning. "Obviously not."

"I jumped right into that one, didn't I?" Genji said. "How do you think Malani feels about . . . uh . . ."

"You?" Kayl said. "I predict if and when we ever manage to meet again, she'll give me a hard time and treat you like the little sister she always wanted instead of me. And she'll want a sample of your DNA. Because of the genetic research thing. But don't worry. She'd never pressure you."

"Maybe she should have it," Genji said. "My genome might help someone. At least there should be a record, especially if something goes wrong with me. I could trust Malani with that, couldn't I?"

"I'm sure you could. You're serious?"

"I'm not sure. But if anyone is going to have it, I think an Owen would be as trustworthy as I could get."

"Thanks." Kayl checked one of the panels in front of him, looking a bit embarrassed by her praise. "Nothing new on here to talk about. Looks like a few more options available among all the people tracking us."

"I thought everybody in the solar system was already tracking us," Genji said. All it took was a telescope, or a link to a shared telescope, and some basic flight software for anyone to maintain a tight track on their current location and their movement.

"Not quite everybody," Kayl said.

"How are our polls doing?" Someone had started tracking

public opinion, and then others had joined in. Despite variations, the polls basically came down to three options—kill them, catch them, or leave them alone, what have they done?

"You're still a lot more popular than I am," Kayl said.

"It's a gift. No, seriously, is everyone in 2140 off their meds? I'm an alloy. They have noticed, right?"

"They've noticed," Kayl said. "There are also a lot more people who want *you* killed as soon as possible than want *me* killed as soon as possible. I'm a traitor to the species, but you're an alien. An alien with human DNA." He looked at her. "Some people are trying to shift that around. Instead of being a human with some alien DNA, they're trying to cast you as an alien with some human DNA."

"They're just getting a jump on attitudes in the 2160s and '70s," Genji said, trying not to let the news get to her.

"That argument was raised then?" Kayl said. "I mean, will be raised then?"

"It was, will be, a common form of personal attack," Genji said.

"But now it's showing up in 2140."

"Because I'm in 2140." She paused to think about it. "We've wondered about this, Kayl. Is my presence triggering debates decades earlier than they emerged in the history I know? Are those issues being confronted now instead of in 2160 or 2170? And is that a good thing, or a bad thing, or something that could go either way?"

"Attitudes haven't hardened," Kayl said. "It's wrapped up with the whole First Contact thing. And the role you've played in that."

"The role we've played in that. Kayl, what if my efforts to prevent Earth from being destroyed in 2180 are actually accelerating everything and will cause Earth to be destroyed earlier than that?"

"We can't know," he said. "But what's the alternative? Do nothing, knowing what's coming?"

"That's not an alternative," Genji said. "Not for me. But you saw what happened on Mars. I was going to intervene and cause some carefully thought-out changes to First Contact. Instead, chaos jumped into the game and we ended up with martial law and everything else. Are we making things worse? I'm not in control of a lot that's happening. Like with Tom Dorcas."

"Tom Dorcas brought that on himself," Kayl said.

"Yes, but you deserve to know that I didn't kill him on purpose." She'd felt increasingly unhappy with not having told him more about that. "I grabbed a weapon from Dorcas's assistant and didn't have time to check what it was but assumed it was a stunner. It wasn't."

Kayl frowned at her. "That assistant was carrying a lethal weapon? Do you think Dorcas knew?"

"There's no way to tell," Genji said, "but based on what I overheard him saying to his assistant, I don't think he would've cared."

"I guess that bit Tom Dorcas in the butt, then," Kayl said.

"More like the center of his forehead," Genji said. "But that particular accident created ripples that are still spreading. I have no idea what changes those ripples might cause."

Kayl shook his head. "It's like Admiral Tecumseh said. The ship of fate has a terrible amount of momentum to it. Changing its vector is hard. And that ship is being impacted by countless forces that we can't even begin to track, like what happened to us with Dorcas. How can we accurately predict how what we do will alter its course? Hey, did you see that latest interview with Tecumseh? She is really holding Earth Guard's feet to the fire."

"I saw it, yeah." Genji eyed the stars outside the lifter. "Our transit to Earth is itself generating a huge amount of attention even though we're only doing it because we have to. I wish I had a window into 2180 so I could see how all of this will play out! We still don't know for certain why I'm still here. Maybe it's because of that 'a cause must exist' theory, but maybe the changes aren't important enough to make inelastic time respond. How much more do we have to do? How much can any one person do?"

"One person changed my future," Kayl said.

"Are you making this all about you again?" But she smiled at him. "I guess that's one good thing I've accomplished."

"We've received another bunch of requests for interviews and lists of questions," Kayl added. "I guess we should try answering them again."

Genji made a face. "At least that way everyone knows we're trying to talk to them but Earth Guard is jamming our transmissions almost right away."

Kayl leaned forward toward his panels. "And here's a new announcement from Earth Guard. No, it's the same thing with the words moved around a bit. 'Earth Guard will intercept the lifter to protect Earth. Earth Guard will make every effort to take the alien and Lieutenant Owen into custody, but will have to respond with necessary levels of force if the alien and Lieutenant Owen attempt to attack when they are cornered.' In other words, they still intend to kill us, but only because they'll have to."

"Is there any chatter from the Dead Zone . . . the Free Zone?"

"Just the same sort of thing we're seeing from everywhere else." Kayl gave her a hapless look. "It's still our best option. We couldn't possibly run past all of the Earth Guard ships protecting the planet, and even if we miraculously managed that, during our entry into atmosphere, we'd be a duck sitting in a barrel for surface-based weapons." He winced. "You've got me saying it."

"I'm controlling your mind," Genji said. "Remember?"

Kayl didn't reply, his gaze on the news reports growing horrified. "A bomb? Aunt Hokulani."

"A BOMB?" MALANI OWEN MADE A FRANTIC CALL, WAITING WITH HER HEART IN HER mouth. "Auntie? What happened? News reports say there was a bomb."

"Yeah," Aunt Hokulani said. "Not a big one. Pretty scary,

though. My porch is wrecked. Good thing my place is one of those reinforced mega-storm-resistant structures built about 2100."

"Are you hurt?"

"Just a little. These paramedics are fixing me up. Are you a doctor?" she asked someone. "My niece is a doctor. She's single."

"Auntie! Are the police there?"

"Sure they are. Aren't you watching the news?"

Malani turned her attention back to the latest reports coming in, seeing the flashing lights and emergency vehicles. Everyone else in the lab seemed to be watching as well, their gazes shifting between the news and her office.

"Excuse me, Malani," Aunt Hokulani said. "These people have some questions."

Malani turned up the sound on her panel, listening, seeing a disheveled Aunt Hokulani speaking to a gaggle of reporters. "Yeah, just before the bomb went off I got a call saying my family was a danger to humanity because we're helping the aliens. We're a danger? The aliens are a danger? Aliens didn't put a bomb on my porch. You see my neighbors? Some of them could've gotten hurt. Not by aliens."

"You don't agree that extreme measures might be justified to protect humans?" a reporter asked.

"You mean, people have to be killed to protect people? Are you listening to yourself?"

Malani relaxed. It was still a scary situation, but at least Auntie was clearly all right.

A moment later Malani was staring at the news report in disbelief.

"When she was at my house," Aunt Hokulani said, "did I see an alien? No. I saw a young woman who was scared of what she'd have to face to help all of us, but who was going to do it. Because she was determined to help us all. What is wrong with that?"

The attention of the news broadcasters had been wandering but suddenly centered once more on Aunt Hokulani. "The alien was at your house?"

"Of course she was. And she isn't 'the alien.' Her name is Selene Genji. She's a lieutenant. Make sure you say that."

"She was at your house?"

"Yes. She spent the night. We had a very nice talk."

"Oh, no," Malani said. "Auntie, did you have to tell them that?" She did a frantic search before hitting the right result to make a call. "Albuquerque Civil Liberties? I need your help. My aunt is about to be snatched off the street by people in biohazard suits using unmarked vehicles, and her home locked down in total quarantine. Yeah. Yeah. That's her. You're watching, too? Is there any way you can get somebody there to protect her before she disappears into some classified facility? Thank you. I am so grateful. I promise I'll get a contribution to you as soon as I can. I owe you. Thanks so much."

Malani ended the call, staring worriedly at the news report.

"Is your aunt all right?"

She turned to see Dr. Jerez watching her. "I think so. The bomb didn't hurt her much. Now I'm trying to make sure she isn't hurt by people claiming to protect her."

"You did the right thing."

"I hope so. Cry havoc and let slip the lawyers," Malani said.

Jerez smiled and took a drink of coffee. "As long as we're on Shakespeare, have you read *Henry VI, Part 2*?"

"It's been a while," Malani said.

"That's the one where those trying to seize power say 'the first thing we do, let's kill all the lawyers.' It's a common laugh line," Dr. Jerez said. "But it's also Shakespeare's compliment to the legal profession. Those who want to take over know the biggest barrier to them is the lawyers helping to enforce the laws of the land and protect the lowest as well as the highest. Lawyers are sort of like white blood cells," Jerez added. "Don't you think so? They protect the body of society from those who would destroy it."

"Maybe," Malani said. "But sometimes those particular white blood cells seem to run amok."

Jerez laughed. "Of course. Who'd deny that? Dr. Owen, is there any vital part of the human body, any function, which can't malfunction? Can't start damaging the body it's supposed to be protecting?"

"I can't think of any," Malani said. "The immune system is particularly prone to that."

"Yes. Going after the body it's supposed to be protecting, and normally does protect. Lawyers are like that. They can cause damage. But they're also vital." Jerez paused in thought. "The human body offers a lot of lessons, don't you think? Everything is interconnected. Mess with one thing in the body, in the genetic code, and other things are going to react. Our bodies are a remarkable collection of improvisations and adaptations and modifications. The guiding principle isn't some ideology. It's very basic. What works? What can get the job done given what's available? What can keep this organism alive as long as possible?"

"That's true," Malani said. "It's all more complex than it seems at first glance, but the guiding principles are simple. Humans tend to strive for some sort of perfection in our lives and our institutions, but our own bodies are lessons in pragmatism."

"Exactly! You said it better than I did." Dr. Jerez eyed her, clearly thinking. "This is some pretty basic research we've got you doing. The lab is going to be standing up a new branch, focusing on whatever we can learn about these Tramontine, and whether that might benefit humanity in some way. I think you'd be a good fit for that."

"That's a big compliment," Malani said, thinking that it would also be a big promotion. "Thank you, Doctor. But, you know I can't promise I'll be able to get a genetic sample from Selene Genji. Even if I get access to her, she might not want to share that."

Jerez waved away her statement. "It's not dependent on that. We have to think about this regardless. Selene Genji. I have to remember to call her that. Referring to her as 'the alien' dehumanizes her." He suddenly had to smother a laugh. "Did I actually say that?"

"Well, it's true," Malani said.

On the news report, more vehicles were arriving at Aunt Hokulani's. Malani watched, tense, hoping the lawyers would get there soon.

It was strange to think that none of this would be happening to her or Aunt Hokulani, none of it would be happening at all, if Selene Genji hadn't pretty much literally suddenly appeared in her brother's life. "She calls herself an alloy," Malani told Dr. Jerez.

"Really? That's an unusual use of the term."

"I think whoever came up with it was trying to avoid all of the baggage that comes with bio-related terms like 'hybrids' and 'crossbreeding' and 'directed mutation.' Especially when those things are related to humans. From what Genji told my aunt, I don't think it worked, but I think that was the intent."

Jerez pondered that for a moment. "I'm not a metals person, but I think alloys are usually created to increase the strength or other desirable properties of metals. Using it for a human-alien cross certainly tells us what the intentions of the genetic engineers who created her were."

"But even she doesn't know the long-term consequences of her genetic makeup," Malani said.

Dr. Jerez frowned. "Ethically, that's dicey, even if her parents signed off on it. Do you have any idea what the benefits were supposed to be?"

Malani hadn't shared any of the things Auntie had told her, but maybe it was time she did. "The biggest one was probably the maximum human life span, potentially doubling it."

"*Doubling* it?" Jerez stared at her. "She could potentially bring that to the human species and we're trying to kill her? Dr. Owen, would you be willing to discuss these things with the senior leadership of the lab?"

"Yes," Malani said.

How might that change things? Hopefully for the better before they got worse.

/////

OWEN SAT WATCHING THE MOVEMENTS OF SHIPS NEAR THE MOON, TRYING NOT TO brood. The lifter was two days out from the vector change that would head them toward the Free Zone.

"Kayl, Aunt Hokulani is all right. We need to have our heads in what's happening here," Selene said. "Not on reports of what's happening on Earth."

He grimaced. "I know you're right, but . . . you saw those lawyers facing off with whoever those other people were. Auntie is still free, thanks to those lawyers, but she's dealing with these things because of me."

"Because of *us*," Selene said. "Mostly me."

"I want to be there to help protect her," Owen said.

"What would your auntie want you to be doing?"

"That is so unfair—"

"What would your auntie want you to be doing?"

Owen looked at Selene. "Helping you. Getting the mission done."

"And keeping yourself from getting killed," Selene added. "Listen to your lead tactical officer. That's me, by the way. How is that closest ship doing?"

Owen roused himself, concentrating on the depictions of movements of ships. "The *Lifeguard* is still closing for an intercept outside of lunar orbit." There was a certain irony in knowing that a ship named *Lifeguard* was bending every effort to kill him and Selene. "But they shouldn't be able to manage it."

"From here it looks like they will."

Owen shook his head, angry. "They shouldn't be able to. The amount of acceleration they're doing is exceeding what one of those ships should be capable of."

"How are they doing it, then?" Selene prodded him.

"They have to be running their primary propulsion too hot. And keeping it there."

"What will happen if they keep doing that?"

She was making him think, making him focus on what they had to worry about. "Potentially they could destabilize their power system."

Selene nodded. "You know what that means, right? I know what that means. The Unified Fleet had older ships that ran into that. It's incredibly dangerous."

"It is," Owen said. "Either that commanding officer is a reckless glory hound, or they're being ordered to do that by Earth Guard brass who don't want to risk us getting away again even if that means risking one of their own ships and crews to try to hit us before we get inside lunar orbit." He paused, his thoughts dark. "If the commanding officer was being that reckless on their own initiative, the brass could have told them to ease off. So it's the second thing."

He pointed ahead along their track through space. "We're entering a region outside lunar orbit that normally only sees interplanetary traffic. With that still nearly shut down because of the First Contact situation, it's going to be just us and *Lifeguard* in there."

Selene nodded, her eyes hooded. "We can evade them because of the Tramontine modifications to this lifter."

"Right," Owen said. "But if anything happens to *Lifeguard* as a result of them overstraining their systems, we're going to be the only ship nearby. That might require some difficult choices on our part, depending on exactly what happens."

"Yeah." Selene leaned forward over the controls in front of her. "The parts printer on this lifter is as basic as they get. But its program can handle a lot of things it can't print. There's something I need to work on. You can go back to worrying about Aunt Hokulani, but I wish you wouldn't."

"I'll inventory the remaining food," Owen said. "And do a physical check of the systems down there. I'm a little worried about the life-support filters."

"Good." Selene was already distracted, focused on whatever she was using the printer software and the available parts files to design.

Before heading down the ladder, Owen looked at the situation again, thinking how glad he was that he wasn't aboard *Lifeguard*.

A DAY AND A HALF LATER, NOT MUCH HAD CHANGED, EXCEPT THAT THE MOON WAS closer, and *Lifeguard* was a lot closer to the lifter. Still running her propulsion too hot. It was like watching a slowly inflating balloon, hoping it wouldn't pop but knowing eventually it would.

Selene hadn't slept much, working over the printer design software with only short breaks. "I've got one thing done," she told Owen when he brought her a meal. "I need the other thing finished, just in case. Is this the last of the taratarabis?"

"Yeah," Owen said. "I figured we might as well finish it off. How do you know what equipment you need to design?"

She sat back, flexing her shoulders. "Can you massage me a little?"

"If I have to," Owen said, pretending to be put upon.

"Thanks." Selene sighed happily as his hands worked on her shoulders and back. "This is still a potential problem on older designs even in 2180, and when I was being trained before that. I was initially assigned to an old ship after training, a really antiquated piece of junk. But the Unified Fleet needed every hull it could get into space. So I went to classes on unique concerns and unique requirements for those aged systems. And instead of a secondary specialty of targeting, I was going to primarily be in engineering."

"Primarily engineering?" Owen asked, surprised. "I thought your primary specialty was close combat."

"It is," Selene said, looking as if she didn't really want to explain this particular thing. "I'd volunteered for that and been turned down, but then . . . something happened, and I was accepted for close combat. Anyway, while I was still on the engineering track we covered this problem in particular, because in wartime there was a lot more possibility of overstraining the older systems in response to emergencies. I don't remember everything, but the software lets me test the design, and I know where the design needs to go, so I'm working my way into reconstructing it all."

Owen wondered what that "something" had been that happened, but Selene clearly was reluctant to go into that. "Why didn't you end up going to that old ship?"

She didn't answer for a moment. "It got blown to hell along with the entire crew."

Owen flinched. *Great job. You stepped in it again.* "I'm sorry."

"Do you want to know the name of that ship?" Selene said.

He eyed her, worried. "What was the name?"

"*Vigilant.* A really old former Earth Guard ship."

Owen stared at her, feeling a strange tightness in his guts. *Vigilant*, nearly forty years from now, wouldn't have had any of the same crew members, might have been modified a lot from the ship he knew. But still . . . "The first time we talked, you got really mad when I said we were aboard the *Vigilant*. Something about mocking their sacrifice. I'd forgotten that."

"I wasn't sure I should ever remind you. I ended up on *Vigilant* after all for a little while, didn't I?" Selene said. "Strange, huh? Maybe I should call *Vigilant* our ship? Maybe our efforts to save the Earth will also result in the fate of our ship and her crew being changed." She glanced at him, smiling very briefly. "We can hope."

Further explanation was halted by the beep of an incoming transmission.

Owen left off massaging Selene to accept the message.

He saw a female commander, one who looked like she hadn't been getting enough sleep. But if she was commanding officer of the *Lifeguard*, that lack of enough sleep wouldn't be surprising. "This is Commander Elizabeth Montoya, commanding officer of the Earth Guard ship *Lifeguard*. Lieutenant Owen, this is the only opportunity you will be given to surrender. Hold your vector until we intercept. Any attempt to change vector will be considered an attempt to escape, and force will be employed against you without further warning. Acknowledge this message and state your willingness to surrender. If deterioration of life support or other systems has left you unable to respond with a message, blinking the primary beacon on your ship will serve to communicate your willingness to surrender. *Lifeguard*, out."

Selene cast a dark look at the communications panel. "They still won't admit I'm on this ship."

"Do you think they'd actually try to capture us," Owen wondered, "or will they just open fire when they're so close we couldn't possibly escape again?"

"Let's not find out," Selene said. "We're going to alter vector before they get in range, right?"

"Just before they get in range," Owen said. "I've noticed when people have a while to set things up and then it gets suddenly changed at the last moment, they have a lot more trouble adjusting on the fly because their minds have spent so much time anticipating one outcome."

"Very good, Lieutenant Owen! I'll make a combat officer out of you yet." Selene bent back to work. "Any chance of more massage?"

"Sure. Why do you suppose *Lifeguard*'s systems haven't failed yet?"

She paused to think. "I'd guess they have some really good engineers nursing those systems along. But even the best can't keep things from coming apart really fast if that ship keeps doing that."

An hour and a half later, Owen strapped himself into the pilot seat. "Vector change coming up. How's that design coming?"

"Done. I was double-checking some things." Selene yawned, reaching for her own straps. "I guess we won't need it after all, though. We're still just out of range."

"Yeah, they're . . . what the hell?"

She followed his gaze to the lifter's panels displaying events in space. "*Lifeguard* is boosting?"

"That's crazy," Owen said, reaching for the thruster controls. "I guess they're trying to sprint within weapons range before we expected it. I'm going to . . . oh, hell. Damn."

Lifeguard's boost had suddenly cut off, along with her primary propulsion. The lights outside on the hull flickered erratically.

"Looks like she's on emergency power," Selene said. "Can they fire any weapons in that condition?"

"Not and hit anything. The particle beams can't shoot at all, and the fire-control systems for the missiles don't have manual backups."

"If those lights don't steady really soon . . ." Selene made an angry growl. "Kayl, they've caused it to happen. Their power system is locked into a self-sustaining destabilizing cycle. In roughly half an hour, that ship is going to blow itself apart along with its entire crew."

CHAPTER 14

OWEN GAZED AT THE SHAPE OF THE DOOMED *LIFEGUARD*, ITS EXTERIOR LIGHTS flickering like the death throes of a badly injured creature.

"Kayl," Selene said, her voice calm in that way it became during a crisis. "I can save them. They'll have full-capability equipment printers aboard, right? That can run off the emergency power?"

"Yes," Owen said.

"Get me a link and I can send them these equipment designs."

"Those will actually work with current human systems?" Owen asked, suddenly seeing questions he hadn't thought of before this.

"Yes!" Selene said. "They incorporate modifications learned from the Tramontine. Just like the sorts of things done to this lifter. Current systems will work with them."

Owen hit the transmitter control, seeing a halting, pixelated image of an ensign appear in response. "I need to talk to Commander Montoya."

"She's not—"

"Commander Montoya, Ensign! Now!"

Montoya's image appeared, the tattered picture streaked with ragged lines. Despite that, he could see the rigid worry on her face. "I'm busy, Owen!"

"We can save your ship, Commander," Owen said. "Lieutenant Genji knows how to fix the problem. She has components you can print out and install."

Montoya's eyes fixed on Owen. "Why?"

"Because I am Earth Guard!" Owen shot back.

"But . . . the alien . . ."

"We are one," Selene said.

"What?"

"I don't stand by and let people die! Let me send you the part data."

Commander Montoya shook her head, having apparently forgotten that she wasn't supposed to be admitting that Selene was aboard the lifter. "Our high-speed data links are down. The low-speed ones keep dropping sync. Nothing complex can get to us."

Selene let out a breath. "Then we have to bring them aboard so you can print them out."

Owen wasn't sure whether he or Commander Montoya looked more shocked by Selene's words. "Selene, they want to kill you!"

"They are going to die if we don't do this!" She looked at him, her eyes demanding. "Kayl, we can't save the world if we're not willing to put our lives on the line to save a few hundred people. Keeping talking to Montoya. I'm going to start bringing the lifter back to meet up with the *Lifeguard*."

Owen took a deep breath. "If you let Lieutenant Genji and me aboard your ship, we can save it."

Montoya stared at him, then reached for a control. "Engineering, status. Probably less than half an hour? It won't stabilize? It won't shut down? I understand."

Commander Montoya spent a precious couple of seconds staring at nothing before she looked at Owen again. "What's your price?"

"Safe passage onto your ship and off your ship. For me and Lieutenant Genji. That's it."

"Genji. The alien. I don't have authority to offer that, Owen."

Selene had been maneuvering the lifter closer to the *Lifeguard* but now leaned over near Owen to enter the call. "Just let me on the ship!"

"We need safe passage—" Owen began.

"They are going to die, Kayl! Let me on your ship, Commander! No promises. Just let me save them!"

Montoya stared at her. "Safe passage," she suddenly said. "On and off the ship. My word on it. I hope you can do what you say you can."

"If I can't, Commander," Selene said, "we'll all die together."

"Make sure you've got the data you need," Owen told Selene. "I'm taking the controls. I'll get us over there faster."

"Thanks. Did I mention I love you? Just in case . . . something."

"I love you, too. Remember what you promised me about suicidal plans."

"This isn't a plan, Kayl."

A moment later she was sliding down to the bottom deck while Kayl lined up on the main air lock of the *Lifeguard*.

The moment he brought the ships into contact, the automated docking sequence took over. Owen launched himself down to join Selene, waiting as the air locks matched up. "I'm trying not to think about what we're doing."

"As long as you stick with me," Selene said. She adjusted her Unified Fleet uniform. "Got to look good, right?"

"Yeah." Owen did the same with his Earth Guard uniform. "What's taking so long? Oh, they're having to mate the air lock on their side manually."

The air-lock doors finally swung open.

Owen saw Commander Montoya right there, waiting, at least a dozen sailors and officers with her, some of them carrying hand weapons.

But Montoya simply nodded to him. "Lieutenant Owen. If you and your companion would accompany me?"

She turned about, seeing the members of the *Lifeguard*'s crew staring past her at Selene. "Open a hole, dammit! We don't have time for this!"

A path opened, Commander Montoya moving quickly, Selene right behind her, Owen behind Selene, passing more sailors who were watching with expressions varying from curiosity to dread to hate.

Owen had never realized how much the inside of a ship in this sort of engineering crisis resembled a haunted house, the emergency lights forming strange patterns of illumination, the darkened areas unnatural, the normal hum of life support silenced so that the sounds of people speaking and moving seemed amplified and frightening.

What made it feel stranger was that he was very familiar with the layout of a cruiser like *Lifeguard*, because it was the same class of ship as *Vigilant*. Except for minor differences accumulated during overhauls and modifications, the deck plan of *Lifeguard* was identical to that of *Vigilant*. Owen might have been back aboard his old ship. He found himself snatching quick glances at the officers and sailors they passed, expecting to see familiar faces. But though the uniforms were the same—the same, in fact, as the one he wore—the people weren't.

They were near engineering when Commander Montoya halted in a repair compartment dominated by the hulking shapes of a couple of big multifunction parts printers.

Without asking permission, Selene went to the nearest, plugging in her data drive and tapping the control panel. "Old. Old, old, old," she said. "Slow. At last. Okay. Got it. Print." Hitting that command, Selene went to the other printer. "Accept the drive, you dinosaur!"

A hand came past her, tapping a command. "That should let you in, uh, Lieutenant."

"Thanks."

That voice was familiar. Owen turned to see Chief Gayle Kaminski. "Chief Kaminski?"

"Hi, Lieutenant Owen," Kaminski said.

"Lieutenant Genji said this ship must have really good engineers. She was right."

Chief Kaminski grinned, the expression filled with tension. "*Vigilant* didn't feel too comfortable after the, umm, accident with the courier ship. I requested a transfer. Sir, everything I know says this ship is doomed. Nothing can stop that self-sustaining cycle from accelerating until it blows us to hell."

"Lieutenant Genji knows things we don't, Chief."

"The survivor? Is that who she is?"

"Yes, Chief."

"We got nothing to lose, I guess."

"How long?" Commander Montoya demanded. "Engineering is estimating less than fifteen minutes left."

"Your old, junk printers are working," Selene said. "It's up to them. Where's an engineer?"

Chief Kaminski pulled herself forward, saluting. "Here, Lieutenant."

"See what's coming out here?"

"Looks like a power regulator that's about to give birth," Kaminski said, her eyes studying the part. "Redundant feedback loops?"

"Oh, thank you, universe, you've given me an engineer!" Selene cried. "You need to replace the standard power regulator coupling with this. See where it ties in?"

"Those the same fittings?" Kaminski asked in surprise.

"Yes. Standard Unified— I mean, standard Earth fittings. Over there. That other one finishing up. See it?"

"That's big," Kaminski said. "Power transfer bloc?"

"Have you worked with Lieutenant Owen? He mentioned you. Best damn engineer in Earth Guard, he said. Yes. You should be able to run some extensions to tie it in."

"Okay," Kaminski said. "But what about the software?"

"These will be transparent to the software, Chief. The software will just see what it thinks are the same components. But the components will dampen out that destabilization cycle. All you have to do is plug them in."

Kaminski looked to Commander Montoya, who nodded quickly. "Do it, Chief. Can you do it fast enough?"

"Let's hope so, Captain. Destry! Muthezi! Orestes! Help me haul these!"

The engineers pushed off with the components.

Selene reached out one hand to hang against a printer, watching them go with worried eyes.

A strange throbbing could be felt building within the ship. It made the hairs on Owen's neck stand on end.

Montoya had been speaking to someone. "My chief engineer says this can't possibly work," she told Owen.

"Lieutenant Genji says it will."

"How does the . . . how does she know that?"

"I can't tell you that, Commander. But believe me, she does."

The throbbing had grown in intensity.

"Five minutes left," Selene said, looking about. "Maybe. What a museum piece."

"You're calling my ship a museum piece?"

"No offense, Captain."

The throbbing was suddenly replaced by what felt as if the ship was shivering. Owen heard cries of alarm from the crew.

"It's okay," Selene called. "Relax. This means your engineers have the parts in place. They're interrupting and damping out the destructive feedback."

"We're out of danger?" Commander Montoya asked, no longer even pretending not to be treating Selene like any other officer.

"Not quite, Captain. But close."

With shocking abruptness, the regular lighting sprang to life, along with the hum of life support. The shivering in the ship's structure vanished.

A call came over the now-working internal communications system. "Captain, this is Lieutenant Commander Biyase in engineering. The power system has stabilized. I don't understand exactly how that happened. We have . . . we have one hundred thirty-one percent power resources available."

Montoya, still looking like someone facing a firing squad with loaded rifles who just received a pardon, blinked in disbelief. "Say again. One hundred thirty-one percent? Stable?"

"Yes, Captain. It . . . it looks permanent."

Commander Montoya's eyes went to Selene. "How long will this patch work?"

"It's not a patch," Selene said. "It's a modification. It'll last as long as your power system does." She rubbed her face wearily. "You can easily manufacture more for other Earth Guard ships. It'll make it easier for you the next time you're trying to run down Lieutenant Owen and me."

"Why?" Montoya demanded. "Why did you do this? Why did you put yourself into our hands this way? You know what Earth Guard orders are regarding you. You know what we were trying to do when the power system destabilized. Why did you do this?"

Selene looked around her at the watching sailors before answering. "Because I do not stand by and let people die. That's not how I was trained, that's not what I do. I am trying to save people." Selene slapped her Unified Fleet uniform with one hand. "We are one."

"But . . . you're not Earth Guard. You're not *human*," Montoya said.

Selene didn't answer, her eyes looking away.

"Commander Montoya," Owen said, "Lieutenant Genji's genetic profile does contain some alien DNA, but maybe that doesn't matter when it comes to her humanity. It didn't matter to her.

Lieutenant Genji came aboard this ship to save the crew, even though she knew she might not leave it alive. She came aboard even though she knew the parts might not print out in time and might not get installed in time."

Montoya eyed him. "The same question stands for you, Lieutenant Owen. I have orders regarding you as well."

"I'm aware of that. Like Lieutenant Genji, I wasn't going to stand by and let sailors die. And I wasn't going to let her face danger unless I was there facing it with her."

"Are you prepared to comply with orders, Lieutenant Owen?"

He took a deep breath. Here it came. "No, Commander. Not voluntarily. I have an important mission to fulfill."

"What mission?"

"Protecting the Earth. Lieutenant Genji and I . . . that's our mission." Owen looked around at the Earth Guard personnel surrounding them. All were staring at him and Selene. Some were carrying weapons. "What's the deal now, Commander Montoya?"

Montoya looked around them as well, and up at the overhead as if reassuring herself that her ship was indeed still intact, then back at Selene. "I made a deal. You kept your end. I'll keep mine."

"Captain!" someone protested. "That alien—"

"*Lieutenant Genji* saved this ship and all of our lives!" Montoya shouted. "Now, I order all of you to stand down. I will personally escort *these officers* back to their own ship. After that, I will notify Earth Guard of my actions and accept any consequences. Are there any questions?"

"That monster—" a chief began, raising a pistol.

The sailors around him wrestled the chief's arm down.

"Let's get you out of here," Commander Montoya said. "You know the way back, Owen? Go first. I'll follow." She pushed off last, moving behind Owen and Selene to keep her body between them and the crew members gathered in the compartment. "Lieutenant Owen."

"Commander?"

"I owe you an apology for stories I've repeated in the past without knowing anything about you. I anticipate this ship will have some problems maneuvering for a while. We'll need to ensure the safety of those new components. You should be able to make it well clear of us if you still have reaction mass available. I can't help noticing how close we are to your being able to get onto a high-speed vector to the Free Zone."

"Is that so, Commander?" Owen said. "You did seem eager to intercept us before we could make that vector change."

Montoya didn't answer for a moment. "I had orders. Make sure they don't get away again. No matter the cost. When the risks kept climbing, I protested and was told to keep on. I should have refused, no matter the cost to me. I didn't, and my crew nearly died. That's why I'm standing up now, letting you both leave. My backbone wasn't gone, but I hadn't used it enough. It's a lot stronger now. You should be able to make it to the Free Zone given the maneuvering problems my ship is going to have. But not everyone in the Free Zone may welcome Lieutenant Genji."

"I'm used to not being welcome," Selene said.

"A few hours ago I wouldn't have questioned why," Commander Montoya said. "Now I can't figure it out. I owe you more than words can express, Lieutenant Genji. I won't forget, although it's very likely I'll be under arrest before long. But I won't forget."

They'd reached the access to the lifter, the lock still open. "Get off this ship," Montoya said. "And good luck."

Selene paused in the lock before entering the lifter, raising her hand in a salute and watching Commander Montoya.

After a moment, Montoya returned the salute.

"Have I mentioned lately that you're insane?" Owen said as he sealed the lock behind them.

"You love me anyway," Selene said, heading for the piloting deck.

"That's because I'm also insane. Were you scared?" Owen added as he followed her and fastened his seat harness.

"After the stuff printed out, yeah. Before that I was too busy to be scared."

Owen reached out to her. "We are one."

"Damn straight." She reached out to touch his hand. "Should that be *our* motto? And are we going to get moving? Because I have a feeling Commander Montoya might not be commanding officer of that ship very much longer."

THE FREE ZONE BOASTED OF ITS INDEPENDENCE, OF ITS NEUTRALITY, OF ITS DEVO-tion to individual liberties. Its automated defenses had been installed by the founders of the Free Zone, a collection of wealthy individuals tired of contributing to the societies that had made them wealthy. As the lifter plummeted toward the landing field outside the main settlement of Utopia, Genji watched those defenses track the ship, wondering how much longer they'd continue to work after the original long-term maintenance agreements finally expired.

After not maneuvering for nearly half an hour, *Lifeguard* had suddenly shifted vector to once more try to intercept the lifter. But the lifter, using the Tramontine-modified propulsion, had enough of a lead that *Lifeguard* couldn't catch it before the lifter was inside the protection of the Free Zone's weapons. Which left Genji in the uncomfortable position of benefiting from the protection of a place she had personally loathed since she was eleven years old.

What would become Utopia Crater in 2169 was, in 2140, a collection of low hills marking larger and smaller towns buried mostly under the surface, lunar material excavated for the structures spread on top of the airtight ceilings and the streets between them as additional protection. Living on the Moon meant being a cave dweller, protected from the radiation and the vacuum on the surface, unable to directly view the astonishing number of stars filling the sky. The largest rounded hill rose nearly six meters above the surrounding landscape, large and small air locks leading into and out of it, the landing field positioned nearby.

"What's the population?" Genji asked as the lifter settled into a landing. Their attempts to call Landing Field Control had been met with automated replies, so they'd picked what seemed like a good spot.

"There's no official count," Kayl said. "Earth Guard estimates roughly ten thousand in the entire Free Zone. But that's not static. There's a hard-core group that stays, maybe three or four thousand. The rest come seeking some sort of paradise, realize the Free Zone isn't it, and leave. But there are always new ones to replace them."

"Let me guess," Genji said. "The ones who stay and never go have the money, because they exploit the ones who come here all starry-eyed and naïve before they leave when their money runs out."

"I don't know much about Free Zone economics," Kayl said, shutting down the lifter's systems. "I do know they keep the Free Zone running on smuggling and fencing stolen goods." He looked over at her. "Which I guess includes this lifter. What are we going to do with it? We could sell it."

"Not yet. I vote we seal it until we find out whether we'll need it again," Genji said.

"Okay, but I don't think we'll need it." Kayl pointed upward. "We've already got a couple of Earth Guard ships up there just outside the range of the Free Zone defenses, waiting for us to lift again. Taking off would be one of those suicidal things."

"Which I have already agreed to avoid," Genji said. "Looks like we'll have to wear suits to get into the colony. If we shed the suits, I'll go into my UV Aversive look again."

"They must know who we are and that we're here," Kayl said. "But I'll wear civilian clothes under my suit as well."

"There doesn't seem to be any reception committee," Genji noted.

After Kayl sealed the lifter, they trudged across the field in their suits, their backpacks little burden, Genji remembering her lessons in Moon walking from when she was younger, putting force into moving forward rather than into rising against the much lower gravity than that found on Earth. "They told me walking on the Moon is like riding a bike," she said. "Learn it once and you always know it. I guess that's true."

"Mars was harder to get used to," Kayl agreed. "But it still felt more natural than this."

They reached the nearest air lock, Kayl cycling it so they could step inside then wait until it repressurized before the inner door opened.

Inside, a long hallway offered views of unoccupied counters and security stations. The only visible movements were those of small cleaning bots automatically collecting the latest lunar dust to seep in.

"Nobody's here?" Genji said. "Not that I'm complaining."

"I guess it's nobody's particular job," Kayl guessed. "The Free Zone doesn't have border controls or a police force. No one else here seems interested in us. Not until Earth Guard posts a reward for capturing us, anyway. Which they will do once they realize that's how to flush us out of the Free Zone."

Reaching the end of the hall, they found a table with three people seated around it, playing games and drinking. "Landing fee," one of them grunted, holding out a hand.

Genji looked around, not seeing any fee charts posted.

Kayl brought out one of the smaller cash cards left to them. "Sure."

The one he handed it to gave the card a disdainful glance. "Not enough."

"It's what we've got."

The man looked over Kayl and Genji, apparently deciding they weren't good targets for a further shakedown. He went back to his game.

"Freelance landing-fee collectors," Genji commented as they walked on. She looked at the empty offices on either side, stripped of any equipment they might once have held. "It doesn't look like the landing field employs many people."

"Of course not," Kayl said. "You know how the Free Zone works, right?"

"I never cared all that much," Genji said, "and after it became the Dead Zone I stopped caring at all."

"There are only minimal fees that are supposed to be paid by those living here to support critical functions, but since there isn't anyone to enforce collection of those fees, everyone stopped paying them." Kayl spread his hands. "Free-lunch city."

"Nice for them. Until the lunch runs out."

"You don't like it here, do you?" Kayl asked as they walked out of the hall into a long street leading between low buildings, the colony roof at the same height as the tallest structures, everything the same dull shade of lunar gray aside from often-faded colorful signs. Even though they didn't need their suits and helmets inside the colony, they kept them on to conceal their identities.

"I can't forget Karachi, Kayl."

"It's 2140. No one here has been involved with that."

"They will be."

Understanding that it wasn't something she wanted to discuss, Kayl let the matter drop.

Why did we have to come here? Genji thought. *I guess we had no other choice to get back to Earth, but why?* She walked along beside Kayl, casting disdainful glances at the businesses on either side of the low-ceilinged lunar roof, most of which catered to the nearby landing field.

And came to a halt so suddenly, her mind reeling, that Kayl took two more steps before hastening back to her. "What is it?"

Genji pointed, wondering if this could really be it. "Pradeesh Ship Industries."

"Yeah." Kayl looked it over. "Small, looks like it's barely hanging on. Why do we care about that?"

"Because it's Pradeesh Ship Industries, and this is the Free Zone, and it is 2140," Genji said. "Don't you realize what that means? Come on."

He followed, with a puzzled expression, as she walked into the front entry, to find a few cluttered offices and workshops beyond. Not a lot of work seemed to be going on, most of the parts visible bearing all the signs of long-ago breakage and being cannibalized for spare components.

A middle-aged man in an executive's suit, but one marked by stains showing this manager had to work hands-on, came out to greet them. "How may I assist you?"

Genji looked him over, trying to control her excitement. Was this him? He looked like the images her mother had shown her. A bit younger, but otherwise the same. "Abraham Stephen Pradeesh?"

"Yes, that is me."

She looked closer, noting that he bore the signs of great grief, still visible in his eyes and face.

"I came to offer my condolences on the loss of your youngest son," Genji said, drawing a startled look from Kayl that he quickly tried to conceal.

"You know of that?" Pradeesh nodded gratefully. "It is still hard. Thank you." He looked upward. "When the aliens came, I wondered, will they come here? Will they reach the Moon in time to save my son? It was a silly fantasy. They did not even reach Mars before my wife and I lost our youngest."

"Are you angry at the aliens?" Genji asked. "Because they didn't save your son?"

"That would be unfair." Pradeesh seemed to be fighting back tears. "And being angry would not honor my son. He was the kindest, gentlest of souls. I will do well in his memory, not seek anger."

Genji smiled, once again trying to control her excitement. It really was him. "You want to go back to Earth, don't you?"

"How did you know? Yes. My whole family agrees on this. The Free Zone is not a frontier. It is a prison. But transport back, and bringing our son with us so he can rest with our family's ancestors, will require taking out a loan we may have great difficulty repaying. Is this what you have come to discuss?"

"No," Genji said. She pointed. "There's a lifter on the landing field. Technically, it's a stolen lifter."

Pradeesh shrugged. "Every ship on that landing field is either technically stolen or simply stolen. Does it need repair?"

"No. I'd like to make you a gift of that lifter."

It was hard to tell whether Pradeesh or Kayl was more astonished to hear that.

"A gift? Why?" Pradeesh asked. His eyes had grown wary.

"I should warn you the lifter has Martian registry," Genji said.

"Martian registry? How did you get it here when—" His eyes grew huge, looking from Genji to Kayl. "It is you? The Earth Guard officer and the one from another place?"

The one from another place. That was probably the nicest possible way to say "alien." Genji smiled again. "Yes. Would you like the lifter?"

"Is it . . . safe?"

"It may be dangerous." She pointed again. "The lifter has modifications to many of its systems. Efficiency, effectiveness, capabilities. Modifications made by the Tramontine aliens. If you examine them, learn how to copy them, sell them, you will become extremely wealthy. That has ruined more than one good person."

"It has." Pradeesh shook his head, running his hands through his hair. "Why? Why would you do this for me and my family? This gift is of immeasurable value."

Genji took a step closer to him to see how he would react, but Pradeesh didn't retreat in fear of her. It really was him. "You had something of immeasurable value taken from you. This gift does not come near to compensating for that. But it may allow you to do much good."

"There is a price," Pradeesh said. "Always there is a price. What is the price of this, one from another place?"

"That you speak your conscience and beliefs to others, and continue to be a good person. Is that price acceptable?"

"I do not understand." Pradeesh seemed to be gasping for air. "You are not from another world, are you? You have come from another realm, to give me this blessing. Tell me this is all true."

"My words are truth," Genji said. "You are worthy of this gift. The lifter is yours if you want it. The price I have named is everything required of you in return. I'll say that a third time to make it binding. There is no other price demanded of you. Do we have a deal?"

"Yes." Pradeesh gazed at her, tears coming again. "Bahisa!" he called. "Come quick!"

A woman a bit younger than Genji appeared, wiping her hands. "Yes? What is it? Why are you so unhappy? Are these thieves?"

"No. No. This is . . . this is . . ."

"Selene Genji," Genji said, nodding in greeting. "And you'd be Bahisa Pradeesh, the engineer."

"You know me?"

"I know of you."

"They . . . they have a lifter . . ." Pradeesh said.

"Give them the access codes," Genji told Kayl.

He first gave her a look that clearly conveyed *I hope you know what you're doing*. "There. Access code and flight codes."

"Repairs?" Bahisa asked. "How bad?"

"It is ours," Pradeesh said.

"What? Father, we cannot afford—"

"Listen! It is ours. Go to the lifter. Examine all of the systems. There should be many modifications. Tell no one of them. We must learn what they are and how to make them."

"But—" Bahisa stared at Genji again, catching sight of her eyes through Genji's suit helmet. "Father! Genji! This is that one!"

"This is an angel, Bahisa. Remember her." Pradeesh turned to Genji. "You asked no other price of me. What can I freely provide that you need? Name it."

"We need someone who can get us to Earth," Kayl said, as if afraid that Genji would say "nothing" and walk away. "No questions asked, no tracers, no tracking."

"Ah, of course you two need this. There is a woman. They call her Midea. Up that way. Big house. No one knows her name, and everyone knows her name. You understand?"

"Yes," Kayl said. "I've actually heard of Midea. She's on a lot of arrest warrants."

"I wouldn't mention that if I were you," Pradeesh said. "Midea can be sensitive. But they say she can get anyone to Earth, and no one in authority will hear a whisper of it. If you wish, I can take you there."

"No," Genji said. "You shouldn't be associated with us. You never saw us. All right?"

"Yes. I understand. If there is ever anything else—"

"I told you my price," Genji said. "Honor it, and we're good."

She led the way out of the building, watching as Bahisa dashed out in an old suit with her helmet in her hand and headed toward the landing field.

"Am I allowed to know what that was about?" Kayl asked, looking unhappy.

"I couldn't really explain," Genji said, looking up and down along the street. "Not in front of him."

"So who is he?"

"Abraham Stephen Pradeesh."

Kayl gave her an annoyed look. "I heard. Why is that important?"

Genji leaned her back against the front of the business, making sure no one was close by and could overhear. "My mother told me about him. She called him one of the great lost opportunities. In the 2150s and early 2160s, Abraham Pradeesh advocated for peace and understanding. People listened to him. But, according to my mother, he didn't have much money, so he could never compete for big audiences with the big names with deep pockets who backed the fanatics. By the mid-2160s he'd already been virtually forgotten."

Kayl sucked in a breath, staring at her. "But you just made him rich."

"Hugely rich," Genji said. "Kayl, in the history I know, the Tramontine modifications on that lifter were the sort of technology that big outfits like Dorcas Funds scooped up and used to become even richer and more influential. But Dorcas is disintegrating because I killed Tom Dorcas."

"Accidentally," Kayl said.

"Right. Instead, now, a whole lot of that money, that influence, will go to Abraham Pradeesh. Not to Tom Dorcas or people like him."

Kayl looked troubled. "But money like that can change people."

"I know. You saw I talked about that to Pradeesh. I don't think someone like him can fall fast enough in one lifetime to reach the pit where Tom Dorcas was. But suppose he does. We end up in the same place where my history went. Every other possible outcome should be a lot better. Possibly a whole lot better, with Abraham Pradeesh reaching and influencing a much larger audience."

Kayl still appeared unhappy. "But is Pradeesh really all that great? How can you judge him so quickly?" He saw the reaction to his words on her face. "Now what did I do?"

"My mother told me that Abraham Pradeesh could have changed the world," Genji said, emphasizing each word. "When I saw the sign for that business, when I realized that Pradeesh had been in the Free Zone in 2140, that we had ended up here, it felt like my mother had known I would be here, had given me that message, so when I had a chance, I could do something. She pointed me here, Kayl. She told me what I should do."

He gazed at her. "You really believe that, don't you, Selene?"

"Yes," Genji said, feeling the sort of utter certainty she rarely did about anything.

Kayl nodded, his eyes on hers. "Okay, then. I can't prove you wrong. I'm not sure why I'd want to try. It's not like we could ever raise that lifter again and survive the attempt. If this Pradeesh can do some good with it, why not?"

"You didn't fight me on this. You're not going to fight me on this?"

"No," Kayl said.

Genji kept her eyes on his. "Maybe my mother sent me to you, too."

He smiled. "You should listen to your mother."

"I'm not joking." She straightened up. "I don't enjoy living in a suit. Let's go see Midea."

THE OVERHEAD LIGHTS WERE BEGINNING TO DIM FOR "NIGHT" TO ACCOMMODATE human sleep cycles when they reached the house at the end of the street. It was big by lunar standards, a mansion two stories high set with its back against the outside wall of this part of the Free Zone colony. Like the other structures they'd seen, it felt older than it actually was, the exterior appearing oddly in disrepair despite the lack of environmental wear and tear. It wasn't a surprise to see the gated entry sealed shut.

Kayl pressed the request command at the gate. "We'd like to see Midea on a business matter."

The image of a bored-looking man appeared. "You have money?"

Kayl held up one of the cash cards from the *Quasar*. "We have enough money."

"Maybe you do, maybe you don't." A buzz sounded, the gate unsealing. "Follow the lights."

The gate let into a wide hallway, lights running along one side to urge them on. Genji found herself stepping carefully, her senses alert. This did not feel like anyplace she would have visited by choice.

But then the whole point was that she and Kayl had no choice. The Free Zone had been a refuge, but it was also a trap.

The hallway led into a large room with a high ceiling. Midea lounged at a big desk near the center, a desk that looked like it had been carved from an asteroid snatched out of space. Was that as ostentatious in the 2140s as it would be in the 2170s? Genji wondered.

There were two tough-looking individuals stationed in corners of the room, their eyes staying on the two visitors.

"We need to get to Earth," Kayl said as he and Genji stopped in front of the desk.

Midea named a price without saying anything else.

Without haggling over the price, Kayl produced one of their larger cash cards, passing it over. Midea accepted it with the look of someone who wished they'd named a higher sum. "Go with Yerovan. Wait where he takes you. When it is time to go, someone will come for you."

Alarms were sounding in Genji's mind as she followed the large man named Yerovan out of Midea's mansion and to a small building down the street. "In here," Yerovan grunted. "Wait."

The inside looked like an abandoned apartment, the appliances, cabling, and other useful materials looted long ago. After closing the door, Genji sat down on a table that had been fastened to the floor and therefore not carried off, pulling off her helmet with relief. The air inside the colony smelled musty and old, but the suit said it was safe. The temperature was a bit chilly, but not uncomfortably so. "I don't have a good feeling about Midea."

"Neither do I," Kayl said, sitting down on what looked like the remnants of a long seat next to a window and also removing his helmet. "What do we do, though? Our options are kind of limited. The longer we stay here, the more people will be looking for us here, and the tighter the blockade Earth Guard will set up around the Free Zone. Not to mention what'll happen when Earth Guard announces a reward for us, which they will when they realize it'll be the best way to get to us here. We need to move fast."

"That's a good tactical analysis," Genji admitted.

"I hate feeling like we're being penned in," Kayl said. "Like we only have one choice, and then one choice, and then one choice. Are we actually choosing? Or are we being herded by fate down a path with no way to turn off it?"

"Is that how you feel? I guess it's hard to tell sometimes." Genji thought about the question. "Maybe if we look at the big things the answer will be clearer to us."

"Big things?" Kayl said.

"You know, life-changing moments," Genji said. "Your father dies, my mother dies, Pradeesh's son dies, I see the Earth die. They happen to us. Do we decide what to do about it, or are we forced down a single path?"

Kayl didn't answer for a while. "You're saying the universe throws things at us but we're still in control because we decide how to react to those things?"

"'Revere your power of judgment.' Marcus Aurelius said we know what is right, that as long as we think things through and follow our best reasons for acting, we'll be in harmony with our-selves and the universe." Genji smiled at him. "With all that's hap-pened since I arrived in 2140, I'm starting to wonder if I understand Aurelius better than I did before. Do you think that's a side effect of time travel?"

"I can't honestly say I've ever heard anyone suggest that." Kayl shrugged. "I don't know. Selene, it's clear that you're certain your mother would approve of what you're doing."

"Yeah." She pointed at him. "And your mother supports you. I've seen those news reports, too."

"I guess I'm more worried about my father," Kayl admitted. "Would he think I'm doing the right thing? What choices would he be making? Would he . . . tell me I'd made the wrong choices? How do I know what he'd be doing?"

Genji considered the question for a while. Kayl had made it clear how much he revered the memory of his father. This was im-portant to him. But how to know what that man would be doing now? "Maybe if we turn the question around we'd get an answer."

"What do you mean?" Kayl asked.

"What would your father not have done?" Genji asked. "Would he have ever agreed to or supported a plan in which an Earth Guard officer was lured onto a ship designed to kill him and then have a destructive atmospheric entry to hide the evidence?"

"Of course not," Kayl said.

"Would he lie to support an official narrative he knew wasn't true? Would he have refused to even consider evidence that contra-dicted that official narrative?"

Kayl shook his head. "If he was anything like I remember, no. You're saying my father wouldn't have backed what Earth Guard's leaders are doing, so he'd approve of my actions?"

"Doesn't that seem reasonable?"

"Yes, it does. But it's also the answer I want, so . . . I can't feel certain."

Genji smiled at him again. "I am. If you are anything like your father, he'd be happy with your actions."

"Do you think he'd be happy with my partly alien partner in life?" Kayl asked, smiling in return.

"How could he not be?"

"Good point." Kayl looked down, clearly thinking.

Genji watched him. After the tension of meeting with Midea, she'd slowly felt the warm glow of having helped Abraham Pradeesh return to her. A glow that made her wonder if this thing with Kayl was really possible, if an alloy could have something that had seemed reserved for full humans. She'd had two other alloys tell her it could happen, but she hadn't believed them. Maybe they'd been right, after all.

"Why are you looking at me like that?" Kayl asked.

How had she been looking at him? "Why do you ask so many questions?" Genji said.

"According to a number of my superior officers in the past, it's a character flaw."

"It's very Tramontine," Genji said, feeling affectionate and whimsical. "Are you sure you don't have Tramontine in you?"

"Tramontine? Alien DNA?" Kayl shook his head. "I'm pretty sure that would've shown up in one of my physicals and health screenings."

"Maybe your spirit is Tramontine."

Kayl seemed taken aback. "Ah . . . maybe. What's this about?"

"Nothing. Just that you seem . . . Tramontine sometimes."

"I have no idea what you mean by that," Kayl said. "I guess I'll have to find out the answer somehow."

"You see?" Genji said. "That is a very Tramontine statement."

"Selene, please don't take this the wrong way, but you're being weird again."

She grinned. "Is that a bad thing?"

A rapid rap on the door interrupted their conversation. Genji recentered her mind on business, preparing one hand for a strike as the other cracked open the door. It was full "night" outside on the street. Was this the escort that Midea had promised? If not . . .

Instead, Bahisa Pradeesh stood outside, breathing heavily. "You have to come. Now."

"What's happened?" Genji asked.

"Midea is betraying you. If you follow her plan, you'll be killed. If you don't follow me now, you'll be killed."

CHAPTER 15

HERE'S A MAN," BAHISA EXPLAINED. "AN UNPLEASANT MAN WHO SEEKS TO impress me. He came by the shop. Drunk. Boasting that I should hook up with him and become his because he was an important man in Midea's organization, and she would very soon come into a mountain of money." Bahisa shook her head. "No one in the Free Zone has a mountain of money. But the news is racing around the Free Zone that such a mountain has been offered for the capture of you two. Midea plans to lead you into a trap so she can collect that money. Come with me and—"

"No," Genji interrupted. "You've warned us. Now, go."

"My family owes you so much. I saw some of those modifications! We have to help you."

"Help me by leaving us here and making sure you're not tied to us," Genji told her, knowing how fierce she looked and sounded. "You're going to be an important engineer." Whose inventions would not, in this history, have to be used to inadequately finance her father's attempts to spread his message. Hadn't Bahisa had to use some of that money to fight Dorcas Funds or some other big outfit over patent infringements? "Your father can't be linked to us. He has to be protected; he has to return to Earth so he can do important things."

"What is this?" Bahisa asked, bewildered. "You speak as if you are prophesying about the future."

"What did I say? Your family cannot be connected to this. Get out of here. We're immensely grateful for the warning. But get out of here. I need your father to help me save the world."

"You know what will come? You seek to save the world?" Bahisa grabbed Genji's hand. "Father was right. I see it, too. Forgive me my doubting. Thank you for honoring our family by making us part of your glorious work. Go to the other end of the settlement. Xenobia. She hates Midea. If she learns Midea is betraying a client, she will seek to help you to frustrate Midea. Go quickly."

With that, Bahisa spun about and disappeared into the shadows.

"Who or what do you suppose they think you are?" Kayl asked.

"I'm not sure I want to know," Genji said, refastening her helmet. "But I also don't want to know what'll happen if we're still here when Midea's people come back looking for us."

"We're going to find out anyway," Kayl said, gesturing up the street.

Three figures were emerging from Midea's mansion, their shapes momentarily silhouetted against the light from the open door.

"Oh, hell. Back inside." Genji got them both inside, looking about her. The abandoned apartment had a lot of obstacles to movement, and not much else. Because at "night" no light from the street was filtering in through windows begrimed by lunar dust, it was pitch-dark in the apartment except for the lights their suits provided.

"They won't expect us to jump them," Kayl said.

"No. And they won't expect to encounter a Unified Fleet close combat specialist. But there are three of them, they're probably good at dirty fighting, and this is their home territory." She looked about once more. "Here's what we'll do."

A couple of minutes later a heavy knock sounded on the door.

Genji, standing back to the side, reached to open it and then faded back against the wall.

The door burst open, one, then another, then a third attacker coming in, stunners at the ready, their attention focused ahead of them at the inside of the apartment, where a single portable light had been set as a decoy.

Genji hit the third attacker hard, following up with a kick that slammed the door closed.

As the third attacker fell senseless, the first two spun about.

Kayl rose from behind the table, slamming a hard blow into the back of the first attacker's head, making him fall forward into the second attacker, both of them tripping over the body of the third attacker on the floor.

Genji moved in, striking without hesitation or mercy.

"I hope I never make you angry at me," Kayl said, collecting the stunners. "I heard bones break."

Genji, breathing in deeply, shrugged. "You can't win a fight without breaking a few heads. They should be out for a while. Let's go see Xenobia."

No one seemed to take notice of them as they walked back down the street through the gloom.

Xenobia's place was easy to spot. Not as grandiose as Midea's, but large and well protected, a couple of security lights gilding the front with illumination.

"Lose the stunners," the gate sentry told them before allowing entry. Kayl obligingly dropped them in the street.

Once again, lights led the way to the owner, but unlike the bright wall lights of Midea's place, the light here was dimmer, almost ghostly, shimmering along the wall as it pointed them onward.

Xenobia's "office" was smaller than Midea's but felt more impressive to Genji. Xenobia sat at her wooden desk, an elaborate board game before her, pondering her next move. On the Moon, the subdued wood of that desk was worth as much as Midea's flashy asteroid desk. The walls were lined with fine tapestries whose colors seemed to be prematurely faded, as if the Moon were trying to leach all color from them and leave everything the same dreary, lifeless gray. The colors of Xenobia's robes were brighter, as if her presence were able to hold off the Moon's malign battle against anything hinting of life.

Also unlike Midea's office, there was no one in this room except her, Genji, and Kayl. It was, Genji thought, an effective display of confidence on Xenobia's part.

"I understand you are in need of my services," Xenobia said, only briefly raising her eyes from her game board. "Your goal is Earth?"

"Yes," Kayl said. "We made a deal with Midea, but she's not honoring it."

"Honor is for fools," Xenobia said. "Business, on the other hand, requires thinking ahead. I have heard of this matter concerning two travelers. Word on the street is that Midea is already celebrating her new wealth." Xenobia smiled in a way that worried Genji. "How unhappy she will be when that wealth slips through her fingers."

"If you're planning on betraying us as well—" Kayl began.

Xenobia silenced him with a gesture. "I have what I need. And one of the things I have is the trust of those who need my services. No one will trust Midea after this. They will trust me. They will come to me, they will pay me. You will earn me far more than whatever we agree upon as my fee." She pondered her game board. "You have two problems. One is escaping from the Free Zone undetected. The other is what happens afterwards, in another lunar colony such as Hamilton, where the authorities will be seeking a pair of travelers and focusing their attention on any group of two.

"There are solutions to both problems," Xenobia added, her eyes going from Genji to Kayl. "There is a route. Obvious, you will think when you see it, but it serves the purposes of some important people in Hamilton that it not be noticed. And I have two other clients seeking to reach Hamilton, and beyond that Earth. A party of four rather than a party of two. Is this arrangement acceptable?"

"Who are the other two?" Kayl asked.

"I do not ask names. I do not provide names. Is this arrangement acceptable?"

Genji nodded to Kayl. Xenobia didn't strike her as friendly, but she seemed very competent, and in some indefinable way more trustworthy than Midea. And that last in particular was what mattered.

Xenobia moved quickly. Within minutes, a guide came to collect Genji and Kayl.

They headed along dark, straight streets toward another side of the colony, Genji watching for ambushes along the way. She became aware that there were other people matching their movements from varying distances, their shapes flitting through the dimness only occasionally relieved by house lights or business lights. More of Xenobia's people providing escort? Or people interested in the reward and looking for an opportunity to collect?

Genji eased closer to their guide. "Who are they?"

The guide spoke without looking at her, his gaze fixed ahead of them. "Mostly Xenobia's, in case someone gets foolish." He touched an insignia on his suit. "This tells everyone I'm Xenobia's, on her business. Everyone knows what happens to anyone who interferes with Xenobia's clients."

He gestured off to the side. "Midea is looking for you. She won't find you before we're in the clear."

"None of these people following us are Midea's?" Genji asked.

"One was, but they had an accident before they could tell anyone. Very sad. Xenobia will send a small contribution to the funeral. It's one of her ways of delivering messages to those who try to interfere."

Reassured, Genji fell back closer to Kayl again.

A rickety mass-transit car took them outside the main colony, through a tunnel clearly in need of maintenance, and to one of the secondary, smaller neighborhoods. There they were met by another guide, who was accompanied by the two new members of their party. Only broad details could be determined through their suits. One was a stout, middle-aged man, the other a girl who might be in her mid-teens or younger.

Reaching a small air lock, they exited the colony, out onto the surface of the planet. The main difference between the gray interior of the colony and the gray exterior of the colony seemed to be the shadows. Where air existed inside, light spread, battling shadows. Outside, light stayed where it was directed and went nowhere else, leaving sharp-edged pits of black.

A small pile of supplies awaited them.

Their guide was swift and efficient. "You're going to walk. Very-low-energy profile so no one can spot you. You'll carry these extra oxygen supplies. Between them and your suit air recyclers you can make it to Hamilton." He looked around at them. "But don't engage in any high-stress, high-consumption activities on the way, or you might find yourself gasping for air before you reach Hamilton."

Kayl was checking some of the other items in the pile. "Full-spectrum liquid-nutrient packs."

"You know how to plug them into your suit?" the guide asked.

"Yeah. How long is this trip going to be?"

"Since you've got to walk, four, five days."

"How do we avoid being seen?" Genji demanded. "There are Earth Guard ships up there. They'll spot a group hiking across the surface regardless of how low our energy signature is."

"Tunnel," the guide said. "Come on."

They were skirting the edge of a crater. It was apparent that over time a rough path had been constructed, with slabs of lunar rock positioned to block views of the path from overhead. Genji eyed the crater, wondering how its shape would be changed by the bombardment of 2169.

A hole gaped ahead of them, leading down into darkness. "There," the guide said. "Just walk. Only one way to go." He turned to leave.

"What is this?" Kayl said. "Wait a minute. Was this part of the subsurface high-speed-train tunnel system?"

"Was," the guide said. "Never finished all the way. They wanted money from the Free Zone to tie us in." Without saying another word, he started walking back the way they'd come.

Kayl led the way down, through an angled shaft with rudimentary steps carved into it.

Following, Genji was startled when they reached the bottom to find herself in a big tunnel bored through the lunar rock, perhaps ten meters across at its widest, the rounded walls smooth and laser straight, heading away from the Free Zone. The only light was that provided by their suits.

She'd ridden the high-speed subsurface trains between different lunar colonies a couple of times in the 2170s while on training missions, one time sitting alone pretending not to notice that no one would take the seats next to her even though she was in her Unified Fleet uniform. Not until a couple of other Unified Fleet members noticed and sat down there.

Had those other tunnels provided any safety when the massive shock wave from Earth's death hit the Moon? Probably not. The Moon itself must have shattered. Everything on it would have been destroyed, everyone on the Moon dying as well.

"It looks safe," Kayl told her on a private frequency so the others couldn't overhear.

"For now," Genji said. "It won't help in 2180."

"That's our job, right?"

His words helped her climb a bit out of the gloomy hole her memories had provided. "Right."

The other two had reached the bottom.

"Call me Ivan," the man said over their common frequency. "What do I call you guys?"

"Guys is fine," Kayl said.

"It's like that, huh? We're going to be together for a while. Why not be friendly?"

"This is business," Genji said.

"Okay," Ivan said. "Fine. I thought you'd sound different."

"Why?"

"No reason."

It was a blatant callout, letting her know Ivan guessed who she was. Perhaps he thought to intimidate her with that.

It would be a long walk to Hamilton.

They started off down the featureless tunnel, the section visible ahead in their lights identical to the section behind. Even though they maintained a steady pace, using the gliding, low-energy Moon stride, it felt as if they weren't really moving but were instead in some sort of purgatory of endless travel, going nowhere and getting nowhere.

Kayl must have felt it, too. "I've got my suit programmed to track our progress," he told Genji. "There's no external check, but it should be fairly accurate. I'm pretty sure I remember how far it was between Hamilton and the edge of the Free Zone."

"Is Hamilton the largest lunar colony in 2140?" Genji asked.

"No, that's Chengqian."

"Oh."

He read the meaning behind that word. "What happens?"

Genji sighed. "It gets a lot smaller," she finally said.

"But Hamilton will be okay?"

"Hamilton will have better defenses. Or better luck. I don't know. I don't remember the details. And in 2180 . . . no one and nothing will be left."

Kayl was silent for a moment. "You told me once how it felt like you were looking at ghosts because you knew what would happen. Does that ever let up?"

"Sure, it does. Comes and goes." Genji looked at him. "I was wondering if you were still alive in 2180. I don't know, of course. But maybe I'm trying to save you, too."

"I'd be pretty old for you in 2180," Kayl said.

"Way too old," Genji said. "I hope you wouldn't have hit on me if we'd met. Not that a lot of full humans seriously hit on me, unless they were drunk."

He didn't answer.

Had she managed to drag Kayl's spirit down? Great.

DISTRUSTING IVAN, GENJI AND KAYL DECIDED NOT TO SLEEP AT THE SAME TIME when the group stopped to rest. Sleeping and then watching in shifts wasn't great, but she probably wouldn't have been able to sleep at all without knowing Kayl was on sentry.

It gave her a chance to see Ivan and the girl. Even though everyone was still in their suits, Ivan had made the girl lie down close to him, close enough to feel icky to Genji. After Ivan fell asleep, the girl had edged away, putting a small distance between them. Otherwise, she stayed passive and silent.

Kayl had noticed the same things. "Something isn't right with those two," he said to Genji as they walked the next "day."

"Agreed." But what could they do about it?

Ivan's mood seemed to sour the longer they walked. When they finally stopped to rest, he shoved the girl when she brought him one of the nutrient packs Ivan had insisted she carry for the two of them. The girl yielded to the shove in a way that seemed disturbingly practiced, as if this was an everyday thing for her.

Genji wondered if there was any way to report Ivan when they got to Hamilton that wouldn't imperil her and Kayl.

Another sleep period, the seemingly endless tunnel and

darkness surrounding them becoming harder to bear. Genji found herself searching for any imperfections in the walls of the tunnel, hoping to see anything that would allow her to track progress for even a few seconds.

The initial oxygen packs had already been swapped out as the suit atmosphere recyclers used up everything they could provide. Genji swallowed the bland nutrient solution, trying not to taste it, rather than drink it slowly in an attempt to fool her stomach into thinking she'd eaten something more substantial. "You know, Unified Fleet nutrient solution in the 2170s will taste just as . . . bleh," Genji told Kayl. "Why can human ingenuity combined with Tramontine technology accomplish such wonders and not be able to make a nutrient solution that doesn't make you gag?"

"Now you've got me thinking about taratarabis-flavored nutrient solution," Kayl said.

"Why did you have to mention taratarabis when all we can eat is this junk?"

/////

ANOTHER DAY IN PURGATORY, GENJI THOUGHT, WATCHING THE UNCHANGING TUNNEL walls move past.

Kayl estimated they were more than halfway there. "The oxygen packs seem to be holding up just as the guide predicted," Kayl told her. "We'll be on the last packs when we reach Hamilton, but we should make it."

"We should," Genji said. "That fool Ivan spends a lot of time pacing when he should be resting. He's burning oxygen faster than he needs to."

"I spotted him feeding something into his suit's medical port. I think he's taking a stimulant during the day to boost his metabolism and get a high. Which will cause him to burn more oxygen. That'll be his problem, though," Kayl said. "We won't have any to spare for him if his oxygen supply gets low."

Genji took a glance at the girl, wondering how Ivan would react if his oxygen ran low.

At the next stop, the girl seemed to take too long to bring Ivan a new oxy pack. She was carrying all of those, too, for her and for Ivan.

"Lazy!" Ivan cuffed the girl a blow on the side of her helmet that made her stagger.

Genji breathed in and out slowly. *It's not my business. I need to focus on the mission. I can't draw extra attention to us. I . . .*

I can't just stand by and watch this.

"Hey, Ivan."

"What do you want?" Ivan demanded.

Genji stood up and took a step closer to him. "I want to tell you that if I see you hit that girl again, I'm going to hit you so hard you'll make a dent in the wall of this tunnel when you bounce off of it."

Ivan stared at her. "You can't threaten me like that. This girl is mine. My . . . responsibility. I have family rights."

"You're going to have some nasty bruises if you abuse her again." Genji turned away and sat down once more, feeling Ivan's angry glare on her.

"Your family rights end where that girl's body begins," Kayl added.

"You going to turn me in?" Ivan taunted.

"Thinking about it," Kayl said.

That finally silenced Ivan for the moment.

But it didn't solve the problem.

"IT'S ABOUT THREE MORE HOURS OF WALKING UNTIL WE REACH THE END OF THE tunnel and the edge of Hamilton," Kayl said, "according to my estimates."

Three more hours. Despite the tedium of the trip through the tunnel, Genji wasn't certain how much she was looking forward to that. There would be a full range of threats from security forces and equipment to worry about, not to mention Ivan, who she had started out not trusting and now regarded as just another threat.

And the thought of what would happen to the girl increasingly bothered her.

But what could they do? Any attempt to notify anyone would likely expose them, likely result in their deaths. And that would mean no help for the girl, a useless gesture that would also destroy any chance Earth might be saved.

How to remove Ivan from the picture without simply killing him? In a way that wouldn't allow Ivan to betray them? There didn't seem to be any good options there, either. Was this a situation where, morally, killing Ivan would be the lesser sin? But she had never killed in cold blood, and starting now felt wrong in many ways.

At least she had a small but good reserve of oxygen left, Genji thought. There wouldn't be any worries about breathing before they reached Hamilton.

She had been watching Ivan, who probably had no idea she was weighing the idea of killing him against her moral compass. For the last several minutes Ivan had been staggering a bit, moving faster for a few steps, then slowing down.

Ivan abruptly turned on the girl. "Give me that," he demanded, reaching for her final oxygen pack plugged into her suit.

The girl flinched back.

"What are you doing?" Kayl demanded. "She needs that oxygen."

"I need it!" Ivan yelled. "I'm almost out! I won't make it! It's her duty to give me hers!"

Kayl and Genji both stepped forward. "If you take her remaining oxygen, you'll be killing her," Kayl said.

"She's young! She can handle it." Ivan turned to face Kayl, yelling louder. "This is none of your business! Get out of my face!"

"I won't let you kill someone," Kayl said, not retreating a centimeter.

"Big man, huh? Big man? Trying to tell me how I can treat my own family? Telling me I have to die?"

Genji saw Ivan's shoulder drop in a way she recognized. Kayl probably didn't spot that, though. She moved in fast.

Ivan's hand swung out, holding a force knife, the field forming the ultrasharp blade almost invisible in the darkness of the tunnel.

Genji's kick staggered Ivan before his blow could reach Kayl, who jumped back when he realized the danger.

"Drop it!" Genji shouted at Ivan.

Instead, Ivan spun about and swung at her. He was slightly hunched over, one arm in front of him as protection, the other with the knife poised to strike again. He wasn't a novice at knife fighting.

Kayl was circling, trying to get behind Ivan.

But Genji could see Ivan watching, and also see him flicking glances toward the girl. "Kayl! Protect the girl! I'll handle this guy."

Kayl hesitated only a moment before backtracking to stand between the girl and Ivan.

"You don't know how much trouble you're in!" Ivan gloated as he moved closer to Genji.

It struck her as unexpectedly funny. "I was just going to say the same thing." Dodging back and forth in a blur of motion, Genji stepped in to deliver another kick, this one sending Ivan flying.

He hit the wall of the tunnel, keeping a grip on the knife, and pushed off, roaring with anger, hurling himself in a head-on attack.

In regular gravity, she might have stopped his charge with some well-placed blows from a braced stance. Low gravity required a different approach. Genji twisted aside, letting Ivan fly past, his knife making a futile swing at her. She spun in midair, a third kick from her accelerating Ivan's leap, putting all the force she could into it, causing him to hit the opposite wall of the tunnel hard while he was flailing around with the knife.

She saw Ivan fall to the floor of the tunnel, the top of his suit helmet peeling upward, and realized that when Ivan hit the wall, his own knife had sliced open the top of the helmet. He had a major breach in his suit, atmosphere fountaining up and out. Her earlier internal debate over killing Ivan vanished from her mind, replaced by her training to save anyone in distress. "Drop the knife, you fool!" Genji shouted. "We need to patch your helmet!"

Panicking, Ivan instead staggered forward, swinging the knife, screaming in a mixture of rage and fear.

Genji closed with him, getting both hands on the knife arm and forcing Ivan to drop it. "Kayl!"

He raced forward, trying to grab one of Ivan's flailing arms and legs.

"Pin him!" Genji called, using one hand to try to open the patch kit on Ivan's suit while the other hand tried to restrain one of Ivan's arms. Ivan had the frantic strength of someone in the throes of panic, frustrating her attempt to restrain his movements.

"Trying!" Kayl cried, cursing as one of Ivan's feet nearly clipped his head.

"Get over here!" Genji called to the girl. "Help us restrain him!"

The girl didn't move, standing with her usual passivity, watching Ivan struggle and scream.

Ivan's screams rapidly faded in volume as the air in his suit vented, only vacuum remaining. A moment later, he fell silent.

Genji stepped back as Kayl checked Ivan.

"Dead," Kayl said. "We probably couldn't have saved him. That's a big breach in the suit. Funny that his own knife killed him."

"His own greed and cruelty killed him," Genji said. Why had she tried to save Ivan's life, anyway? Feeling angry over the senseless death, feeling guilty for having wanted Ivan to die and her own relief at knowing the problem of Ivan had been solved, she rounded on the girl. "Why didn't you help? Why did you let your father die?"

"He wasn't my father," she replied in a voice dulled by lack of feeling.

"Not your father?" Genji exchanged looks with Kayl. "Who was he?"

"I . . ."

"Who was he?" Genji repeated.

"There are places," the girl said, "where poor families still sell daughters into marriages to older men with money."

"That's illegal everywhere," Kayl said, recovering before Genji could. "Even in the Free Zone."

"There are still places," the girl said.

Genji stepped close to the girl. "What's your name?" Her voice had gone from harsh to gentle.

"Krysta."

"How old are you?"

"Fourteen. Fourteen and a half." Krysta blinked, her face still emotionless. "I was sold when I was eleven."

Genji walked away from her, fighting a surge of rage. Stepping close to the body of Ivan, she gave it a vicious kick.

"Don't worry," Kayl said, his voice calmly reassuring. "You'll be safe now, Krysta. We'll make sure you get somewhere safe, to people who will treat you properly."

Krysta finally showed some feeling. "Not Earth Guard. You can't tell Earth Guard."

"Why not?"

"Because you're them. I know you're them. Ivan knew. He was going to turn you in for the reward when we reached Hamilton."

Genji turned back to her. "Krysta, we won't hurt you. No matter what you've heard, we won't hurt you. You're safe with us."

"I know. You stopped him from hitting me. And you protected

me just now." She suddenly became animated, looking from Genji to Kayl. "I won't tell on you."

"We'll get you to Hamilton," Kayl said. "You'll be safe there."

"No. No," Krysta protested. "Don't you still need me? They're looking for two of you. If there are three of us, you'll be safer."

Genji shook her head. "It's dangerous for you to be with us."

"I want to go back to Earth! Please! I'll pretend to be your daughter."

Krysta didn't have any idea how much that concept would rattle her, Genji thought. "You're a bit old to be . . . our . . . daughter."

"A sister, then. A sister to one of you. Or a niece. I have an aunt. I used to wish she'd find me and help me. Back when . . . back when I still wished."

Genji sighed, knowing when she was beaten. "Kayl . . ."

"I know," Kayl said. "All right, Krysta. We'll get you back to Earth. From this moment on, you're going to be okay."

"Am I really? I really am?" Genji heard Krysta's voice shaking, heard the tears in it. "He's gone. I hate him so much. It's all right to hate him so much, isn't it?"

"Yes," Genji said. "It's all right. But leave room in yourself for something besides hate. If you want to thank us, leave room for something else inside you. How is your oxygen?"

"Okay, I guess."

"Kayl?"

"I'm good," Kayl said. "A little lower margin, but we shouldn't run into any more reasons for extra exertion. How about you?"

"I'm fine. Didn't break a sweat."

"You usually don't," Kayl said.

They left Ivan's remains lying there as they resumed walking toward Hamilton.

It was only an hour later as they trudged along the final stretches of the tunnel that Genji realized Kayl had made a joke about her alloy abilities. Not a criticism, not a worry, but a shared joke. "That was funny," she said to Kayl.

"What was funny?"

"It took me a while, okay?"

THE TUNNEL ENDED SUDDENLY IN A WALL OF LUNAR ROCKS THAT HAD BEEN CUT AND formed and sealed into what appeared to be a fairly massive barrier.

"Over here," Kayl called, pointing to the right side of the barrier. "Three openings in the side of the tunnel."

Genji came close to examine all three. They were spaced up the wall, leading into passages that angled forward and farther to the right. "Which one?"

Kayl checked each one carefully. "Did you notice this?" He pointed to the bottom of each entrance. "This one has dust on the entry. So does this one. That one doesn't."

"Meaning the third has been used enough for the dust to be whisked off by boots," Genji said. "Is that Earth Guard training?"

"Sort of," Kayl said. "We get law enforcement classes sometimes. Examining a crime scene, and anti-smuggling, looking for clues to hidden doors and stuff."

"And I thought you were just the Master of Flight." Genji looked back. "Are you doing okay, Krysta?"

"Yes."

"We don't know what's up ahead. I'll lead, Kayl will be right behind me. You follow and keep us in sight."

"Okay."

Genji eased into the passage, using her light to illuminate the sides, top, and floor. Once inside, the disturbance of dust on the floor was even more obvious. There weren't any signs of danger, so she moved on cautiously.

About one hundred steps later she reached an air lock.

It could easily hold the three of them, so they all got inside and cycled it. "I am so looking forward to taking this suit off," Kayl said. "And eating something decent."

The other side of the air lock opened into a warehouse. Stepping back, Genji saw that from this side the air-lock door appeared to be a clothing locker of some kind attached to the wall. Someone had scrawled "Pevensie" on the nameplate.

There weren't any signs of alarm systems or surveillance systems, so they wended their way through the warehouse, Kayl pointing out the stolen and smuggled contents of the crates they passed. The warehouse eventually led to a series of doors and passages that finally let out on a small side street.

Kayl looked about them in surprise. "We're inside Hamilton. Using a path that totally bypasses all the border checks at the official entrances. I wonder who in Hamilton likes having that way of getting in and out without being spotted."

"You're not planning on notifying Earth Guard, are you?" Genji asked.

"Not now. But if we get through all of this alive and save the Earth and everything, I will let them know."

Going back inside one of the rooms the smuggling route had led through, they shed their space suits. Genji put on her UV Aversive jacket, gloves, and hat to hide her skin, as well as the big sunglasses to hide her eyes. Kayl was in a generic civilian outfit that he described as 2140 work casual. To Genji's relief, Krysta's outfit proved to be threadbare but otherwise respectable. "We'll get you some new clothes," she told Krysta.

A couple of their burner phones easily linked to the Hamilton network, providing maps and other information. "There's a flight to Earth leaving in five hours," Kayl noted. "Still some seats available. It'll land in Tanegashima, near Kyushu. Is that okay?"

"Tanegashima is still there?" Genji asked.

Kayl flinched. "I really wish you'd stop saying things like that."

"It wasn't destroyed. Not until 2180. It was replaced by a new facility. Can we afford to wait around for another flight?"

"I'd rather not," Kayl said. "If Earth Guard discovers we're out of the Free Zone, they might lock down all flights from the Moon."

"Let's get tickets, then," Genji said.

Kayl fiddled with his phone. "We can't buy them using these phones because of the ID-link requirements, so we'll have to go to the landing field and use one of the kiosks there."

A walk to the nearest mass-transit station let them board a surface bus tied to a single rail in the street. Genji watched the streets of Hamilton roll by, thinking that even though the buildings were all constructed of the same gray rock as those in the Free Zone, there had been much more in the way of attempts to add color to the streets. Much of the visible colony ceiling had been painted dark blue. The streets were lined with rows of trees and bushes, all thin from racing upward against such a low-gravity field, all of the trees having been trimmed to keep them from reaching the ceiling. She had disliked nearly every moment spent in the Free Zone's Utopia. But Hamilton was livable in ways that went beyond breathable, fresh-feeling air and controlled temperature.

As the bus went past the center of the colony, some of the buildings rose to four stories, the ceiling higher to match them. Genji remembered being in one of the tall buildings over thirty years from now, going up to one of the restricted levels rising above the ceiling of the colony, the stars and the lunar surface visible on all sides and through skylights. She'd been seven years old, traveling with her mother.

"What are you thinking?" Kayl asked.

"Happy memories," Genji said. "What?"

"I just . . . it doesn't seem like you have a lot of those."

"I guess I don't." She smiled at him. "I've made a lot more, though."

Hamilton colony's Miranda spaceport was significantly smaller than Genji remembered from the 2170s, but it was still bustling with passengers. To Genji's relief, there didn't seem to be a high level of security here. In fact, some of the security stations were on automatic instead of having human guards overseeing them. Was Earth Guard that complacent?

Their false IDs and anonymous cash cards proved easy to use at third-party ticket kiosks here. "How should we fly?" Genji asked Kayl. "I guess it'd be easier to hide among the crush in sardine class."

"No," Kayl said. "The exact opposite. Earth Guard and other authorities know people trying to smuggle themselves or others usually travel sardine class. And they think they 'know' that people with any money are less likely to be lawbreakers. First Class gets minimal screening and minimal attention. It keeps showing up as a problem in reviews of security screenings, and it never gets fixed, because too many people 'know' they need to focus on the poorer travelers."

"It's nice to have an Earth Guard officer around at times like this," Genji said.

"I hope it's also nice at other times." He tapped the kiosk. "Three first-class fares. Private compartment."

"How much is that costing us?"

"You really don't want to know, Selene," Kayl said. He held up one of the anonymous cash cards they'd found on the *Quasar*. "But Dorcas Funds is paying for it. Which IDs should we use?"

"These," Genji said. "Krysta can use this one. We haven't employed it yet."

"And . . . we're done." Kayl stepped back, indicating the disposable data card with their tickets on it. "I don't know about you, but I am seriously hungry."

Genji nodded, suddenly aware of just how empty her own stomach was. "We'll get Krysta new clothes and then we'll eat. What sort of food do you like?" she asked Krysta.

"Umm . . . fried . . . chicken? The nuggets?" Krysta looked as if she expected to be reprimanded for making the request.

"And French fries?" Genji said.

"Can we really?"

On the way to a food court classy enough to not call itself a food court, they paused at a clothing storefront to print out some new clothes for Krysta, who acted deliriously happy as she looked at herself in every passing reflective surface. As Krysta paused at another window to model her reflection, Kayl touched Genji's shoulder and nodded toward a nearby news feed. She looked, seeing a blaring word scroll. Alien Saboteur Nearly Destroyed Earth Guard Cruiser. Only Heroic Efforts of Crew Saved Ship.

"No good deed goes unpunished," Kayl said.

"That never changes, does it?"

"That official narrative may hold for a while, but the crew of the *Lifeguard* will talk regardless of whatever orders they have to say nothing. They're probably already passing back-channel messages to friends on other ships. And once they go on liberty and get a few beers in them, they'll be competing to try to impress everyone with their stories." Kayl shrugged. "It may be a while before they go on liberty, but this official story will crumble over time."

"I hope we're both still alive to see that," Genji said. "What's the matter with people, Kayl? Why do we build institutions that make it so hard for good people to get things done right?"

"My father," Kayl said, "used to joke that it was so people like him would always have jobs trying to fix them." His eyes shaded with sadness for a moment.

"Him and his son," Genji said.

Once in the food court, modeled as an outdoor garden with enough real trees and bushes to feel like individual tables had some privacy, it turned out that Krysta not only loved French fries and chicken nuggets; she also drank coffee like a sailor, black and lots of it.

Genji watched Krysta wolf down vat-grown chicken and French fries, thinking, trying to process her feelings. She realized that Kayl was watching her and looked away. *Our daughter.* Still a very strange idea, still a very frightening idea. Would she ever welcome it? But, for now, this girl needed them.

It was like Rear Admiral Tecumseh had said. Contemplating the fate of billions was very hard to process. But the fate of one person? She had no trouble at all feeling the weight of that.

She'd been unforgivably careless, watching Krysta rather than their surroundings, a fact that became alarmingly apparent without warning.

The voice speaking close to them was firm and authoritative. "I didn't expect to see you here."

CHAPTER 16

GENJI TENSED HERSELF FOR ACTION, BUT WAITED, ANGRY WITH HERSELF FOR having been distracted by Krysta. Why had whoever this was alerted them instead of calling in a mass of security personnel first?

Kayl looked over, his worried face lighting up in surprise. "Yolanda? Is that really you?"

A female officer sat down in the fourth chair at their table. "It's me. Been a while, Kayl. How are you doing?"

Kayl shrugged. "You know. In trouble with my superior officers. On the run for my life. Same old."

"Uh-huh." Yolanda spared a glance for Genji, her expression troubled. "I heard from Hector."

"And?"

"He told me someone we once knew, and someone with that someone, were good people trying to do good things."

"And?" Kayl repeated.

"I was on the fence," Yolanda said. "I love Hector with all my heart, he's a wonderful guy, but he's not always the brightest star in the heavens. Like, he wanted us to invest our retirement in Dorcas Funds, and look what's happening to that."

To Genji's own surprise, she spoke up. "Pradeesh Ship Industries."

"Pradeesh?" Yolanda said.

"They haven't listed yet," Genji said. "They will. Jump on it."

"Okay. Investment advice from, uh, an unusual source." Yolanda studied her. "I'd never guess. I mean, I can see some of your skin around your mouth. But the way you talk, the way you act, you seem human."

"Thank you," Genji said.

"She is human," Kayl said.

"Are you saying she doesn't have alien DNA?" Yolanda asked.

"Some of her DNA is alien," Kayl admitted.

Yolanda sat silently for a moment. "Do you know Carmen Demetrios?"

"Demetrios?" Kayl asked. "I don't think so."

"She's been my best friend forever. She's aboard the *Lifeguard*. I guess you guys didn't have time for introductions with all the officers." Yolanda paused again. "Carmen told me what really happened." She looked at Genji again. "She told me the real reason why she's still alive. What should I call you?"

Genji spread her hands. "We seem to be on a first-name basis, so feel free to call me Selene."

"Selene. Thank you, Selene. I owe you big-time. That got me off the fence. That, and realizing if the Earth Guard brass are lying about that, what else are they lying to us about? I guess Hector made a good call with you two."

Yolanda's eyes went to Krysta. "I almost thought it couldn't be you, because of your third party here."

Krysta huddled down in on herself under that gaze. "They saved me," she whispered.

"Saved you? From what?"

"Him."

Yolanda gave Kayl a demanding look.

Kayl shook his head. "She was sold as a child bride when she was eleven."

"Eleven?" Yolanda shook her head. "That's impossible. That doesn't happen anymore."

"It did to her," Kayl said. "We encountered the guy who bought her. This isn't something she made up."

"But that should've registered in the population databases," Yolanda insisted. "An eleven-year-old girl can't simply vanish and not be noted."

Genji listened, letting Kayl take the lead on this. She didn't want Yolanda rejecting the idea because an outsider to Earth Guard was pushing it.

"I don't know how her parents, or the guy who bought her, gamed the databases," Kayl said. "But I'm learning a lot of things that are supposed to be impossible are happening in ways we're not seeing."

Yolanda frowned, shaking her head. "I'm having trouble accepting this. I mean, I'm not accusing the girl of lying, but . . ."

"How did Selene and I make it to Mars?" Kayl asked her. "And then to this spot on the Moon? Without being tracked, without leaving footprints? Shouldn't that kind of movement have shown up in the databases?"

"That's . . . a very good question," Yolanda said. "It's not one I want to think about, but you're proof something isn't working the way it should." She took another look at Krysta. "So this poor girl really—?" She inhaled sharply. "You said you met the guy. Where is he?"

"Dead," Krysta said. "He can't hurt me anymore."

"Dead?" Yolanda looked from Kayl to Genji.

"We didn't kill him," Kayl hastened to tell her.

"Though I might have," Genji said. "If I'd known then."

"I don't blame you," Yolanda said before addressing Krysta again. "Sweetheart, do you want to come with me? I can get you to people who help kids like you. They're really good people and will take really good care of you."

Krysta shook her head firmly. "I want to stay with them. They protected me. They saved me. They're going to take me back to Earth. I can help them get to Earth, so I will." After the burst of words, she sank into silence again.

"Did they ask you to help them?" Yolanda asked.

"No. I knew I could help them, so I will. That's all."

"We told her how dangerous it is," Kayl said. "But she's pretty insistent."

"Well, she's right," Yolanda said. "The whole system is keyed to look for a pair, not three people who look like a family group. What are you going to do with her once you get to Earth?"

"Find a good place for her," Kayl said. "I promise."

"Coming from you, that's good enough for me." Yolanda sat back. "I reviewed the latest status update this morning. You know that rogue Earth Guard officer and his alien, uh, girlfriend? I'm sorry, Selene. How should I refer to your relationship with Kayl?"

"He is the one who shares my life," Genji said. She couldn't marry him, but girlfriend simply wasn't an adequate description. And Kayl seemed happy whenever she said that.

"So, life partner?" Yolanda asked. "Okay? Those two are trapped in the Free Zone. Earth Guard is finishing the last details of a fine-mesh net of ships and equipment and personnel around the Free Zone that an ant couldn't get through without being spotted. It's just a matter of time before they're run to ground."

"I'd hate to be in their shoes," Kayl said. "That's really quick work for Earth Guard."

"Yeah," Yolanda said. "We've all been amazed at how fast it was stood up. Rumor is a couple of up-and-coming captains have been relieved for cause because they didn't move quickly enough."

"That's new," Kayl said. "Up-and-coming used to be a get-out-of-jail-free card for people who had problems actually doing things. Where does Earth Guard think that rogue officer and his friend are trying to get to?"

"Earth, obviously." Yolanda gestured with a nod. "But to do that, they have to get out of the Free Zone and into one of the other colonies on the Moon. Security isn't just really tight around the Free Zone, but also focused on anyone trying to enter any of the colonies closest to the Free Zone. To do all that, they stripped equipment and personnel off other duties, like screening passengers at the spaceport. After all, those two have to get out of the Free Zone and into a colony before they can try to board any ship for Earth, right?" She leaned forward. "As you pointed out, there's no way you should've been able to get to this spot. How the hell did you do it?"

"That's an operational secret for the time being," Kayl said.

"Let me tell you, there is going to be a major crackdown on smuggling related to the Free Zone," Yolanda said. "It was one of those things everybody thought was too hard to deal with, but having the rogue officer and his partner in life flee there for safety has created a lot of public focus on the whole Free Zone problem. Changes are coming."

"I hope for the better," Genji murmured, wondering how those changes would impact everything else.

"Getting back to Mars and operational secrets," Yolanda said, looking at Genji once more, "there are some videos going around that we've been told were doctored. But I have it on a clear vector that those videos are authentic. They show two missiles disappearing."

Genji nodded as she ate another fry. "Pocket disruptors."

"Pocket disruptors? How do those work?"

"I can't remember," Genji said. "I do remember that they're short-range defensive systems. No danger to anyone not attacking the Tramontine ship."

"Do you happen to remember exactly what their effective range is?" Yolanda asked.

"No. I can't remember that, either."

"A real ally," Yolanda said, "would not hesitate to share that kind of information."

"A real *smart* ally would hesitate to share that kind of information until she was sure it wouldn't be used to try to kill her again." Genji flicked a smile at Yolanda, one that lasted barely a second.

"Can you tell us anything about what's happening on Mars?" Kayl asked a few moments later, clearly trying to break the silent-appraisal staring contest going on between Genji and Yolanda. "Are things on Mars with the First Contact negotiations going as smoothly as press reports claim?"

"Pretty much," Yolanda said. "Not nearly as quickly as when negotiations started, but they've got a solid foundation to work from." She cocked another look toward Genji. "Earth Guard is denying it, and officially the negotiators are still only issuing general statements, but more and more accounts credit a certain alien spy for laying that foundation."

"Have you heard anything about Captain Yesenski?" Genji asked. She'd been worried about him ever since escaping Mars.

"Yesenski? Sure. Let's see if I can remember any of it."

"I'd like to know, too," Kayl said.

Yolanda grinned. "It's no secret the brass are furious with him for letting you two escape. But it's public knowledge that Yesenski rescued the negotiators during what everyone is calling the Forty-Eight-Hour Martial Law on Mars, that he got the First Contact negotiations back on track and got the whole martial law mess calmed down without anybody being killed. The Earth Cooperation Council has already passed a resolution thanking Yesenski. So, Earth Guard brass can't touch him. Yet. Have you heard about Rear Admiral Meng?"

"The press is reporting that he was relieved from command of the Earth Guard ships at Mars," Kayl said.

"Meng is now awaiting court-martial for a laundry list of failures. I guess his fate is supposed to encourage the rest of us to try harder." Yolanda switched her gaze back to Genji. "I already mentioned one of the officially banned but often viewed clips in Earth Guard. There's another, of a certain alien berating Meng for how poorly his ships did trying to catch her."

"How do people in Earth Guard feel about that?" Kayl asked.

"There's a split. Some are really unhappy to see an outsider calling out Earth Guard for failures. But there are others saying she's got a point. Are we Earth Guard, or are we just glorified space traffic cops?" Yolanda eyed Genji again. "You told him you've got combat experience in space. How?"

"That's a little hard to explain," Genji said.

"It's true, though," Kayl said.

"I watched videos of the way you went through those soldiers on Mars. It's easy to believe you've been in some tough learning environments. Where are you from, Selene?"

Genji considered the question and how to answer it this time. "Somewhere it'll take forty years to reach."

"Another star?"

"Not exactly. Hopefully when I get back there, if I live that long, it won't be the place I left."

Kayl leaned forward, trying to divert the conversation again. "Yolanda, whatever you've been told, what Selene said on the Martian Commons is true. She is here to help the Earth, and to try to protect human lives."

"Protecting the Earth and human lives is what Earth Guard is supposed to be doing," Yolanda noted.

"That's what Earth Guard is supposed to be doing, yes," Kayl agreed.

Yolanda eyed him silently for a few moments. "I wouldn't take that from many people, Kayl. But I guess you've got the right to say it. That whole courier-ship thing. But I still think Earth Guard has important things to do."

"I agree," Genji said. "If Earth Guard's flaws can be addressed, if it can be put on a different vector, it could prevent . . . a lot of problems."

"You sound like one of Tecumseh's disciples," Yolanda said.

"Rear Admiral Tecumseh told Selene she'd want her on Tecumseh's staff if the admiral was still on active duty," Kayl said.

"Tecumseh? Said that? To Selene? Swear you're not making that up."

"I heard it," Kayl said.

"That means you're one of the disciples, too. No wonder Earth Guard brass is gunning for you." Yolanda rubbed the back of her neck, looking out across the food court. "You're not going to hang around Hamilton, are you?"

"We'll be gone soon," Kayl said.

"Good. I'm not the only one here who might recognize you. Not that I've seen you. It's been years since I laid eyes on that Kayl guy. Last question, Kayl. Big question. The aliens. Your assessment. Good, bad, or indifferent?"

"Good," Selene said.

"I'd expect that assessment from you. Kayl?"

"Definitely good," Kayl said. "I was on their ship for days. It's full of families. They don't want to fight or conquer. They just want to learn things."

Yolanda eyed him with a trace of awe. "What's the ship like inside?"

"Fantastic. Amazing system integration. Beautiful ship. Very livable."

"If you survive this, Kayl, try to get me a ticket to see that. Deal?"

"Selene is your best bet for that," Kayl said.

"No problem, Yolanda," Genji said. "You and Hector both. Kararii fessandri etheria."

"Huh?"

"It's Tramontine. It means 'my words are truth.' It's sort of a binding personal commitment thing."

Yolanda gazed at her for a long moment. "Thank you. I've never received an alien pinkie promise before. That's a deal, then. Look, I've got to get back, and my lunch break got used up in conversation. Are you guys done with those fries?"

Genji saw a panicky look appear in Krysta's eyes. The girl looked ready to leap onto the table to protect the fries. "Go ahead, Yolanda. It's the least we can do. Krysta, relax, I'll get you more fries."

"And more coffee?" Krysta asked hopefully.

"No," Genji said. "You've had too much already. If you drink any more coffee, we'll have to peel you off the ceiling. Drink some water. And finish your chicken before you eat any more fries."

Genji wondered why she had the weirdest feeling that she'd just heard her mother talking.

"Good luck," Yolanda said as she stood up. "Kayl, back when we were hitting Magsaysay with the group, the guy you were made me think of an old quote. I'm glad that you still make me think of it. 'Here only—a right mind, action for the common good, speech incapable of lies.'"

Genji spoke up to finish the quote. "'A disposition to welcome all that happens as necessary.'"

Yolanda raised her eyebrows at Genji. "You've studied Marcus Aurelius?"

"My mother liked his ideas. But, just to be clear, I disagree with Aurelius on that last. I'm not accepting something that happened. I'm trying to do something about it. That, to me, is what's necessary."

"And I'm with her on that," Kayl said. "You would be, too, if you knew the details."

"I'd like to hear them someday. For now, I'm trusting you, Kayl, and the . . . the woman who saved my friend's life." Yolanda nodded to both of them. "I'm glad I met you, Selene. I mean that. I sure wish you'd tell me where you came from, though."

Kayl watched her walk away before turning a concerned look on Genji. "Selene, something occurred to me just now. Suppose we hadn't gone back to help *Lifeguard*. Suppose you hadn't risked your-self that way, and *Lifeguard* had blown up. We would have made it to the Free Zone at nearly the same time, where things would have played out the same, and probably would have made it to Hamilton at the same time, too. When Yolanda saw us here, she wouldn't have been thinking of her friend who was still alive and who had told Yolanda you saved her. Instead, she would have thought about her dead friend, and the official Earth Guard report claiming the loss of *Lifeguard* was due to alien sabotage."

That wasn't a pleasant thing to think about. "She would've turned us in for certain, regardless of what Hector had told her," Genji said. "Our first realization that we'd been spotted might have been when security agents sealed off this eating area."

"You did the right thing because it was the right thing," Kayl said. "Not expecting any reward. But you got one, we got one, anyway."

"A good deed that got rewarded?" Genji said. "I didn't think the universe allowed that. I would've done it anyway, Kayl. You know that, right?"

"Of course I do." He paused. "My father would have said that we only received that reward because we did what we did without any thought of reward."

"Have I told you that I think your father was a pretty wise person?"

Kayl smiled. "That's another thing we agree on."

YOLANDA'S DESCRIPTION OF THE SECURITY SITUATION EXPLAINED THE MEAGER number of human guards scanning outgoing passengers. But . . .

"She could have mentioned they're using DNA samplers," Genji grumbled. "How are we supposed to get past those?"

"It's okay," Krysta said. "I can get us through this."

"How can you get us through this?" Kayl asked.

"It's a trick Ivan had me do a lot so no one could use his DNA to identify him." Krysta must have seen their skepticism. "It really works. Every time."

Approaching the DNA sampler terminal, Krysta walked close to Genji, their arms linked. At the sampler, Krysta extended the hand on her arm linked with Genji when it was time for Genji's sample to be taken. Then she extended her free hand into the sampler for her sample, before running back to Kayl to link an arm with him, and repeat the fake sampling.

The lights on the DNA sampler glowed green, green, green.

"Move on," the bored, overworked guard said.

"It always works," Krysta said. "The guards never pay attention because they expect the AIs to monitor the sampling, and the AIs never alert as long as the sampler gets a sample."

"Why didn't the system alert on three passengers having the same DNA?" Kayl wondered, looking concerned.

Krysta shook her head. "Ivan said the systems just register it as the same passenger being screened multiple times. There's some default that assumes the IDs are entered wrong because they had so many problems before matching IDs to DNA with the new systems. I think that's what he said to his friends. As long as the DNA sample doesn't cause an alert, the security guards and the AIs don't worry about it."

"I am learning so many things," Kayl said. "None of which are making me happy even though we're benefiting from them."

Genji saw long lines and slow examinations underway at the entrances for the lowest-priced fares, just as Kayl had predicted. And, again just as Kayl had said, only a single guard was watching over the arrival of the first-class and business-class passengers, waving them on after their ticket cards were approved by the scanner.

Even in the first-class line, though, there seemed to be more attention being paid to couples traveling together. Their group of three didn't attract any special notice.

The private compartment wasn't huge, but it was private, and very comfortable. The four chairs, each wide enough to accommodate two people if passengers were so inclined during the flight, could automatically turn into beds. A large panel on the "outside" wall acted as if it were a window. A snack bar was conveniently located on the opposite wall. There was even a private toilet in the back of the compartment.

As well as an actual human flight attendant. "If you need anything, just ask. The menus for meal service are available at each seat, along with a wide variety of entertainment options. Individual privacy screens can be raised and lowered about each seat."

"I hate to think of all those people crammed in shoulder to shoulder in the lower decks while we enjoy this," Kayl said.

"I feel guilty, too. But if we want to reach Earth safely, we need to be able to travel without eyes on us." Genji shed her sunglasses, jacket, and hat with a sigh of relief.

"That is so cool!"

"What?" Surprised, Genji saw Krysta staring at her.

"Your skin! I never got a good look at it before. Can I do that? Can you show me how to do that?"

Genji realized she'd been staring back at Krysta for several seconds, dumbfounded. "You can't— Krysta, no, I can't show how to do that. I was born with it. And you don't want to look like this."

"Why not?"

It was too much. How to explain anti-alloy prejudice? "Kayl?"

He nodded to her before speaking to Krysta. "Okay, I agree with you that she looks really good—"

"Kayl!"

"—but right now there are a lot of people trying to kill anyone who looks like an alloy. So, bad idea."

"Maybe someday?" Krysta asked.

"No," Genji said. "Never. You don't want to look like this. That's all there is to it."

"Okay." Krysta looked down. "Your eyes are pretty, too," she added in almost a whisper.

It was as if she wasn't simply in the past, Genji thought, but in some alternate universe where all the rules were different.

Or would that just be a description of any past for anyone looking back from any future?

Waiting for departure was a special kind of hell, wondering if at the last moment Earth Guard personnel or soldiers or special police would come charging onto the lunar-to-Earth shuttle. But at the scheduled time, the shuttle sealed its air locks and rose from the spaceport.

Kayl leaned his chair back. "I am so tired. I think I'll sleep for the entire twenty-six-hour transit time."

"What's the matter?" Genji asked. She'd gotten a lot better at reading him.

"Just some things I need to think about." He looked out the "window" as the Moon's surface fell away, the shuttle rising to accelerate toward Earth.

They sat silently for a while, enjoying the sense of being safely on their way. Genji, acutely aware that this "safe" ship could still easily become a trap, found herself unable to sleep.

Krysta had curled up next to Genji in the same chair, her head resting against Genji's chest as she slept. Genji watched her, still trying to adjust to a time where full humans had no trouble doing something like that with an alloy. "What are we going to do with her, Kayl?"

He rubbed his chin, gazing at Krysta. "There are some good places that would take her in."

"I don't want to just drop her with someone and not know what happens to her. We promised her she'd be safe."

"Yeah." Kayl looked out the "window." "If I can figure out how to safely contact my mother or Aunt Hokulani once we're back on Earth, I can ask them for recommendations."

Genji looked up at him. "Your mother? Aunt Hokulani? Would they take her in?"

Kayl appeared startled by the idea. "Selene, I can't volunteer them for something like that."

"Will you ask them? Please?"

"You don't even know my mother! You don't even know what she's like!"

"I know you. And she raised you," Genji said.

He gave her a defeated look. "All right. *If* we can safely contact my mother or Auntie, I'll ask them. I will not pressure them."

"I wouldn't ask you to. Have I told you how wonderful you are?" Genji looked down at Krysta. "Look at how sweet she is. You can't see the pain when she's sleeping."

"I know someone else like that," Kayl said.

"Really? If I can succeed at our mission, maybe some of my old pain will be easier to bear." Genji shook her head. "How could anyone do that, Kayl? To their own eleven-year-old daughter?"

Kayl made a face. "Earth Guard has been involved in a great deal of law enforcement activity. That sort of thing shows you a lot of the less attractive sides of a lot of humans."

"You don't have to tell me about the less attractive sides of people," Genji said. "Why do we still believe, Kayl? Why do we still think risking our lives for others is worth it?"

"We've speculated that we're both insane," Kayl said. "But I think we're also alike in a very important way. You and I can't stop seeing the good things. No matter how the bad things try to bludgeon us into submission, we keep seeing the stars instead of the dark between them."

"You are so Tramontine sometimes."

That earned her another startled look. "I'm beginning to suspect that's one of your highest compliments."

"Don't let it go to your head." Genji bent her head down toward Krysta. *Our daughter.* Would that feel like this?

But any daughter she had with Kayl would also be an alloy. Would also face what she had faced. How could she do that to a child?

That was an issue that would never arise, though. There was a much heavier responsibility riding on her.

"I'm going to save the world," she whispered to sleeping Krysta. "Even if I have to save it one life at a time."

OWEN WOKE FROM A FITFUL SLEEP TO SEE SELENE BESIDE HIS SEAT/BED, THE PRIvacy screen rising into position. She climbed in next to him. "The kid is still out like a light, and there's no telling what tomorrow might bring. How about it, Master of Flight?"

"I didn't want to disturb you," Owen said. "You looked so content, holding her."

"Did I? It did feel nice. But it also feels nice holding you. In a very different way, of course. Let's take it slow," Selene said, moving to press her lips against his.

That proved much easier said than done, but Owen certainly wasn't going to complain.

THE NEXT "DAY," OWEN WATCHED SELENE AND KRYSTA. THEY WERE TRYING TO PLAY some sort of game that involved guessing and gestures.

He could see the uncertainty in Selene. How many friends had she had growing up? Most of them had been fellow alloys, Owen suspected. And how many girls younger than her had she gotten to know well? There probably hadn't been any babysitting jobs for alloys, even if the current people-watching-people fad hadn't faded by then in favor of once again letting AIs handle watching the kids. What age had Selene been when she joined the Unified Fleet in a world ravaged by war? Seventeen years old? Her mother dead, her life devoted to fighting a merciless war Selene had only offered Owen brief glimpses of, against opponents who literally would be willing to destroy the Earth in the name of "saving" it. How much room had that life left for typical social interactions?

It was painfully apparent that Selene didn't know what she was doing with the younger girl and was trying to spot cues in whatever Krysta did.

But Krysta, whatever her earlier life had been like, had been ripped from her childhood at the age of eleven. For the past three years, her social interactions must have been extremely limited as Ivan sought to keep their real relationship secret. Owen caught her snatching glances at Selene, attempting to figure out the right responses and actions.

Watching the awkward ways in which Selene and Krysta were trying to interact was both touching and sad in a very profound way. One of them reflected the problems today that most believed to be solved and gone, while the other embodied the failures to come that would cause unimaginable loss.

But the game ended in small bursts of laughter. "Where did you learn that game, Lieutenant Genji?"

"My mother taught it to me," Selene said. "It was very popular in . . . someday."

"In someday?"

Sensing the need to provide a distraction, Owen pointed to the data crawl on the window. "I need to talk to Selene about what we're going to do when we land."

"Yes, Lieutenant Owen." Krysta had apparently decided she should refer to them both by their formal titles.

"Krysta," Selene said, "you understand that you can't call us those names where anyone can overhear, right?"

"Yes, Lieutenant Genji. I understand that."

Selene yawned and came over to share his seat. "How bad do you think security will be at Tanegashima? It's not a major spaceport, is it?"

"It's big enough," Kayl said.

"Is there something else on your mind?"

"The mission." Owen had spent more time awake than asleep during the flight, even when Selene was sleeping alongside him. He'd once been fairly certain that while there were some flaws and gaps in the legal and security environment that kept society running and people safe, on the whole there weren't any big problems. Though, in retrospect, the example of what had happened to his father should have caused him to question that more than he had.

That had been before he'd encountered Selene. Since then, he'd seen in detail how the wealthy were not just bypassing but simply ignoring the rules. He'd learned that supposedly foolproof systems like the DNA sampling checks had gaping holes in them known to even a small-time thug like Ivan. The tunnel between Hamilton and the Free Zone, which should be on every security chart, but wasn't. Just how easy it was to acquire burner phones and false IDs and cards to make totally anonymous cash payments. How much of an underground economy and society was built around all of those?

Not to mention how dismayingly easy it seemed to have been for Lieutenant Selene Genji to be slapped with an effective death sentence based solely on her genetic profile, and how easily someone had decided that Lieutenant Kayl Owen should die along with her for the sake of a good cover story.

On paper, the current society and institutions were solid and effective.

But he had now seen that much of that picture was an elaborate simulation, imperfect AIs and compromised databases and complacent or corrupt officials combining to create a false image of "all is well."

Selene had said the slow collapse of institutions like Earth Guard in the 2150s and 2160s would feed and reflect growing violence and extremism in the following decades. How could anyone prevent such massive societal structures from crumbling? But if he and Selene couldn't figure out ways to reverse that process, saving Earth might be beyond their reach.

"The mission?" Selene said. "That's my brave Earth Guard officer. I'm sorry I got you involved in this, but I'm very happy you're involved in it with me."

"I got myself involved," he reminded her.

Their conversation was interrupted by a soft chime, followed by an announcement.

"Attention, all passengers. Attention, all passengers." The announcement sounded routine, even cheerful. "We regret to inform you that as a result of the current security emergency, this ship will not debark into the Tanegashima Spaceport Terminal. All passengers will be screened as they leave the ship onto the landing field, where they will then receive individual interviews and checks. We regret any delays these extra security measures may create. All passengers are reminded of the need to comply with legal security instructions, and the potential consequences of failing to do so."

"That's bad," Owen said to Selene, feeling his guts tighten.

She nodded slowly, rising from her relaxed position next to him. "Krysta, there's something you have to promise me. We may run into a lot of danger when we land. If I tell you to drop down and stay down, I want you to promise me you will, whether it's on this ship, or on the landing field, or in the terminal. Anywhere. Drop down and stay down. Don't follow us when we run. Don't get up until a police officer arrives and asks who you are. Then you are to tell the truth. Don't lie to the police. They can't help you if you lie to them. Promise me all that."

Krysta looked upset. "But I'm going to help you. And stay with you."

"Krysta, we promised to protect you. And that might mean not exposing you to the risk of death on our account. Promise me. Drop down and stay down and tell the truth about everything to the police."

"Except Yolanda," Owen said. "Don't mention her."

"Right. Except that."

"All right, Lieutenant Genji," Krysta said, her voice trembling. "I promise."

Another announcement started. "Due to extra security at the spaceport, and extra screening requirements, our landing has been shifted from Tanegashima to Wallops. Shuttles will be available for suborbital hops from Wallops to Tanegashima for all cleared passengers. Our planned landing time will be moved back one half hour while we await escort into Wallops."

"Escort?" Selene said, her voice quiet.

Owen leaned close to the "window," modifying the view. "I think I see them. A pair of aerospace fighters coming up to meet us."

"Kayl, these can't be routine 'emergency' procedures. They're bringing us into Wallops. They're focusing on this ship. Somehow, they realized we might be aboard it."

"It sure looks like that." He pulled out the sort of small paper notepad most people carried to write untraceable and untrackable notes to each other. "Krysta, see this name and contact information? If we get separated, and you don't know what else to do, call my aunt Hokulani. She'll help you."

Selene was looking about their compartment. "No parachutes available this time."

"Do you really think they'd shoot down an entire ship full of people to try to get us?" Owen asked her. A moment later he realized that even he couldn't be sure of the answer to that. Not anymore.

Selene's hand grasped his. "No matter what happens, Kayl, remember the mission. And remember that I love you. You made an alloy feel . . . like being an alloy only mattered in good ways."

"That's how I see you," Owen said. "You've made me feel . . . like I can make a difference. Not just to you. To a lot of people."

"You and that hill of yours," Selene said. "I guess it's always been my hill, too."

"I love you," Owen added. "Let's try to get out of this alive. Both of us."

What if they didn't? What if this was the end of the line?

Had Lieutenant Selene Genji managed to cause enough changes to alter the fate of the Earth? Or had there been too few, and too little an impact on history, and Earth was still doomed to be destroyed on the twelfth of June 2180?

"We are one," Selene said, her hand tight on his.

"We are one," Owen echoed her, watching the aerospace fighters still rising toward the shuttle, the surface of the Earth so close beneath them, but still so far away.

ACKNOWLEDGMENTS

I remain indebted to my agent, Joshua Bilmes, for his ever-inspired suggestions and assistance. Thanks also to Robert Chase, Kelly Dwyer, Carolyn Ives Gilman, the spirit of J. G. (Huck) Huckenpohler, Simcha Kuritzky, Michael LaViolette, the spirit of Aly Parsons, Bud Sparhawk, Mary Thompson, and Constance A. Warner for their suggestions, comments, and recommendations.

The quotes from Marcus Aurelius are taken from the Penguin Classics edition of *Meditations*, translated by Martin Hammond.